THE COMMAND

DAVID POYER

D0126881

St. Martin's Paperbacks

THE COMMAND

Map by Paul J. Pugliese

Library of Congress Catalog Card Number: 2003028058

ISBN: 0-312-99181-9
EAN: 9780312-99181-4

Printed in the United States of America

St. Martin's Press hardcover edition / June 2004
St. Martin's Paperbacks edition / July 2005

St. Martin's Paperbacks are published by St. Martin's Press, 175 Fifth Avenue, New York, NY 10010.

10 9 8 7 6 5 4 3 2 1

TOMAHAWK

"There can be no better writer of modern sea adventure around today."

—Clive Cussler

"An absorbing narrative that whips along the author's usual firecracker pace . . . *Tomahawk* is very much a book of to-day."

—*Norfolk Virginian-Pilot*

"Poyer's characters are well-developed and frequently complex. His description is vivid. And he certainly knows the navy."

—*Jacksonville Times-Union*

"Sharp-edged . . . [a] tense tale."

—*Florida Times-Union*

"*Tomahawk* is a book of many levels. On the surface, it is a book of suspense—spies, secret missile strikes, murder . . . Dig a little further, and there is an officer who is troubled deeply by the effects of the weapons that he is developing."

—*Proceedings*

"The intrigues of bureaucracy have a ring of authenticity . . . if you're into military thrillers, you'll like this book."

—*Wisconsin State Journal*

"A gritty thriller."

—*Microsoft Network*

ACKNOWLEDGMENTS

Ex nihilo nihil fit. For this book I owe thanks to Bob Berkel, Steve Boyer, Ina Birch, Wayne Burch, Al Chester, Katharine Cluverius, Mike Cohen, Donald J. Davidson, Drew Davis, Bart Denny, Mona Dreicer, Ernest Duplessis, Marie Estrada, George W. Fleck, Clive Foster, Sohrab Fracis, Sloan Harris, Michael Holm, Donna Hopkins, Bill Hunteman, Chris Borroni Huxtable, Sarvar Irani, Deborah Lee James, Marty Janczak, Sean Jenkins, John Kirby, James King, Ted Koler, Shea Kornblum, A. J. Magnan, Bob Malouin, Edison McDaniels, John McEleny, Peter Mercier, Paula Mills, Joe Navratil, Gail Nicula, Paula Paschall, Jim Pelkofski, Lin Poyer, John Pucky, Sally Richardson, Josea Salam, Scott Schwartz, Sandra Scoville, Asia Sharif-Clark, Matt Shear, Denny Shelton, Denise Strother, Terry Sutherland, Chan Swallow, Jim Tankovich, Bill Valentine, Kimberley Walz, Mark Young, and many others who preferred anonymity. Thanks also to Commander, U.S. Atlantic Fleet; Commander, Second Fleet; the Eastern Shore Public Library, the Northampton Free Library, the Joint Forces Staff College, and to the crews, goat lockers, and wardrooms of USS *Deyo* (DD-989) and USS *George Washington* (CVN-73). Thanks to USS *Donald Cook* for the names of her ship's boats, and to personnel of R/V *Gosport* and USS *Hue City* for live training in boarding and search. My most grateful thanks to George Witte, editor and advisor of long standing, and to Lenore Hart, best friend and reality check. As always, all errors and deficiencies are my own.

THE COMMAND

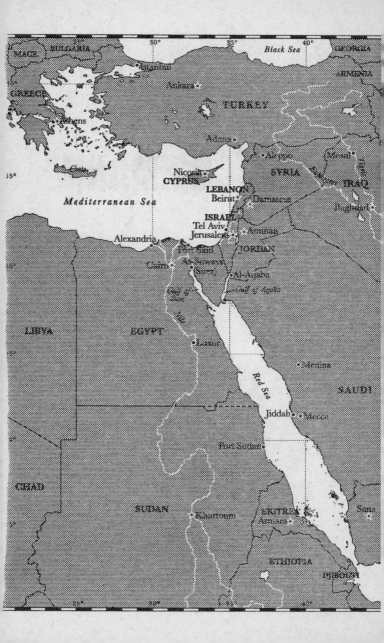

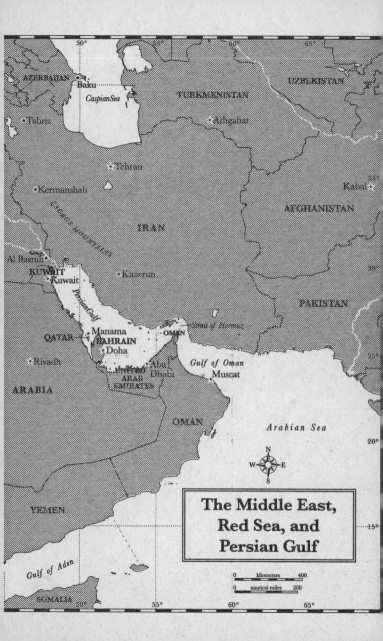

The Middle East, Red Sea, and Persian Gulf

The single best augury is to fight for one's country.

—Homer, *The Iliad*

PROLOGUE

1992: Central Asia

The mountains were silver and cobalt and jet. They flashed like jewels in the golden rays of the declining sun. Waterfalls arched over shadowy gorges. They were pristine and stark and very beautiful, and above them, floating in the crystal air like distant planets, towered range after range of the Himalayas.

The base lay where the road ground upward from a dusty plain. For years the Soviet flag had flown above it. Its guard towers had been manned by the elite security troops of the Twelfth Department. For a while, after they left, the flagpole had been bare. Then, one night, had disappeared, leaving only a wrenched-off stub embedded in the concrete.

Now the bunkhouses stood empty. Armor, heavy trucks, self-propelled howitzers waited in forlorn rows on the dusty hardstand. The guards had been hastily organized by a newly and equivocally independent state. The tanks, the artillery tubes, the other weapons might or might not belong to that state. Like much else in the wreckage of an empire, their status was . . . unclear.

The base commander was eating rice and lamb shashlik by the light of a kerosene lamp when his subordinate, a captain, barged in without knocking. Neither was Russian, though they wore threadbare Soviet uniforms.

The captain explained in great distress that one of the special weapons seemed to be missing.

"When was the last inventory?" the commander asked, fingers halted halfway to his mouth. A clump of rice detached itself from the ball and fell to the floor.

"Three months ago, when you arrived."

"But they must be counted! Every day!" the senior officer shouted, flinging his bowl down. It shattered, and rice and meat splattered the planks.

"Yes, there's an inventory—a count—we sign for them at each guard change," the captain stammered. "But—well, you'll see. But you have to come!"

The jeep wouldn't start. There was no money for parts or repairs, or even blankets for the men, and the winter nights at this altitude were cruel. Usually no one got anything on payday, either. The commander reflected he could hardly blame his troops for looting the buildings for scrap metal, gutters, wiring, furniture, doors, windows. He'd seen small arms in the marketplace in town, and prisms and sight telescopes and radios, obviously from tanks. The two officers seized rusted bicycles instead. As the captain shouted to a grizzled sergeant to sound the alarm, they cycled with soft-tired wobbly haste across the compound.

The bunker was sunk into the earth. It was surrounded by barbed wire, light towers, and a sign that warned of great danger, special security, severe penalties. But the wire hung loose, the lightbulbs had been stolen, and the guard who met them was drunk.

The captain pointed to a lock that looked impressive, but wasn't locked. The alarm panel was dead; outside power had been sporadic for a long time, and there was no fuel for the base's generators. The commander nodded silently, expression menacing. Sensing disaster despite his condition, the guard staggered after them, muttering and weeping, as they entered the cage and moved from weapon to weapon.

It looked as if six bulky shapes filled out their gray plastic shrouds. But when the commander ordered the sniveling guard to pull them back, only five of the oblate cylinders met the eye. Where one had rested on a transport dolly, cardboard ration boxes had been stacked and cleverly shaped. The dolly was gone, too.

Staring at the remaining weapons, at the ranting, reeling trooper, the broken strands of rope and skid marks on the concrete floor, only one conclusion remained to the commander: where there had been six 203-millimeter nuclear artillery shells in his custody, there were now only five. Behind him more guards poured in, pointing rifles, shouting in a babble of Kazakh, Uighur, and Russian.

"These shells weigh a metric ton," the captain said, wringing his hands. "This took many men. A truck. A crane. Someone knows how they got in here, who they are, where they took it."

The old sergeant came in, and snapped to attention in the rigid Soviet style. He reported that the guard company was present and accounted for except for two men. He gave their names.

"Chechens," the captain said, face paling. "Oh, God is great, God is great. It was the Chechens."

"We must report this at once." The commander's voice was outraged. "Close the gates instantly. Post double guards. Muster patrols in trucks to search the town. Get me the Defense Ministry. Also the Russian liaison. We will find who did this, and where the thieves have gone."

A truck engine faltered, then roared into life. A shot cracked as a stumbling recruit dropped his rifle. As his troops scattered, shouting, the commander slid his hand into the back pocket of his uniform trousers.

To feel the tight thick roll of American currency nestled there.

PART ONE

DUST AND SMOKE

1

Pier 8, Norfolk, Virginia

Glancing through the porthole in the at-sea cabin, the tall man in choker whites checked the sky. Overcast but clearing. The wind light, the air warm. He rubbed his mouth. It might turn out to be a good day after all.

Daniel V. Lenson, Commander, U.S. Navy, had spent most of his career in destroyers and frigates. Some of those tours had been enjoyable. Others had not, and he'd seen shipmates die, had killed other men, and come close to dying more than once. Five rows of decorations were pinned above his breast pocket. The topmost was light blue, set with small white stars. His sun-darkened face was beginning to show the years at sea. Sleepless nights and tension had crimped crow's-feet around the gray eyes and scattered silver in his sandy hair.

His watch gave him ten minutes until he took command of USS *Thomas Horn,* a helicopter-capable Spruance-class destroyer. Just now he was having weak coffee and sugar cookies with the skipper he was relieving. For someone who was turning over command, normally a time to celebrate, the balding little man seemed tense and disappointed.

"You heard about the three envelopes?" Ross said, turning his cup in gnarled fingers. Dan wondered why he was so nervous, as if in the waning minutes of his watch some disaster might still overtake him. As to his own feelings, the less said the better.

Post-traumatic stress disorder, the civilian shrink had called it. From being caught and tortured by Saddam's Mukhabarat. That was behind the icy sweat, the breath-stopping sense of impending doom. When he declined her prescription, she said he could try to go on without drugs. But if he gave in to his fears, avoided stressful situations, or showed panic, the terror that hunted beneath his conscious mind would take over his life.

He cleared his throat. "Three envelopes?"

"Fella comes on board to relieve, the outgoing CO gives him three envelopes. He says, when you get in trouble, open the first envelope. When you get in real trouble, open the second envelope. And when you're ass-deep in gators and there's no way out, open the last one.

"So sure enough, the fella screws up and he opens the first one. It says, 'Blame your predecessor.' So he does, and it works. Then later on he gets in real trouble. He opens the second envelope, it says, 'Reorganize.' So he does that, and he's out of the shit. But then at last he gets in real, real deep kimchee and can't see any way out short of a court-martial. He opens the third envelope."

"So what's it say?"

"'Prepare three envelopes.'"

Dan chuckled, but then the silence came back. They'd gone over everything they had to talk about. Unfortunately, what he'd learned hadn't contradicted his first impression, which was of a ship that needed attention.

He'd heard things were less than rosy during his precommand training. The regional engineering training and readiness inspectors said *Horn*'s engineering department lacked leadership. A master chief told him the ship got a present when it passed its reexam for certification. The second recurring theme was sexual fraternization. Dan took waterfront tales with a grain of salt, but the fact they were going around wasn't good.

Four men had been standing on the quarterdeck as he'd come up the brow the week before. By the time he'd finished saluting, only the officer of the deck remained. When crew scattered at the sight of khaki, something was wrong. His unease grew as he filtered through the spaces, talking to chiefs and white hats, learning who the shitbirds were, what gear was due to fail and which was bulletproof. He'd met department heads and reviewed inventory letters. Spot-checked ammo and crypto materials and the controlled equipment like night vision devices and handheld radios and computers. Signed the admin and relieving letters, and looked over the disbursing officer's audit of cash on hand.

Now he had to stand in the noon sun and show them their new skipper.

A trilling tone from the ship's service phone. Ross flinched and snatched it off the bulkhead. "They're mustered." He stood too fast, knocking over his cup. The dark fluid just missed Dan's whites.

Looking at the oily black liquid dye the carpet, suddenly he didn't feel well. A shadow moved over his perception, darkening the very light. He didn't want to go out in front of these people. Didn't want this command. All he had to oppose to fear was duty. That and the blue ribbon he wore. Which attested, like the Cowardly Lion's medal, that he had once been brave.

He followed Ross out into sunlight and the wind.

Standing on *Horn*'s flight deck as a cloud strains the sun into searching beams of golden light. Looking down past the Sea Sparrow launcher to the after five-inch, its tapered barrel centered and elevated.

Spruances were no longer the most modern destroyers in the fleet. But they were bigger, roomier, more comfortable than the Gearings and Knoxes he'd begun his career on. They carried antiship Harpoons between the stacks and Tomahawks forward. A tug churned by, screws whipping the Elizabeth River into malt frappé. He held the salute as the honors tape played over the 1MC, the ship's public address system. As a smiling, glasses-shining Commodore Saul Aronie, Commander, Destroyer Squadron Twenty-Two, passed between saluting sideboys. The sun was blazing now, right in his eyes. He was standing with Ross and Ross's wife, what was her name, he couldn't remember whether it was Cecilia or Cynthia or Cindy.

His own wife couldn't make it out of D.C. With the new administration, Blair had moved from Senate staff to the executive branch. It was one of those long-distance relationships. The week after the wedding, he'd been off to the Naval War College, while she briefed the new administration's transition team.

The day was as bright now, the wind as warm as his glance out the porthole had promised. The crew were phalanxed ranks of white. The commodore settling into his chair, adjusting his sword. At the podium, Dan's new exec. From behind he contemplated the small waist, the swell of her hips. This would take some getting used to.

Claudia Hotchkiss was a head shorter than he was, an energetic woman with apple cheeks and dusty blond hair. She looked like the actress who held the torch for Columbia Pictures. The same enigmatic expression, too. *Horn* would be the first warship in history to deploy to a combat zone with an integrated male/female crew. Hotchkiss had served in oilers and ammunition ships and had done her department head tour aboard *Mount Whitney* before screening for exec. She stretched on tiptoe to reach the mike. "Captain Carter Llewellyn Ross, commanding officer, USS *Horn*."

Ross lifted his cover, smoothed what was left of his hair. Gripped walnut-stained plywood and faced the ranks, the seated rows of guests, with the embattled crouch of one resolved to tell the unwelcome truth, come what may.

"Commodore Aronie; Commander Lenson; distinguished guests; officers and men of USS *Horn*. Thank you for joining me on this morning, on what should be a happy occasion.

"It should be happy; yet for me, it is not.

"I must speak out against what is happening to this navy I have loved and served."

A stir rippled across the sailors, listening at parade rest.

Here and there Dan caught a bark, a grunt, a low, questioning growl.

"The United States military cannot be a laboratory for social change. We cannot allow the freedoms civilians take for granted. Nor can we accede to every fad or frenzy that agitates the body politic. We see this in the current attempt to welcome to the armed forces those who are not only condemned by Scripture, but dangerous to cohesion in battle.

"Linked to this is the attempt to place women in harm's way, aboard warships such as *Horn*."

The murmurings swelled to agreement, approval. Hotchkiss was straining forward like a small pit bull on a tight leash. The commodore sat motionless, legs crossed. His face had lost its tolerant smile. But he made no move to interfere. Dan understood. This was Ross's swan song. For the only time, maybe, since he'd joined the service, he was free to say exactly what he liked.

"Now, I have nothing against women. My parents taught me to respect and honor and care for them, as Cindy I think will attest. My daughters are smart and capable. That's not why I'm uneasy with those who, for their own political gain, are thrusting females into places they don't belong.

"Battle is a brutal business. It requires choices and actions no woman in any culture is prepared for. It also takes total concentration. Concentration that will be disrupted when young men and women are attracted to each other—or sidetracked from their jobs by the kinds of accusations and rumors that are inevitable in a mixed environment.

"Women personify creation and caring. In many ways, they're better than we are. Kinder, more helpful, more willing to sacrifice for those around them. They alone are capable of perpetuating and nurturing the species. This is their great mission."

Ross took a breath, flexed his fingers on the podium. He didn't look at the commodore. "Men are fitted for another task. Defending the home; and by extension, the homeland. There is a hard edge in us. Even, at times, cruel. It must be tempered by a warrior code. But in combat that ferocity makes it possible to win. Without it, defeat is inevitable. And the loss of all we've labored to win. Freedom. Democracy. Maybe, our very survival. The world may be at peace now. But as Plato said, 'Only the dead have seen the last of war."

"My own career is ending. I have no desire to stay. I have only respect for Commander Lenson. He is a war fighter. Like Petty Officer First Class Thomas W. Horn, the ship's namesake, he bears the highest decoration for courage our nation awards: the Congressional Medal of Honor. I wish him the best. But I don't envy the task he faces, because it's against Nature and God—to make warriors out of women, to ready a gender-mixed unit for battle."

Ross paused for a moment, gazing off over their heads. "Maybe I'm a stick-in-the-mud," he said, almost softly. "What they call a traditionalist. But what was our navy built on? The *traditions* of honor, of confidence in our brothers in arms, and, ultimately, of victory. That's what I learned off Vietnam, and on deployments to Westpac and the Med. From the men, the *men,* who went before me. Stretching back in a chain to Steven Decatur and John Paul Jones.

"The navy's downsizing. Well, we can build more ships the next time danger threatens. But without those core traditions, will we still have a force that can defend the land we love? Tradition unites us. It inspires us. It sustains us in the hour we face death. Without it, I fear for our future—and for our country."

He paused again, as if about to say more; then his eyes fell on Aronie's. Dan saw no signal passed, not so much as a blink. But the captain's face closed, and he ducked his head. "I will now read my orders."

While he read out the paragraph of terse navalese, Dan unfolded himself. He joined Ross and turned the page to his own orders. "Proceed to the port in which USS *Thomas Horn* may be and upon arrival, report to your immediate superior in command, if present, otherwise by message, for duty as commanding officer of USS *Horn.*" He faced Ross.

Snapped his hand up in a swift and perfect salute. "I relieve you, sir."

"I stand relieved." Ross returned the salute and shook his hand. Quickly, perfunctorily, without meeting his eyes. They both faced Aronie. "Sir, I've been properly relieved by Commander Lenson."

"I have relieved Commander Ross, sir."

"Very well. Congratulations, Carter. My best wishes to you, Dan."

When they sat, all eyes turned to Dan. Who stood shifting from foot to foot, presented with a dilemma.

The spotlight at the change of command belonged to the outgoing skipper. The incoming CO was expected to confine his remarks to wishing his predecessor well. Yet Ross's words required an answer. He couldn't let the crew go with them ringing in their ears.

Was Ross right? Were they trying to force something that in some deep way cross-grained how the universe was built? He absently pressed his ribbons above his heart, making sure they hadn't come loose.

He didn't deserve the medal. The glances it earned him, the startled salutes. By tradition—that word again—every man in uniform saluted the wearer of the Congressional. But since the navy had awarded few decorations of any kind in the Gulf War, compared to the other services, Dan wondered sometimes if he'd gotten it to fill some ambiguous and unutterable quota.

And the even more sobering story he'd had at third hand: that the U.S. Navy hadn't put him in for the award at all, that he owed it to a personal nomination by General Norman Schwartzkopf, who'd ordered the Signal Mirror mission.

He cleared his throat. Looked out over the sparkling river, the bay, imagining the sea beyond that. Its implacable fury. Its intolerance of human error, of weakness, of any lack or shortcoming. He didn't want to face it with a divided crew. But he couldn't insult Ross on his last day in command.

To hell with it, he thought. If the guy didn't want to get

stepped on, he shouldn't have brought it up. He snapped the book closed on his prepared remarks.

"Commodore Aronie; Captain Ross; honored guests; officers, men, and women of USS *Thomas Horn*. Good morning.

"We are here today to honor Carter Ross and to thank him for his service. A long service, going back to USS *Morton*, DD-948, on the gun line off Vietnam. A period that saw the vanquishing of the Soviet Bloc and the end of the Cold War, that he'll now cap with an honorable retirement.

"It is for us to pick up the torch he sets down and to carry it into an unfamiliar world. One without the old verities, the old enemies we knew for so long.

"But constant change is the law of life.

"*Horn* will lead in that change. Pursuant to legislative initiatives, we've been selected as the test ship for the Women at Sea program. This is a great honor, and due no doubt to the fine record you've all racked up under Captain Ross's leadership.

"I have a great deal of respect for Carter Ross, and for those who believe, as he does, in the importance of tradition. But in one respect I have to disagree with them.

"Women have been serving at sea in tugs, tenders, oilers, for almost twenty years. Now they're taking the next step. *Horn*'s been tasked with making sure the mixed-crew concept can work. And we *will* make it work. Because in combat, we have to fight together, as a team, or we'll all go down. I've been there. I know it's true."

Now the flight deck was quiet. No murmurs of agreement, but neither, he noted, of dissent. The women, who'd looked dismayed at Ross's remarks, seemed to have gained heart.

"All standing orders will remain in effect until further notice. Again, I look forward to serving with you."

There, that was enough. He pushed his sword behind him and perched again on the green baize-covered chair. Feigned attention as Aronie began his remarks, lauding Ross and going over the ship's deployments and awards during his command. Keeping his back straight, looking interested, while his gaze roved over the audience. He caught the eye of the command master chief, Woltz. The senior enlisted man nodded slightly. Met next the glower of the outgoing engineering officer. Dan had already told him he'd be leaving. Other than that, they were strangers to him.

They looked so young. Even the chiefs! What had happened to the grizzled, profane E-7s who'd instructed him as a fresh-caught ensign and sustained him as a lieutenant? The department heads looked like callow boys or self-conscious college girls.

He blinked, seeing suddenly, in their places, the crew of *Reynolds Ryan,* so many dead in the icy North Atlantic. Of USS *Turner Van Zandt,* lost in the hazy Gulf. Of *Bowen* and *Barrett* and *Gaddis* and the other ships he'd served in. Just as young. Just as unformed.

Did he have what it took to command them, to take responsibility for their lives?

Aronie finished by presenting the outgoing skipper with the Meritorious Service Medal. The benediction pronounced, Hotchkiss dismissed the crew. Usually the ceremony was followed by a reception in the hangar, coffee and bug juice and a sheet cake cut with a sword. Instead, Ross and his wife left at once, passing down the line of sideboys as the pipe shrilled.

Aronie lingered, talking to Hotchkiss. When Dan came over, they looked up. "Commodore," he said.

"Congratulations, Lenson. You're making history."

"I hope so, sir."

"I've seen female soldiers on duty in Israel. They'll do fine. And you're taking over with enough time to get everyone used to working together before you deploy. I'll be in touch tomorrow. We'll discuss what has to be done before the joint task force exercise."

Dan said that'd be fine, he'd be aboard all day. Hotchkiss nodded past him, and a moment later bells pealed out. "DESRON Twenty-Two, departing," said the 1MC.

Aronie got into a sedan on the pier. And suddenly Dan was alone. A curious sensation, to be an isolate amid the bustle of the in-port quarterdeck. He caught furtive glances, swiftly averted as men passed. Woltz, and Camill, the operations officer; a young chief named Marty something. He wanted to say something to break the ice. Crack a joke. But he didn't. His presence inhibited them. Perhaps even intimidated them.

He wasn't one of them anymore.

Now he was the captain.

2

When the chief broke them from quarters, the shortest sailor in the back rank took her hat off and wiped her forehead down, then her neck, and the back of her neck. The officers got to sit in the shade, but they put the enlisted out in the sun and made them stand for the whole thing. She'd sweated through her whites. Hobbling aft on her bad ankle, hoping to catch a breeze off the river, she could smell herself, and it wasn't good.

The kind of smell that took her back to boot camp. Where the same sweltering heat came up off the grinder.

In Orlando, Florida. In August. Wearing two pairs of socks, dungarees, an undershirt, a long-sleeved shirt over that, the utility belt (holding a black raincoat, neatly folded and tucked, and a canteen of warm water from the barracks scuttlebutt), and to top it off, a black garrison cap. What better color to absorb heat. Same color as the asphalt, radiating back that Disney World sun. And the constant yelling. The sweat rolling down your body. Carrying your drill rifle in the same position, arm crooked at waist level for hour after hour till your shoulder bunched in excruciating cramps. To the point you dropped cadence on purpose, just to get dropped for push-ups on the hot asphalt. Even though it burned your hands.

GSMFN, gas turbine mechanic fireman, Cobie Kasson had reported aboard *Horn* that morning fresh from gas turbine A school at Great Lakes. Or not exactly fresh; she'd managed a week at home with her mom and daughter in Lafayette, Louisiana. Kaitlyn was three now, a bundle of energy outdoors, absorbed with her new kitten in. The navy had changed Cobie so much it was a surprise to find her daughter almost the same; a little older, that was all. Her mom said she'd grow up fast once she started kindergarten. Hugging her frail body, her chicken-wing shoulders, Cobie had wished that would never come. Wished, too, that they could be together.

That was her dream. To have her own place, not to have to live aboard ship or in a barracks.

She'd never thought of herself as military material in school. Her first job was at a tire store. That was where she met Toby, when he came in for new mufflers for his Mustang II. After she had Kaitlyn, she got put on as night desk at the Econo Lodge. It didn't take long to get fed up with that, especially getting held up by a crack-crazed asshole with a gun. Then the owners sold to a new chain. The maids and servers said new management would lay off all the desk people and rehire. And sure enough, she opened a paper somebody left in the breakfast bar one day and read an ad for her own job.

The Gulf War started that night. The staff gathered in the lobby to watch the bombing of Baghdad. One segment was set in some kind of command post. Men and women watching flickering screens. Another segment showed women loading bombs onto planes. All at once her life seemed trivial. Making snap decisions about whether or not to send out for more breakfast bagels. Her grandfather had been in the navy. She had a picture of him in his sailor suit. He'd enlisted at sixteen, right after Pearl Harbor. So when they told her she'd have to reinterview, take a cut in pay, she'd gone downtown to see the recruiter.

All of which made her first day aboard *Horn* a sick joke.

She'd spent last night at the transient BEQ. Bachelor enlisted quarters—she was learning the shorthand that condensed everything down to initials. It was OK, almost like a motel, except people were yelling and playing music and carrying on all night long. She didn't get much sleep, and her ankle hurt like hell even after she ate ibuprofen.

She'd been running downstairs, Week Seven, when she missed a step and fell. Then that night they had to run a mile and a half. It wouldn't have been so bad if they hadn't had to stand for seventeen hours a day. All the girls in her company had swollen ankles. They told her she should see the doc. But nothing—absolutely nothing—was going to keep her from graduating. So she'd kept running, and ate Midol one of the girls smuggled in. But now even when she wasn't on her feet the ankle still hurt. She hoped she hadn't fucked it up for good.

When she got on the bus, there'd been three girls on it already, sitting together. Ina, Patryce, with a Y, and Lourdes. Ina and Patryce were third class, senior to her. Cobie was glad there'd be other women in the engineering department. Ina said in a cute English accent she'd heard there were only about twenty women and three hundred men on the ship they were assigned to. Lourdes was a fireman, too. She was Mexican, and Cobie got the impression she didn't understand the other girls when they talked fast or used slang.

As the bus got closer, she saw the ships past a field of tall iron tanks. Like big gray buildings, with the sun flashing off their windows. The water, green and rippling in the sun. They pulled onto the pier, and Ina pointed out a canvas sign along the gangplank: USS THOMAS W. HORN. VALIANT MEN. She looked at it twice, then realized it must be the ship's motto.

The heavy girl, Patryce, said, "Think they named the ship after the guys?"

"What do you mean?"

"Three hundred horny guys. Well, I get just as horny as they do. So horny *Horn,* look out. Here we come. Hell bitches in heat."

Cobie limped her seabag up the ramp into a blizzard of

faces. The girls were shunted here and there, but none of the guys looked at them. In the passageways they twisted to slide by, like just touching them would infect them with something. Then Control, a big room with panels of gauges she recognized from the Hot Plant at Great Lakes. A chief told them this was home now, if they had a problem to come to him first.

Deeper still, down and aft. To aft female berthing, 3–382–3–L. A huge fan coil unit roared just inside the door. Past that were many narrow metal bunks with blue curtains, stacked three high. Close-smelling, hot, with gray terrazzo decks and fluorescent lights hanging on springs. At one end an escape trunk led up. At the other, a head with two urinals, one toilet, and two sinks smelled like a truck-stop restroom. A sawed-off shell casing painted red, and a sign, TAMPONS HERE NOT IN THE SHITTER. YOU CLOG IT YOU CLEAN IT.

Her own personal space turned out to be a top bunk with a bleed air line as big around as her chest suspended four inches above her face. A motor droned on the other side of the bulkhead, and an emergency breathing pack was mounted where her feet would go. A high school–type locker smelled like something had died in it. At the bottom lay a withered pack of Trojans.

She suddenly felt trapped. Scared. The ship smelled like oil and paint and a heavy funk underneath, like some guy who sweated hard and didn't shower enough. Guys were real territorial. She knew that from when she'd decided to clean out Toby's Mustang. The berthing space felt safe. But outside of that she didn't see any other girls, just one woman in khakis she'd glimpsed down a passageway. That reassured her a little, the woman officer.

She ended up many decks below the last light of day or breath of air, down metal ladders and bangy gratings. In front of five hostile-looking jerks in scuffed boots and blue coveralls, sitting around in front of a worn console in main engine room number one, Main One. A tall stubble-chinned guy with hollow cheeks, a crew cut, and sweat circles under his arms stuck out his hand. He had dark eyes and looked at her out of the sides of them, no hint of a smile. "Petty Officer First Class Helm. You'll be workin' for me."

"Cobie Kasson."

"Where you from, Cobie?"

"Louisiana."

"Yeah? Whereabouts?"

"Lafayette."

"Kasson, that a Cajun name? You like that zydeco stuff?"

"It's my mom's name. She's from Idaho. She raised me after my daddy left."

"Lemme guess. Straight out of boot camp, A school, Hot Plant, four-year obligation, that right?" She nodded. "How'd you do in school?"

"Eighty-two."

"That's not too good, is it?"

"I was UA for eighteen days."

UA was unauthorized absence, AWOL, going over the hill. The other guys looked up from polishing their boots, reading their comics. They went back to them when she said her daughter'd got sick and the navy wouldn't give her compassionate leave. They'd restricted her for the rest of A school and docked her pay.

"Well, they teach a lot of stuff at that school we don't use here. See, this ship was built in 1977. How many cars you see on the road from '77? The gens are shit, they gave 'em to us off the *Haylor.* And the waste heat boilers, I don't know why they put those things on here. We have to make the parts, or buy 'em out in town."

"Well, I'm eager to learn all I can and start to—"

A second class rattled down the ladder, saw her, looked away instantly. He said, riding over what she was saying, "Chief says we got to cough up another mess crank. That ditzy B-bitch got the monthlies so bad she can't get out of her bunk. The em-dee-em-ay wants somebody else."

"Hell with him. We ain't on the hook. If she's sick, he got to go to another division."

"Bolo says he's countin' bein' on the rag same as sick-leaved off. He wants another guy or none of us are eatin'."

Cobie felt her heart sink. Not mess duty. Not the day she reported aboard. But to her surprise Helm said, "Ricochet, get your ass down there. And wash your fuckin' hands before you stick 'em in our food."

X-Men thumped to the gratings. "Fuck that, man! I just got off!"

"You're only back on till the . . . regularly assigned person feels better." Helm smiled at her.

Ricochet left, not looking happy. The first class got up and said casually he'd take her around, give her a tour of the space. When they were out of earshot, pulling themselves up the smooth greasy-feeling handrails to the next level, he said over his shoulder, "What's wrong with your leg?"

"Just twisted my ankle a little." Guys didn't want to hear about what was wrong with you. Your headaches or stuff. Toby sure never had.

"Uh-huh. Well, listen. Some of these A-holes are going to act weird around you. Don't take it personally. Chief engineer, he laid it on us certain things are written in concrete from the get-go. If any of the guys get caught screwing around with you people, it'll be the wrath of God come down. Captain Ross don't want any hanky-pankying on his ship. Wants us to concentrate on our jobs, not on our lib-a-do. You know what that is?"

She told him yeah.

"So don't take it wrong if the guys don't talk to you. There'll be some shit— There'll be some stuff—"

"You can say 'shit' and 'asshole,' Petty Officer. My ears lost their virginity back when I worked at Ray's Tire and Auto."

"Uh-huh, well, like I was sayin', there'll be shit along the way, but we're gonna work it out. And you just call me Mick, you don't need to do that Petty Officer Helm stuff unless there's an O around."

"An 'O'?"

"An O. A zero. You know, an officer. Or Chief Bendt. You got to work together, you don't do that day to day. Anyway, you got a rack? Oh, yeah, the women's bunkroom—we call it the Mustang Ranch." He'd grinned. "Okay, we got a change of command this morning, you better hustle and get your whites out of your seabag. Remember to come right back after, we got a lot to get done today. You can meet the Wizard of Oz when we fall in. Flight deck, whites, half an hour, go."

So that now as everybody milled around the helo deck, gradually dispersing, Helm took her over to meet the khaki. Master Chief Bendt, the "Top Snipe," was short and harried. Gray-black hair grew out of his ears, and his tobacco-stained fingers trembled like a rabbit's nose. He looked at her for a half second and said to get her lined up fast, issue her coveralls and gear, they'd be getting under way soon for the exercise. Then he turned away, nuking a cig. The main propulsion officer, Lieutenant (junior grade) Osmani—the Wizard of Oz, right—was younger, and not bad looking. Rangy, his uniform tailored better than the chief's, with a dark complexion. He shook her hand, but his look skated around the fantail, the sky, everywhere but at her. "What's up with the ankle?"

"I sprained it in boot camp. Sir. It's feeling better, though."

"Been on a mixed ship before?"

"This is my first ship, sir. Boot camp's integrated now, though."

"Well, you'll like this better than boot camp. We'll see some good liberty ports, we're a MEF deployer."

"I'm not sure what that is, sir."

"Mideast Force, means we deploy to the Persian Gulf. So we'll see a Med liberty and then do the Suez Canal. Jebal Ali and Bahrain, maybe Oman. You'll see the world, Fireman Kassie."

"Kasson, sir. I'll try to do a good job for the division."

Osmani said to come see him if she had any questions, then let her go. She looked around. Helm was gone, but Ina stood by the door that led down to the main deck.

"So, wot're you doing this afternoon, love?"

"I didn't sleep much last night. Maybe I better just crash."

"Oh, no, you don't. 'Ow's the Strip sound? One of the fellows in my division has a van. Be at the brow at fifteen hundred. Wi' your bathing suit."

She shuddered at the thought of her boot camp–issue suit, all she had with her. Well, maybe she could buy something. "Who else's going?"

"Me and Patryce, maybe Lourdes. Might be a girl from S-4, too. Come on, we'll have some sodding fun before we get under way. A bar. A dance place."

She winced even thinking about dancing, on this ankle. But she didn't want to get marked as a loner. So she said, "Well, okay. If you're not going to stay out real late."

"Where you 'eaded now?"

She remembered then Helm wanted her back in Main One. He was probably waiting for her there. She told Ina this, then limped quickly down the ladder and started changing with the other girls in the noisy crowded compartment. Two dozen sweaty women shouting at each other and throwing clothes and spraying deodorant.

She grinned suddenly, buttoning her denim workshirt with KASSON stamped on the front. A sailor, aboard her first ship. Learning the gear. Tonight she'd hit the beach and hammer down a few brews.

Then her fingers slowed as she remembered what the new skipper had said. About being headed into danger, everyone having to pull together if they were going to make it. He sounded like he knew what he was talking about.

Who could tell? She might even be going to a war.

3

Naval Special Warfare Development Group, Dam Neck, Virginia

You! Sasquatch! Out, out, out!" Marty Marchetti yelled, kicking the biggest turkey out of the van. The name had just come to him, but it seemed to fit. The other melonheads rolled and tumbled out, too, fingers carefully lifted off triggers. They hit the ground running, sprinted fifteen or twenty yards, heads bobbing, sand spurting up from their boots, and flopped down clumsily, or went to one knee, racking the slides on their weapons to feed the first round.

The ground was speckled with silver coins of sun and moving blurs of shadow. A breeze from seaward brought the crash of the surf. But here in the close, trapped air of the pine woods back of the dunes, everybody was sweating. He was, too, under the harness, gear, the life vest he insisted every man who'd volunteered had to wear today.

The candidates for USS *Horn*'s Maritime Intercept and Boarding Team, and Marchetti thought what a sorry bunch they were, wore blaze orange float coats and green nylon pistol belts and black leather holsters. They wore steel-toed work boots. They wore blue *Horn* ball caps and high-impact goggles and carried the weapons they'd just been issued like they were afraid of them. This would be close quarters battle. Where you didn't see the guy who wanted to kill you till you were practically face to face.

He got them moving toward the red-roofed building that waited ominously beyond the whispering pines.

He oriented and scanned, looking for the enemy, but
didn't see them. They were there, though. He'd seen them go
in: two black-clad figures who moved with a graceful lope,
more a shuffle than a run, heads weaving, scissoring to cover
each other as they ran.

"Sweep Two—"

"Who's that, Senior?"

"Krippner, Danchuk—you two take the right flank.
Sweep Team One, stay with me. And talk to each other, goddamn it."

This kind of work was out of their line for destroyer
sailors, but then again, not that far out, considering where
they were headed. He'd done a hundred and two boardings
over his last two deployments. Over that time he'd come to
realize the navy wasn't giving the whole small-arms readiness, ship's security, boarding and search thing anywhere
near enough attention. It was low tech. No computers or
missiles. Just one of those brown-water missions the navy
always tried to push off on the marines or the coast guard or
the reserves. The boarding team on a Spruance-class was
typically one or two of the gunner's mates dogging whoever
their chiefs or division officers thought liked running around
with a rifle or, worst case, whoever they didn't want in their
own rate.

They made it to the building without taking fire, though
he felt exposed as hell. The guys in black were in there
somewhere, waiting. He hustled the team in through a
hangar door, shouting, trying to get them talking to each
other. But their voices seemed to travel out and then stop,
lost beneath the cavernous trusswork ceiling. This shadowed
air smelled like old gunpowder. No glass in the windows,
but lots on the floor, a green jagged glitter like the aftermath
of a riot. Rusty Conex boxes and steel plates and old torpedo shipping containers were scattered across the stained
concrete.

He sucked air, eyes darting from gloom to gloom. The
weapon was heavy, and he had to keep bringing it up,

searching over the barrel for a face or a flash of movement. Where the fuck were they?

Suddenly, there they were. A ragged rapid *crack crack crack crack*. The number-one team was trying to get around one of the containers without getting shot. They discussed it, too loudly, then gave it a try. A clumsy high-low, and the second one stepped out, fire clattered, two guns going full auto. The kid did a half turn and stumbled back, mouth gaped. A splotch of red oozed over his life vest.

The second team was supposed to be working up the right side, giving them supporting fire, but one had decided to anchor himself behind cover. The other was more aggressive, Marty liked the way he moved, low and graceful, holding his weapon in line with his eyes. Lizard, he called him in his mind. Yeah.

Marty moved after them. The kid looked back, saw him, winked. The other guy still frozen behind cover. Hopeless. Forget him.

A round came out of the darkness so close past his ear he felt the wind. He was silhouetted, goddamn it, should have closed the doors as he came in. He ducked back, then came out sprinting, firing a burst as he went to keep their heads down. He made it to the barrier, and yelled, "He's to your right—my two o'clock." Saw the big guy looking to him, uncertain, and yelled at him to get the fuck out of there.

Sasquatch did, and instantly caught a round to the head. He gripped his skull and staggered back behind the wall. Marty hesitated. Two down. It was all going wrong, maybe they should just try to get out. No. They had to go forward. But nobody was going to move until he did.

He faked left and came out of cover running and firing blindly into the dark. Too late, saw the guy aiming at him from behind a wall. He tried to get his sights around, put fire on him, but instead heard the *whap* of a solid hit to the center of his chest. Like getting smacked with the tip of a whip—stinging pain succeeded instantly by numbness. Wet droplets sprayed his face. He felt his legs go in shock and surprise.

"Okay, that's enough." The range safety officer blew his whistle and stepped out of the corner. "Sorry, that isn't gonna do it. Let's try that again."

And he got to his feet as they lowered their rifles and checked their magazines, pulled paintballs out of their pockets, reloaded. Breathing hard, legs shaking, because it was all just too fucking much like the real thing.

Gunner's Mate Senior Chief Martin A. Marchetti had been in the U.S. Navy for seventeen years. He wore his hair buzzed, stood a fathom even, and pressed three hundred pounds. Elaborate Chinese dragons in four colors uncoiled down from shoulders on which every muscle group stood out in relief. He'd brought the guys out today to try out for what various navy pubs called the VBSS, SART, MIB Team, or Tiger Team. The guys who reacted fast, shot straight, and thought ahead, he'd keep.

Getting the ship's boarding and search team up to speed was part of *Horn*'s pre–overseas workup. But not a big part, to judge by the training schedule. All the squadron weenies wanted was a couple of boat drills and some paper punched at the range.

Marchetti didn't think this set the bar high enough. The guys in the black outfits and masks were from SEAL Team Six, based here at Dam Neck. He wasn't going to get his boys anywhere near their standards, but he could give them some idea of what it was like to get shot at.

They squatted on the grass, listening to the safety officer, Devlin, in a flight suit, black turtleneck, and black ball cap, explain how to take a corner. "A ship's made out of corners. If you can control them, you'll win the engagement. This is a game of percentages. You get them on your side—strong side, weak side, cross fire, communication, mind-set— you'll walk out instead of getting dragged out."

This he could use. But along with listening, Marty was watching the men around him. Who was tuned in. Who didn't care. Who'd kept up on the run that morning. You didn't have to be able to run five miles to board and search a ship, but you had to be in good shape. Especially if things went to shit.

Like they had for him, a couple of times.

At lunchtime Devlin said he was going to the Shifting Sands, did Marchetti want to ride over? So he made sure Goldstine had the weapons and ammo locked up—they'd shoot live fire that afternoon on pop-up targets—and sent the rest of them to the mess hall. He got into Devlin's Ram and they went over to the club.

They were drinking Diet Cokes at the bar, Marchetti admiring the titanium Luminox on Devlin's wrist, when a hand fell on his shoulder. "Martini Fucking Machete. I thought that was you."

"Jeez—Zebie?" He flipped the other chief's lapel. "They making jerkwaters like you master chiefs?"

"Just got to be in the right rate, guy."

Zebie Chesko was heavier than he remembered. A lot of guys let themselves go once they put on khaki. Marty flashed on a slim youngster smoking a Lucky in front of a five-inch thirty-eight. They'd been seamen then, on the old *Albany.* He introduced Devlin, told Chesko his division was doing some tactical training.

They ended up at a table, waiting for steak sandwiches and listening to Faith Hill in the beer-smelling dim. Chesko said he was at the shipyard in Portsmouth. He was in Virginia Beach to check out a rental for the last summer his daughter would be with them before she went to Hollins on a basketball scholarship. What was he doing? Marty said Rosa was history. The last he'd heard, she was a receptionist at a funeral home in Chattanooga. Chesko said that sucked. Marty said it actually didn't, the sex was the same, but the dishes piled up. And he was on *Horn,* ginning up to head back to the Gulf.

"*Horn?* No shit, you on the fuckin' USS *PMS?*" Chesko put down his beer. "Hey, know why they let women in the navy? So the officers can fuck face to face for a change."

"Women?" said Devlin.

Marchetti said, "Not in my work center, thank God. They're mostly in the hole with the snipes."

"We got them all over the yard now. Hard hats and tool belts and little bouncing cheeks. Their minds are on their fuckin' wombs, not their fuckin' jobs."

"Not like some guys I know, do their thinking with their dicks." Marchetti toasted him with his burger.

"So, what's it like?"

"Fuck if I know. They only been there a couple weeks," Marchetti said. "I don't think they're gonna stay, myself. It's tough duty, destroyers."

Devlin didn't say anything. Marchetti got the message very loud: the only tough duty was whatever SEALs did. He didn't buy it. He figured, him and Devlin, even money. But it wasn't worth starting trouble over.

"It's just buying votes," Chesko said. "Fucking liberals, trying to brownnose the lezzbos. Like at the yard. We're plowing billions into ship mods so they can sit down to pee while we're scrubbing sonar upgrades because there's no funding. How about you, Chief? When you gonna get them in the SEALs?"

The waitress came over to check on them. All three men watched her ass as she walked away. "We'll never see them in special ops," Devlin said. "I get a few at the range. Some of 'em can shoot. But that's not all there is to it."

Chesko said, "Take my advice, don't let it start. I remember when they first put them on the tugs, my fuckup detector went off. Most of 'em was dykes, but if they got pregnant, they got a admin discharge automatic. That was bad enough, you train them and then they want out, so they forget to take their pill. But now, babysitting's gonna be part of the defense budget. Like, they're thinking, now the Russians are gone, we don't have an enemy anymore, what do we need the military for?"

"We've got other enemies," Devlin said.

"Sure, this is just a breathing space. But Slick Willy's so hot to load us up with fruits and feminazis, sometimes I wonder if he's actually trying to fuck us, so when the fucking Chinese land . . . Hey, I ain't no dittohead."

Marchetti said, "I like Rush all right. He's got the right idea."

"Well, he's out there sometimes . . . but, like, one of my collateral duties, I get to escort people to the decommissionings and shit. Last week I get this female E-8, she's bulging out to here in her maternity uniform. I still got scars from biting my tongue. I wanted to ask her what the fuck she was gonna contribute if war broke out the next day. And some guy probably's still walking around a first class because of her."

"It's not gonna be good," Marchetti said. "You can tell that already."

"Ask any guy on the tenders. They'll tell you, it's a circus." Chesko told a story about a salvage and rescue ship out of Little Creek whose CO got caught porking the ops officer in the backseat of a ship's van the command chief had fixed up as a love wagon. "And even if they ain't fucking themselves silly, one thing always made me respect a guy was, he went through the wickets to get what's on his sleeve. All these split-tails got to do is keep showing up and they make rate. What kind of skipper you got this time?"

"Tough to tell," Marchetti said, trying to think what kind of CO he had. He'd seen the guy at the change of command, then he came down to the chiefs' mess, and then around the ship here and there. Actually a lot more often than he'd used to see Ross. "He's got a shitload of sea time. And a Congressional for something he did in the Gulf. I don't know what, but—"

"A Congressional?" said Devlin.

Chesko said, "I thought you had to be dead."

"Well, this dude's alive," Marchetti said. "His wife's some heavy hitter in D.C., too."

"That why he got the ship?"

"Hey, fuck if I know, man."

"What's he think about the girls?"

"He probably don't like it any better than we do." Marchetti took his last bite and said through it, "It's just not ever gonna be possible just to be a team, you know? There's always gonna be the sex thing. No matter what. So that's all she wrote for me, you know?"

Chesko said, looking at his plate, "You want those fries?"

Marty pushed back and told him no, go ahead. His old shipmate slopped catsup on them as the others looked on with the unspoken contempt of men who stayed in shape. "I know they can fly and all that shit, but one of these days we're going to get mixed up with somebody who knows how to fight. They're gonna get captured and raped and start ratting the other POWs out. Then, you watch, everybody's gonna say, 'Why didn't the military tell us they were gonna get hurt?' Hell, we already got ships that can't sail because there's too many of 'em knocked up to go to sea."

Marty didn't say anything, but Chesko was starting to irk him. Probably because he was putting the mouth on his ship.

Devlin glanced at his watch. "Ready?"

Chesko said he had to pony home to mama-san, give him a call before they deployed, they'd get together. Marty said yeah, they'd have to do that.

Walking to Devlin's truck, Marchetti said, "I don't know how much these melonheads are going to pick up in an afternoon. Or even if I'm going to keep too many of this bunch."

"I see a couple you can lose without hurting anything."

"I figure whatever they learn, it can't hurt. We'll just have to work at it."

"Right," said Devlin. He buckled the seat belt and adjusted it. Then squinted through the windshield. "But if you can get one thing across . . . Machete? That what he called you?"

"Yeah."

"Your team. The mind-set."

"I'm listening."

"You've got to make a decision. Are you the hunter, or the prey?"

Marchetti said, "Okay."

The SEAL said, squinting into the sun, "I say that having

been in a few gunfights. Remember, a lot of the guys you'll go up against, they've never had to take on a real opponent. Don't be afraid of them. Let them be afraid of you."

"Got it," Marty said.

"You're going to make mistakes. You might even get shot. But as long as you're still shooting back, you're not dead. And even if you die, if you've trained him right, the guy behind you will win." Devlin looked at him level. "If you can pass that on to your team, you'll be okay."

He nodded.

"Ready for the Killing House?"

And Marty Marchetti said yeah, he was ready to strap it on.

4

Off the Virginia Capes

Some weeks later Dan was in his at-sea cabin, just behind the bridge, talking to Lieutenant Herbert T. Camill.

"The Camel" was the operations officer, one of the department heads. He'd grown up in Muncie and gotten an NROTC commission at Ball State. His shaved head glowed in the overhead light. He spoke ver . . . y . . . slow . . . ly, with pauses not just between words but within them. They'd been out to sea every week since the change of command, and every time Camill went on the net, Dan itched to snatch the handset away from him. But he'd come with a solid recommendation from Tactical Action Officer School. He also had a full multiwarfare drill schedule planned, set to start slow and peak with the joint task force exercise. This morning Camill was briefing him about Evinrude, the electronic surveillance package they'd take to the Mideast with them.

As soon as the Camel left, the phone trilled. Hotchkiss, was he free? Dan said sure, wondering why the exec always called first. He'd told her his door was open twenty-four-seven. As long as he lived aboard, and they had so much ground to make up. "Meet you on the bridge," he told her. They were making their approach to the Capes, and he liked to be on hand when they were in sight of land.

One of the electronics technicians was coming aft as he went forward. "Petty Officer Leatherbury," Dan said.

"Morning, sir."

"Tweaking the TACAN?" A radar beacon that friendly aircraft could use to home in on the ship.

"The new board's in, she's doing good now, sir."

"How about those fifty-cals?"

"Fired them again yesterday, sir. Still rusty on what to do when it jams, though."

He was working his way through the crew. Five or ten minutes with each man. Something Chief Woltz said Ross had never bothered to do, that he hadn't even seemed to know some of the chiefs. Dan felt he owed it to the men he served with to at least know their names. To know a little about each one, where he was from, if he had a family, what he hoped for from his time in the navy.

He tried to use those minutes to get his own message across, too. That admin inspections and meticulous cleanliness were less important now than honing combat skills, firefighting, and damage control. That everyone aboard would qualify with the pistol, rifle, shotgun, and fifty-caliber machine gun, no matter what their job on the watch, quarter, and station bill.

In fact, he'd been unpleasantly surprised, looking over the records with Hotchkiss, to see that although their deployment date was rapidly bearing down on them, his crew wasn't fully trained.

He couldn't pull Ross's famous first envelope on this one. It wasn't his predecessor's fault. Cut past the bone on personnel and operating funding, the navy had pulled its training cadre out of Guantanamo Bay. The Gitmo experience dreaded, suffered, and valued afterward by generations of sailors—isolated weeks of grinding training, varied by nights on the gun line in case the Cubans came through the wire—was no more. These days, the Afloat Training Group did an assessment, identifying areas the command needed to focus on. The ships did tailored training in home port, finishing with a battle problem. The up side was, it cost less. The down side was, the ship ended up training itself. In

Horn's case, with the women joining either from noncom-batants or straight from boot camp, the learning curve would be even steeper.

Together with the problems in engineering, he'd even thought of reporting to Aronie that *Horn* couldn't meet her sailing date. It might not end his career, considering he'd just taken over. But he'd decided not to—yet.

So when he spoke to each man or woman, he laid the prob-lem in front of them. Along with his solution: to go to full-time training, every possible day under way, and a final battle problem refereed by observers. This would cut down on time with their families. But he owed it to those families to bring them back. And last, he told them that if things really went to hell, the women would be just as much on the line as the men. So instead of bitching about them, they'd all better help train them. He'd backed up the one-on-ones with a shakeup of the watch bills, to make sure everyone knew a new era was here.

There was grumbling about things like actually setting Condition Zebra when they went to general quarters instead of simulating it. Zebra was the highest level of compartmen-tation, sealing every hatch and scuttle below the waterline. The downside was it stopped ventilation and crew move-ment. But most seemed to agree. The navy didn't salute in-doors, but you could greet a skipper pleasantly or grudgingly. So far, the reactions were reserved, as if they'd taken in what he said but were suspending judgment.

Spruances had wide, spacious pilothouses, with big square windows angled outward. In the morning sun they flooded the bridge with light. "Captain's on the bridge," the boatswain announced, and the officer of the deck came in at once from the port wing, where she'd been examining a col-lier behind them through her binoculars.

Lieutenant Lin Porter wore her dark hair back in a pony-tail. Intense, meticulous, with a roundish Slavic face, *Horn*'s new engineering officer had taken a grip on the confusion below. She'd demoted two chiefs, fleeted first class up to re-place them, and reorganized the engineering office. Porter

had served aboard *Yellowstone* and *Recovery* before an ex-
change tour with the newly reunited German Navy, where
she'd gained the experience on gas turbine engines she'd
need on this tour. She was married to a Marine Intruder pilot
who'd probably retire and sell insurance when his squadron
transitioned to the F/A-18. Porter reported on the contacts
around them, courses, speeds, closest points of approach.
Dan liked her no-nonsense, deadpan delivery.

Land was a dark green line sketched beneath scattered
clouds. He looked at the chart, glanced at the radar repeater.
Satisfied everything was in hand, he went out to the wing.
The boatswain of the watch, Antonio Yerega, was taking the
cover off the padded leather chair reserved for the commanding officer. Dan was hoisting himself to a position of
vantage when Hotchkiss came out carrying her signature
loaded clipboard. "Good morning, sir."

"XO. What's on your mind?"

"I finally got through to SURFLANT, got the revised
services schedule. *Nicholson* may drop out of a gun shoot
Friday. We can have her services if we want. Also, got a
call from Com Second Fleet. Admiral Niles is back from
Europe."

Dan asked her to load a briefcase with the ship's schedule, the current maintenance plan, and the training plan and
have it on the quarterdeck when the brow went over. He told
her to have one of the junior officers there, too.

Coming in through the Hampton Roads Bridge-Tunnel. The
murmur of the plotters, the navigator calling ranges and distances to hazards and obstacles. *Horn* passed the rocky
riprap of the tunnel islands and pivoted to look down the
line of gray ships nestled at the Naval Operating Base, Norfolk, Virginia. Dan sat back, trying with all his might to
relax.

Ross had let his officers maneuver only in the open sea.
Never during underway replenishments and pier approaches, when the danger of collision was highest. It had

probably kept his blood pressure down, but the result was they were afraid to handle the ship and uncertain in close quarters.

Dan had decided to work with Hotchkiss first. As the bow passed the clifflike stern of USS *Nimitz*, she reported, "Sir, I have the conn."

"Very good, Commander. Watch that offsetting wind."

He tried to look calm. Spruances had two controllable rotating pitch screws. Below twelve knots, the ship's speed was a function of the pitch of the blades; the shaft itself rotated at a constant rate. Above twelve, the screws stayed at maximum pitch and the shafts sped up. The turbines reacted fast and had a lot of power. Normally, you approached a pier at an angle, shallow or sharp depending on the wind, and stopped engines to let the ship bleed off speed. But today's berth was all the way inboard, past a destroyer and an amphib already alongside pier five. The north face of pier six, on their starboard hand, was stacked deep with nested ships, further narrowing their maneuvering margin. Claudia would have to run straight in, despite a brisk northerly breeze, then move *Horn* bodily sideways, into that wind, to place her alongside the pier.

A crackle of radio from the pilot informed him the tug was made up ahead of the pivot point on the starboard side, with a power tie-up. Hotchkiss opened with a forceful rudder order lining them up, then dropped the pitch to slow. *Horn* moved along at a good rate, but began shedding speed as she passed the pierhead. "Left five degrees rudder," Claudia told the helmsman.

She sounded confident, but Dan was getting light in his seat. With a car, you turned the wheels left, the rest of the vehicle followed. With a ship, you put the rudder over and the stern moved. Left rudder, stern moves right, bow swings left, ship goes left—eventually. It was the "eventually" that got you into trouble. His spine was rigid when she said, "Right full rudder." He sank back gratefully.

Now they were passing the amphib, lined up down the midpoint of the dock. Civilians called piers "docks," but to a seaman, docks were the water spaces between the piers. *Horn* was still moving too fast for comfort, but Dan thought he read the exec's intent; a swifter passage to the berth meant less time for the wind to work. Unfortunately, the bow was swinging to starboard now as the rudder took effect.

"Port engine back full. Starboard engine back one-third."

Good, she was using the engines both to slow the thousands of tons of moving metal and to twist them to port. Dan blotted perspiration furtively from his forehead. Enlisted men looked down from the amphib's bridge. One pointed at Hotchkiss, who gave him an annoyed glance, then turned her back.

Horn was slowing. Slowing . . . He felt the moment loom, then slide into the past when he'd have stopped his engines had this been a steam-powered ship. But gas turbines responded more quickly. There, she was ordering "All stop." The lee helmsman slid the throttles back, and suddenly seven thousand tons of destroyer was perfectly motionless, perfectly placed, parallel to her berth and fifty yards off. She'd stay there for only a few seconds, though. Then the wind would begin carrying her down on a Dutch frigate so close to starboard Dan could have beaned the guys gawking from her deck with a baseball.

"Rudder amidships. Captain, can we have the push boat now?"

"Captain" meant in this case not him but the pilot, a confusing form of address but traditional. The pilot put his handheld to his mouth as Hotchkiss strolled over to Dan. Close up she wasn't as cool as she'd looked from yards away. Wisps of hair from under her cap clung to flushed skin. She gave him a questioning glance; he cleared his throat and blinked, looked away.

Beside and below them the tug was blasting out diesel smoke. The engine vibrated the air. Something was making him uneasy. Just as he realized what it was, Hotchkiss went on tiptoe to peer over the bulwark.

"We don't seem to be going anywhere," she said.

The momentary stillness was gone. They were drifting downwind, away from their berth. Dan stood in his chair to look down over the splinter shield. The tug's skipper was staring up through his windshield. A middle-aged, reddened face. Their eyes met, and the other shook his head rapidly.

"*Clelia Gracie*'s dropped gears," the pilot said, relaying off the handheld.

"Just fucking great," Hotchkiss said. He followed her gaze across to the Dutch warship. The strip of water between them was narrowing as *Horn*'s drift accelerated. Yet still he waited, forcing himself to stay nailed in the chair.

"I'm going to need help here, sir," she said, several beats before a male officer would have.

He came out of his chair. "Left hard rudder. Port engine back full. Starboard ahead full." In the pilothouse the chorus, "Captain has the conn." Glancing down, the tug's master still shaking his head. A *whoop, whoop* from the Dutchman; his collision alarm, he was shutting his watertight doors.

His only remaining chance to avoid a low-speed but still unpleasant, expensive, and diplomatically embarrassing collision was to get his bow into the right angle the pier made with the quay wall. The maneuver would also push his stern perilously close to the Dutchman. But under the suddenly increased drive of the screws the bow was already pivoting. His glance crossed the pilot's. The man said another tug was on its way, ten minutes. Dan nodded, but they both knew it'd be over by then, one way or another.

As he walked briskly to the port side, the bridge team flattened against consoles. Hotchkiss followed. Good, she was still in the game. Watching and learning from the Old Man. While that Old Man, anxious but trying not to show it, braced his palms on the bulwark and eyed a swiftly widening gap of brown water fingernailed with scalloped wavelets. The wind was stronger than he'd thought. Spruances had high superstructures, a lot of surface for the wind to grab. Maybe he wouldn't be able to pull this one out of his ass.

"Engines stop. Both ahead one-third. Rudder hard right."

Now the bow was nearly in line-heaving range, though the stern was swinging far out, but in the process *Horn* had gathered forward momentum. The quay was marching up on them. Its cracked concrete face was so near he saw a rat watching from behind a bollard. "Engines stop," he shouted into the pilothouse, registering the repetition of his command, the ping of the engine order telegraph.

It wasn't enough. He looked down to see the boatswain's mates staring grimly across at the pier, lines sagging in their hands. Too far to throw.

One trick left. "Right hard rudder," he shouted; then, "Engines ahead full."

Heads whipped around in the pilothouse. He leaned over the splinter shield, waiting, listening.

And suddenly it gripped him. A gush of cold sweat all over his back. The instantaneous and swiftly increasing fear he might turn and run. Or worse, stand mutely frozen, unable to respond or react.

At the edge of his mind, something began to glow. A thin, pale edge, like a white-hot steel blade seen end on.

He heard the engines start to whine, and cut them off. Hearing his voice high, almost out of control. Hoping it wasn't too late, that he hadn't stood rooted too long and missed his chance.

The stern halted its downwind drift and nudged twenty yards to port. The momentary shot of water through the rudders had kicked the stern to windward, but hadn't increased their forward velocity that much. Maybe they could still brake with the lines, before they slammed the delicate dome below the bow into concrete and mud.

He eased out a shaky breath. Told the phone talker, calmly as he could, "Put over lines two and four."

Two and four were the spring lines that tended aft, the only ones that could brake the forward momentum he'd built. The line guns popped. Orange ribbons uncoiled in the air. And thank God, the handlers on the pier grabbed the vivid filaments as they drifted down and began hauling them in hand over hand, first the lead line, then the nine-thread, and last the heavy elephant's-trunks of mooring line. The handlers dropped the bights hastily over the bitts, then took to their heels.

He looked down again at the forecastle crew. They were edging back, too, but the chief was shouting at them to stand fast.

"Check two and four," he said.

Hotchkiss spoke for the first time since turning over the conn. "Not hold them, sir?"

Dan rethought. "Checking" meant one turn on a chock, braking the outrunning line with friction. "Holding" meant making it fast, stopping the ship dead—unless, of course, the line snapped. And it was true they were not slowing fast enough.

The rat stood suddenly on its hind legs, seeing the bow towering above it. Then tore for the shelter of a Dumpster, speed laying it flat along the ground.

"No, we'll check them. If we hit the quay, too bad. If we part a line, we'll kill somebody on the fo'c's'le." He shouted into the pilothouse, "Rudder hard left. Engines back full." And to the phone talker, "Put over one and six."

A chattering groan rose below them. Nylon, biting and slipping over steel as it absorbed energy. White smoke burst off the bitts. *Horn* reeled, tilting. He felt the astern bell taking effect, but too late. The quay wall slid out of sight beneath the bow. He closed his eyes, bracing for the crunch.

When seconds passed without it, he opened them again. Nothing had parted, and they hadn't hit the quay. He breathed out, looking around at those who watched from bridges and forecastles, who'd gathered, like spectators at a suttee, to witness his self-immolation. Said to Hotchkiss, "Okay, you've got the conn back. Remember your engines are still astern. Your rudder's still right, and you've still got the tug alongside."

The windlasses began going around, slowly warping *Horn* into her berth, while Dan stepped back where no one could see him, lifted his cover, and smoothed a shaking hand over his sweat-soaked scalp.

The Second Fleet flagship was moored close enough to walk to. His briefcase was waiting at the quarterdeck, along with Lieutenant (jg) McCall, the strike officer. Strike was the re-name for what had been missile officer on his previous ships. Kimberley McCall was rail-thin, as tall as Dan, and carried herself in a way that straddled boyish scrawny and model elegant. She was from Savannah and proud of it, single and into tennis, parties, and getting her MBA. Dan told her they'd be visiting Vice Admiral B. F. Niles. Had she ever heard of him?

"Yes, sir. 'Nick' Niles. First African-American three-star. Commanded *Barney* and *California*. I hear your paths have crossed before."

"What?"

"You worked with him at Joint Cruise Missile Projects. Back when the test beds were crashing, and nobody knew why till you found out. They told us that story at Tomahawk School."

Dan remembered it: how he'd frozen his butt off lost in Saskatchewan and only survived by burning the fuel out of the bird. "Sea stories get improved along the way. And Admiral Niles and I haven't had the happiest of relationships."

"Any idea why he wants to see you, sir?"

"I'd guess it has to do with Women at Sea. But we'll find out when we get there."

They fell silent, swinging along the waterfront. Gray prows grew, cast their shadows over them, fell behind. The smells of river, fuel oil, steam, exhaust. Passing enlisted muttered, "Good morning, sir, ma'am." Dan noticed them eyeing McCall. She was humming under her breath.

Mount Whitney was the East Coast command ship, a swollen gray blimp spiky with antennas and dishes. A staff officer took them down a hushed, carpeted corridor. In the flag captain's office a Jack Mathias introduced himself and gently detached McCall. She'd not be required, he said. The admiral would see *Horn* alone. Mathias grimaced apologetically, like a proctologist's nurse. Dan's mood of disanticipation sank another notch.

"Lenson," Niles rumbled. He didn't get up or ask Dan to sit. Just reared back in the padded chair, pale-palmed hands locked behind his bull neck. Dan tried to swallow his nerves by inspecting him back. But Niles's Certified Navy Twill khakis looked as if they'd just come from the tailor. Three silver stars flashed like rhodium-plated shark's teeth at his collar points. He looked more grizzled around the edges but otherwise the same: massive, beefy, and pissed off. Even the jar of Atomic Fireballs on his desk might have been the one Dan had sampled in Crystal City, years before. The flag captain was lingering in the doorway. Niles pointed a finger pistol and blew him away.

Dan opened with, "Good to see you again, sir."

"Bullcrap. You hate my guts. And notice I'm not saluting your Congressional."

"I hadn't noticed, sir."

Niles blinked like a rhino contemplating a charge. "I have no idea how you got it. Or a command. It wouldn't have happened if I was on the board. I have no idea how your wife fixed this dames-at-sea fiasco for you either, but we're going to unfix it just as fast."

"She had nothing to do with it, sir. I got the CO selection before she was named assistant secretary. And it's not a fiasco. Not yet, anyway."

Dan remembered too late, contradicting Niles wasn't the way to get on his good side. The pouched eyes burned even redder. "Well, just to make it clear, we aren't going that way."

"What way, sir?"

"Women do the job on the auxiliaries. But we don't need them aboard combatants."

"It's good to hear your policy on that, sir. I was hoping to get some guidance as long as I was here."

"I'm sure you were. It's horseshit, and we're not going to stand still for it."

"Who is 'us,' Admiral?"

"The service leadership. He keeps pushing this, he's going to see a backlash he won't believe."

Dan wondered why a black man would be so set against integrating women. But obviously being black didn't mean you were a liberal, a lesson Nick Niles seemed to live to personify.

Niles was looking out the curtained porthole. No, not a porthole, more like a round picture window. "Lenson, I have a problem with your commanding one of my ships. A big problem. Usually you Academy guys understand the concept of obeying an order. But it didn't take with you. You were out sick that day, or something. To you a command's not a *command,* it's some sort of *suggestion* from above."

"I work within the system, sir. As long as possible."

"And when you decide it isn't?"

"I try to take responsibility, and act. I know that can't be officially encouraged. But if any service has a tradition of independent action, it's got to be us."

"I see. It's not direct disobedience. It's *taking responsibility.*"

Dan didn't bother to answer again. He sounded defensive even to himself. The worst of it was, at some level, Niles was right. He *did* regard power as intrinsically suspect, and thanks to the shrink, he thought he knew why. Growing up with an abusive cop for a father didn't give you the warm fuzzies for authority figures.

"And as far as the *system*—you have no idea what the system even *is*. You think you're smarter than we are."

"No, sir, I don't—"

"You think you're holier, or more ethical, or something. But we have the big picture and you don't. You react too fast; you don't think things through. God! You resigned once. How about trying it again?"

"Sorry, sir. I like command."

"I can't believe you got a ship," Niles said again. He shook his head, like a stymied water buffalo. "But since you did, I'll be watching. No more Lenson adventures. No more *hanging* people. Fuck up, just once, and you'll be on the beach. Let's see you stay in with a relief for cause in your jacket."

Dan was still standing, at an almost reflexive brace. Niles stared at him for some seconds more, then picked up a red-striped message folder. Leaving Dan unsure whether the interview was over. "Are you done with me, Admiral?" he said at last.

And Niles said, just as he had years before, "Oh, *I've* had enough. Get the fuck out of here."

His hands shook, his fists were balled. Mathias's glance was pitying. Dan stood in the passageway, trying to regain control. Fighting the murderous gloom that shadowed everything he saw.

Then, from nowhere, he wondered: What am I so upset about? Niles didn't like him. So what? He'd never expected to make O-5, and here he was. Never expected to get a command, and he had.

Maybe he was just numb, but suddenly it just didn't seem to matter that much. He'd been shipwrecked, torpedoed, and tortured. Led men in combat. Where did Niles get off telling him he wasn't a good officer? To hell with Niles's opinion of him. And everybody else's, too.

McCall came striding down the passageway, cool gaze seeking his. He watched with only the most perfunctory attempt to hide his admiration. Damn! She *was* good-looking after all.

5

Manama, Bahrain

Three blocks outside the main gate, in the rundown, predominantly Shi'a neighborhood west of the U.S. Naval Support Activity, a dark-eyed woman with a surgical mask over her face peered down at the body sprawled on the pavement. Blood and fluids stained the road. The driver stood beside the truck, smoking; the bicycle, crushed flat, was still pinned under the big double rear tires.

"He must have died instantly," the traffic sergeant said in Arabic. "The wheel passed over his head."

Aisha Ar-Rahim said a short *du'a* asking for help. Then she knelt and pulled the bloody sheet back, careful to touch it only with rubber-gloved fingertips, releasing the olfactory bouquet of the violently and recently dead.

The pathologist at Glynco, where she'd gone through federal law enforcement training, had warned the students before their introductory forensic autopsy. Blood, he'd said, was only part of that mingled smell. Its metallic tang could be flavored due to recent ingestion of foods, drugs, or alcohol. The lungs, liver, and kidneys all had peculiar odors. Bone had little smell, unless it was heated, as in amputations. Of course, any tissue that had been burned—in this case, from contact with the truck's exhaust pipes, muffler—would have its own aroma. And finally, organ contents—bowel and bladder—would be part of the collection. Their odors were dependent on many things, including metabolites of vitamins, asparagus, alcohol, coffee, drugs, diseases, and, of course, the bacterial mixture in the feces.

Breathing through her mouth, after that first necessary whiff, she studied what lay beneath.

The skull had been crushed. But the face had not been destroyed. The right cheek hung down, exposing teeth carameled with tartar. She pressed the flap of flesh back into place, restoring the face to where she could visualize it in life. Black hair, brown eyes, weathered skin. Mustache, but no beard. About thirty, at a guess.

Aisha was from Harlem, New York. This was her second month in Bahrain as a special agent, specializing in foreign counterintelligence—although so far she hadn't done any of it in her two years with the agency.

Which up to now, she thought, had been nowhere near this exciting. Though it was hard to see this as a high point.

Typically, a duty call would be answered by an admin person. The "investigative assistant," a fancy name for the secretary, would notify the duty agent. After hours, after 5:00 P.M. or on the weekend, like now—it was Saturday—base security would contact the duty agent directly, who would then respond.

Which she was doing now, since the resident agent in charge was in Naples at the moment. When they'd told her where the body was, she'd started to put on a pants suit she often wore when she had to go off base. Then changed her mind, and chose instead a light but capacious *abaya* dress with long sleeves, low heels, and a scarf, which she'd converted to a *hijab* before getting out of the car. In the black leather purse locked in the white Suburban were a cell phone, a heavy, silver-toned badge with the seal of the Naval Criminal Investigative Service, a container of Mace, handcuffs, a little prayer rug, just big enough for her face and hands, that she'd bought on hajj, and a nine-millimeter SIG Sauer P228 loaded with 115-grain Cor-Bon +P+ hollow points.

She asked the police sergeant, in Arabic, "Tell me again why you called us."

He smiled nervously, obviously still unclear who she was, though she'd already explained. "He has American ID."

"You're telling me he's an American?"

"No, that he has American ID."

She remembered to keep her voice softer, more polite than she would have if this was a crime scene investigation in the United States, or within the walls that sealed the American enclave from the Arab city around it. "May I see it, please?"

She flipped through the documents in the noon sunlight. The sergeant looked uneasy, keeping an eye on the passersby. The women were all in black, covered from head to toe, only darting eyes visible. Some tugged children. The men wore the long white cotton *thobe* that was the national dress of the island. The sergeant cleared his throat, and they dropped their glances and walked quickly past, sandals scuffing up dust.

Aisha compared the ID with the face she'd jigsawed together. The photo was good. The ID was good. The trouble was, Base Security said Achmed Hamid Khamis had been fired the year before. Not only that, he'd been in his fifties, and weighed 110 kilos. The broken body under the sheet would barely weigh 60 and was twenty years younger.

"You'll take charge of the body?" the sergeant said hopefully.

"What other identification did he have?"

He showed her, reluctantly. An Omani passport, but in a different name from the base ID. Blood had soaked into one corner, bright arterial red, like raspberry juice. Same man, same face, but a different name. Another photo ID. Reading the Arabic with some difficulty—she spoke it better than she read it—she found it was a Bahraini driver's licence in the same name as the base ID. But this photograph was of a different man, with a longer jaw and smaller eyes, one of which did not look directly at the camera.

"Have you called the SIS? Major Yousif?"

"No, I haven't."

"It's your decision, of course, But this may be something he'll want to look into."

The sergeant went back to his car, shooing children away from it. They scattered, throwing clods of earth at him and some at Aisha, too. He shouted and they fled, brown bare feet kicking up in the sunlight.

Left with the body, she turned the head to one side and then the other. Looking for scars, tattoos, earrings. Bone shifted beneath her fingers. They came away wet with a thin, clear, slimy liquid she figured must be cerebrospinal fluid.

With a quick, violent jerk, because she hadn't seen enough of this yet not to be horrified and disgusted, she peeled the sheet down to the waist and lifted the shirt. The trousers were black polyester with a cheap belt and brass-tone buckle. Above it, the midriff had been can-opened. Here, yes, bowel contents, urine, the warm organic gushings of shit and death.

She covered it again, swallowing to keep nausea from overwhelming her, and went on to inspect the hands. You could tell a lot from hands. These were ringless. The watch was a cheap Casio, still running despite the impact.

She was thinking of fingerprints—she had a portable kit in the car—when she turned the unresisting, still-warm hand over. On the underside of the wrist, just above where the cuff of the long-sleeved shirt would cover, was a smear of ballpoint. She lifted it to the sunlight, trying to make it out. Arabic lettering, but smudged. Stretching the skin and looking closely, she thought it said *Imaamah*. She didn't know what the word meant. But that, after all, was what photographs were for.

Yousif arrived just after she put her camera away after close-ups of the truck, the bicycle, the face, the midriff, and the smeared letters on the wrist. Bahrain wasn't so large an island he couldn't have come direct from headquarters. He was in the British-style uniform of the Special Intelligence Service. He bowed with a tight smile. "*Sabaah el-khair*, Agent Ar-Rahim."

"*Sabaah an-noor, Raa'id Yousif*."

"*Kayf haalik?* How is your health today?"

"Praise to God, I am well," she said. "And you?"

"Praise to God, well." He looked at the body. "American? Is that why you are here? Or is the driver one of yours?"

"Neither, I think. Though the sergeant thought he might be. He has a U.S. base ID, but it's"—she searched for an equivalent for the word "bogus," but didn't know any— "*mosh kowayes,* no good," she finished.

"Is that right?" He looked into her car. "Where's Robert?"

"In Naples."

"I see." He looked at the body again, but didn't touch it. "The sergeant says you found something else amiss with his papers."

She showed them to him, and he nodded halfway through her explanation and took them. He picked at the military ID with a thumbnail. Flipped through the passport, peering at the visa stamps. Then pocketed everything as an ambulance filtered down the narrow street. "We'll take care of it from here," he told her over his shoulder, switching to English. Which he spoke almost flawlessly, only having trouble with the *f*s, as she'd noticed Arabs often did.

"You'll take care of it?"

"He's obviously not one of your people, he's not in your records. And the death occurred in town. So he's my problem. *Raqeeb!* Sergeant!" Switching back to Arabic. "Any of these scum see what happened?"

"They say he made a turn without looking and the truck was backing out."

Aisha said, "I'm wondering what he was doing with a base ID."

"I wonder that, too. Did you take prints?"

"Not yet. Do you want me to?"

"No, we'll do it at the autopsy." He used the English word, as if he thought she might not know the Arabic.

"So you'll do an autopsy?"

He smiled at her. "*Inta betettallam.* Oh, yes."

"Can I be there?"

"Of course. I'll call you when it's scheduled."

"And if you find out who he is, meanwhile, will you let us know?"

"Most assuredly," Yousif said, smiling. "We will share everything we find out with you. Just as we always do."

He was addressing her as *ya saiyyida;* formally, but was there an undertone of humor? And if so, what did it mean? Men in white were unloading a stretcher. She waited, but Yousif said nothing more, and a few minutes later she went back to her car.

Crime happened in every community, and that was true of the military, too. The Naval Criminal Investigative Service looked into any crime involving naval personnel, from grand theft to murder. It conducted criminal investigations, contract fraud, counternarcotics, and counterintelligence work. Its jurisdiction was worldwide. Agents were civilians, not military, federal law enforcement officers, equivalent to those in the FBI, CIA, or DEA.

Aisha was an assistant resident agent in charge in Bahrain. She and the senior RAC, Robert Diehl, provided law enforcement, counterintelligence, and force protection for the thousand personnel on the base, as well as for those aboard the ships that called here for fuel, repairs, and liberty. She also occasionally choppered out to the battle group in the Gulf, though another agent handled most of the shipboard cases.

Ninety-five percent of service people were good to go. Unfortunately, she and Bob and the third agent in the Bahrain office, Peter Garfield, got to deal with the other five. Occasionally she found the work interesting, but more and more recently, she felt it didn't really challenge her. The best she could say about it was, she got to sharpen all her law enforcement skills, including diplomacy and language, when she got the crime and counterintelligence information from her foreign law enforcement counterparts—like Major Yousif.

There were some people, of course, who didn't think she ought to be here. Or wondered why she was.

It had started at the Special Federal Agent course. Fifteen weeks in the Georgia summer. She'd done all right on crime scenes, firearms proficiency, hand-to-hand, arrest procedures. Finished the Criminal Investigator segment number three in the class. But she didn't seem to have a legal mind, and she'd blown the crim law final.

The next day the director had called her in. He'd sat tapping his fingers and looking out at the pines. Then swiveled his chair and said, "I had high hopes you were going to be one of our agents, uh, Miz Ar-Rahim. But we can't compromise the requirements for graduation."

"I understand."

"That's something I refuse to do. On the other hand, we're under pressure to increase the number of female and minority graduates we can field. And someone with your— background—"

"You mean being African American, sir? Or being an American Muslim?"

"Both. You're a—pretty special asset, as far as we're concerned."

So maybe she wasn't DOA yet. She waited.

"We've been trying to think out of the box, some other way we could solve this. And maybe we have one, if it's something you were willing to sign on to."

Since her other scores were so high, he'd offered her a "qualified" graduation, contingent on her passing a retest on the legal section of the final in six months. Her first assignment was the San Diego field office, with the normal caseload for new agents: burglary, larceny of more than fifteen hundred dollars, suicide. The low point was an autoerotic death at the marine barracks. The lance corporal had gotten his sexual gratification by tying his web belt around his neck and hanging himself from the transom while watching porn videotapes. Unfortunately, the chair slipped. As a new agent, female, and growing up as sheltered as the Muslim community had kept her, it had been a disturbing investigation. But she'd passed both the retest and her ninety-day probationary.

The NSA at Bahrain was her first overseas assignment.

She'd been here just long enough to meet the major players, though she couldn't say she felt comfortable with them. Especially the locals, like Major Yousif and his boss, the minister. Muslim, like her. But there was a difference. She wasn't sure exactly what it was. She was still working on that one.

Sometimes she thought it had taken leaving America, to make her feel, for the first time, American.

Aisha had grown up in Manhattan. Central Harlem, 135th Street. Her father had converted to Islam in 1964, when he heard Malcolm X at the Audubon Ballroom. Her mother, a Baptist from Worth, Illinois, had become a Muslim when they married. She'd taught her and her sisters to do *tasbih* with their fingers, and how to make their *wudhu*.

She'd been three years old when she realized not all the thousands of people on the street that never stopped humming and thundering outside the walls of their apartment were like her family, or dressed like her family, or prayed like her family.

She knew she lived in the biggest city in the world. Her mother was from Worth, outside another big city called Chicago. She didn't remember anything about the Carolina place her grandma and her aunts talked about when they sat in the kitchen and drank beer. That was where Grandma was from, back when Grandpa had come north to work in the factory.

She remembered Worth: the Fourth of July parades, Worth Days in September, with the parade and the flea market. When they went to church with her grandma, no one there mentioned Allah. They stared and whispered when she did, and told her to pray to Jesus instead.

Every summer her grandma took her to the carnival. Her favorite was the pony carts. The yellow one was hers. She wondered if that ride was still going around. That old metal cart with its layers of buttery enamel so thick it looked melted at the edges, and the chips here and there showing it had always been yellow, coat after coat, all the way down to the silvery core.

Then one day Grandma died, and they never went to Worth again. And she and Zara and Layla and Fatima had gone to the Clara Muhammed School, and grown up in Harlem and yet not in Harlem, in New York but not in New York, in America, yet not really. Instead they lived in another nation inside America, surrounded by the close-knit, self-isolated world of the old Nation of Islam that fiercely walled off the idolatrous and licentious and above all white world outside. That bought from its own, learned from its own, stayed with its own. That was only gradually waking to the worldwide Islam Malcolm El-Shabazz had grasped in the last years of his life was out there. The bigger, freer world she'd always wanted to see. Always wanted to be part of.

And now, she was.

As she let herself into the narrow second-floor office, an enlisted man glared up from a vintage olive-drab Selectric. "Hi, Kinky," she said.

"How you doing, ma'am."

The office was the size of a Comfort Inn double, with gray metal desks and file cabinets and a refrigerator-sized evidence safe. Racks of three-ring binders and cardboard evidence boxes. Kinky was the investigative assistant, a desiccated little man with black-framed glasses and a change-purse mouth tucked under a prissy mustache. He wore the old-style dungarees and a *Belleau Wood* ball cap, as if he was still aboard ship. His paychecks said Rossetti, but everybody called him Kinky. She'd never asked why. She didn't want to know.

"Get that call about the body in Quraifa?"

Quraifa was where the Arab had gotten run over. Where the kids had thrown mud and yelled insults. Sitting at her desk and turning on her computer: "Yeah. I checked it out."

"One of ours?"

"I don't think so."

She waited for the screen to come up, then typed in her password. It didn't work again. The computer security people insisted the password be a random string of numbers and letters, even punctuation signs, so it was impossible to guess. Which meant nobody could remember them, so they had to write them down somewhere. She slid her drawer open and looked at where she'd penciled it inside. The machine recognized her then and told her she had mail. She said again, "I don't think so. We'll probably leave it for the locals. Anything for me?"

"The backgrounds are piling up again."

She sighed. The Defense Investigative Service did background investigations for military security clearances. But DIS agents didn't go overseas, so Washington sent the investigations for personnel posted there to the service-specific agents in the field. Who considered them a pain, so the junior agent ended up with them. Other than that, there were reports on pending investigations that had to go out, naval messages to release. She went through them and returned her phone calls. One was from the base exec, who'd heard about the body and wanted to know what was going on.

When she was done with that, she was face to face with the backgrounds again. She still didn't want to do them. The computer was running slow, so she put it on cleanup and sat thinking, as it ran a little icon of a disk taking itself apart and putting itself back together over and over again.

She found herself thinking about the dead man again. Who had he been? Where'd he gotten the base ID? That'd been his picture on it. But the bicycle hadn't had a base sticker. Which meant he hadn't kept it on the base, possibly hadn't been on the base at all—maybe. Unless he parked it outside and walked in. But she couldn't see him doing that, it wouldn't stay there long, not in that neighborhood. And . . . with an Omani passport. That wasn't out of line. They came to the island for jobs; the Omani economy sucked and Bahrain's was booming. But why was he using two names? And why didn't the crushed face match the picture on the driving license?

She picked up the phone and dialed the ID section of base security. The woman who answered had a singsong Puerto Rican accent. She checked the files again, for Achmed Khamis and also for the passport name, Al Shatar. Aisha heard a keyboard clicking. "Ma'am? Like I told the officer who called this morning, Mr. Khamis was discharged from base employ in June of last year. Mr. Al Shatar, we don't got nothing under that name."

She said thank you and hung up. Looked at the computer, as it chugged away revising its memory. Sometimes she wished she could do that. Erase images she didn't care to keep.

Like blood and feces. The slippery feel of cerebrospinal fluid. She'd never seen violent death that close. Maybe that was why she couldn't concentrate this morning.

The screen flickered, came back up with her familiar desktop. She wished there was some way she could put names into it, have it go away and search some worldwide database. But there wasn't. Maybe in twenty years. Not now.

She sighed, pulled out the first background investigation, and went to work.

6

Cherry Point Operating Areas

Well before dawn but still unseasonably warm. Like every day so far this time out, three hundred miles off North Carolina's Outer Banks.

Dan carried his coffee onto the wing as radios hissed and voices discorded, turning over the watch. Around him the night glittered with far-flung lights, the pulsing beacons of aircraft like itinerant stars. A new moon like a paring of machined titanium silvered the black and restless sea.

The Joint Task Force Exercise capped the outgoing Med and Mideast Forces' predeployment training. The Blue Force was the *Theodore Roosevelt* battle group. The Red, or Opposing, Force, simulating a fictional opponent named Kartuna, consisted of the Mideast deployers, eked out with players out of the East Coast ports, and Canadian and German units as well. Their last exercise before leaving the States, and Dan hoped *Horn* showed up well before the lieutenant commander and two chiefs who'd boarded the day before to be their exercise observers—read, evaluators and graders, in the final report that would go up the chain of command.

The last two weeks had been a crescendo of eighteen-hour days. Revising the battle bills, conducting the underway engineering demo, cruise missile tactical qualification, last-minute school billets for the aircraft controllers, picking up the data transfer disks with the canned Tomahawk missions, and the thousand other tickets and wickets as their deployment date bore down.

A week ago, one of his officers had broken. The auxiliaries officer, a jaygee whose previous experience had been in fleet support ships. She not only didn't know the plant, she had a bad habit of turning valves without following the Engineering Operating Sequencing System procedure. After the second sewage spill Dan had gotten her, Hotchkiss, and Porter together in his stateroom. Halfway through the counseling session she'd jumped up, crying, and run out. Dan had yelled out of his door, "Auxo, I'm not finished with you yet." But the only answer had been a sob.

When he turned back, Porter had gone white. "Maybe I'd better go see what I can do."

"There's nothing you can do, Lin. If she can't take a reaming, what's going to happen when we have a main space fire, or major flooding? I want this lady off my ship by close of business."

"That'll end her career," Hotchkiss said. Not disagreeing, just pointing it out.

"Then she'll have to find another one," Dan told her. "She may be a nice person. That's not the point. If she clutches under pressure, she'll kill her shipmates. I'd do exactly the same for a guy who reacted like that." He waited. "Am I wrong? This is the time to tell me."

And, at last, they'd both shaken their heads. And the next morning there'd been an empty bunk in Officer's Country and a chief in charge of A division.

Yeah, he'd pushed everybody, and he wasn't too popular just now. According to his grapevine, some of the wives were having dark thoughts about what their husbands were doing with female sailors aboard. As long as they didn't write their congressmen . . . As for readiness, they'd flubbed several exercises in the workup phase, but had come back the next day after reorganizing and retraining deep into the night. But there were still too many glitches, errors, misheard communications, overlooked safety procedures.

The sun was heating the horizon from beneath like a

torch under slowly reddening iron. He caught one of the
phone talkers eyeing him through the window. The boy instantly looked away, but he straightened in the leather chair,
trying not to look as wrung out as he felt.

"Ready for this, Captain?"

He and the observer/liaison shared sticky buns as the
horizon brightened, as the sun suddenly squeezed up, like
one of Niles's Atomic Fireballs spit out by the puckered sea.

He hadn't heard another word from Niles. Only silence
from on high.

The boatswain's mate brought out his gas mask and their
new antiflash gear. Not Navy issue, but heavy, clumsy hoods
improvised out of fiberglass cloth and gloves that were
meant for aircrew. Wearing them in the heat meant pouring
sweat and itchy rashes. But Dan had seen too many men die
from burns to worry about comfort.

He rubbed his face. Wondering if he was asking too
much, if he was projecting on the outer reality the shadow
that lived now within. Was it forehandedness? Or paranoia?
The world was at peace. Why should he expect his people to
train in the dark, taking mock casualties, taking hits, losing
power, drill after drill till they were ready to drop?

But he couldn't help the suspicion, intuition, that somewhere under that eastern sky they'd come face to face with
something they'd best be ready for. Not a test, or a drill, or
an exercise. Something real. Something menacing. Something powerful.

He didn't even know what it might be.

Only that it was there.

Zero-nine-thirty. He picked up the rolling shape in his
binoculars. A government-leased survey ship, flying for the
purposes of the exercise the flag of a "hostile neutral," the
People's Republic of Micara. It was idling three miles
ahead, in what his scripted geography chart showed as the
Strait of Benaventa. *Horn*'s embarked helicopter had completed the threat assessment and was drawing a smoke line
back in their direction, coming up on bingo fuel state, when

low fuel compelled her return. Yerega watched him. When Dan nodded, the boatswain's hand was already on the 1MC switch.

"Now flight quarters, flight quarters, all hands man your flight quarters stations. Stand by to receive Blade Slinger 191. No hats are to be worn on the weatherdecks. No eating, drinking, or smoking aft of frame 292. All unauthorized personnel stand clear aft of frame 292. Now flight quarters." He released the switch, then depressed it again. "Away the visit, boarding, and search team. Deck division stand by the port RHIB."

Horn heeled beneath them, turning into the wind, and he watched the incoming machine grow and grow and at last pass behind the hangar, too close to see.

The boarding and search went well at first. One of the RHIBs, the twenty-foot rigid-hull inflatables that had replaced the old motor whaleboats, cast off and half-planed, half-wallowed across the green swells. It circled the other vessel for a visual check, then closed to board over the stern. They found the stowaways. But one crewman had a rifle concealed under a windbreaker on his lap, and none of the boarding crew bothered to search him. The chief observer said he could have mowed down every man on deck before they could get their pistols out of their holsters. Also the boarding team had no climbing gear, no keys to their handcuffs, and so on down a long list of shortcomings and miscommunications.

Twelve hundred, noon, after a wolfed lunch of grilled cheese and fries that felt like it had wedged six inches down his gullet. "Range to the carrier?"

"Forty-one miles, sir."

"Captain, we have a low-flying contact just popped up 031 nine miles, outbound."

"Bridge, TAO, hold air contact bearing 005, range 32 nautical miles . . . Come to 160 for two minutes, then come back to base course."

The Combat Information Center. "Combat." Sitting in the

blue leather elevated chair while around him in a space no
bigger than a good-sized living room eighteen people
worked in dim blue light. Five different conversations were
going on over sound-powered phones and radio headsets.
Helo land/launch, battle group common, fleet antiair warfare
control net, the surface control circuits, and screen commander circuits.

Combat was laid out concentrically, though it took familiarity to distill that arrangement from the dozens of screens,
circuits, tote boards, and comm gear that festooned every
flat inch above the green rubber decking. His chair overlooked the tactical action officer's station, the surface
weapons controller, and the Harpoon and Tomahawk engagement planners. To his left, tote boards listed the ships
involved in the exercise, the day's call signs, and *Horn*'s
comms status. Behind him was the dead-reckoning tracer—
dark at the moment, since no antisubmarine play was scheduled. Those could be considered the inner ring. Farther out,
along the bulkheads, were the underwater fire control panel
and the helo controller's station, with a grainy black-and-
white TV that showed the flight deck, empty, at the moment,
as just now a refueled 191 was twenty-five miles distant,
checking out a contact suspected to be USS *Briscoe*. To the
left were the fire control radar consoles, gun control consoles, and, along the forward bulkhead, the electronics warfare stack, nav table, and the Tomahawk launch console. On
the far side of the bridge ladderway was the curtained-off al-
cove of sonar.

When he'd started out, a captain fought his ship from the
bridge. Now destroyer COs fought from Combat. Dan intended to spend the bulk of his time here, at least until he
was satisfied Camill could defend the ship in his absence.
Directly in front of him the TAO was working the radar re-
peaters and radios and the blue screens of the JOTS, the
Joint Operational Tactical System, like a croupier on a heavy
night. He was drinking coffee with one hand, tapping at a
keyboard with the other, and carrying on two different con-

versations over the air while reporting over his shoulder to Dan about a generator bearing failure light the helo said just came on. Dan told him to bring him back in, get the generator checked out.

"Sir, OPFOR commander wants to know why we're not moving out there at flank speed."

"Let me talk to him." Dan informed Hotel Juliet, the Red Force commander, about the trouble light and promised he'd be proceeding north at flank speed as soon as his aircraft was secure on deck.

Sitting back again, one segment of his consciousness monitoring the sputter of speech and the jerky prance of digital symbology, another reflected on how free-form and inchoate operations at sea seemed now. The navy had once moved across the face of the planet in great ordered formations. At Armageddon battle groups would march in great phalanxes into the northern waters of the USSR, while submarine fleets collided north of the Greenland-Iceland-U.K. Gap. Flag officers had plotted strategy that stretched across time zones, and commanding officers followed written orders and stayed in their sectors.

Now Blue and Red and merchant traffic interpenetrated, zones overlapped, no identity was certain. Chaos had been loosed on the deep.

Camill, interrupting his increasingly gloomy thoughts. "Sir, prefire brief complete, safety walk-through complete, we're ready to start."

"Make it so," Dan said.

Of four attacking aircraft, *Horn* splashed one. The designators reacted slowly and had trouble keeping the radars on the targets. The combat direction system dropped track while they were being passed from the consoles. The automatic tracking systems either failed or were applied haphazardly. When the hits started fires, the repair parties reacted hesitantly and probably would have passed out from smoke inhalation because their masks didn't fit right. The main space fire drill and mass casualty drills dissolved into confusion and recrimination. They were even less ready for chemical attack.

Nineteen hundred in the wardroom. Officers, chiefs, tactical petty officers held up the bulkheads, nodding with fatigue. They presented weather, equipment status, operations, intelligence, and rules of engagement. They discussed Q-routes and frag orders. The observer-liaison reminded them of the data collection requirements, sheets that had to be filled out hour by hour so that after the exercise ended their tactics could be graded.

Twenty-three hundred. He tossed in his at-sea cabin, tormented by dreams. They switched between his father and the Mukhabarat torturer named Major al-Qadi. The dream was bad enough. But then he came to the part where they doused Sergeant Zeitner with fuel and set him on fire. It was that, the smell of oil and flame, that jerked him awake.

Only to remember, sweating, staring into the darkness, it hadn't been a dream. And that he himself had not been as brave as Zeitner. He didn't deserve the decoration he wore, or the respect.

He lay with palms blanking his eyes, denying, minute by minute, the voice in his heart that told him to take the pistol out of his safe and make the guilt and terror stop. He kept telling himself this voice lied, that it was trauma, stress, the aftermath of torture. But he didn't believe it.

It came to him with dreadful certainty that he was going to do something irreversible. Shoot himself, or go mad, or pull up the dogging bar on the watertight door next to his bank and step out into the dark sea.

The bridge buzzer went off beside his ear, and his whole body jerked. He grabbed it and half barked, half moaned, "Captain."

The officer of the deck said they had a contact at eight thousand yards, closing, with a closest point of approach of two hundred yards. He stepped into his pants and got to the bridge barefoot to find it coming in fast on his port bow, a containership or cruise liner, much larger than *Horn*, a huge and confusing array of white and red lights that made no sense to the eye. The little Furuno radar was obviously not giving correct courses. Combat seemed to be tracking not the ship he was looking at, but another ten degrees off and fifteen thousand yards away. He could not slow his engines, the reflex action in a serious and quickly worsening situation; another contact was following them close astern to starboard, reducing their maneuvering room to zero, unless he cared to cut across the steadily nearing ship's bow.

And to his horror, faced with the necessity for immediate action, his mind did not respond. He seemed to be back in the dream, suspended, yet at the same instantly conscious of others around him waiting for orders.

Inside his skull seethed dazzling white pain and the smell of burning fuel.

He put his hands out in the darkness, groping, and felt cloth. His shaking fingers dropped to the knobbed controls of a radar repeater. He leaned forward, hammering his knuckles into them over and over. Till the pain penetrated the milling turmoil of what passed for his mind. He took a deep breath. Then another.

At last, though he could not have said from where, an order occurred to him. He gave it. Then another.

He escaped by putting all engines on the line and accelerating out of the closing jaws. But as he walked aft on trembling legs, seeing blood drip black from his hands in the red passageway light to explode inky ellipses on the buffed and slanting tile, Dan Lenson reflected with utter cold lucidity that the greatest danger to USS *Horn* might be the tormented brain of her commander.

The exercise peaked the next day in an intense swirling battle that had no clear front and no clear development and no clear outcome, except that everyone seemed to be getting clobbered. Hostiles, neutrals, unknowns popped up, seethed, and vanished between the imaginary landmasses. Cruise

missiles from nowhere blitzed *Theodore Roosevelt*. Two Red
Force units were sunk by air strikes, one by surface-to-
surface missiles, two more by Blue submarines, while Blue
suffered from mines in the approaches to Kartuna City and
from land-based missiles while transiting the straits. As far
as he could judge, if the referees hadn't kept "reconstituting"
sunken ships and shot-down aircraft, the exercise would
have ended after the first hour with the destruction of every
unit from both sides. *Horn* was hit over and over, and the observers imposed casualty after casualty as the day went on:
missile strikes forward, midships, and aft, class A fire in
supply berthing, class A fire in the admin office, flooding in
Aux One, flooding in the Mount 51 passageway, class B oil
fire in main engine room number two, flooding in shaft alley,
electrical power failure forward, ruptured firemain piping.
On and on till the crew slumped glassy-eyed to the decks.

It was a sobering foretaste of an all-out littoral action
fought with computer-aided data availability and long-range,
high-speed weapons. He hoped the U.S. Navy never faced
an opponent of even roughly equal numbers and weaponry.
The carnage would be immense and the victor anybody's
guess. Like the confused and bloody nights off Guadalcanal,
where shadows loomed suddenly from the dark and the first
who drew would either win the gunfight or bear the crushing
responsibility of blotting out the lives of fellow Americans.

This was the kind of war *Horn* might be headed for.

This was the kind of war they had to be ready to win.

Dusk, and they were steaming north along the coast. Lights
twinkled on the horizon. He looked toward them, wishing he
could get ashore. Just for an evening. Just to be no longer the
captain. He'd never understood before, watching those he'd
served under, second-guessed, criticized, how crushing
heavy it all could weigh.

Instead he nodded to Yerega, who flicked switches and
handed him the mike.

"This is the skipper speaking."

He paused, hearing his voice echoing, then went on. "The JTFEX is over. The observer-liaison team has just given me our raw scores. In some respects we've done well. In others, not so well."

He went over the shortcomings: failure to set Zebra, absences from watch stations, inadequate training of firefighting and damage control teams, improper readiness of casualty power cables, inadequate marking of casualty power terminals, unfamiliarity of personnel with dewatering procedures. Then he paused.

"To sum up: I'm not happy. My choice is whether to accept our performance, go to the Gulf the way we are, or to go back and do it over.

"I don't like that first choice. We're going in harm's way. It would not be fair to you, nor to your families, if I took you there less than fully prepared.

"*Horn* will no longer accept mediocre performance. Our new motto says it: 'Aggressive and proud.' I believe we can be the best ship in the United States Navy. But to get there, we'll have to do better.

"We have clearance to enter port, but I've advised the squadron we won't be alongside tonight. I've asked our observers to help us conduct additional training tomorrow. And the day after, if necessary. Until we're ready to fight our ship, and save her when she's hurt."

He lowered the mike, then set it back in its receptacle. Catching the bridge team's looks of resentment and disappointment. That was okay. Nothing in a skipper's billet description said he had to be liked.

The faces of the dead haunted him. He wasn't going to add to their number.

He owed his men—correction, his *people*—no less than that.

7

Mashhad, Khorasan Province, Northern Iran

The city was a thousand years old. Its name meant "Place of Martyrdom." Most of its inhabitants were not yet awake, though here and there chimneys smoked, fires glimmered, where bakers were preparing the morning bread. The cool air was an acrid musk of wood smoke and saffron and centuries-dry dust. In an hour the muezzins would call the city to wakefulness and prayer, but now it lay sleeping under the stars.

The third team had been at it since midnight, in a littered, oil-reeking loading bay with a rolling steel door to conceal their work lights. First to be chain-hoisted into the truck were two rusty but incredibly heavy half-inch-thick steel slabs. They fit flat on the bed of the rented Fiat. On top, wrapped and taped in black plastic bags, went twenty kilos of the Polish explosive the man who called himself Malik had brought with him.

After that, the bricks. With muffled grunts, they stacked them along the left side, up to the scarred metal ceiling. Thick, heavy pavers, dug out of a road sometime past and left at a corner of the plastic company's sprawling and dilapidated site. Malik had lighted up seeing them, and drawn them into his diagram. They boxed the bricks into place with plywood and braced them with planks.

In the darkness they trudged in and out of the factory, carrying sacks and containers. The second team had bought what they carried here and there around the city, from dealers and resellers the first team had located months before.

The three who labored this morning had never met their predecessors. The first party to arrive identified the target and visited it. They paced off distances, observed guards, took photographs, and drew up the attack plan. The second team arrived after the first left. They assembled the materials; truck, tools, road maps, weapons, and the ingredients of the bomb itself. Malik had provided detailed specifications, and nothing they bought was out of the ordinary for men who carried cards identifying themselves as working for the Mashhad Plastics and Associated Chemicals Company, Ltd. Sacks of urea pellets. Concentrated acid in carboys. Plastic surgical tubing. Steel beams and sheeting. Half a ton of used bolts, stripped from derelict cars before they were crushed in a junkyard north of town.

The men now stacking sacks and carboys around the central charge were Baluchis. Sebah Sahaba, Gulbeddin Hekmatyar's militants from the highlands between Iran and Afghanistan. Malik had met them at the bus station two days before and bunked them on mattresses in the abandoned factory.

Yesterday afternoon they'd slaughtered a lamb, cooked it in a steel drum dug into the ground, and feasted on hot baked meat with handfuls of saffron rice and pine nuts and spring onions and sweet cakes and crunchy sweet melons, drinking the sweet Iranian Fanta. Then gone together to a *hammam,* a local bathhouse. They'd soaked in the steam and let the body-washer peel the grime and tension from them with rough cloths and hot water, then eaten icy sherbet of vinegar and sugar, and drunk many cups of strong thick coffee flavored with anise. A boy had brought them fresh ripe pomegranates, so ripe and juicy that, broken open, they looked like lacerated and bleeding flesh.

The men had laughed and joked then, relaxed and loud, young and brash.

This morning they shivered in the wind, and stared at nothing.

Malik flicked his cigarette away and came into the glare of the work lights.

He was not tall. His black receding hair was trimmed and combed. His eyes were rather sad behind plastic-framed glasses. Flecks of some dark material were embedded in his left cheek, above where his beard began. His left eyelid sagged, making him look sleepy, or cynical. It was actually muscle damage. He wore a rumpled gray polyester suit jacket, blue trousers, and a striped shirt with the collar open. Clicking a flashlight on, he climbed into the truck and inspected what they'd done. Then jumped down again and directed the others as they lifted precut I-beams. These went along the right side, fitting so precisely between floor and ceiling they remained upright, wedged in.

The men listened as he explained again the sequence of events, and how it would be brought about.

Not long after, the sound of drums broke the stillness of the night. Then the wailing of the muezzins began. Metallic-sounding, electronically amplified, their voices soared and fell in an eerie, distant, repetitive polyphony.

> God is most great! . . . *God is most great.*
> I testify that . . . *I testify that*
> There is no god but God! . . . *There is no god but God!*
> And that Mohammad . . . *And that Mohammad*
> Is the Prophet of God. . . . *Is the Prophet of God.*
> Come to the Prayer! . . . *Come to the Prayer!*
> Come to the Salvation! . . . *Come to the Salvation!*
> Prayer is better than sleep. . . . *Prayer is better than sleep.*
> God is most great. . . . *God is most great.*
> There is no god but God! There is no god but God!

As they rose from their salaams they glanced at the man in the shadows. "You do not join us?" said one.

He shook his head. "I am not worthy."

"Truly, you are."

"Truly I am not, my brothers." Malik spoke quietly. "To-day you are His true and beloved soldiers, who will purify the earth of those who defile the true Islam with this false cult of saints. Remember what the Prophet, *sallallahu alayhe wa sallam,* said before his death: that a curse be upon those who took the graves of their prophets as mosques. We are all His instruments. But you are His firstborn sons. I bow down to honor you, and wish you the tranquillity that comes before battle."

"Truly, it is so. That we are but His instruments," said the man who would drive the truck. He licked his lips, frightened, but making his voice bold. "But you're still one of us, brother. May His peace be upon you."

They recognized this as more compliment than truth. This man had come from far away. And Malik probably wasn't his real name; Malik was the angel in charge of hell. Yet he knew his dangerous trade. His clear, liquid Arabic marked him as educated, but he also spoke good Farsi and reasonable Pashto and no doubt other languages, too. But there was a gulf between them.

"I am merely the willing servant of God. God is great!"

"God is great!" Their shouts echoed in the loading bay, under the glare of the electric light.

The city was the holiest in Iran, a country drunk with holiness since an aged ayatollah had toppled a dictatorial emperor. Here lay Ali Riza, great-grandson of the Prophet, and the eighth holy and infallible imam, who had been murdered in 817 A.D. Beside him slept the storied Caliph Harun al-Rashid, scholar, poet, warrior, the most magnificent of all the caliphs, correspondent with Charlemagne, hero of *A Thousand and One Nights.* Omar Khayyam was another poet buried not far away, at Nishapur; but in Mashhad, poets, though respected, did not rank with imams.

Imams were holy leaders in line of succession after Muhammad's cousin and son-in-law Ali, whom the Shi'a held had been blessed by the Prophet as his rightful inheritor. Great merit could be earned by pilgrimages to their tombs. Especially to that of the *shah-i-ghariban,* Emperor of the Exiled, patron of the lost, the hopeless, and the damned. So that as centuries ebbed, marbled courtyards, golden-domed mosques, museums, and minarets had risen. Its library gathered the largest collection of handwritten Qur'ans in the world. British and Russian had played the Great Game in its alleyways, and in 1912 a bomb had ripped through the sanctuary, permanently estranging the Shi'ite world from the Muscovite bear.

Today was a holy day of mourning for Hussein, grandson of Muhammad. All over the city, at hundreds of inns and hotels, thousands of pilgrims rose and washed and prayed. They streamed into the streets, where first a trickle, then a flood floated through the predawn darkness, converging in an echoing shuffle and the sigh of prayer.

The team scrambled up into the truck. Malik kept looking to the eastern sky. The silhouettes of mountains loomed against the gray light of coming day.

The chain-link gate swung open, and the Fiat pulled out onto Quarani Tohid, Quarani Street, a wide, spotlessly swept boulevard. It roared slowly south, teetering heavily on overloaded springs. Malik followed in a white Datsun sedan with a battered-in fender. He stayed well behind the truck, blinking involuntarily each time it bottomed out.

His hands tightened on the wheel. A green pickup had pulled out from a side alley. It accelerated up to the Fiat, paralleling it on the four-lane street. In it he could see two of the feared and omnipresent Iranian religious police—the *komiteh.* They could stop any vehicle, question or jail anyone, simply on suspicion.

It moved up alongside the roaring, smoking truck, and he took his foot off the gas, dropping back even farther as one of the *komiteh* leaned out, looking it over. Then relaxed as the police vehicle pulled off and vanished down another street.

The driver wasn't from Mashhad, but he'd driven the route several times, practicing, in the sedan. Still in the near darkness, threading among the groups of pilgrims as they gradually converged on the huge tomb and mosque complex, he drove slowly, at no more than thirty miles an hour. Then, a quarter mile short of the golden dome, the truck pulled to the left and descended a ramp.

The Datsun kept straight on, passing the central square. Malik peered through the windshield. Thousands of pilgrims gazed up at the glowing bulbs outlining minarets and domes, the colonnade, and the arched portal that led to the interior and ultimately to the holy burial chamber in a sparkling wonderland of light and beauty.

He'd visited that chamber. Had entered, men separating from the women as they did so. Had checked his shoes and strolled in stocking feet through the marble paved courts, the silver balconies of supplication, examining the inlaid tiles and mirrors, the intricate inscriptions. Had prostrated himself before the magnificent golden *zarih* that protected the ancient tomb. Had watched the other pilgrims with sad eyes, noting as they entered from this direction and that.

And had smiled, heart racing with excitement, as he realized how it could be done.

The truck was underground now. The three sat crowded together in the cab. One reached under the seat from time to time, stroking the steel buttplate of an assault rifle. He kept hoping for the tranquillity that was supposed to come to the martyr. But only touching the gun seemed to give him any comfort. The driver concentrated on driving; the one sitting in the middle held a hand-drawn map on his lap, directing him. It had been drawn by a man on the second team, who'd taken a job inside the shrine, repairing the plumbing in the pilgrims' washrooms.

The tunnel road circled the immense complex, leaving the spacious courts and open areas at ground level free for the pilgrims to enter and congregate and wander from porch to porch and shrine to shrine. It was a service access, the

walls neither enameled tile nor fine marble but rough concrete spaced with fluorescent tubes covered with yellowing
plastic. Signs pointed to various exits from the ring.

"Dar al-Sa'adah," said the man with the map suddenly,
pointing. The driver pulled off, and the truck twisted into a
maze of smaller passages. At last he downshifted to first
gear. The motor slowed, laboring as it pulled its weight up a
short, steep incline.

On the porch between the Golden Balcony and the dome of
Hatam Khani some three hundred women and small children
were gathered, waiting.

The porch—actually an enclosed hall of access—
gleamed with semiprecious stone and shining gold. The
floor was smooth, brightly colored marble, scrubbed and
waxed to spotlessness. A shallow trough showed where millions of feet over the centuries had passed through a golden
door. The walls were covered to head height with thousands
of intricately carved tiles incised with verses from the Holy
Qur'an. Above that, across the upper wall, the sixty-six
couplets of the elegy Malk-ush-Shu'ara Saboori Mashhadi
had pronounced over the murdered imam were inscribed in
the lovely intricacy of Nastaliq script. The whole interior
was brilliantly lighted by hundreds of bulbs nestled in immense nineteenth-century chandeliers of the finest Bo-
hemian crystal.

The golden door, closed now but about to be opened, led
into the Zari-i-Mutahhar, the Holy Burial Chamber itself.
The women peered toward it, praying and speaking in
hushed voices. An infant cried out, but was hastily rocked
and kissed back into a restless, fidgeting silence.

The bearded man in the gray suit coat stepped on the accelerator again. The minarets, the lights fell back in his rear
view. He drove south, careful to avoid the throngs that
spilled now onto the streets. They were singing. The words
came indistinctly through the closed glass. Glancing again at
his watch, he turned on the radio. Leaned to tune it to a local

station, and increased the volume till it drowned out the
hymns. He examined the mirrors again, looking for police or
any sign of interest in him. There was none.

Lighting a cigarette, listening to a discussion on the radio about milk production, he drove slowly and carefully
out of town.

The man who'd kept touching the Kalashnikov pulled it
from beneath the seat and chambered a cartridge. He
slammed the door open, jumped down, and walked back to
guard the rear of the truck.

Inside the cab, the driver, sweat running down his face,
reached behind the seat to pull a thick cable into the light. It
was made up of four fuses. Each was covered by transparent
plastic surgical tubing. Their ends stuck out, cut and frayed
apart to expose the core. The driver flicked a lighter several
times. But no flame emerged. Finally the other pressed in the
cigarette lighter, on the dash. Seconds later it popped out,
glowing cherry red.

When all the threads were burning, fizzling up a thin blue
sulfurous smoke, they bailed out of the cab to either side,
drawing Russian-made automatics.

At that moment the green pickup pulled up the ramp behind them. The man with the Kalashnikov saw the *komiteh*-
men at the instant they saw him. They were armed only with
heavy sticks, but they charged out of the pickup and up the
ramp at him without hesitation, shouting and brandishing the
clubs. He pulled the rifle close to his body and hosed out a
burst. The bullets blasted them backward.

The bomb went off in two stages, separated by milliseconds.
The first detonation, the five kilos of explosive on the right
side of the truck, fired the heavy steel I-beams sideways and
upward through the ancient brickwork and plaster between
the underground access and the reception hall above. They
crashed through bricks and lath and the thin sheathing of
marble and tile on the plinth, mowing down the women who
stood closest to the wall.

Then the main charge went off. This second explosion was so powerful the plates only resisted for a time too short to measure before they gasified in the expanding fireball that stamped the truck frame down into flattened steel, and blasted apart the heavy masonry foundations, dating back to 1602. But before they disintegrated, they and the mass of heavy brick focused the blast, sending a half ton of rusty rivets and bolts through the freshly torn hole.

Moving faster than bullets, heavier and even crueler in their jagged irregular shapes, the thousand-pound fragment-charge cut down the waiting crowd in a welter of blood and torn flesh, jewelry, cloth. They sheared off arms and hands. Smashed through faces and skulls, punctured bodies, tore through lungs and eyes and stomachs.

Some of the women had grasped toddlers by the hand. Others carried infants beneath their chadors. These, too, were torn to pieces by the flying steel, then flayed by the shock wave, lungs and arteries and sinews torn apart in an instant and blown through windows and mirrors.

Their surroundings turned instantly from decoration into instruments of murder. The immense nineteenth-century chandeliers disintegrated into millions of shards of impaling-sharp crystal. The inscribed tiles, cut with the holy concentration of craftsmen intent on the worship of God, became a hail of ceramic projectiles.

A horrible bloom of torn meat, shattered bone, and bright blood sprayed out across the lovely calligraphy, across the holy words of the Prophet of Mecca.

The shock sent a tremor through the building, popping lightbulbs, setting the walls and pillars swaying above the thousands of pilgrims. They instantly concluded an earthquake had began, and began herding out into the open air.

In the wrecked porch, smoke billowed from a gaping hole in the floor. For a moment the terrible sound seemed to have wiped out all sound. Then the echoing silence slowly yielded. To cries, gasps, prayers. To a slowly rising chorus of terror and screams and pain.

• • •

Outside the city the Datsun stood parked by the side of the road. Not far away uphill, lethargic sheep milled slowly in a wire pen, or lay on the dusty ground, not even blinking as flies crawled over their eyeballs.

The man called by the name of the angel of punishment watched smoke rising above the minarets. Listened to the wail of sirens. The radio babbled with horror. A reporter spoke urgently from the courtyard of the shrine. He wept as he described the bodies being carried out. Scores of dead. Hundreds injured. Blood. Slaughter. Death.

He stood smoking as more sirens joined the lament. It sounded as if the Baluchis had parked in exactly the right spot. The announcer, voice shaking with outrage and fury, spoke of gunmen shot down in the ring tunnel.

Heroes? He cocked an eyebrow. Perhaps, in their way. Simple men, who believed. Damaged men, filled with hate.

Tools, to be used.

As he'd used such tools before.

He wondered now whether he'd put enough acid in the mix. Maybe next time he'd add more.

In the pen, a herder or lot manager came out and began sifting feed into a trough. The animals slowly congregated, but they didn't seem eager to eat. The small man glanced his way a couple of times; then walked over.

"Komak bokonam?" said the Iranian.

A northern-flavored Farsi. "Your sheep seem tired," Malik told him, in the same language, though he knew his accent would sound strange.

"They've been that way for some time. The lambs—they don't grow like they should."

"You might consider feeding them something to pep them up. There are such things."

"Are there? I'll have to look into that," the herder said, bending to feel along a lamb's flank.

The man went back to the car. He watched for a while longer, listening to the frenzied voices on the radio. Thinking about them, and about the sheep, and about where he was bound next.

Then only a tracing in the air of dust and smoke marked where he had been.

8

Norfolk, Virginia

Dan woke on an upper floor of the Omni Hotel to find his wife already up. It was early yet. The windows were still dark, the river beyond a swatch of blackness. The shaded desk lamp was glowing.

Not moving, not letting her know he was awake, he lay watching her.

Blair was tapping busily on the notebook computer her aide carried around for her. The half-moon glasses she wouldn't wear in public were perched on her nose. She worried at her teeth with a pencil eraser as she stared at the screen. The front of her hotel bathrobe was open.

Blair Titus was as unlike his first wife as it was possible to get. Where Susan had been dark and spare, Blair was tall and pale and blond. Even now, breasts exposed by the unbelted robe, her utter concentration gave her an air of inaccessible professionalism. This, he knew, was a front. She had a passionate, even reckless side. But he'd seen her other persona, too. Fixing a careless witness or pompous general with a pointed query, which every attempt to evade would only widen the wound.

Her relationship with authority was different from his. Where he both envied and suspected it, neither position nor rank intimidated her. She had a doctorate in operations research, a juris doctor degree from George Mason, and a stepfather who owned six thousand acres in Prince Georges

County, Maryland. He could see how insecure men found her threatening and reacted with hatred that was really fear.

They'd met on the deck of a tanker in a sandstorm, when he was exec of the foredoomed *Turner Van Zandt* and she the defense aide for Bankey Talmadge. And again in Bahrain, where one night had interlocked their lives like enzymes recognizing the molecule that might complete them. Agreeing the odds were against them. Until one day, as he stepped out of an isolation ward, she'd persuaded him they had to try.

Blair had started as a presidential management intern. From there she'd gone to the House as a junior staff member, then to the Senate, tracking political favors and working the military beat. Then to the Armed Services Committee staff when Talmadge had taken over as chairman. She'd briefed the candidate on military issues during the campaign, and Les Aspin had asked for her by name for Defense. When the list came through, her job was manpower and personnel. She'd sailed through her hearings, one of which he'd managed to get down from Newport to catch.

Taking over her Pentagon office, she'd told him, was harder. Over a hundred military and civilians and five appointees. She worried about being the first woman in the post. How she felt awkward at parades—everyone watching and she couldn't screw up. He'd been able to give her a couple of tips; how to put military people at ease, and when to take the reins.

It wasn't a traditional marriage. They grabbed weekends and holidays together, scheduling meetings around each other's commitments. Once in a while they had a few days together in the apartment she rented in Alexandria. He honestly didn't know if it was working. They were just both so damned busy. And now here he was off again.

Then she turned her head and smiled, and he set aside his doubts. Whatever the future brought, he had this moment. This and a few more, moments of fulfillment and love, like jewels set into an iron bracelet of duty.

"No bad dreams?"

"Not tonight."

"That's good. I didn't wake you, did I?"

"Hell, no. It's well past 0400. What're you doing?"

"The staff did a draft of my remarks, but they can't seem to get them through the hotel's fax."

"You can do that kind of stuff off the cuff. What, are you worried about it?"

"I like to have something in my pocket."

"I thought I was the only one who wasn't sure what he was doing."

For that he got a glance over the glasses. "You wanted command, right? You didn't want the staff job."

"I wouldn't be right in legislative affairs, Blair. Sooner or later I'd tell them what I thought of them."

"Yeah. You tend to do that. So what's the problem?"

"I guess, this whole assignment."

"What about it disturbs you?"

"Why I was selected for it, for one thing."

"Why would the navy possibly select you for *Horn?* Well, let's see. Surely not because of your combat record. Or your sea time. Or your Silver Star and Congressional. That couldn't have had anything to do with it."

"I'm not sure that's true."

She took her glasses off and leaned forward, and her robe fell open even more. "Dan, let me speak from the SecDef perspective. You're something we don't have very many of anymore. We've got policy wonks, and acquisitions guys, and hardware and systems and logistics types. What we don't seem to be generating are war fighters. You can argue the reasons for that all you want. I know you've got opinions on the issue."

"I sure do."

"I don't have any insight into the selection process. It's service level, opaque to us. But I think that's precisely why you were chosen. What's more, you've got an open mind. You can give this concept of putting women in combatants a fair trial." She bent to look out; he saw past her the first emanation of dawn rising from the river. "Yeomen in World War I. Transport pilots in World War II. The navy started them off in transports and hospital ships in the seventies. But so far, they can't serve on warships."

"Because Congress says they can't."

"Title 10 U.S. Code, para 6015. For years Congress said the code was there because the services wouldn't accept women. And the services said Congress forced them to continue their exclusionary policies. But Panama and Desert Storm fixed that. Twenty-three women got the Combat Action Ribbon from the Marine Corps alone."

She touched the computer, keeping it awake, and went on. "Actually, they *can* serve on combatants, as long as they're temporary billets. Legal officer on the *Independence.* If they're civilians, they can serve in the replenishment ships that refuel the battle groups. The EEOC under Title 7 forced us to let female engineers and technicians accompany combatants on sea trials. So they *can* go to sea, and they *do* go to sea . . . and keeping them out of ship's company looks more artificial every year. Now the Defense Advisory Council has called for bringing down those statutes. And I agree."

"I sort of thought you would."

"It's not because I'm a woman, smart-ass. The manpower figures say we have to. I've tested the waters with the chiefs. The air force chief of staff needs pilots no matter what's between their legs. The Marine Corps's against. The army's divided. The navy's the swing vote. That's why we need a demonstration."

"*Horn.*"

"In order to overcome a statutory prohibition, we have to do a test program. There's policy riding on you, Dan."

"With what as the ultimate agenda?"

"There's no agenda. Maybe DACOWITS has one, but DoD as a whole does not. Or if we do, it's to make use of women up to the point where the down side cancels out the up side. Right now nobody knows where that is. The Hill might decide there should be no statutory limits."

"Not even ground combat?"

"Women are *already* in ground combat," Blair said, gesturing with the glasses. "Look at the army. Women can drive supply trucks though a combat zone. But they can't man an Abrams. If you were going to attack somebody, would it be a tank or a truck full of ammo?"

"The truck."

"One soldier in Desert Storm, she was trained as a radio operator. They needed truck drivers instead. They showed her how to drive in forward gear, the sergeant told her he'd instruct her in reverse the next day. Only that night the Iraqis attack across the berm and she finds herself driving a tanker full of fuel through an Iraqi minefield, and she can only do it in forward gear."

She paused, looking into her screen as if into an oracle. "My deepest suspicion is that we're not really talking about whether women can do these jobs. Everybody knows they can. If they can be street cops in New York, firefighters in L.A. And I don't think it's about keeping women from being killed. Women die in every war. I think some people want to exclude women from *killing.* And the reasons for *that* make very interesting speculation."

Dan rolled over, finding the conversation somewhere between fascinating and beyond him. "Such as?"

"All the way from feminist theory to the archetype of the murdering mother."

"Huh. Well, regardless, I'm getting the feeling certain elements want *Horn* to crash and burn. Or want me to."

"Are you saying the naval establishment wants it to fail?"

Dan thought of Niles. "I don't know. Maybe. Maybe that's why they assigned me."

"Oh, of course. Good *God.* You don't say things like that to that exec of yours, do you?"

"I'm not married to her."

"Dan, I've noticed that when it comes to this issue, maybe eighty percent of the guys just want somebody next to them who can do the job. Another ten percent are gung ho for the women. And there's ten percent who are just assholes. Whatever a girl does is going to be wrong, just because she doesn't belong in the club."

"Where do I rank? Angel or asshole?"

"I'd count you in the eighty percent. Which is fair. But you have both supporters and enemies at high levels. Some will try to help you. Others will try to torpedo you. Most will just hang back and watch. I'll help you all I can, but—"

"No, Blair. No offense, but please don't try to *help* me in any way."

"As I was going to say, I don't think you want me to. So let's leave it at that, okay?" She looked back at her computer, frowned, pushed her glasses up again.

His gaze traced her neck into the robe, and from nowhere came the memory of Hotchkiss's flushed skin, the fine hairs of her nape. The double image pushed metal up his cock. He shifted his legs. "Turn that thing off and come over here."

"That an order, or an offer?"

"A threat. Turn it off, or I'll tell CNN what we did last night."

"Blackmail."

"Absolutely. And you know what any hint of sexual irregularity would mean to the image of this administration."

She acknowledged the thrust with a twisted smile. Glanced at the computer again; then shut it down. "You know, I've got something riding on this, too."

"On *Horn?*"

"I've told some important people that this initiative's going to show how well women can integrate. If you look bad, I will, too."

He felt a sudden flare of resentment. Everybody had to put the pressure on. Like the song. Just put the load right on me.

"Slide over," she said, turning off the lamp. Dropping the robe, and standing; a graceful curving shadow that grew larger and larger until it eclipsed the dawn.

Screwed, shaved, and showered, he pulled the plastic off a fresh set of whites as she cursed the inventor of panty hose. *Horn* was due to get under way for the first female combat deployment at noon. Making this an official media circus, he thought darkly. Three-star equivalents, like Blair. COM-NAVSURFLANT. He'd heard nothing from Second Fleet staff, which he hoped meant Niles was going to skip it. He threaded a new white belt. Clipped on a pewter buckle with the ship's crest and sawed the rest of the belt off with his pocketknife. Occupying his hands with routine, while his mind ran free.

Blair turned from the mirror in the cobalt blue suit she favored for TV. "One last hug."

He said into her ear, "The last? How about at the pier?"

"The under secretary and the captain? Not exactly the tone we want to set."

She was right, of course. Holding her, he wanted her all over again, but more; wanted not just the physical contact, but to be with her for more than a snatched day or two. Like a criminal on the lam. How had he maneuvered himself into this? His classmates had normal marriages. Normal families. He had an ex in Utah and a daughter he never saw. For a second he imagined letting the ship go without him. Wouldn't that make Niles's day.

"What's funny?"

"Not much, when you think about it." He kissed her again. "I don't want to leave. Not with you staying here."

"I told you, I might be able to work something to come out to the Gulf. Now that we have a permanent presence there. I'll let you know if I can."

All he could think to do in answer was hold her tighter than ever.

They had breakfast, then split up. Blair's official reason for being here was as a member of the Defense Advisory Committee on Women in the Services. Three other members joined them as she was signing the tab. Other than a marine colonel, who was in uniform, Dan had no idea who they were. Just competent-looking women in civilian clothes. Blair treated them as equals, which would put them pretty far up the political food chain.

Pier 6 berth 2, time 1000. The 1MC echoed from the ship. "Now muster the color guard with the officer of the deck on the quarterdeck." A yellow poly rope was stretched across the pier, holding back those who'd come to see their husbands, sons, and, in a few cases, daughters and wives off.

Four bells sounded as he neared the brow. "*Horn,* arriving," the 1MC announced.

The first thing he did was tell the officer of the deck to strike the pier barrier, to let dependents aboard as long as they stayed topside. His people wouldn't see their loved ones for six months. The least he could do was let them say goodbye. He checked with Hotchkiss as to their readiness to get under way, then went out on deck again. He told each family how proud he was of their service member, what a good job he was doing for the ship and the navy. One woman said she'd never heard anyone say a good thing about her son before.

His mood darkened again as he saw the cameras.

They were lined up on the fantail, filming the crew as they came aboard. A lieutenant commander he didn't know was with them. Dan pulled him aside. "Who the hell are you?"

"Com Second Fleet public affairs, sir."

"Who are all these people?"

"Media requests, sir. National media!"

"Okay, but why are they here?"

"They *asked* to be here. They're the press, and you're news."

He got his temper under control and was looking around when he saw Woltz. The command master chief was talking to a reporter. Their heads were together, and the newsie was scribbling in a notebook. Dan caught "fucking sailorettes" and "dangerous."

"Master chief."

Woltz froze. "Yessir, Captain."

"You and the chief master at arms make a last tour below. Make sure no one's aboard who shouldn't be."

"Aye, aye, Captain."

The reporter said, "The chief was telling me nobody wants the women aboard."

"Did he?"

"They're not used to going to sea. They don't know their way around."

"Most of them have been to sea before. Oilers and ammo ships and tugs."

"How's the crew feel about them?"

"They're all sailors to me."

"That's not what I asked you, Skipper. Is there resistance from the enlisted men?"

"I told you, they're all sailors to me." He sounded pompous and evasive even to himself. Worse was knowing now where the command master chief stood. The chiefs' mess was key to how well the ship worked. He didn't need trouble there.

Eight bells. "Undersecretary of Defense for Manpower and Personnel."

Dan held the salute as Blair came up the brow, stepping carefully on the slick metal treads in low heels, and faced the flag and then him. She looked very good, indeed, and the sailors on deck stared when he dropped his salute and she took his arm; then, smiling, thought better of it and simply shook his hand.

A cameraman shouted, "Here comes one of 'em."

He turned back to see a chubby girl boarding. One of the engineers. Patty something . . . no, Patryce. Patryce Wilson, electrician's mate third. A gloss-lipped black woman with a microphone thrust it forward, almost knocking her down. A moment later the others were shouting, too, asking whether the men had hazed her, if she had a boyfriend aboard, if she was sorry she'd come to *Horn*.

Dan said to the public affairs type, "Get them off the fantail. Now."

"Sir, we can use the exposure. We—"

"Get them off my ship!"

Heads turned, but simultaneously he was dragged backward by both arms. He was about to react violently when he realized it was Hotchkiss, on his right, and Blair on his left. "Let go of me," he told them.

"No, sir. Please. Don't antagonize the press."

"I'll deal with this," Blair said coolly. "Step back, Commander." It took him a moment to realize she was talking to him.

"Berenicia Savage, isn't it? Blair Titus. We went to Somalia together, do you remember? Did you want a statement on what this ship means to the services?"

"Oh, Blair . . . Just a moment . . . This young lady was telling us about how well she's getting along with her male com—compatriots."

"That's fine." Blair smiled at the girl, who looked bewildered by the cameras and attention, and at the same time radiant, fulfilled, like a game show contestant who's just scored. "I'm glad to hear it."

"Does this mean the navy's recovered from Tailhook?"

"I don't know if we'll ever recover from Tailhook," Dan said, catching the PAO's warning glance but not caring. "We defeated a dictator. We liberated a country. The country respected the military again. Then a few drunken louts made us all assholes again."

Savage's eyes lit. She held the microphone out. Blair closed her fist over it and pushed it away. "What the commander *meant* to say is that today is an epochal event in the history of the U.S. Navy. Women went to sea with Stephen Decatur in the War of 1812. Today they're going again, as combatants. Now let me introduce the other members of the Defense Advisory Committee on Women in the Services."

He gave the VIPs a quick tour of the spaces, including women's berthing, which, thank God, Hotchkiss had made sure was squared away and the signs taken down. When they were standing on the bridge and Boatswain Yerega was explaining the layout, the marine colonel murmured congratulations on *Horn*'s JTFEX results.

"I'm sorry?"

"I was told your overall score was one of the highest in the battle group. That's outstanding, Captain. Positively outstanding."

He was saved from a response by the "DESRON Two Two, arriving." He took his leave politely, inviting them to coffee and cake in the in-port cabin after they'd completed their tour.

Aronie had come without an aide. He looked relaxed and fit. Dan offered to take him to his cabin, but the commodore said he'd seen the admiral's sedan arriving. He'd just wait on the quarterdeck.

Keeping his voice below the output of the band, which was tuning up on the pier, Dan said, "I heard we came out better than I, uh, expected on the JTFEX."

"Indeed you did. That was outstanding."

"Sir, the chief observer shared his comments with me before they left the ship. We weren't as good as that."

"How good were you?"

"Average. If that. We worked on the sore points after the exercise, but in the exercise itself, I have to say, we didn't show up all that well."

The commodore said blandly, maybe a shade too smoothly, as if he'd rehearsed the answer, "Well, that's not what came out of the pipe on my end. They must have done a recount somewhere between you and me."

Dan thought this was interesting, but was stopped from pursuing it by the 1MC again. "Naval Surface Forces Atlantic, arriving," it said. He and Aronie stepped forward and saluted side by side.

As sailing time approached, Dan saw the official visitors off, then the families. Hotchkiss stationed the sea and anchor detail. The tug showed up, not the *Clelia Gracie,* he was glad to see. The band played "Anchors Aweigh" and "Proud to Be an American" and "The Girl I Left Behind Me." Dan wondered at this last but figured it was the standard repertoire. Blair gave him a chaste peck beneath the quarterdeck awning and left. She wasn't big on long farewells, and neither was he. The longer they took, the worse he felt. Then the admiral left, and last, Aronie.

The commodore shook Dan's hand firmly. "We're getting under way shortly, too. See you on the other side of the pond."

"Aye, aye, sir."

"You'll do fine. You've got a great bunch of people here."

At least in the military, the junior guy always got the last word, Dan thought. "Yes, sir," he said. "We'll do our best."

Too late, when Aronie was on the pier, he remembered he'd wanted to straighten out that matter of the observer's comments. Around him families were weeping openly. Children clung to their mother's legs, waving to Daddy. He wished his own daughter was here, or that she'd called. Well, she was almost grown. She didn't have time for a dad half a continent away.

The tug hooted. He rattled up ladders. Hotchkiss saluted. "All stations manned, ready to get under way."

He looked to where Blair's car was already pulling out, to where families waved flags, to the homeland they'd not see again for half a year. Then turned to the waiting faces on the bridge. Smiled, more confidently than he felt.

"Okay, XO, let's get this show on the road."

PART TWO

RED SEA

9

Cobie was down in Main One, washing down the GTG. Main One was main engine room number one. The GTG was the gas turbine generator. She was getting used to talking in acronyms, even when she didn't know what they meant. Like the little platform everybody called the IR flat, but when she asked what IR stood for, nobody knew. She was getting used to a lot of things. Or trying to, anyway.

After three weeks of standing three-section watches across the Atlantic and past Gibraltar in it, she was *real* used to Main One. Nickels and dimes, like the guys told her most gas turbine ships stood: five hours on, ten hours off. She worked here and spent most of her off time here, too, unless she wanted to lie in her bunk or go to the ship's store, if it was open.

The first impression you got coming through the access at the top of the compartment was gratings. Level on level of boot-polished shiny steel, going down and down. Going out on them took an effort of will, like believing you could walk on air. The gratings were set in terra-cotta-colored I-beams with thin pipe handrails painted glossy black. Through them, way down below your boots as the whole space tilted, you could see the shaft going around steadily, usually not all that fast, but giving the impression of tremendous power. The IR flat—a flat was like a deck, in the engineering spaces—was just inside the access, with parts lockers and a couple of

mats and the guys' weights and not much else. You went
down the ladder past the huge white insulation-wrapped intake and exhaust ducts for the engines and generators, and
you were on what they called the boiler flat. Above the gray
padlocked steel cases of the reduction gears.

Here you had to choose between another ladder down or
to turn right past the silver-gray, heat-radiating drum of the
waste heat boiler, with the steam traps hissing behind curtains of white vapor too loud to speak over. Past that was the
1S switchboards. The next level down was the PLCC flat.
PLCC meant propulsion local control console. Threading
between racks of firefighting hose and control panels and red
Halon tanks, you worked your way around the tractor-trailer-
sized boxes of the engines themselves to the console the on-
watch used to control everything.

You could peer through a thick window into the sound-
proofed interior of the isolation module. A jet engine, same
as in an airliner, a DC-10 or a C-5. Looking in you couldn't
see much happening, even when they were running, just
stainless tubing and hoses and suspended like in midair the
long dully gleaming barrel of the turbine itself. It was
screaming in there, the temperature was over fourteen hundred degrees in the combustor at full power, but all you saw
was the light glowing on it and the safety chains swaying
like some unseen hand was shaking them.

Then past that and down yet another half level you came
to GTG number one. Another gas turbine, but smaller than
the main engines, it ran at a constant speed to drive the generator. Its exhaust ran the waste heat boiler that provided
steam for the ship, hot water for the showers, and steam for
the mess deck's kettles and all that.

Below that was the lower level, with the engine foundations and the coalescers and fire pumps and the complicated
hydraulics for the screw pitch control mechanism, and all
the lube oil pumps and filters and tanks. Petty Officer Helm
wouldn't let her touch the lube oil. It was synthetic MIL-
SPEC-23699 stuff that ate rubber seals. It would give you
dermatitis and paralysis and birth defects. He worked on it

himself, with rubber gloves and a rubber apron and a face shield. You were walking on diamond-treaded steel floor-plates by now, and pulling them up showed you nothing below but the sea chests where pipes came in through the bottom, and red-painted steel, and slowly roiling water that was the bilge.

That was Main One. Main Two aft was pretty much like it, but she didn't see much of it or the aux spaces or Control because Helm kept his watch section busy doing qualifications and cleaning the steam traps and doing all the other stuff they had to do to keep the engines and generators and pumps running. It wasn't as hot down here as she'd thought it'd be, but it was so noisy everyone had to wear ear protection and shout at each other. It had been rough all the way across. She carried trash bags in her coveralls to throw up in. Ricochet was worse. He was puking nonstop. He lay on the IR flat whenever he could because he said there was less motion up there.

Her watch section was five people. Helm and Ricochet, whose real name was Sanders but everybody called him Ricochet because when he walked down the passageway he bounced off one bulkhead then the other. GSM3 Pascual, who everybody called the Porn King because he had a stash of books and magazines and tapes under his bunk he rented out by the hour. He read *Velvet* and *Superman* and *Vero* on watch. She'd opened one he left on the PLCC. All guys with huge cocks coming in women's faces, the women rubbing it into their tits. Only you could tell it wasn't real come because there was so much of it. She figured probably dishwashing liquid. Whenever she came across one of his magazines after that, she dropped it in the bilge. And Akhmeed, who had a little mustache shaved narrow and came from the Philippines and didn't want to talk about anything but his truck.

It was Akhmeed who'd cut her down after the guys taped her to the overhead. The taping wasn't so bad. What was embarrassing was having to wear a rubber glove on her head. You stretched the latex wrist over the top of your skull and your eyes and your nose. Then blew out until the fingers erected like a rooster comb on top of your head. You had to go around the ship flapping your arms and crowing. She'd come face to face with the exec by the Coke machine. Who'd yelled at her to take the fucking glove off her head and get back to her work space, this was a ship not a frat party.

But now the hazing was over and Chief Bendt had called down on the 4MC to wash down the GTG because they were going into Palma this morning. Helm had shut it down and told her to do the washdown with Sanders. She got her tools together and made sure the temperature was under 110 degrees. If it wasn't, you could warp the blades spraying cold water on them. She climbed into the isolation module and started disconnecting the air lines and hoses. The ship was rolling and her mouth was watering and she didn't like being in there. All somebody had to do was dog the hatch and light off the turbine and she'd cook. Nobody'd ever hear her screaming. So she kept the door propped open. She could hear the guys talking outside about why the rotor rings were sparking.

"We replaced the brushes and sandpapered the rings."

"Is it the rotor? Is it warped?"

"Naw, it's them rotor worms. They get into it and eat out at it from inside."

"What kind of zit brain you think I am? You're fuckin' so lame, man."

"Yeah, fuckin' lame, you scammer. Red on the head like the dick on a dog."

"At least when I fart you smell something, man. Not just dry old cobwebs."

"You're the fucking head of the class, man. Like when they told you to go see the chief engineer and ask her for twelve feet of fallopian tube."

She climbed out and told Helm he could spin the motor now. You spun it at low speed from the panel, about two thousand RPM. Meanwhile she went up the ladder to the upper level and poured half a gallon of BNB into the wash tank. She didn't know what the initials stood for, just that it was like a detergent. She cracked the valve to pressurize it, then went back down to the generator and carefully opened the solenoid valve next to the module. A hiss came out of the open door, but you never actually saw any water. It went in the engine and out the exhaust and evaporated when it hit the hot tubes in the boiler. She gave it one shot with the BNB and two rinses with fresh water. Then climbed back in to reconnect.

"You got *Girls Go Wild,* number eight? I got to get geared up for Palma. One of the hull techs, he was telling me there's like thousands of English girls there. They hear an American accent, they take 'em off right there."

Pascual's voice: "Sure, I got it. Two dollar an hour. Never been looked at. You be the first one."

"You don't need porn, dickhead. You need a testicle transplant."

"Your bitch got you so pussy-whipped, you don't even read porn."

"I never said I read it. But I look at it."

"Save yourself some money. Go to the ship's store, buy some Baby Ruth bars, and go down to Aux 2. Give them to that Wilson chick, she'll take you in the trash compactor room."

"I heard that Borromeo say somethin' about that, but I figured it was bullshit. He's so full of it. The great Latin lover."

"It ain't bullshit. She'll clear your fuckin' tubes. The av mechs snuck her into the back of the bird. Sealed her up airtight, three guys at once."

"Fuckin' women at sea. Fuckin' port-a-pussy . . . sumbitch thought this one up, he oughta get a fuckin' medal. This little one you got, she's got a cute little ass on her. Anybody hooked up with her yet?"

Sanders, sounding confused: "What? Who? Kasson? No, she don't . . . she ain't . . ."

She put her head out and saw two losers from one of the work centers aft. They looked startled seeing her head come out of the enclosure. She snapped, "Ricochet. Clear those tags and set up for a manual start." They muttered and drifted off.

They moored before lunchtime at an industrial part of town. Big heaps and wooden bins of reddish clay rose inland. Somebody said it was what they made Spanish tile out of, like for roofs. She looked ashore eagerly. It was her first overseas port, unless you counted Rota. Fortunately she wasn't in the duty section. They had to sit for a preliberty brief in the mess decks, then everybody went down to the compartment to get ready.

Ina was already dressed when she got there. She had her hair back in braids and was wearing white shorts and running shoes. She looked about fifteen. Which was not necessarily bad, Cobie guessed. Better than coveralls and shitkickers. She waited in line for the shower, thrilled when the water came out hot, and scrubbed the fuel stink off her. Back at her locker, she hesitated between her two civilian outfits. A dark red sundress—God knows what she'd been thinking. Maybe drinking wine in Rome in the Colosseum by moonlight. Uh-huh. Or else jeans and a T-shirt. She unpinned her hair and brushed it out, wishing it would lie straight, but with all the humidity from the hole it kinked up like an unraveled rope.

Patryce Wilson came out of the shower and strode through the compartment naked except for flip-flops. Cobie looked away, remembering the overheard conversation. It was just locker-room bullshit. When a woman acted friendly, some guys took it as an invitation, and once the stories started, everybody had to top them. Like the retards by the generator that morning. "Patryce, you been here before?"

"Palma? Shit, yeah, lots of times. I'll take you to some cowboy bars. We'll get shitfaced. Speak any Spanish?"

Cobie said she didn't, only "Muchas gracias," and Wilson said that was too bad, Spanish men were fun. "Hey, how about Lourdes?"

"She's gotta speak Spanish. Don't Mexicans . . . yeah. Don't they?"

The ear-piercing whistle she hated, then the 1MC. "Liberty call, liberty call. Liberty call for duty sections two and three. Liberty expires on board at 0200 for second class and below. Now liberty."

"You get her, I'll get Ina."

"She's already dressed," Cobie said to her back. Then looked at her makeup kit, hardened and cracked in the heat of the berthing compartment. With hasty, out-of-practice daubs, she began making herself up.

Ina didn't show for the longest time, and Lourdes had to go back for her purse. Everyone had to sign out with a liberty buddy. Patryce told them to sign out two and two, if they signed all four together they'd have to come back together. By the time they finally got to the gate the bus was gone, disappearing over the hill. Patryce said it didn't matter, they'd go to the mall till the next one.

The mall was built into the side of a hill. They had to climb past about five hundred little motorbikes parked below it. Girls and guys were pulling up and leaving. Cobie eyed the girls. Spandex ran rampant. They wore it tight, black stretch pants, or painted-on jeans with big clunky shoes. The guys were swarthy, with dark hair slicked back, kind of greasy looking. There was a Pizza Hut, but it wasn't like in the States. Everything was in Spanish and the pizza tasted funny, but they had Tanqueray and orange juice for two dollars a pitcher. The waiter was a hunk. Patryce called him "stud muffin." Cobie had a glass of T&O and then another, listening to Patryce tell about the artist guy she'd met up at the castle the last time she was here and how she raped his thing.

After that things started getting fuzzy. So instead of one thing, and then another thing, there were scenes, like postcards. Like snapshots in a cruise book. Our Port Visit in Palma.

ON THE BUS TO MAGALOUF

They pull themselves on giggling and screaming and the bus driver gives a sour look but nobody cares. The ship rents the buses and there's nothing but *Horn* dudes aboard anyway, and they're noisy, too. There's nothing the driver can do.

Looking out as the straining engine carries them uphill and then down, through a city. She blinks, fascinated at the passing cars, shops, people. All the signs are in Spanish. Sure, what else! This isn't fucking Bumfuck, Louisiana, anymore. She doesn't feel exactly safe, in a funny way she's never felt before. What if somebody asks her a question? She took Spanish at Acadiana High, but right now she can't remember hello or thank you. Behind them the guys have the windows down, hooting at the babes on the street. They're smaller than Americans, with long dark shiny hair. Most are wearing dresses, some, the ones who look like office workers, pants suits.

The bus drives for a long time, out into the country, up and down hills and ridges. Then they see the sea again and tall buildings. It looks like Fort Lauderdale, where she went on the senior trip. The guys are going nuts, throwing things out of the window, until a first class tells them to knock it the fuck off if they don't want to get everybody restricted to the ship for the rest of the cruise.

A paper bag comes back, hand to hand, somebody stole one of the pitchers from the Pizza Hut. The bus bumps, and it runs down her neck onto her shirt and she says angrily, "Shit. Fuck." And Lourdes is rubbing at it with a paper napkin from her little purse.

THE DAIQUIRI PALACE

Magalouf's like a TV show about the rich and famous, a long curving beach with hotels and clubs. The Daiquiri Palace is a two-story blue house with an outside bar overlooking the beach, then farther down a little concrete wall. Then nothing but beautiful, fine white sand, and beach chairs lined up like tombstones, that regular, except where people had pulled them together and were lying on them. She has her suit on under her jeans so all she has to do is pull her clothes off. The sand's so hot it burns her feet, but the water's warm and blue. Back at the bar somebody's riding the mechanical bull. They're yelling and screaming, and when he falls off, everybody dumps beer on him. Then some guy from Oklahoma gets on, and he can actually ride. They carry him around on their shoulders, then pour beer on him, too, and throw him in the water.

SHOPPING ON THE STRIP
There are lots of English girls out shopping. The clerks are Spanish, but they all speak English and French and probably two or three other languages, too. She starts to feel like she didn't get a good-enough education, listening to them switch from one language to another. She gets to talking with one of the English girls. Everybody goes to Palma or the Canary Islands, she says. Ina here's from England, Cobie says. The English girl's curious, wants to know if Ina plans to go back. Ina says no, she's a Yank now.

Cobie buys a new swimsuit. A two-piece, made in France. It's expensive, but she really likes it. It makes her look taller. She wishes she wasn't so damn short.

THE COWBOY BAR
Patryce takes them there in a taxi. She says you can meet Spanish guys there without a lot of Americans around. Cobie isn't sure she wants to, but they're following Patryce because she knows where everything is. Only when they get there it's closed. So then Lourdes says she's hungry, and they go to another place, all dark wood inside and heavy wooden tables and the menu's all in Spanish, which Lourdes reads to them. Everything's roasted meat. Beef and lamb and pork. She'd like chicken, but there isn't any, so she has beef.

Now it's starting to get dark. Cobie feels sick, almost like throwing up, from the T&O and the beers and all the meat, but she keeps trying to think about something else and it goes away.

THE TATTOO BAR
Another bar, she's not sure where, someplace on the Strip. Guys from the ship in back. Lots of mirrors. Paintings on

the walls. A little old guy with a beard is hunched on a stool with a bottle of Jack Daniel's and shot glasses on a metal tray painted in an Arabic pattern. The tray's cool, her mom would like it. Maybe she can find one at one of the shops.

The guys are getting tribal tattoos. Complicated designs on their chests and arms and shoulders. Barbed wire. Lion's heads. The old guy doesn't speak English. He pours shots of whiskey and shows them other designs. Butterflies. Teddy bears. Rainbows. Unicorns. He points to her neckline. A rose design looks pretty. She could feature that. But then the machine buzzes and blood runs down the guy's arm who's getting tattooed.

She's scared, but Ina gets a unicorn in a field of flowers, its hooves in the air. Cobie takes another shot of whiskey. At last she lies down on the damp blue plastic and peels down her jeans. The machine buzzes. She bites her lip at the sudden blazing pain, whispering softly ouch, ouch, ouch.

THE DAIQUIRI PALACE, AGAIN
Back on the beach. It's cool now, and somebody lights tiki torches. Everybody's drinking daiquiris a woman shakes up at the bar. They go swimming again. Her back stings when the saltwater hits it. There are more girls now, women the guys picked up and brought back to dance and swim. The English girls are going around topless, showing it off like they just invented tits.

Patryce takes her top off first. She teases Ina and Cobie when they won't. Lourdes tells her she'd better put it back on and stop drinking, but Patryce tells her not to be a poop. They're not gonna get to do this once they get to the Gulf, she'd better go back to the fucking ship if she's going to spoil her fun.

Cobie tries to ride the bull, but the shaking makes all the food and booze come up and she hunks all down the front of her new bathing suit. She rinses it off in the house, then goes

into the water to wash her front off. But when she comes out
her top's gone from where she left it on one of the lounge
chairs. Then somebody hands her another daiquiri, and it's
kind of fun walking around with the night wind on her chest
and the guys all trying to act cool, like it's nothing. They
take their shirts off, too, and pretty soon they're playing
drunk volleyball down on the beach.

IN THE BATHROOM

She has to pee bad but doesn't want to do it in the water.
Something brushed her legs the last time she went in and
now it's dark. The light's off when she goes into the bathroom. She switches it on and sees Wilson's head in this
guy's crotch. His wet shorts are on the floor and Patryce's
going up and down on him. Bartlett, who runs the ship's
store. A big dude who jokes about how he'll give them a
break on the Slim Jims. Patryce's eating his Slim Jim now.
It's huge and glistening, almost blue. Cobie stares. She's
never seen a black man's dick before. His eyes open and he
smiles at her over Patryce's head. She looks away quickly,
hesitates, then goes into the stall and closes the door and
pulls down her bottom. She has to pee forever, like she's
soaked the whole ocean in through her skin. Meanwhile
they're grunting and thumping on the other side of the parti-
tion. Finally she wipes herself and rushes out, bare feet
clammy on the concrete. It's wet with piss and beer and saltwater and gritty with sand.

   Outside the torches are still flickering but everything
feels different. Her back burns where she got tattooed. She
feels sick and dizzy and the beach is going around and
around, like when you're down in the hole and the ship's
rolling. Lourdes is standing alone, hugging herself. Eyes
wide, looking scared. Some guy's shirt's hanging on the rail-
ing. Cobie pulls it on, not caring whose it is, and the next
thing they're on the bus, then there's the ship, and the ladder,
and her rack. That's the last thing she remembers. In her
fucking rack, with the motor droning next to her ear and the

ship spinning and spinning like it's all going down the toilet. Vortex. To
        nothing
        but
        black.

10

Four days after they left Palma for operations with the battle group, the word arrived. Along with lessons learned, COMIDEASTFOR instructions, and rules of engagement. The binder of messages and references was two inches thick.

Dan flipped through it on the bridge while Hotchkiss and Camill stood waiting. The sun glared and swayed. A blue sea was running. A burnt-orange haze glowed around the horizon. Over the years Dan had watched that dirty halo creep farther and farther out over the Med. *Roosevelt, Anzio, Cape St. George,* and the amphibious ready group lay thirty miles behind them. *Horn* was out ahead in a screen station, maintaining tabs on aircraft and surface contacts as Task Force 61 plowed toward far-off Crete, with the sonar chanting its eerie, lilting whine.

He rubbed his temples, glancing at a chart of the northern Red Sea the exec had propped against the window. Operating areas and warning zones were outlined in red and green and purple. He read through tab after tab, orders, mission, rules of engagement, logistic requirements.

Horn and *Laboon* would detach as the battle group passed 28 degrees east, about the longitude of Rhodes. Operating as Task Unit 61.1.7, under tactical command of *Laboon*'s captain, they'd transit the Suez Canal and "inchop"—change operational commanders—to Commander, Mideast Force, for duty in the Red Sea. Their mission would be enforcing U.N. sanctions by interdicting traffic to and from the port of Al-Aqaba, Jordan, the transshipment point for imported goods and exported oil trucked out the Iraqi back door.

At its northern end, where it bounded Egypt, Saudi Arabia, Israel, and Jordan, the Red Sea split into two estuaries. The Gulf of Suez and the Gulf of Aqaba branched off like an index and little finger extended to ward off evil. The two U.S. ships would be operating either just inside or just outside the entrance of the Gulf of Aqaba, depending on which sector the Senior Combatant Commander assigned them on arrival. The British, French, and Australians each had a frigate on the Red Sea station. They'd be refueled by an oiler out of Jubail; mail and spare parts would stage out of Sicily via a weekly C-9.

The Red Sea. He'd transited it in *Van Zandt* during the Iran-Iraq War, on the way to Operation Earnest Will. Had run it again in the strangely fated *Oliver C Gaddis,* on her way to the Far East. But he'd never operated there long, not at night, in close proximity to land, under an air threat. And most of his people had never been here before. Many had never deployed before.

Maritime interdiction operations, MIO. Not the most technically challenging assignment he could imagine, but maybe that was for the best, given they'd just gotten here.

"Set up a preaction briefing. All officers, chiefs, tactical petty officers. How about during the canal transit, while we lay over?"

"Aye, aye, sir."

He studied their faces. When he'd joined the navy, a black ops officer would have been unlikely, a female exec unthinkable. Their smooth young faces filled him with vague alarm. But he hadn't been any older when he'd filled their shoes. . . . He swung his legs down. "A thorough briefing," he added. "I want everyone to see the big picture, not just his, uh, not just their own little piece of it."

Camill left, but not Hotchkiss. "Captain, a word?"

"Sure."

"Alone?"

"At-sea cabin?"

"That's fine, sir."

Dan looked at the officer of the deck. Resisted the temptation to check the radar. He wasn't going to micromanage them, much though he wanted to. The tote board gave him no surface contacts inside fifteen thousand yards. . . . He felt uneasy leaving such kids in charge. Was this how Jimmy John Packer had thought of him, back on *Reynolds Ryan?*

"Captain's off the bridge," Yerega shouted behind him as the door to the pilothouse swung shut. He went down a short passageway, passing the nav shack.

His at-sea cabin was the size of a bathroom in a middle-class house. A leatherette settee stood along the starboard side beneath a blue-curtained porthole. Forward of that was a small desk with a shaded light over his notebook computer. Inboard was a shower and water closet. That was it. The reward of the general, he thought, is not a bigger tent. He pointed to the settee, then raised his eyebrows as she closed the door. "We need it closed, XO?"

"Maybe so, sir."

She looked calm and self-possessed, as usual, but slightly flushed. He couldn't tell whether it was anger or excitement, but it was intriguing. He steered his mind away from wherever it was going. "What you got, Claudia?"

She unclipped manila and spread the photos on leatherette.

They were of Palma. At least, the first two. The others were of *Horn* sailors having fun on liberty. On the beach. His heart sank as he thumbed through them. Eyes bleary, breasts bouncing as they ran into the sea. Lifting bottles, mugging for the camera. Not exactly pinup material, but that wasn't the point. The Bacchae had gotten drunk and naked, too. At the peak of their revels they'd selected a man, chased him down, and torn him into bloody lumps of flesh.

"They're all over the ship," Hotchkiss told him. "Lin Porter walked into the first-class lounge in the middle of the movie. She found this set on the table."

Dan looked through them again, playing for time. But Hotchkiss must have gotten the wrong idea, because she said sharply, "Do you find them exciting?"

He decided he'd better miss her point. "What I find interesting is that they're enlargements. Not Polaroids."

"Which means they were printed aboard."

"In the Evinrude spaces," Dan said.

The intel weenies were the only ones who had darkroom capability. He turned the photos facedown and cleared his throat. "It's not what I'd call good news. But it's not the end of the world, either. Sailors are sailors, I guess, of either gender. Sometimes they get drunk on liberty. Sometimes they display poor judgment. Occasionally they've even been known to take their clothes off."

"With all due respect, I don't like that comment, sir. It strikes to the root of the problem on this ship, and I think it requires corrective action."

So the pink tinge to her ears was anger. He filed that for reference, and leaned back, clasping his knee. He gained a few seconds from the phone, which beeped to inform him of a crossing contact on the starboard bow. He told the officer of the deck to maneuver to avoid and to make sure CTF 61 and CTG 61.1 had the same track data. Then shuffled the pictures and squared the edges, careful not to look at them again, and put them back in the envelope, wishing it was as easy to get the issue out of sight.

"Okay, you may have something there. What's your suggestion? How should we handle it?"

"We need an outside investigation."

He quelled his first impulse, which was to say that might be overreacting. Instead he went to the porthole and pushed the curtain aside, looking out.

Beer and partying and the shirts come off. Some might see it as harmless. But Tailhook had changed the way the U.S. Navy thought about what had once passed for innocent fun. If it pissed Hotchkiss off, he'd better think about it again.

On the other hand, reporting it up the chain of command

would mean what Aronie and Blair had asked him to do, make this experiment work, would go up in smoke.

Or was he starting to think like the senior officers he used to hate? Covering his ass. Trying to keep bad news from going upstairs.

No, this wasn't about him. They were all in unfamiliar waters, the leadership as much as the rank and file. He didn't think a couple of topless pictures were a big deal, as long as he didn't know about them. But the longer he pondered, the more he saw that now they'd found them, the leadership had to react. To let it go would send the message it was okay to ridicule and belittle the women. Inviting Blair's hostile ten percent to go a little further, and a little further after that.

To react too harshly, though, would drive the splinter of the male crew's irritation under the skin, to fester and turn ugly.

When he thought he was there, he turned from the sea. "I'd like you to hold off taking it outside the ship. At least for now. I'm not ruling it out. It may be the way we'll go eventually, but before we do, I want you to conduct your own investigation."

"An XOI?"

Dan said yes, an XO's investigation. He told her to start with Lieutenant Sanduskie, the intel officer, to find out who'd developed the photos, presumably using the ship's equipment, chemicals, and paper. That should lead to whoever had snapped them. Hotchkiss asked how she should charge him, and Dan suggested Article 134, disorders to the prejudice of good order and discipline. He then stopped her dead by saying, "I want the women charged, too."

"I'm not sure I heard that right, sir. That's blaming the victim."

"Not quite. If one of my male sailors decided to disrobe in public, I'd expect to see him at mast. Granted, it's a topless beach, but it's still conduct prejudicial to good order. Discipline applies to all hands." He glanced at his watch and said, more harshly than he actually felt, "Clear?"

Hotchkiss hesitated, then nodded.

"As long as you're here. I want the chain guns and fifties

manned as we go through the Ditch." She started jotting on
her clipboard. "Make it a rule, as long as we're within sight
of land in the Red Sea and Gulf, I want the ship's self-
defense team manned up. Check the rotation and get more
people trained if we need to. I want at least three sections
qualified. We'll stay in three sections in Combat, too, with a
qualified TAO on watch at all times.

"Second, once we get into this operating area, we're going to be doing a lot of MIO. Make sure we're taking a strain
on our boarding team; they're not going to have a lot of time
to break in. We'll get there, and probably an hour later we'll
have to put guys over."

"Want me to get more people qualified there, too?"

"If we need to. I think Marchetti's got one team already,
but back-check the weapons officer on that. I already told
you about food . . . Camill's working on the chop message . . . I guess that's all for now."

A tap on his door. The duty radioman. "Sir, message from
CTF 61."

Hotchkiss got up, too. As she left, she brushed so close he
could smell her hair. Strawberry scent. He looked after her
as she went down the passageway, fanning himself with the
message, before he saw the radioman watching him, eyebrows raised.

11

Manama City, Bahrain

The smell of strawberries took him back—to his college days, carefree, or as carefree as a young Arab could be trying to get good grades and make his parents proud.

Back to the days in America.

The man who'd called himself Malik in Iran, Rafiq in Buenos Aires, and other names in many other places, sat under fluttering blue canvas awnings in the Marina Corniche, looking over the sun-gleaming gulf and eating fresh strawberries and frozen TCBY yogurt with a plastic spoon. His thinning hair ruffled in the hot wind. His narrowed gaze, watching the pedestrians promenading past, laughing and chattering and playing music on cassette decks, seemed to see everything and yet nothing at all.

The Sudanese passport tucked into the breast pocket of the cream linen sport jacket showed him without the plastic-rimmed glasses he'd worn in Mashhad, without the beard, with only a carefully trimmed mustache. With his high narrow forehead and prominent nose he looked a little like Anwar Sadat. The name in that passport was Doctor Fasil Tariq al-Ulam. He wore light slacks and a yellow shirt, unbuttoned at the throat, and pens in a pocket protector. A gold-toned Casio calculator-watch. A wedding ring. A cigarette smoldered in an ashtray. He'd spent the afternoon strolling the waterfront. Coffee at the Phoenicia. The hourly show at Dolphin Park. Another coffee at the Marina Club, where he'd struck up a conversation with one of the boat owners, and spent twenty minutes examining a chart of the harbor before taking the table in the café.

The chill sweetness numbed the roof of his mouth. How did they get fresh strawberries here, he wondered. Fly them in?

He looked out over the beach and felt the hot wind like the breath of the Devil. Heard the flutter of canvas. Smelled a tang of wood smoke.

With that smell another beach floated up in memory. Far away, and long ago, but he'd never forgotten. Who could forget something like that? He could not.

He could not.

He could not.

He'd taken a job with the Vietnamese. That summer that seemed to him now the longest season of his existence, heavy, dirty, dangerous work far out on the Gulf of Mexico. Himself young, eager, friendly, someone people liked. A good guy, the Americans said. The shimmering water, the heat, had not been unlike the sea on which he looked out now.

Then, he'd admired America. He smiled bitterly to himself.

Three semesters a year learning the engineering he'd make his life's work. The teachers spoke English too swiftly to understand. But the books were patient. And yes, the West was attractive. There'd been alcohol. And blond Southern girls, with their soft speech and flirtatious ways. They said he was dreamy. They called him Omar. He met them at bars. A few drinks, then back to his apartment.

Closing his eyes he recreated the tangle of sun-browned limbs, the fine golden hairs inside the parted thighs of blond cheerleaders who called him darlin'. Slipping white panties from the tanned hard bodies of tennis players. They passed notes to him in class saying they wanted to stroke his fancy. Or pressed their breasts against his back in the library, when he was trying to study. They fucked without shame, eyes blue as ice staring into his. Later he saw them with other men, and they met his reproachful stare with amusement at his anger. At Star Trek cons he slept with Romulans, Vulcans, Klingons, Kohms. With Commander Uhura, her high boots tumbled on the floor as he violated the Prime Directive again and again.

But that summer his hands calloused and his fingernails broke, and he picked up shrimper's Vietnamese and learned how to keep engines and winches, injection jets and coolant pumps running when there weren't any parts to fix them with.

That August the *Hônh Phúc* threw a wheel and another boat towed them in to Cameron, on the pass to Lake Calcasieu. He'd gone ashore to get away from the stink of shrimp and diesel fuel, and walked till the sea left his legs. By then he was far out on the beach. He stopped at a bar. Then it was night, and he heard the music, and followed it out into the wind and the sand grated under his sandals and he walked down between the dunes to where the surf roared glimmering in the moon.

On another beach decades later, he closed his eyes again. Listening to a truck going by behind him, on the wide smooth highway that bordered the Gulf where the emir held sway.

He must have heard it then, too, but mingled with the surf his ear could not distinguish that deep-throated throb, huge pistons firing up and down in the brutal syncopation of tribal drums. Because walking down out of the dunes he'd found a dozen men gathered around a fire.

They must have thrown gasoline on it, to get it blazing so high in such a short time. The flames streamed up from huge crooked logs of bleached driftwood. Jagged scars showed where they'd been dragged across the sand.

Barrel-chested, muscled, their vests and leathers were studded with bright metal and dangling with chains. They wore boots and wristbands, head wraps, heavy rings that flashed in the firelight. They passed bottles from hand to hand, and the smell of marijuana came with the crackle and heat of flame. The firelight flickered on their machines, slanted in black shoals. He had not realized here existed no obligation to welcome the stranger. Had just walked past, sandals digging into the cool sand.

Someone had called out. And something in his voice had given him away, when he answered.

"Hold on there a minute," a contemptuous voice had said, when the light fell on his face. "Look what's tryin' to sneak up on us. Where you think *you're* going? Wherever you think, you ain't."

He'd known then to run, at least, but someone else had dropped his beer and tackled him, slamming his face into the sand.

He'd begged, but up in among the dunes they'd pushed him from one to the next. Made him strip off shorts and T-shirt, sandals and underwear. Then made him kneel in the sand.

He tried to laugh. Naked. Alone. Hoping once they saw he was harmless, wouldn't fight back, they'd let him go.

Then one of them, coming up from the fire, had picked up a pointed stick.

Alone at the café table, the slight dark man who'd passed through so many identities he had no longer any name at all sat motionless, staring out at the sea.

At a little after three o'clock another plodded into the shade. He was heavyset and bearded, with a wide, sunburned nose. He wore the thobe, the long white shirt or robe many wore on this island on the street or in the shops, especially during the hot season, and a *ghutrah* on his head. Their gazes touched, then slid off. Al-Ulam took sunglasses from his jacket and slipped them on. They looked around the café, noting those others who sat sipping coffee or lemonade or beer, foreigners mostly. At last the new arrival shuffled to his table. Murmured in classical Arabic, "I still feel the loss of Al-Quds, like a fire in my intestines."

"What excuse have I to surrender, while I still have arrows, and there is a tough string for my bow?"

The other bowed. "Peace be to you, sir. Do I address the honored Abu al-Ulam?"

"I am Doctor al-Ulam."

"I am Rahimullah bin Jun'ad. We are honored to have you among us."

"May God increase your honor, Rahimullah bin Jun'ad," al-Ulam said politely, waving to the seat. "Please, sit down. Join me."

The heavyset man glanced at the cigarette, but said nothing as the waiter listened and presently brought freezing glasses of sweetened lemonade tinkling with ice.

There was no hurry to their talk. They became acquainted gradually, both wary, both formal. Al-Ulam learned bin Jun'ad had two sons and that he was a customs clearance manager for InterFilipinas International, a shipping company. He was originally from Yemen, but had lived in Bahrain for twenty-two years. He in turn told the other rather less, and only part of it true.

As two dark-haired beauties came swinging along the corniche, bin Jun'ad frowned. Flicked stubby fingers in their direction. "Are these *muhajaba?*"

Al-Ulam thought this might be the first approach to their business. As bin Jun'ad closed his eyes, he admired them. They were bold, attractive. Their skirts did not cover their legs, their scarves did not cover their hair. As they clicked by on high heels, he caught the hot glance of dark eyes.

"They must be foreigners. Indians? Lebanese?"

"Unfortunately, they are our women; but seduced by the devil, and the West, which serves him. This regime"—opening his eyes, bin Jun'ad gestured at everything around them, speaking in a thick low murmur unintelligible a few feet away—"is *jaahili:* ignorant, false, deeply corrupt. The land is *kufr,* the law *kufr,* the regime *kufr,* the people *kufr,* all save a few. The al-Khalifas and al-Sauds permit this evil."

"The shadow cannot be straight, when the source is not."

"Indeed. They call themselves Muwahhidun. But those who have knowledge say that to use man's law instead of shariah, and to support the infidels against the Muslims, turn those who do so into *mushrik,* those who are no longer in Islam."

"You are eloquent," al-Ulam told him.

The stubby fingers fluttered. "No, Abu, I am an ignorant one. But I am a Qari; I have memorized the Book. These spewers of filth call adopting the ways of the polytheists modernism. But did not the Prophet, peace and the blessings of God be upon him, say, according to al-Bukhari, and ibn Maajah and others: 'Whoever brings anything new into this affair of ours that is not from it, it is rejected from its doer.'" Bin Jun'ad glared out as more women passed, laughing and commenting as they watched a young man run along the beach.

"Those whom I serve in the name of God, *subahanahu wa ta'la,* do not hold with those who shirk their faith," said al-Ulam. He rattled ice, set the glass down. "The word of God is simple to know and easy to obey. All has been set forth clearly. A command is a command. Is that not simple enough?"

They fell into a debate about whether the women who had just passed were *kufr* only, or fully *kaffir.* Whether, following the test of ibn Taimiyyah, the great imam and scholar who had died in prison in 728 A.H., their corrupt way of life doomed them to hellfire as Muslims, or whether the essence of unbelief manifested in their way of life had sunk so deeply within them they had left the fold of Islam. Bin Jun'ad quoted the hadith of ibn Abbaas that most of the inhabitants of hell were women who had committed *kufr* in various ways, illegal intercourse, or temptation, or simply being ungrateful to their husbands. They debated this for some time before bin Jun'ad asked if al-Ulam had been in Afghanistan.

"Truly, I have."

"Recently? Or in the past?"

"Both in the past, and recently. With Mullah Omar and Mullah Ahmad in Kandahar."

"Is it a just regime, as we have heard?"

"The *imaamah* of Mullah Omar is pure and clean and wholly Islamic. You will not see women parading like whores or masquerading as men in the schools. They are put away, the foreigners are gone, and the people live in all things according to the word of God. I have seen the wonders occurring in that country. In the Sudan, also, we are building the jihad."

Bin Jun'ad said respectfully, "When you said you had been there in the past, did you mean as a *mujahid?*"

"I was living as an engineer in Egypt when the call reached me. I left my family and followed the path of jihad."

"Where did you fight?"

"I fought in two actions, but I was not the bravest. It would inspire you, to see how the brothers charged with their Kalashnikovs and did not falter. The machine guns cut them down right and left, but the rest went on, shouting God is Great." He waited as the other murmured the phrase, too, then went on, "One day we captured eight of the godless ones—the Russians. We made them kneel, and looped detonation cord around their necks, leading it from one to another. Their heads leaped off in perfect arcs."

"Isn't God merciful," bin Jun'ad breathed, eyes blinking rapidly.

"We drove them out, and then their power collapsed in their own country, too. After that, we realized nothing was impossible. One superpower has fallen. Now it is the turn of the second."

"I am told you have worked with the Sheikh. Do you know him? The Sheikh?"

He debated how much to tell this man. He hadn't survived this long by trusting others. This Qari had known the password, and he voiced the right opinions, but by speaking of the Sheikh, he was touching on matters better unsaid. The one al-Ulam followed was so reclusive he himself had never met him. The Sheikh didn't trust telephones, for example. He sent his instructions on videotapes or by hand-carried notes. Or most securely of all, by word of mouth, through men who could be trusted because they could be killed.

Which was why since Afghanistan the man bin Jun'ad was calling Abu, honored son, had not lived in any country for longer than a year. In the Gulf War he'd carried messages between Iraq and a Saudi group Saddam had counted on to support his invasion. But that group had been suppressed by the Saudi police. He'd barely escaped, using another false passport, to refuge in the Sudan.

But year by year the pace quickened. He was found trustworthy. His skills were honed and appreciated. He'd gone to Argentina, Azerbaijan, Bosnia, to Pakistan three times, to Yemen, Egypt again, then Saudi Arabia, Britain, Algeria.

And most recently to Iran.

But more and more these days, he found himself tiring of travel. He'd started a fishing company in Sudan, using the Sheikh's capital, but building his fleet with the profits. His boats spent more days at sea than any of his competitors', with fewer breakdowns and less theft. He owned six now; when he returned he hoped to buy two more.

Finally he said, "To us, Qari, the most exalted commandment is to kill the idol worshipers where we find them. Is your heart ready for this?"

Stubby hands spread. "Bones must break and limbs must fly, so the true religion may stand. I and mine are ready to help."

Al-Ulam said, "So far, those who wage jihad have struck either against the sectarians, those outside the *lofel,* or against the regimes which support the Zionists. But in the end, these are puppets.

"We are not frightened of this so-called superpower. It is corrupt and decadent, and, above all, it does not want to fight.

"We must strike the enemies of God, and two stand foremost: the Greater Satan, the Americans, and the Lesser, the Jews themselves. It is God's command, to carry on until Al-Quds is free and Palestine is free, and the Kingdom of the Two Holy Places is free of their presence and taint.

"This is my business here, my friend. Tell me now, does it meet with your approval?"

Bin Jun'ad's pug face shone as if lit from within. For a

moment he struggled to speak. Then whispered, like one given at last the land he'd worked as a laborer all his life: "There is no turning back from the ultimate victory of God."

Presently bin Jun'ad suggested they go to a nearby mosque for the *zuhr,* the noonday prayers. They rose, paid, and passed out into the glaring sun.

They walked together down the Tarafa bin al-Abd, scanning passing faces and cars. Evidently he'd made his point, because bin Jun'ad said, "If that is why you are here, we must make decisions. There is a place we can talk. But we must be careful. The security service is active here. An English dog is their chief. They spy on us to protect the ruler, and the Crusaders. This is where they repair their ships. At this moment, fortunately, the police are concentrating on the cultists, who are politically active against the regime."

"The Shi'a?"

"They attempted an armed coup ten years ago and were put down. There was another plot last year. Their Hezbollah are even more dangerous to us than the police." The Yemeni lowered his voice as a foreigner came up behind them on the sidewalk. "We must not appear together, after this. Especially considering we'll be working in the Shi'a part of town."

Which turned out to be in the Makarqah quarter, south of the Gold Souk. Bin Jun'ad didn't own a car; he said the island was small enough that when he needed to travel, a taxi sufficed. After prayers and discussion in the air-conditioned basement of the mosque, they walked for some time through the quarter, passing and repassing certain streets. Al-Ulam didn't object. Better to be cautious. Bin Jun'ad explained they also rented a house south of the city. The first brothers to arrive had worked there under the cover of setting up a fishing business.

"Fishing," al-Ulam said. "That's good."

"It let them buy equipment and travel about. The second team is waiting for us now. Do you have money? Is there anything else you need?"

Al-Ulam said he had enough, and more was there if it was needed; praise be to God, there were many who provided for those who fought the unrighteous.

Their destination was on the third floor of a narrow building on a narrow street lined with shops. The first floor was a shoemaker's; the second sold cell phones. The third and uppermost, reached by worn steps, was a small apartment. Whoever had lived in it before had taken most of his furniture; what remained was a table, some folding chairs, and several mattresses.

Three young men bowed as bin Jun'ad introduced them. Abdulrahman, Nair, and Salman. The local talent, like the bearded Qari, tended to be the weakest link. They were guides in unfamiliar territory. But as the time for the action neared, some wondered if too many of their Muslim neighbors would die, or they remembered infidels they liked. Sometimes they bragged to their friends about the great act of jihad that was going to astonish everyone.

When that happened, they had to be silenced.

He glanced through the single low window down at the street. "Qari, do you have the findings of our brothers, the first to come here?"

"They left this." He pointed to a computer on the table.

Al-Ulam grunted approvingly. A new Sanyo, with hard drive, scanner, printer. A phone cord coiled down the stairs.

The first team, who'd reconnoitered the targets, was out of the country by now, except for the leader, who'd been killed in a bicycle accident. Abdulrahman, Nair, and Salman would buy whatever was necessary for the action. Only when all was ready would he turn again to bin Jun'ad for those fanatics who'd would actually drive, carry the bombs, throw the grenades—the "useful idiots" who, if captured, could say nothing, for they knew nothing.

He started the machine, waited while it booted, and inventoried the directory. Instead of opening the files, though—they'd contain only gibberish if opened by accident or by someone probing the system—he first opened the scrambling program. Shielding the keyboard with his body, he entered the passwords and user identifications, then opened the file.

He read in silence, while the others waited.

The first team had identified two possible targets in Bahrain. The first was the American naval base. Bin Jun'ad had put them in touch with a friend from the mosque, a believer who worked in the fuel supply facility. This man had taken one of the men from the cell onto the base with him. They'd photographed the gate area and the fuel pier. They'd thought of sabotaging the pier, blowing up the valves with grenades, then using flares to ignite a raging fire in the harbor. But they later evolved a better plan: driving a truck onto the base during the huge Fourth of July rock concert and "Back Home" celebration that would pull hundreds of Americans together in the Desert Dome.

Al-Ulam studied diagrams, photographs, schedules. Detonated at the right point, a bomb would bring the dome down on the revelers. The death count might be close to a thousand.

The second possible target was an apartment building in the new suburb of Juffair. A new sixteen-story building, where American support personnel lived—contractors, visiting officers, civilian personnel and their families. This attack, too, would be via truck bomb, not unlike the one he'd built at Mashhad.

He cocked his head. The problem was, he had no explosives. He'd managed to bring detonators; they were easily concealed in his shaving kit. But the stocks of Polish plastic were exhausted. He could improvise something. But improvised explosives were never as potent as the manufactured article.

"What are you thinking?" bin Jun'ad wanted to know.

"I'm considering how to build the bomb."

The rotund man in the thobe smiled cherubically. "You're going to be pleased at this. Our man inside the base? He had a friend with access to their weapons storehouse. It was expensive to deal with him. But together they brought out almost a hundred kilos of American plastic explosive."

Al-Ulam looked again at the screen. It showed the ground floor of the apartment building. He could see where the supporting pillars were located. The plastic would serve as the heart of the charge; the rest he could buy locally. Diesel oil, nitrate . . . His heart pounded with the same passion he'd felt in Buenos Aires, in Algeria, at Mashhad. Sixteen stories. No one in it would remain alive.

"That is good news," he said. "Good news indeed."

12

The Great Bitter Lake, Suez Canal

Now muster all accused, witnesses, and chain of command in the wardroom for captain's mast. Maintain silence about the decks."

Marty Marchetti stood at parade rest. *Horn* was at anchor, but the waiting men still swayed in the passageway. He flexed his arms behind him, feeling the burn from a hard workout in the cramped rubber-matted weight room aft. Pain was weakness leaving the body. He'd heard that once, and it had stayed with him.

Like the anger stayed with you, when one of your guys was getting railroaded.

The starboard side 01 level passageway zigzagged out around the wardroom, the wood-grained metal door of which was closed as, he supposed, the captain and exec settled on what was going to happen in a few minutes. The chiefs had already sat in judgment, and the exec had done her quizzing the day before. His guys stood in line with the others, with, to his surprise, some of the bitches, too. He couldn't get used to them. Gave him a start when he'd come around a corner and there was a pair of tits.

For some reason it seemed like he always went through the Ditch at night. The scenery: not worth looking at, even if you wanted to stand topside in suffocating heat and biting flies and gnats so micromean they bit you on the way down when you breathed them in. For hour after hour they'd bored through the narrow, dead-straight canal. He wondered why they called this the Holy Land when God had wasted so little time on it. It was flat and dead, and the villages that lined it were broken down and poverty stricken. They'd dropped anchor in the lake not long after dawn, to let the northbound traffic go by before proceeding on the second leg down to the Red Sea.

He stuck his chin out as somebody cracked the door. "Chiefs and div-ohs can come in," Woltz, the command master chief, said. "Witnesses, too."

He was the nearest to the door, so he went through first, with Chief Bendt and Lieutenant Osmani behind him. Then Gerhardt, the radioman, and Mr. Camill, because the communications officer was on anchor watch, and Lieutenant Sanduskie and Chief Andrews, the cryppies. They looked lost out of their little shack up on the 03 level, like hermit crabs blasted out of their shells.

The wardroom smelled of burnt coffee with an aftertaste of mold from the ventilation ducting. The tables were moved back to the bulkheads, except for the long one where the captain stood.

Lenson was looking at the records in front of him. He was in cotton khakis with his portable radio clipped to his belt. He looked tired, his long frame pelvis-braced against the table. They ran into each other sometimes in the weight room. Marchetti was a lifter, but the captain spent most of his time on the treadmill, cranking off miles. Behind him the yeoman stood ready with more folders.

Marty ended up in rank with the other chiefs and division officers and department heads, to the captain's left, directly across from where the exec stood. She looked focused and vindictive. He'd have to spend the whole mast looking at the gap in her front teeth. He closed his eyes and rolled his shoulders.

"Atten-*hut*," said the exec. The captain said, almost too soft to hear, "All right, we ready? Bring in the first victim."

The door opened for a thin boy in dress whites and a white hat. Marty followed him with his gaze, trying to beam encouragement. Goldie was the armorer for the boarding team. He was matched pace for pace by Chief Forker. Forker was a joke as master at arms, a roly-poly with a tentative voice who didn't swing as much weight in the chiefs' mess as the ship's sheriff ought to. He murmured, "Halt . . . hand salute . . . sound off."

"Gunner's Mate Third Class Gowin Goldstine, reporting as ordered, sir."

Lenson nodded. He looked at Goldstine as he stood at attention, then down at the papers.

"Goldstine, you are suspected of committing the following violations of the Uniform Code of Military Justice. Article 134, disorders to the prejudice of good order and discipline. You do not have to make any statement regarding the offense of which you are accused or suspected. Any statement made by you may be used as evidence against you. You are advised that a captain's mast is not a trial and that a determination of misconduct on your part is not a conviction by a court. Further, you are advised that the formal rules of evidence used in trials by court-martial do not apply at a captain's mast." The captain held up a paper. "I have a statement here signed by you acknowledging you were advised of your legal rights pertaining at this hearing. Do you understand the rights explained therein?"

"Yes, sir." The response was barely audible; the yeoman took a step forward with his steno pad, to hear better.

"Do we have a witness?"

"Witness, step forward," said Forker. "Sound off."

A girl stepped out of ranks and came to attention, a pace behind Goldstine. Marchetti looked her up and down. The rat. "Fireman Cobie Kasson, sir."

"Witness, what can you tell me about the accused's involvement in the offense?"

Marty noted with contempt she looked more nervous than Goldie, and he was the guy actually at mast. He tried to guess how stacked she was, under the baggy coveralls, then remembered he didn't have to. He'd seen the pictures.

In a quavering voice she said she'd been on the beach,

had several drinks, and had her top stolen. The other women were going topless and she didn't think it through, just joined them. If she hadn't been drinking, she wouldn't have done it.

"Petty Officer Goldstine took the pictures?"

"I saw him with a camera. Taking pictures of Ina and Patryce—of the other women there, too."

"He took one of you?"

"Yes, sir."

"Did you pose for it?"

"No, sir. I didn't pose. I didn't see him taking it."

Lenson said, looking at his papers, "If you didn't see him taking it, how do you know he took it?"

"I saw the flash go off. When I looked, he was doing something to the camera."

"So you mean, you didn't see him in time to stop him taking it."

"Yes, sir."

"How did it make you feel, knowing these pictures were circulating among the crew?"

She hesitated. "Humiliated."

"Do you have anything to add or change in your statement?"

She didn't. Lenson shuffled paper, then asked Goldstine, "Would you like to ask any questions of this witness?"

Goldstine shook his head. He shook it again when the captain asked him if he had any other witnesses he wanted to call, or evidence to present.

"Any personal statement to make, Petty Officer?"

"Yes, sir. I think I made a mistake there, sir."

Lenson set the folder aside and leaned forward, looking at the man before him eye to eye. The radio hissed on his belt, but did not speak. "So you admit taking these photos?"

"Yes, sir."

"What was your motivation?"

"Well, sir . . . just to get shots of the girls. The women."

"Why?"

"Well, they took their shirts off, sir. And we was all pretty shitfaced . . . drunk. I figured as long as they were showing it off, it was all right to take a picture."

"All right. Let's see. One of your shipmates goes ashore. He gets loaded. Has to piss. He leaves his wallet out on the table while he goes to the head. It's all right to take his money?"

"No, sir."

"Excuse me? I can't hear you."

"No, sir. It wouldn't be right to do that."

"See the point I'm making?"

"I think so."

"That you protect your shipmates, even when they're not at their best." The petty officer nodded miserably. "All right, everybody's got a nice buzz on, you take some shots without thinking too much about it. But the next day, you're sober. You could toss the film over the side. You could ask the women what they want you to do with it. Instead you take it up to the cryppies. Then pass the prints around for everybody to drool over. Whose idea was that?"

A swallow, a pause. Finally Goldstine murmured, "Mine, sir."

"Nobody else involved?"

"No, sir."

Marchetti watched the skipper turn this over. He didn't look like he was buying it. Of course, it wasn't Goldie's idea. He'd told everybody in forward berthing about the pictures, and somebody told him, hey, why not take them up and get prints for everybody. He'd told the chiefs this. But Marty had taken him aside afterward and asked him why he wanted to get other people in trouble. Why not take the rap like a man. He was glad to see he was taking his advice. A stand-up attitude was better in the long run. Down in the spaces, when no khaki was around.

"Very well," Lenson said. He looked at Marchetti. "Senior Chief? What have you got to say for your man here?"

Marty cleared his throat. "Sir, Goldstine's a hard worker. This was an error of judgment, but think about what he was looking at."

Lenson had been regarding the man in front of him; now he looked startled. "Sorry, Senior. What exactly do you mean?"

"Well, sir, just that he probably ain't had any since we left the States, and suddenly there's these chicks with their boozooms waggin' in the sea breeze. It'd be hard to look away. He probably didn't think twice about taking a picture."

"That's the point. That we think about what we're doing."

"Seems to me they should of thought about what *they* were doing, too."

The captain's gaze sharpened. Marty met it, not giving any ground. Goldie was getting railroaded, and the fucking exec was driving the train. The girls start stripping, he'd have done the same thing. At least nobody'd tried to grab a handful. CO had to see that. Unless he was getting confused by cunt, too. Marty looked from Lenson to the exec. Possible? Likely? There were rumors.

"I'll be dealing with them in a few minutes, Senior. Let's stick to what I asked you."

"Goldie's good to go, sir. Doesn't need supervision. I don't keep nonperformers around."

The division officer spoke up, too: he was dependable, this was a momentary lapse of judgment, and so forth. Lenson turned back to Goldstine. "Well, performance counts. You seem to be someone who contributes to his division and his ship. Anything else to say?"

The petty officer mumbled he was sorry, he'd apologize to the women involved. Lenson listened carefully, examining his face.

"All right, I hear you. Making a personal apology, that's a good start. However, the fact remains you've damaged *Horn*'s camaraderie and trust. I'm going to hold you to account for that.

"You'll be restricted to the ship for the next forty-five days and perform extra duty for that period of time. Reduced in rate to the next inferior rate . . . to be suspended for six months. If you come before me again, anything of this nature, expect to be hammered."

"Yes, sir."

"Any questions?"

"No, sir."

"Dismissed," Lenson said to the master at arms.

Everyone relaxed, shaking out the kinks. The captain checked with the bridge on his radio. Then it was time for the petty officer who ran the darkroom, or what passed for one, a small compartment with a sink. Lenson came down harder on him than he had on Goldstine, pointing out he was a first class, expected to be preparing himself for the responsibilities of chief, who'd misused government facilities for a frivolous purpose.

"You're married. Right? A family man. Got a little boy. Davy. Do you take cheesecake shots of Rhonda and pass them around on the mess decks?"

"No, sir."

"Why not?"

"I respect her, sir."

"And your shipmates? Who keep the ship running, keep you in steam and hot water and hot chow? Keep that 440-hertz power going for your listening equipment? You respect them, too?"

"Yes, sir. I respect them, too."

He stood rigid, and Marty knew why. With a first-class crow and a security clearance on the line. The captain went on about how he'd violated his trust, misused his position, abused his shipmates. He kept asking why he'd done it, but the best the IT could come up with was how it was all a joke.

"Yeah? Tell me why it's funny," the captain wanted to know. At last the accused just stood there. He got forty-five days restriction to the ship, extra duty for forty-five days, and a bust to second class . . . suspended for six months. His shoulders dropped in relief.

This time when the accused was dismissed some of the khaki started to leave, too, but the CO said sharply he wanted them to stand fast.

One by one, Lenson called in the women whose pictures Goldstine had taken. He gave them each the warning, showed them the photos, and asked them to explain. Then told them he'd already punished the men who had taken, developed, and distributed the photographs, but that they, too, had to behave like adults when they were representing their ship and their country. One after the other, he restricted them to the ship for forty-five days and gave them a week's extra duty. One of the women, an English-sounding girl, cried at attention, silently, tears leaking down her cheeks. At that Lenson softened his tone, adding they weren't on his shit list, he just wanted to make sure they got the message. But she got the same punishment as the others.

Marchetti was in the passageway one deck down, headed for the chief's mess to adjust his coffee level before the boarding and search drill, when he heard "Got a minute, Senior Chief?"

It was Commander Crotchkiss. And he was gonna have to be real careful not to forget and call her that to her face. "Yes, ma'am."

"Want to buy me a cup of joe?"

He held the door for her and wedged himself behind the too-narrow table while the mess crank got mugs. They were the only ones in the compartment. Through the door leading to chief's berthing he could see the bunk curtains drawn back, jackets and towels hanging from the bunk bars. Everyone was out on deck, supervising. Hotchkiss stirred creamer into the Black Bear. "MIO training this morning?"

"Board and search in fifteen minutes."

"Live fire? Small arms?"

"I don't think the Egyptians would like that here in the Canal."

She sipped. "Chief, I feel hostile vibes coming off you. What's eating on you?"

"My troop got a raw deal this morning."

"Which troop?"

"Goldie. Goldstine. The one the skipper whacked for taking the pictures."

"You think he should have walked?"

"It was on shore. They were letting off steam. If it was some hairy asshole mooning the camera, nobody'd have given a shake about it. But they're girls, so everybody goes apeshit."

"You don't want us here, do you?" Hotchkiss asked him.

"You asking straight out?"

"Sure."

"Women got no business aboard ship, ma'am. Like this topless business. Goldstine got pulled off the twenty-five-millimeter for this mast, you know that? Captain wanted the fifties and the chain gun manned while we're at anchor. But what are we doing? Getting distracted by some bullshit nonissue."

He took a breath, expecting her to snap back, but she didn't interrupt. So he said, "Level with you, ma'am? They can do a lot of stuff good as the guys can. But that ain't the point. It isn't how much they cost. Or what's fair, or unfair. I'll tell you what I'm afraid of. That they just aren't gonna come through when the crunch really comes."

"Well, we're here," Hotchkiss said, coming back at him at last. "So no matter what your personal feelings are, Senior, it's your job as much as it is mine to make things work out. I hope you agree with me there."

He said reluctantly, "I know it's ship's policy."

"That's good. Because I want you to consider putting some of our *Horn* women on your boarding and search teams."

Oh, Jesus, no. He barked coffee into his fist. "Well . . . ma'am . . . we already have all our billets filled. Both teams."

"There must be somebody you think would be better off somewhere else."

Actually, there were; useless goofballs who bitched and couldn't rappel, losers he'd planned to leave in the boat during any real opposed boarding; but he liked the idea of having to drag along a girl even less. It must have shown, because Hotchkiss said, "If I get you a woman who's better than one of them, how would you feel about that?"

"You show me one who can pull herself up a thirty-foot line hand over hand, I might take her," Marty grabbed out of the air. Figuring there might possibly be one or two total steroid Olympic buffarillas who could actually do that, but none he'd seen on *Horn* could. "Send me one of those and I'll teach her to do fire and maneuver. But until then I don't think it's a good idea."

"I'll send you one you can train," Hotchkiss said.

He glanced around the mess, made sure the cranks were back in the galley. Then leaned forward, taking her eye to eye. "Ma'am, no. Due respect and all that, but this team will be carrying live ammo. Climbing jacob's ladders. Rappelling up stacks of containers and busting off locks with sledgehammers and crawling through bilges and holding crews at gunpoint, and most likely sometime during this deployment we will have to tee off on some actual bad actors who do not want us sniffing their assholes. Smugglers. Stowaways. Iranians who hate our guts. We will get in their faces. We will wrestle them to the deck and put cuffs on them. We might even have to light them up if they come at us with a knife or a gun or a cargo hook. I'm not taking someone who can't react aggressively. It wouldn't be fair to her, and it sure as hell wouldn't be fair to the guy whose back she's supposed to be covering."

The exec had gone stiff. Her green eyes were narrow now. "You'll obey orders. Like everybody else aboard."

But he'd had enough. Getting up, he said, "Commander, you can't order me to take anybody I consider dangerous to the team. I'll take that one to the captain. And I don't think he'll go your way."

"Now muster Blue and Gold boarding and search teams in the helo hangar with GMGCS Marchetti," said the 1MC.

He waited, arms folded, as the last few men came up from the locker where the small arms and ready ammo and boarding party equipment were kept. They fell into loose ranks, pointing weapons at the overhead as they checked actions, buckled on pistol belts. Seven guys in each team.

When he was a seaman, they'd have just been called port
and starboard. Now they were the Blue Team, the Gold
Team. It did sound better. Goldstine and Sandoff came hus-
tling forward with the M-60 for the RHIB.

The army had gotten rid of the .45 Colt automatic and the
M-14 rifle years ago, but that was what the navy still carried
aboard ship. "Machete" himself toted a black pump-action
Mossberg with ghost-ring sights and a full-length magazine
of triple-ought buckshot and solid lead slugs he could
switch between in a fraction of a second. Along with a Ka-
Bar strapped to his thigh, a handheld Saber radio, his boarding clipboard, a police-style D-battery Maglite, cuffs,
chemical agent, and a canteen of water. The team wore
steel-toed combat-style boots and blaze orange float coats
and dark blue coveralls. Their *Horn* ball caps were all the
same, no gold braid, no chief's anchors, no rank insignia.
No name tags, and they didn't call each other by their real
names, either. Just to give the shitsuckers they boarded less
of a handle on them. He went down the line, doing an inspection arms, making sure each man had all his gear and a
full canteen.

Then he sat them all down in a circle on deck and started
passing out paper. Boarding and search wasn't all rappelling
and pointing guns at people. You had to know basic math,
first aid, restraint, legal stuff. He had a Farsi speaker this
time, who said he knew some Arabic, too. Seaman Second
Barkhat, a little dark wiry guy they called Deuce.

They were going to do tanker inspections, stop fuel and
weapon smuggling into Iraq. So he started off by telling
them what he knew from doing the same thing in the Gulf.
What to look for: recently painted areas, fresh concrete, hidden tanks in the chain lockers, tanks with water made to float
on top of the oil somehow. But most shippers didn't get that
cute. He told them to take out their conversion tables.

"So, say ship's records list a fuel tank capacity of two
hundred metric tons and it topped off two days ago in its last
port of call. The question's gonna be, how much tank
stowage, in cubic feet, is the ship going to need to hold this

much fuel? Because if he's smuggling fuel or crude, the only way we're going to find it is to match the tankage we find and what's in it against his constructed or installed fuel tankage and what's supposed to be there for his legal fuel to get wherever he's going and back. The difference will be what he's trying to smuggle. If they can hide it in amongst the fuel tankage, they can walk past us with two thousand tons of contraband crude." He took a breath. "Now, how do we know what he tells us is diesel fuel is really diesel fuel? Who knows the specific gravity of gasoline?"

"Point seven three five is gasoline," somebody said behind him. "Point nine is heavy crude. Point nine five is bunker C oil."

The stocky blonde in coveralls had baby blue eyes and a round face. "Patryce Wilson," she said, grinning at the guys on the deck. "GTE third. XO sent me."

He put his hands on his hips. "Sorry, lady. We're full up."

"You the senior chief? The one they call Machete? She said all I had to do was pee up a rope."

The men grinned at each other. Marty cleared his throat, unsure how to take this but not liking it. "I said you had to climb a rope, not piss up it. That one."

He pointed to the two-inch hemp line that went up to the ceiling of the hangar. Every time they mustered he made the team climb the rope. At first without gear. Then, as they got in shape, with full gear. It might save their lives to be able to get up, or down, the side of a ship, a stack of containers, an escape scuttle. Just getting aboard a rolling trawler in heavy seas took a lot of physical strength.

Wilson looked at it. She wiped her hands on her coveralls, then took a jump. She got a few feet up, then stalled out. Hung there.

A chuckle, a snigger went around.

She twisted her legs in the rope, resting. Then hauled herself up, inch by inch, locking the line with her boots at each hitch. Marchetti didn't know where she'd learned that one. She grunted and farted, and the guys groaned, but now they weren't laughing.

She got to the top. Way up in the overhead. Hung there, puffing. Then started to slide.

Marty started forward, wincing. She was letting the rope slip through her bare hands. He reached out, but she said in a muffled voice, "Hands off, till you get invited." Then let go and fell in a panting, tumbled pile.

"There," she said. She got up, looking at her hands. Wiped them on her coveralls, leaving dark patches.

"Nice job," he told her contemptuously. "I'd high-five you, but I just had my dick in my hand."

"Don't let that stop you. I just had my finger up my snatch." She planted herself down with the men.

This dirty-mouthed bitch snapped back like a nylon line. He just needed a little time, to figure out how to ditch her. Though probably, like most girls, she'd drop out all by herself, once it got really tough.

"All right," he said, "We'll call you . . . a supernumerary. Any of these limp ladies wimp out, you step in. That should motivate you melonheads. . . . Your teammates are Crack Man, Sasquatch, Lizard, Snack Cake, Deuce, Amarillo, and Turd Chaser. Your name'll be . . . Spider. Cause you climb like a sick one.

"Okay, that's enough, listen up. Now we're going to talk about a UN 986 Letter and what's gonna be on it and what's not. Pay attention, because we're gonna be doing this for real starting about two days from now."

They bent their heads over the handout while he went on talking. Thinking, beneath what he was saying, that she still didn't belong here. He wasn't going to let her put the team, the mission, at risk.

But he'd take care of that his way.

13

Oparea Adelaide,
Northern Red Sea

The high sharp mountains lined the coast, lavender violet in the morning, red as candlelight through wine in the evening sun. They cut the horizon jagged and cruel for miles inland and never seemed to be out of sight, no matter where *Horn* went in the narrow band of sea that slipped like a crack through the most storied desert on earth.

All the coasts looked the same, brown, hot, barren. The steady northeast wind was lip-cracking dry. It brought a fine invisible dust that lodged in the pores of the skin and could filter through a watertight door, especially if there was precision machinery on the other side. The dryness was only occasionally varied with a land squall that fogged the air like batts of fiberglass packed around the slowly moving ship.

Over the past weeks Dan and *Horn* had come to know the upper portion of the Red Sea well. It was shallow, except in the shipping channels, which ran from the scatter of islands at the foot of the Gulf of Suez south more or less down the center of the Red Sea itself. And narrow: at its widest it was only a hundred miles across, and up in the tributary gulfs the coasts closed in alarmingly. It felt strange being under way on patrol where one could see land on either hand.

This early July morning he stood sweating in the pilot-house, alternately looking down at the chart and out at the mountains as the quartermasters laid out a revised oparea grid that had just come down from the commander, Task

Group Red Sea. From Commodore Cavender Strong, Royal Australian Navy, embarked aboard HMAS *Torrens*, a River-class frigate of British lineage. His force consisted of *Torrens, Horn, Laboon* and a French destroyer, *Georges Leygues*.

Dan had not yet met Strong personally, but he'd gone on the scrambler phone with him the day *Horn* reported in.

Strong had laid out their assignment in spare sentences. The coalition group had been here for a year. Their operating area was bounded by the Sinai to the north, the Hejaz to the east, and the coast of Egypt to the west. The entrances to both the Gulf of Suez and of Aqaba were choked with small jazirats, islands, and coral reefs and sand shoals. The islands were low and rocky, with few lights or other navigational aids. The commodore emphasized Dan should take the utmost care when transiting and not to depend on any one navigational method. The year before, a British warship had grounded on the Sha'b Ali on the way from Suez, not even reaching her patrol area before she had to turn back on a long voyage homeward.

Essentially, Strong said, they were conducting a modified blockade, although the word "blockade" could not be used publicly. "Interdiction operations" or, better yet, "enforcing UN sanctions" was the preferred phraseology. They were here to prevent embargoed goods from reaching Iraq and illegally exported oil or oil products from leaving it.

It was a delicate assignment. They'd be inspecting not just Iraqi flag vessels, but ships from every nation bordering the Indian Ocean and many from farther away. Few of these countries liked Westerners and many considered their presence a violation of Islam, or, at the least, an insult to local sovereignty. They could expect diplomatic protests, legal threats, and occasional danger, especially for the boarding parties. The best approach was to go in with overwhelming force behind you; but to act with as much courtesy as the master concerned seemed responsive to. Allegations of excessive use of force or other illegal or dangerous acts would be subject to judicial review.

Strong had positioned his force in three sectors, two
blocking positions south of Sinai and one in the Gulf of
Aqaba. Each unit spent three weeks on station and then a
week transiting to her liberty port and back, usually
Hurghada, but to Jiddah about every third trip off the line,
for the English-speakers, or Djibouti, for the French. An
oiler came up from Jiddah once a week with free Saudi fuel.
Limited amounts of fresh food were available, but the choice
was small and the cost high. The U.S. units would most
likely prefer to rely on the joint defense logistics system now
operating in Saudi. Strong had then sketched out his operating procedures in sentences dry as the air, emphasizing
again the danger of reefs, tidal currents, and squalls, especially in the Gulf of Aqaba itself.

Here at the intersection of the great Y formed by the in-
tersecting gulfs, sea traffic divided. As it came up through
the central passage from the Indian Ocean, by far the greatest part turned west for As-Suways and the Canal—and the
Med and Europe and America. Those ships, gigantic oil
tankers plowing along so low in the water their freeboard
was barely visible, and huge liquid natural gas tankers with
their white bulbous tanks of refrigerated gas, were not the
concern of the multinational force. Their lookout was for
those that turned east, bound for Jordan and Israel, Al-Aqaba
and Eilat. For as remote and deserted as the land around
them was, an astonishingly numerous cavalcade of coasters
and merchants marched steadily as foraging ants through
these narrow passages.

In her first week on station *Horn* had boarded and
searched twenty-two ships. So far they'd found no oil, no
weapons, no contraband, and had nearly come to grief one
hazy night on a course laid too close to the westward reefs
off the Jazirat Shakir.

Which brought them to this summer morning. Fortunately, Dan thought, seeing what was taking shape on the
chart, it looked like the day would be clear. Because Strong
had ordered them to the inner station. They'd transit the

Madiq Tiran, Tiran Strait, and take a blocking position in Oparea Sydney, sixty kilometers inside the Gulf of Aqaba.

He shook himself awake and went out on the starboard wing.

Early though it was, the air was so hot it parched throat and nose instantly. The sun glared up from the flat water and down from the sky. The panting heat, the concentrated light, warned that it would really be searing by, say, thirteen hundred. He balanced on his heels, blinking grit from his eyeballs as a tanker transited the horizon with the inevitability of mercury rising in a thermometer. A thin brown haze boiled off its stack into a sky brilliant blue directly overhead, hazy tan with suspended dust lower down.

He looked down. As *Horn*'s hull rolled through blue transparence it churned the sea into a roiling, turbulent, somehow colder-looking lamination of translucent jade, a milky greenish film that slid aft slowly and was replaced again and again. Not for the first time, he wished he was swimming in it. To strap on a mask and drop over the side . . .

But duty could not be evaded. Not even for a moment.

The door dogged behind him against the heat and dust, he looked at the chart again, and picked up a pair of dividers. Pricked off distance, and ran numbers through his brain.

"Bring her around to zero-niner-zero," he told the officer of the deck. "And bring her up to standard. We'll set the navigation detail ten nautical miles off the Madiq Tiran."

Cobie was in the women's head, glad to be off watch at last. She was looking forward to breakfast, then maybe half an hour on her back with her eyes closed. But first, something more important.

She carefully blotted the dregs from a bottle of clarifying lotion across some pimples that had appeared at her hairline. Little, white-hearted buggers. She'd never had an outbreak there before. It was all the sweating they were doing down in the hole. Helm said this was nothing compared to a steam plant, but in the last few days the temperature in Main One had gone over a hundred and ten. Coveralls, forget it. She wore dungaree bottoms and a tee. The guys went around in gym shorts and bare chests. It looked good on some, not so good on others.

Hair on guys, you could keep it. Looking at them one after another in her mind, like flipping pages in a magazine. Akhmeed, not her type. Ricochet wasn't that fuzzy, but he wasn't built either, his chest thin as a little boy's.

She cocked her head, looking into her eyes in the mirror and smiling just the littlest bit. If she had to pick, she'd go for Mick Helm. A decent build. Not hairy all over. And he liked her, too. She was picking up something there, not just a work center supervisor trying to get somebody new off on the right foot.

When she shook the bottle again, it was empty. Fa-a-wk, she thought. She thought of going to shorts and a sports bra. Imagined the Porn King looking up from *Hustler* to check her out. No way in hell.

She was wondering where she was possibly going to get more Clinique when she heard a *whoomp* and a scream from back in the compartment. She dropped the bottle and ran to the door, looking the length of women's berthing.

Smoke, lots of blue smoke . . . and yellow light, flames. Coming from the outboard stack of bunks, up against the hull. Coming from . . .

"Goddamn it," she yelled, and grabbed the extinguisher off the bulkhead.

Her bunk tier was flaming black oily smoke. The heavy extinguisher almost dragged her arms off. But she towed it bumping and scraping across the terrazzo. Some black dude gaped in from the passageway. "Class Bravo fire," she screamed at him. "Call DC Central. Call 211."

"God, what is going on—"

"Cobie, what happened—"

The other girls had leapt from their bunks. Now they were yelling and screaming and rushing around. One was cursing, trying to get her emergency breathing device on over her head, catching it on her braids. Cobie banged the extinguisher down and pulled the pin. "Back off," she yelled to Myna, who had the bunk below hers. She was trying to claw her bedding off, trying to get to something under it. "Get out of there! That's a fuel fire. Give me a clear shot."

"Fire, fire, fire in the Lezzie Locker! That is . . . right, sir . . . fire in compartment 3–382–3–Lima, after women's berthing. Repair five provide. Fire in compartment 3–382–3–Lima, after women's berthing. Repair five provide."

The blaze was fierce, considering it couldn't be thirty seconds old. It ate into the plastic bunk cover. Cobie couldn't help getting a lungful, and started to cough.

By the time she and Ina had it out, spraying purple K powder and beating it out with towels, the compartment was opaque. Girls were staggering around coughing and gagging, arms full of tapes and clothes. Some had the transparent plastic bags of the breathing devices inflated over their heads, as if their brains were being eaten by alien jellyfish. She lowered the nozzle and leaned against a bunk frame, panting.

The repair party investigator edged through the door. She waved him over and pointed to her bunk. A total mess, burnt and dirty, with smoke marks smeared up the bulkhead. And covered with the gritty purple powder. She looked at her rack of tapes. The plastic cases were melted. Totally ruined.

All at once she thought, I could have been *in* there.

She turned abruptly, dropping the extinguisher, and bolted for the head.

Chief Forker got hold of her when she came out. Still sweating from throwing up, but she felt better. Now there was lots of khaki, including, standing in the door, the exec.

"That your bunk?" the paunchy chief master at arms asked. "Kasson?"

"Yeah. Myna here's in the middle, the girl in the lower must be on watch—she's one of the auxiliarymen."

"Were you smoking?"

"I was in the head when it started, Chief. And no, I wasn't. I don't smoke. Nobody smokes in the compartment."

"Nobody? Ever?"

The chief's bland disbelief enraged her. She grabbed his arm and towed him to her bunk. Pointed to the smoking mattress. "Smell that, Chief. Get your nose right down into it. That's right."

He looked up. "Lighter fluid?"

"Some kind of fuel. With a pretty high flash point."

Forker peered suspiciously into the overhead. She could almost scream . . . "It wasn't a *leak*," she said tightly. "Somebody poured it here, or threw it, then lit it."

A level voice said, "You're saying, arson."

"That's right, ma'am," she told the exec. "It's just lucky there wasn't anybody in one of these bunks."

Hotchkiss looked grim. The other girls murmured uneasily. Forker looked at the door, seemed to be measuring a line between it and the bunks. He cleared his throat, as if they should all stop yakking and listen to him. "They came in, maybe with the stuff in a cup or something. Threw it, lit it, then left. You say you were where?"

"In the head."

"See anybody come in?"

"I was looking in the mirror."

Somehow he managed even to make a nod an insult. "Anybody else get a look at anybody didn't belong in here? Well, o-kay . . . I guess we'll have to investigate. But I wouldn't count on getting the guy. If it was a guy."

"What do you mean by that, Chief?" said the exec. Cobie saw she was getting angry, too. "They live in here. Why would they torch their own compartment?"

Forker lifted his eyebrows. "I seen bunk fires before, ma'am. Half the goddamn time it's somebody trying to get back at somebody pissed them off. Just about always, somebody right there in the same space."

He turned away to the repair party guys. They were recoiling their hoses, backing out. The 1MC said, "Class Bravo fire is out in compartment 3–382–3–Lima. Reflash watch is set."

She looked after his retreating back, shaking. What did

that mean? Wasn't he even going to try to find out? Then a
hand tightened on her arm.

Close up, the exec had little lines around her eyes. Her
lips were chapped and grim. "We'll find out who did this,"
the commander told her. "I know what you girls have to put
up with in the work spaces. But this is too much."

Cobie looked back at her bunk. At the twisted, burnt rem-
nants of all her letters. . . . "I hope so, ma'am," she said.
"Before somebody gets killed."

Through a bright noon *Horn* hunted with a turbine whine
and a creaming hiss of foam. To port the rocky tip of the
Sinai and the flat-topped, chalk-colored cliffs of the Ras
Muhammad. To starboard, low barren islets, uninhabited
and unmarked save for the occasional stranded wreck left
from the 1972 war. The navigation team sang a litany of
courses and distances.

Dan, in his bridge chair with a stack of traffic on his lap,
tried to avoid fixating. It was hard, with the jewel-like tones
of reef patches and the lighter brown of drying boulders so
close in to port. The traffic separation scheme sent northbound vessels east of the reefs, southbound west. The east-
erly channel was wider, but it was all too damn tight.
Fortunately, as Strong had said, there was no air threat. Iraqi
aircraft had been grounded since the Gulf War, and Egyptian
and Saudi activity was limited to the occasional patrol aircraft that obligingly squawked its identifying IFF. Dan still
kept Condition Three watches manned in Combat and on the
weapons stations, though.

Hotchkiss, clipboard under her arm. The worry about
close quarters receded, to be replaced with a different appre-
hension. One could run one's career aground in other ways
than the gnash of steel on coral. He hesitated, then beckoned
her. "Exec, what you got?"

"We need to talk about this situation."

"The fire in women's berthing."

"That's right." She moved in close and held out a soda
can. Dan let her put it under his nose. A petroleum scent.

"What is it?"

"Most likely distillate fuel, marine. Could be a couple of other things, including lighter fuel. Which we sell in the ship's store."

"Great, that narrows it down. Dusted?"

"No prints. Or so Forker says."

"You don't sound convinced."

"I think it's beyond either his capabilities, or his motivation. To put it bluntly, he doesn't give a shit who did it or why."

"Do I need to recalibrate him?"

"No. You need to sign this."

The clipboard held a message to COMIDEASTFOR, requesting assistance from the Naval Criminal Investigative Service station in Bahrain. COMDESRON 22, COMNAV-SURFLANT, COMSECONDFLT, and the JAG office in Washington were info addees. Along with arson in the berthing space, it mentioned the photo incident and other insults to the female crew. A pattern of gender discrimination and harassment had escalated to an attempt on women's lives. In as many words, it said USS *Thomas W. Horn* was sick and needed major attention.

"Well, now," he said.

"You send it, we get to the bottom of this," Hotchkiss told him. "You don't, I resign and go to the press. Sir."

"That sounds like a threat."

"It is. I have to protect these kids."

"I have to think of all my crew, Claudia. I understand where you're coming from. Believe me."

"Do you?"

"Give me one more chance to prove it," he told her. "I need to take this to the senior enlisted. They're the only ones who can solve this."

"They're the ones who *encourage* it. Like your command master chief. And Forker. And that testosterone-laced prick Marchetti."

"I know how you feel," Dan told her. "But I don't think a witch hunt's the way to handle this. Three months is not a lot of time to change two hundred years of tradition. And regardless of how impatient we get with the pace, blowing it open with higher command, and with the media, isn't the way to make progress."

"Or to advance the CO's career," she said. "Is it?"

He stiffened in his chair. Almost spoke angrily back, but restrained himself. Remembering the times he'd felt exactly the way she did. Not about women, but about the other things that seemed to get overlooked or set aside when the men at the top put their own interests first. She'd carry out her threat. He could see it in the set of her lips.

"Neither yours nor mine," he said at last. "And I'm closer to the end of mine than you are to yours, Claudia. The navy needs officers like you. Let me work this a little longer. I promise you, I will work it."

"Don't stonewall this," she told him. "Sunlight on crap is the only way it ever gets cleaned up. The navy doesn't change by itself."

He opened his mouth to contradict this, but had to close it. As far as he could remember, she was right. The U.S. Navy didn't change unless the alternative was ruin. On the other hand, once it did, that, too, became Tradition. That massive institution ratcheted forward in microscopic increments, with bursts of sparks and deafening noise and heat, but it never ratcheted back.

"Put that in your safe," he told her. "Give me one week. Then, if you still want to send it, I'll sign it without changing a word. That's a promise."

She stood still. Then nodded curtly, and was gone.

He breathed out, leaned back. Feeling drained. Was this all going to be a bust? He hated to think so. Everyone had worked so hard.

No, he thought. I have good chiefs. They'll come through.

At his elbow, the comm petty officer cleared his throat. He remembered the traffic, still on his lap, and went through it quickly, penciling the appropriate department where there was any chance of misunderstanding.

• • •

By 1700 they were on station, under way at bare steerageway between the incoming and outgoing traffic lanes. Dan
left the bridge after a renewed warning to Osmani, who'd
just qualified as officer of the deck, to maintain a 360-degree
awareness. He had no desire to get run down by a sleepy
tanker skipper.

He took his place at the wardroom table, freshly showered and feeling more human than he had most of that day.
Baked haddock, one of his favorites. The first bite was
halfway to his mouth when his radio sounded off. "Captain,
bridge."

"Go."

"Message from the commodore via voice, Captain, re-
layed through *Georges Leygues*. Intercept, board, and
search."

He started to say, "I'll be right up," but instead stopped
himself and told Osmani to have the TAO plot a course and
speed to intercept and get back to him. He got halfway
through the fish before the wardroom phone rang.

"Now away the boarding and search team. Section Gold.
That is, away the boarding and search team. Team Gold
provide."

Marchetti came to, pulled from the depths of exhaustion
and the strange dreams he got when he had to sleep in a hot
compartment. In this one, he'd been a helicopter pilot in Somalia. Wounded and left behind, with thousands of pissed-
off skinnies with guns searching for him. A nubile Arab
woman had hidden him. He'd undressed her, been on the
point of entering a velvety softness. For some reason they'd
both been speaking German. He stared at the underside of
the bunk above, hearing the ship creak and sway around
him. Then swung out and dropped into his coveralls, stacked
around his boots fire-station style. He bloused the cuffs and
buckled his belt and was ready to go. Pulled his cap off the
bunk light and was out the door, through the mess. The other

chiefs were eating. He grabbed a biscuit off Forker's plate and gnawed at it as he went up two decks.

Goldstine was handing out the weapons and ammo at the ready locker. The guys grabbed their iron without expression, haggard, silent. Too many boardings. Too many condition-three watches. He'd thought they might get a break, running in to Aqaba. Guess not. He slung the shotgun and stuck the .45 he'd started carrying as backup in his belt. "What is it this time," he asked the boarding officer, Ensign Cassidy. A porky, scared-looking kid who didn't seem to have any idea how to lead a boarding team—or anything else. It didn't seem fair the chiefs had to train the officers. Marty figured they'd given him Cassidy to either harden him up or break him, and so far the odds were not good.

"Motor vessel *Yazd*. Bound for Aqaba. She hove to on the radio call."

"Flag?"

"Iranian."

On the rolling fantail the red plastic-and-nylon jacob's ladder was laid out ready to drop. He saw the other ship, tilting slowly back and forth ahead. *Horn* was making up on it, slipping through deep blue four-foot seas. A rust-streaked white deckhouse on a black hull. No net gear. Maybe a thousand tons, the typical small merchant that ran around from the gulf. Heaving to on the call was a good sign. More than once in the last few weeks they'd had to chase them down, threaten them, before they hove to. *Horn* rolled to a sea, and the choking hot breath of turbine exhaust blew down on them. He didn't need that, looking at a two-mile ride in a small boat.

"Go ahead and load," he told them. "Mags only, chambers empty."

Fear, the port RHIB, came up from astern with a rocking roar, leaping over the wake that dragged behind *Horn*'s vertical stern. The coxwain raised a glove, then twisted the wheel to come in. "Kick that ladder over," he told one of the men, then looked back along them, lined up ready to go.

Crack Man, Sasquatch, Lizard, Snack Cake, Deuce, Amarillo, Turd Chaser.

The supernumerary, Wilson, stood back a few feet, weaponless because he'd told Goldstine not to issue her anything. He waved her back impatiently. Seven men plus himself and Cassidy. It made for a crowded ride but the semi-inflatables could carry more than the old rigid whaleboats. He didn't miss them. Just the fact the soft side of the RHIB wouldn't crush your arm or your leg if you got caught between it and the hull paid their way as far as he was concerned.

"Gold team, move out," he shouted, and swung over the rail.

The helo was up. Standard when they ran a boarding and search. A close pass, letting the target see the barrel of the gun poking out of the door, tended to meek down your average merchant master. Plus with all the protuberances and gear the SH-60 had fitted it looked even more dangerous than it actually was. It roared low, then curved away, gaining altitude, leaving caramel smoke and a racketing roar.

He pulled his attention back to clinging heavily loaded to a swaying ladder above a turbulent sea. He glanced down to where the RHIB surged and lunged, then dropped. Landed in the floorboards. He unfouled the sling and moved aft, perching on the gunwale. It got wet back here but he didn't mind. One by one the guys picked their way down the ladder and dropped. When Cassidy held up a hesitant hand the coxswain gunned it, the bow hook tossed off the painter, and they surged forward so suddenly he almost toppled backward.

From sea level the target looked much farther away than from up on deck. All he could make out between the passing waves was its stack and mast, tilting back and forth. Rolling like a pig in shit. The RHIB jostled toward it, the coxswain taking it slow. The heavy seas shouldered the boat left and right, pushing it around as if it were made of Styrofoam. A sea burst over the gunwale and soaked them. At least you were cooler when you were wet.

He licked sweet salt from his lips, and sucked a heavy odor of burning fuel, different from the familiar smells of *Horn*. The motor vessel's exhaust smelled like cheap diesel, like at a truck stop in Georgia, and he started to feel ill again. Sasquatch was already gagging over the side. For a big guy, he got sick easy.

"Hurry it up, God damn it," he yelled at the coxswain. Who shrugged as the chopper roared over again, a hundred feet above their heads.

But he nudged the throttle up, and they started slamming through the waves, jarring like they were hitting solid banks of gravel. Looking ahead, he saw the target closer now. Weeping rust. A deserted afterdeck. The crew was supposed to be up forward, so the helo could keep an eye on them. The painted legend YAZD and beneath that a squiggle he figured was whatever Iranians spoke.

Suddenly it loomed over them, a startlingly high wall of rough, rusty steel and flaking black paint. Marty eyed the rope ladder dangling from the stern. Not the quarter, the stern. Oh, well. . . . It slipped from sight as they continued ahead, doing a circuit, looking up at the bridge. He couldn't see into it from this angle, but he didn't see any heads. Nor any antiboarding measures. Sometimes they tried to make it hard. Welded steel spikes to the hull. Epoxied the bases of busted bottles along the deck line. Wrapped barbed wire along the handrails. As they rounded the bow eight or nine scruffy-headed, swarthy men gazed down at them. Some looked bored, others ticked.

"Horn Gold, this is *Horn*, over."

He said into the radio, "Horn Gold. Go ahead, over."

"They giving you any trouble?"

"Not aboard yet. Over."

"The master said the French boarded him already."

"So why we searching them again?"

"Beats me. Commodore said to."

Okay, great. He said roger, out, and holstered the Saber as the coxswain aimed them for the ladder. The bow hook got it and hung on as *Fear* seesawed violently. Turd Chaser got his

gloves on a rung and swarmed up it, bolt cutters bobbing
where he'd slung them over his back. A moment later he
stood at the top, hand on holster, staring around. When he
beckoned, Amarillo hit the ladder.

When Marty got to the afterdeck, the team was out in
their perimeter. But their weapons pointed at nothing but
flaking steel and battered bitts and what looked like a metal-
mesh goat pen. The vacant, seedy, rolling deck felt creepy,
like boarding a ghost ship. But *Horn* rode a couple of hundred yards off, and the helo clattered overhead. Aside from
that, all he could see was mountains, far off to the north.

"Bridge?" said Cassidy. He nodded. Shotgun at port
arms, buckshot in the tube, he led them forward.

The master said his name was George. He sounded pissed.
In a small, smelly room behind the little enclosed bridge he
pulled a folder from behind a bolted-down, corroding type-
writer. "I tell you, French inspect already. Two day ago."

"And we're inspectin' you again," Marchetti told him.
"Like having gravy on your cake. You can stay up here or go
forward with your crew. Your choice."

George spat on the dirty deck. He threw the folder down
contemptuously. "You take us off bow soon," he said. "Too
much sun." And left.

Marty picked them up and fanned the documents out. She
was registered in the Grenadines, wherever that was. "We
got lucky," Deuce said, pointing to an ancient photocopy
machine.

They could see the crew through the windows, sitting
with backs against bulwarks and wildcats in the eyes of the
ship. Bedraggled, unshaven, in torn denims and dirty field
jackets. They were all smoking. Dead in the water, the vessel
careened back and forth with a long pendulum roll that set
Marchetti's teeth on edge. From below came shouts as the
sweep teams went through the next deck down. He had three
teams of two. Amarillo and Crack Man were on the bow
guarding the crew. Sasquatch and Snack Cake were going
through the crew's quarters and mess decks, and Turd

Chaser and Lizard had headed for the engine spaces. After they made sure all the crew was topside, they'd move them somewhere they could keep an eye on them—most likely the mess decks. Then start the actual search, opening holds and tanks, taking soundings and samples. He wondered again why they were reinspecting if the French had really given them a clean bill on the inward passage.

Cassidy pulled himself up into the pilothouse as the helo buzzed past in a blast of sound. A close pass down the starboard side. "Got the sounding log," Marchetti yelled to him.

It showed a ballast tank, four cargo tanks, and two fuel oil tanks, along with fuel oil service and settling tanks and freshwater tankage. All quantities were given in square meters. He handed it to Deuce along with registry, manifest, bill of lading, a crew list, and a sheaf of individual licenses and documents. The crew was Iranian, Syrian, Pakistani, Greek, Russian-Ukrainian. Some of this was in squiggly writing, and he told Deuce to see what he could make out of it. There didn't seem to be any UN form and they had to call the master back to scowlingly retrieve it from another folder.

The 986 form showed clearance for a cargo of animal feed, Indian tea, bagged flour, and raw jute. He compared it to the printout that had come over from the Maritime Interdiction Center. *Yazd* had been inspected many times before. It looked like this was her regular run. The database from the previous inspections, bumped against the log and the other onboard documentation, gave them a benchmark to check on crew changes or out of the ordinary cargo or itineraries.

The photocopy machine hummed. Light chased across the bulkhead. Marchetti passed a hand over his wet forehead. The enclosed quarters, the extreme roll was getting to him. Changing from one ship to another in midocean set off bad things in his inner ear. He went outside and gripped the handrail, looking across to *Horn* until the nausea backed off. Down on the forecastle the crew laughed, making gestures up at him. He made a gesture back at them. They stopped laughing, then got up unwillingly as Crack Man motioned them up.

Back inside, he grabbed the copies of the tankage diagrams and went below, planting his boots carefully on worn steel rungs.

Belowdecks was dim and spooky. He flicked a switch but nothing happened. The crew had turned off the generator, or else it was broken. He looked into the mess decks, wrinkling his nose. Insecticide, curry, greasy meat, old cigarette smoke. A movie poster showing an Indian woman dancing with a bear. A flash of the woman in that afternoon's dream, dark-haired, wide-hipped, full-lipped. Scattered newspapers in incomprehensible alphabets. A gray cat stared insolently from the sideboard, where it was licking a plate.

A central ladder well wound into the depths. He pulled his .45 and worked the slide. Fuck the rules. The passageways creaked as the steel fabric rolled around him.

Two decks below he glimpsed one of the teams moving past the ladderway, the lead man ahead, pistol drawn. Then the other, covering him from the other side.

He was watching the roaches scatter in a deserted stateroom when he heard shouting, scuffling, a thud. "What's going on down there?" he yelled, rounding the ladderway, sliding down on the greasy handrails without touching the treads.

Snack Cake and Sasquatch stood over a guy lying on the deck. "He jumped out at me," Snack Cake said.

"So you coldcocked his ass?"

"Only a little bit."

"Fuck, man." Marty bent over him, helped him to his feet. The Iranian, or whatever he was, wasn't very big. He wasn't young, either. Blood streamed from matted hair into a gray-streaked beard. He looked to be about sixty, and not a lot of tread left. "Shit. This ain't gonna look good."

"Asylum," the geezer said, perfectly plainly.

"Huh? What'd he say?"

"Asylum. I want asylum in U.S." He smiled through the blood. He had terrible teeth.

"We're not in that business, Pop," Marchetti told him.

"You give me asylum, I tell you where it is."

"Where what is?" said Lizard.

"Shut up," Marty told him. To the old man he said, "Oh, yeah? Well, too fuckin' bad. We already know."

"You know?" Pouchy eyes closed in cunning. "No, you don't. Or you wouldn't be down here."

"Uh-huh. Well, maybe. You would be—"

"I am Saloman Rashik."

"Uh-huh. Rashik. Okay, Liz—"

"Lizard. Not 'Liz.' "

"That's what I said, Liz. Take him back to the fantail and get him bandaged up. Then hold him separate. You know the drill from there. Don't let the others see we got him. Sass, I'll cover you, which way you going from here?"

They reassembled on the bridge with Cassidy after forty-five minutes of going through the tankage and the cargo. Actually they gun-decked the tankage. Nobody smuggled oil into Iraq, and *Yazd* wasn't a tanker anyway. Cassidy said the chart markings and fixes checked out. There was more animal feed than the bill of lading specified, but since there was no UN restriction on it, they couldn't argue with that. The master had wanted back on the bridge. He glowered from a folding chair, arms folded.

"Who's this Rashik dude?" Marchetti asked him.

"Who?"

"Ra-sheek. Rashik."

The master shrugged and rolled his eyes. "An old man of no use. He kills bugs. He cooks. That's his cat."

"He's from where? Lebanon?"

The captain said no, Syria, and he was a troublemaker and a liar. He stole from the others in the crew. Rashik was a piece of shit. He could ask anyone. Marty thought about that, then crooked a finger at Cassidy. They went out on the little wing, where "George" couldn't hear them.

"Whattdya think, sir? He says he'll show us where it is if we give him asylum."

"But what is it?"

"He won't tell us unless he gets what he wants. Or at least

something in writing that says he gets it, if he comes through."

"He's just jerking our chain," Cassidy said. "We already searched this rustbucket. And the French, before us. You heard what the master said. A shit-for-lunch, a thief, a liar."

"Sometimes it's your scumbags come through for you," Marty told him. "They're always looking for a better deal. We could see what he's got to offer."

The lieutenant said he could work it a bit if he thought it was worth it.

Marty borrowed a pack of Vantages from Crack Man and went aft. He sat down with the old guy and offered him a cigarette. They went back and forth for about twenty minutes. The Syrian, or Lebanese, or whatever he was, kept saying he'd show them where it was if he got asylum. Marty said he couldn't make any promises, but maybe they could help him if he showed them what he had. Somewhere in here he realized the guy wasn't as old as he'd thought, he was only about forty, but he looked hard used. He said if he did that and they left him aboard, the master would have him killed. He wanted to be taken off. The cat had to come, too.

"You say there's something aboard, huh? Contraband?"

"What?"

"Something smuggled? What is it—oil?"

"Not *oil*." Rashik's nose wrinkled in contempt. "These are American cigarette? They don't taste. Is tobacco in them?"

"Work with me, I'll work with you."

Eventually they got down to what it was: pipes. Rashik said he'd seen them being lowered into the after hold late one night. "Pipes" sounded harmless, but when Cassidy reported it to the ship, the word came back to check it out, and meanwhile hold the informant separate from the rest of the crew.

So Marty and Crack Man and Sasquatch and Turd Chaser—they called him that because he was a hull tech, the closest the navy got to plumbers—climbed down into the after hold and started tearing it apart. Before, they'd sampled; now they dug. They hauled and strained at the stacks of feed.

In the terrible oven heat of the closed hold the cottonseed waste or whatever it was had rotted into what you found in a sink drain when you took it apart. Oozing through the jute bags, it stained coveralls and hands fertilizer brown. They panted through their mouths, trying not to smell what they were standing thigh-deep in. The beefing and bitching started. Rats rustled at the corners of their vision, burrowing away from the sudden activity. But at last they got down to the ceiling-boards, right down to where he could shine his light through the rusty bottom into the fetid stinking roach-crawling bilges.

He straightened, disgusted, dizzy with the closed-in heat. "Fuck it," he said, wiping a sleeve over his dripping face. "That's enough. There's nothing here."

"You want us to restack this shit?"

"Fuck it. They can do it." He waded toward the ladder, trying to shake crap inches thick off his boots, like walking through a hog yard.

Then his gaze stopped.

On a swipe of green paint, back by the after bulkhead. Where they'd stacked the bags as they burrowed down.

The team cursed anew but he drove them back to work. Bags tore as they manhandled them, releasing fresh showers of what looked like smashed-flat coffee beans. It made a slippery paste underfoot as they struggled hundred-pound sacks from one end of the hold to the other.

But gradually as the after level lowered, a patch of paint came into view. Same color as the rest of the hold, but cleaner. New.

He sent Crack Man topside for a fire axe, and took a roundhouse swing in the middle of the painted area.

Plaster or concrete flew apart with a cracking sound. "Son of a bitch," Lizard said.

Marty grunted. He hacked around the edge till he was tired, then handed the axe to Sasquatch. Clouds of white dust filled the thick air. Finally Marchetti told him to back off. He crept forward, pulling his Maglite off his belt.

The beam showed him a void extending back under the

fuel oil service tanks. Its inner walls were dark steel. He
looked back to where his shotgun was propped and felt to
make sure the .45 was still at the small of his back.

Then bent through the hole, and duckwalked into a space
maybe four feet high.

Carefully dunnaged into the space with baulks of piny-
looking wood were perhaps two dozen cylindrical brown
objects. As he crept closer, he saw the brown was a thick im-
pregnated kraft paper wrapping material. He slit it with the
Ka-Bar. Beneath was . . . he couldn't quite made out what.

He rapped it with the knife, but that didn't tell him anything. Just that it was a shiny metal tube a foot in diameter
and maybe eight, ten feet long. There were no markings on
it, although there was writing on the paper. Too faint to read,
but he thought it might be German or Dutch. They didn't
look like much. If he'd fallen over them stacked outside the
engine room he wouldn't have given them a second look.
But they were hidden so there was probably a reason. He
backed out and climbed out of the hold and reported back on
the radio.

Dan was on the scrambled freq to Commodore Strong for
the fourth time that afternoon. He was telling him he'd decided to leave his search team aboard that night. The master,
expostulating fiercely he'd known nothing of any contraband, had been told to start the engines and steam back toward the mouth of the gulf. She lay now directly ahead of
Horn, plodding along at nine knots. Dan told the officer of
the deck to check in by radio with Ensign Cassidy every fifteen minutes and warned Cassidy and Marchetti to keep
Yazd's crew under close supervision.

Strong was saying, "Make sure your men keep close control. Once you lay hands on them, these smugglers will scuttle rather than turn over evidence. Especially if they're Iraqi
and have families in country."

"Aye, sir."

"I've reported our discovery up the line. *Laboon* will relieve you off Ras Muhammad, after you transit the strait.

You'll escort your detainee to Jiddah, where the Saudis will take him to a security area off Bahrain while his case is decided."

"Aye, aye, sir. What happens then?"

"They off-load and evaluate the cargo. Eventually the ship's auctioned as a captured smuggler. To deter the next owner the Iraqis approach." He heard the commodore clear his throat off-mike, then come back. "Unfortunately, our best customers at the auctions are the other smugglers, the ones who've made it and gotten paid. They buy the captured ships, and the whole cycle repeats itself."

"That doesn't sound too productive, sir."

"Well, one hopes we are putting something of a dent in Saddam's rearming. At any rate, a well-done to you and your crew. MIC out."

"*Horn,* out," Dan said, and hung up the red phone. He looked out at *Yazd* again, plodding along against the backdrop of the mountains. Thin high clouds hovered above the distant peaks, growing darker as the day closed.

"Now all chief petty officers, first class petty officers, assemble in the chiefs' mess. All chief petty officers and first class petty officers, assemble in the chiefs' mess."

He glanced at his watch. Swung his legs down, and went below.

Dan had asked Forker to get the enlisted leadership together. He stood in his in-port cabin, steadying himself against the sway of the ship. Debating, in the last minutes before he faced them, what would be the best approach.

Hotchkiss wanted to take it outside the skin of the ship. The criminal investigators. Commander, Mideast Force. But he still thought *Horn* could do this herself. If she found her own answer, it'd be a hell of a lot healthier than one imposed from outside.

Because if it broke outside, she was lost. She'd be shattered for years, if not forever. Another repeat of Tailhook, another reek of cover-up and U.S. Navy closed-mindedness.

Nick Niles would rub his beefy hands. But from what

Blair had told him, Dan didn't think this clock ran backward. If the *Horn* experiment blew apart, the extreme feminists in DACOWITS and Congress would take over Women at Sea and kill any chance of proceeding with any semblance of goodwill. Splitting the service down the middle, with quotas, lawsuits, years of bad publicity. He could kiss his career goodbye, too, but that didn't seem as important as what it'd do to all the guys and gals who'd striven to turn the ship around after Ross's lackluster regime.

But he couldn't do it, the XO couldn't do it, a wardroom full of officers couldn't do it. Only one community could turn the crew around.

Forker stood by at the door to the chiefs' mess. Dan nodded, and the chief master at arms jerked it open.

"Attention on deck!" They came to their feet in a surge, cigarettes hastily stubbing out. The air was a blue haze already.

"Carry on," he said, and took the center. The chiefs and first class stood around the edge of the compartment, crowded back into the berthing area. Some with arms folded: a bad sign. He caught Hotchkiss's eye. Good, she needed to hear this, too. He raised his voice. "Can everyone hear me? Good.

"I guess everybody's heard what happened this morning in female berthing. Some anonymous coward set a fuel fire. Endangering not just the lives of the sailors in that compartment, but everyone aboard. It's arson, and if someone had gotten killed—and we had three people report to sick bay for smoke inhalation—it'd be murder. And this meeting would be the beginning of a murder investigation."

He let that take effect. Some nodded, expressions sober. The ones who'd seen what fire could do at sea, most likely.

"Somebody doesn't like having women aboard. Okay, he's got a right to his opinion. But when it comes to destruction of property and threatening the lives of his shipmates, that's where the right to an opinion ends.

"If the guys in this room want a witch hunt, a no-date policy, and the NCIS aboard tearing us apart, I'm ready to go that way. The message is written. It'll wreck this ship. I can see that far ahead. And I think you guys in this compartment *are* the ship. You put your sweat equity into making her what she is today, the best-prepared strike destroyer in the U.S. Navy.

"But somebody aboard wants to destroy everything we've worked to build.

"Before I kick this upstairs, I want to try to fix this one last time through the people who lead this ship. The chiefs and senior petty officers, the work center supervisors. The seamen and junior petty officers listen to you. The younger sailors follow your example."

He paused, looking at their faces; wondering if he was getting through. Maybe to some. Enough? The right ones? He had no way of knowing.

"I will say that I have ways of finding out who set that fire. When I do, he will not enjoy it. I will make an example of someone who values the lives of his shipmates so little.

"Here's the offer I'm making to anyone who doesn't want to be with the command program. I want you to pass it on to every one of your men.

"I don't care what they think about women in the navy. They're here. The problem's not the women. The problem is certain people's attitude.

"So let's talk to that attitude. You men know who the cases are in your division who feel that way. Tell them this. From me.

"You can't serve with women? Then get off *Horn.* Say so now. I'll sign your letter and transfer you off. But if you don't get with the program, you'll be sorry you ever met me. If anything like this happens again, you will go through every refinement of the military justice system I can locate for you."

There, that was enough. He nodded curtly, and turned, and they made way for him to leave.

Outside, Forker looked both anxious and impressed. "Well?" Dan asked him.

"You láid it out for 'em, sir. Unfuck this, or die."

"I don't think that's exactly the way I put it."

Forker looked as if that *was* exactly the way he'd put it. "Anyway, that laid it on the line. I don't think we'll see any more fires."

"I hope you're right, Chief. But I want to find out who set this one."

He stopped in his in-port cabin to get his gym gear. Looking around the empty stateroom, he suddenly felt everything he'd done that day was wrong, too late, too feeble, and not enough.

Was Hotchkiss right? Was he covering up a problem he ought to hand over to the investigators? Covering his ass to save his career, the same thing he'd hated and resented in those above him? Only time would tell. Unfortunately, with Claudia Hotchkiss on his six, he didn't have much of that.

Even worse, whoever had done it might strike again. Killing someone this time. How would he live with himself then?

He stared out the porthole, rubbing his mouth as night came to the Red Sea.

14

Manama, Bahrain

The big white Suburban was assigned to the office; it wasn't hers. Aisha had bought a Hyundai in San Diego, but it was in Staten Island now. Her mom didn't drive, but her dad took it to Jumah service every week to keep it in running condition.

She was waiting when the door opened, and a large man in a dark suit and maroon figured tie looked in. "Want me to—"

"It's okay, Bob. I'll drive."

Bob Diehl was the size of a soft drink machine. His face was droop-cheeked and saggy-eared, like a basset hound's. Tentlike slacks draped over cordovan loafers. Bahrain was his last station, his last tour. An old-line agent, he both impressed and repelled her. He and Kinky were always telling each other jokes, worn-out puns and remarks about faggots and women. On the other hand, she'd seen him in operation a few times, like when he'd "counseled" a petty officer who'd been stalking a girl at the Desert Dome.

Diehl had been in submarines before joining what was then the NIS. He had been an agent for twenty-four years, as long as she'd been alive. Sitting in on that interview, she'd realized how many times he'd done this and how well he knew the screwed-up young sailors that made up most of their clientele. First he intimidated the kid, letting him glimpse the big .357 Magnum revolver the older agents carried. Then he told a joke, about what you called an Arab with a hundred girlfriends. The answer was: a shepherd. Then he clarified exactly what the kid had been observed doing, characterizing it in the most rancid and dismissive terms possible.

And then scared the shit out of him, laying out what would happen if anything like this happened again. He made the process look effortless. Made the suspects, usually petrified and sometimes not too bright to begin with, say what he needed them to say. In fact, she had the feeling he could make them say anything he wanted, true or not.

The senior agent hesitated, then went around to the passenger side and opened the door for a tall, hook-nosed officer in tropical whites. Aisha pulled her purse out of his way. When he slammed the door, and she heard her partner's door slam, too, she turned the key.

Today was the monthly security liaison committee meeting, where the local police and counterterrorism people shared information with the resident intelligence community. The Ministry of Justice and Islamic Affairs was also headquarters of the SIS, the Bahraini security police. Brigadier General Bucheery would chair. Commander Hooker, as head of security at the Naval Support Activity, was invited, as were the security liaisons from the various embassies. He'd asked her to come along to listen to the side conversations in Arabic—he wanted a typed report afterward—and Diehl had invited himself.

She was leery of Hooker. He didn't say much, and his expression never changed. The agents didn't work for him—their chain of command went separately from that of the military up to the director, who worked for the secretary of the navy—but they had to work together, and they all had to work with the lawyers. Hooker sat quietly for the first mile, then said, not turning his head: "Anything on the thefts in 138 yet, Bobby?"

Diehl rumbled cigar-phlegm from the back. "Not yet."

"I hoped you'd have something by now. The captain was on me about it again this morning."

Neither agent said anything. "Nothing?" Hooker persisted. "Do I need to take this investigation?"

"No, sir," Aisha said. "We're working on it."

"What else have you got going but that?" Hooker persisted.

Diehl took that question, and she concentrated on driving. The Bahrainis had abandoned the British habit of driving on the left years ago, but unfortunately they'd kept the roundabouts. You had to stay sharp on the free-for-alls on Palace Avenue and King Faisal. She steered the heavy vehicle expertly as Diehl explained the theft was only one of several investigations in progress. One was a credit card scam. Then there was the guy they were hoping to turn into a cooperating witness and catch whoever was selling hashish on base.

"I'm not interested in those now," Hooker interrupted. "The pressure's on about this shortage. That's dangerous stuff to have wandering around."

He was referring to a recent theft of explosives and small arms. Building 138 was the wire-ringed, high-security armory area that held equipment for SEAL detachments and other high-security items. The day before yesterday, a routine inventory had revealed four nine-millimeter pistols, fifteen fragmentation grenades, and at least forty kilos of demolition explosives missing.

"We dusted for prints and took pictures of the locked area," Diehl began. "The locks weren't cut, so it wasn't a penetration from the outside."

"Who has access?"

"The officer in charge, the NCO, four storekeepers. We've interviewed them all, with negative results."

"Interviewed how?"

"The usual. Drill 'em and grill 'em. I gave them a good working over."

Aisha had been there. He'd had one of the kids crying. But none had confessed to knowing anything about the missing weapons and explosives.

"These are military members? Marine or navy?"

"Two marine, two navy. Their NCO's a gunnery sergeant. He reports to a supply corps lieutenant. You probably know him."

"The NCO, the OIC, they have access?"

"Not alone. It's a two-key system."

"So you've got absolutely nothing?"

"We've just started, Commander," Aisha told him. She kept her eyes on the road. More than once, she'd caught him staring at her. "We did the first-pass interviews, that's all. We'll let them stew a little and call them back in."

"Well, don't let it go too long. Anybody you like?"

A storekeeper second had avoided her eyes all through the interview. He was cool, didn't know anything, but he'd shifted on his seat to avoid confronting her, even when it meant facing Diehl. He was from Detroit. His name was Childers, but the others referred to him sometimes, she'd noted, as Jaleel.

"There might be one," she said, glancing at the rearview. The cross street to the palace was coming up. She got in the right-hand lane and signaled.

"Who? Which one?"

She didn't want to answer that, both in case she was wrong, and in case she was right—in case they had to take the man to court-martial. Better to keep what they suspected to themselves, until they were ready to bring charges. And as it turned out, she didn't have to, because a faultlessly uniformed constable in white gloves was swinging open the gates to the palace. "Here we are," she said brightly, and pulled in.

The ministry was new and white, like every government building on the island. When she'd got here she thought at first it was like coming home. More like home than Harlem, with the kids yelling and throwing dirty snowballs when she and Zara walked to the madrassa. Here she heard Arabic in every shop and street, accented differently than the Nation taught it, but still the fluid lovely language the angels spoke, laced with compliments and whimsy and the familiar words of the Prophet, peace be upon him. An administrator from the Awali Hospital had asked if he might take her to lunch. She'd daydreamed about leaving her job and living here.

So sometimes it felt like home. And then there were times when it didn't, not at all.

Like when she'd been bending over a dead body, and children had thrown mud clods at her. Calling her "American devil." How had they known? Of course, of course, the huge white car.

Hooker got out, and she started, recalled from her thoughts, and followed the men inside.

The conference room had been furnished by the Swedish consortium that had built the palace. It was all blond laminate and recessed lighting. There was a back-projection screen for briefings. Steaming silver urns and trays of cookies and succulent Iraqi dates waited on a side table. The servants, or waiters, or whatever they were, were straightening chairs and offering coffee and tea. Hooker went straight for a paunchy, sharp-bearded Arab in a spotless silk thobe. Aisha got coffee, checking out the room as she sipped.

The men wore uniforms, business suits, or the white robe and headdress. She was the only woman. The Bahrainis had a few in their charities and their labor and social affairs ministries, but they didn't appoint them to the security organs.

Bahrain was an Arab state, but it had hosted first the Royal Navy and then the U.S. Navy for many years. The air force had operated from the base at the south end of the island during Desert Storm. To the tourist, the island looked free and open, with its glamorous hotels and night clubs where liquor flowed. To business, it was a haven. When it became obvious the island's oil reserves were running out, the government had created a free-trade sector that pulled shipping companies, banks, and merchants in from all over the Mideast.

She hadn't learned any of this from Diehl. He didn't care about anything outside the walls of the base. In fact, he'd

made cracks about the locals she hadn't liked at all, although
she hadn't said anything. No, she was just the good little
Muslim girl . . . She'd picked it up talking to the locals,
mainly wealthy Sunni women she met in town, in the stores,
when they made *salat* together in the little prayer areas in
the malls. She loved to shop and buy clothes for her mother
and her aunts, and there were beautiful modest fashions here
and what else did she have to spend her money on? The
women were surprised to hear she was American, and out-
spoken in setting her straight. The rest she got from her own
reading, the local papers, *Al-Hayat,* the *Gulf Daily News,* the
Middle East Economic Digest.

For the less well-off residents, especially the Shi'a,
things were more tightly run. The State Security Court could
detain persons without charge or trial for up to three years.
The Security and Intelligence Service had hundreds of
agents and there were rumors of torture. But the emir hardly
ever executed anybody, enjoyed a joke, and—she'd heard
from a flight attendant she ran into one night at the Al
Hamra—enjoyed the women he invited to his personal
beach, far from the eyes of ordinary Bahrainis.

A stir at the door announced a stiff, graying man in a
British army uniform. Major General Sean Gough had
headed the SIS for twenty years. He surveyed the room,
talked briefly to a dark-browed man she recognized as the liaison from the U.S. embassy, and thus, she figured, the CIA
chief of station.

Then he saw her, and immediately came across to bow
over her hand. Cold blue eyes studied her from a foot above
her head. "Sister Aisha," he said in fluent, Saudi-accented
Arabic. "*Assalamu alaikum wa rahmatullahi wa barakatu.*
How good of you to join us again. You and the commander
are most welcome."

"Thank you, General."

"Unfortunately I have an unpleasant issue to raise. Either
with you, or—perhaps—"

"What is it, General?"

Hooker, back from his conversation with the Arab. He didn't look happy to see them together. "Good morning, General."

"Commander." They shook hands. Gough said, in fluting British English, "About to remark to your charming young protégée. Hearing unsettling things about the security on your base. More precisely, the security of your explosives. Not good news for those of us responsible for keeping the lid on the kettle, so to speak. Eh?"

"Sir, I'd like to—"

"No, no, Commander. Not in front of the natives. Call you this afternoon. A cozy little chat. Eh?"

Gough winked at her and turned away. Aisha could tell Hooker was furious just from the set of his fingers on the china cup. She moved away in case it should shatter.

To bump into Major Yousif. The SIS man smiled down. "*Ya Naqueeb Ar-Rahim*," he said, addressing her by a police rank. "*Ahlan, ahlan.* Welcome, welcome, a happy occasion. It seems to be written we are to meet again and again. Why do you think that is?"

"Maybe because we're both cops."

"You're the first Arabic speaker the Americans have sent us. Fortunately for us, the CIA has not yet reached that level of expertise."

"They just haven't told you," Aisha said. "Pretending you're stupid is an old American trick. You'd be surprised how well it works."

He chuckled. "Oh, no. I've been taken in all these years." He didn't have an unattractive laugh, like some men. She noted he didn't wear a ring, either.

"Not to ask questions where they're unwelcome, but how well do you get along with the Americans? Or I should say, the other Americans?"

"Fine. We're used to looking different, different religions and nationalities." This wasn't exactly what she thought, but you didn't tell a host country security agency anything that didn't reflect well.

"That's hard to imagine. We Arabs have what I have often thought of as a centrifugal tendency. But then, our colonial history, the boundaries we were left with . . . and then the tragedy of Palestine. So you're both Muslim and American."

"I don't see why I can't be both."

"You must have your own opinions."

"I certainly do."

"May I ask what they are?"

She decided to change the subject. "What did you find out about the man who died in the Quraifa? You were supposed to invite me to the autopsy."

"I'm sorry. It slipped my mind you wanted to be there. It was routine. What did I find out about him? Nothing, I'm afraid. That's why I never got back to you. The passport was false."

"The Bahraini license?"

"Real, but not his. Reported lost some time ago."

"So the decedent found or stole a driver's license, and used that name to get a base ID?"

"The base ID was false, too."

She said, surprised, "It was real. I checked it."

"A high-quality forgery. Clearly so, under ultraviolet. We weren't sure either, until the lab report." He caught her expression. "Correct. Someone on the island is making forgeries good enough to fool your gate guards. We're trying to find out who. We're still trying to find out who this man was, too, and why he was here."

"Will you keep me informed?"

"Always."

She thought, And yet you didn't tell me any of this until I asked. But then someone was saying, "Shall we take our places?" and she nodded and went back to sit with Hooker and Diehl.

Alternating between English and Arabic, the security minister read a long address from the crown prince. It was about popular participation and economic reform, and how necessary these were if the country was to move to a higher

level of productivity. How citizens had to motivate themselves through education and innovation to build a modern
society. How governmental officials had to set an example in
morality and sincerity and be prepared to make
sacrifices . . . She tuned out and stared out the window at the
fingernail of distant blue visible far out over the nodding
palms and the roofs of the city.

The boilerplate over, one of the departments briefed on a
resurgence of unrest among the Shi'a. Israeli suppression of
the Palestinians had put hate for Israel and America in the
air. Here that translated into resentment of the ruling family.
He warned everyone to be alert for riots and possibly new
acts of terror. Next was a report from what seemed to be an
unofficial Saudi liaison, or perhaps he was official—everyone seemed to know him and he wasn't introduced, so she
couldn't tell. His report was about the spread of religious extremism, but his definition of "extremism" seemed vague.
The first part was in English; the second, Arabic. She could
follow most of it, though she missed a word here and there.
The Arabic segment was about "polytheist" missionaries,
and how to "welcome" them—actually, how to block their
activities and find pretexts to ask them to leave the country.
The Saudi seemed concerned the Bahrainis weren't taking
the problem seriously.

Aisha caught Gough's glance, evaluating how she was
taking it. She smiled back. Caught a blank look on the face
of the CIA man—it was going past him—a politely interested expression on the face of the security minister.

For a moment she tried to imagine the tightrope *he* must
be trying to walk. On one side, literally, they were right
across the causeway, the Saudis. On the other, the British
and Americans. The Iraqis threatening from up north. The
Iranians, coreligionists of the Shi'ite majority, across the
Gulf. On one hand, bazaar fundamentalism, whipped up by
the repression and house-bulldozings in Israel. On the other,
pressure from the steadily educating middle class to demo-
cratize. Beneath it all, the knowledge that soon the oil would

stop flowing and Bahrain would become again a barren, wa-
terless desert.

No, she didn't envy him at all.

Like all Arab meetings, when it was over everyone scattered
instantly. In seconds the room was empty. Diehl tilted his
watch. "Half the fuckin' day shot in the ass."

"You don't need to use language like that, Bob."

"D'you copy any of that? What they were sayin'?"

"Most of it."

"Anything worth hearing?"

"It'll all be in my report," she said.

Hooker came back from talking to a heavyset white man
she thought was FBI. "Let's go. We've wasted enough time
here." He still looked furious, and she knew it was about the
missing explosives and guns, and even more, that Gough
knew about them. Which meant he had sources of information inside the base.

"What were you talking to the general about?" he wanted
to know as soon as they were in the car.

She said, startled, "To Gough? Nothing. He was just
showing off his Arabic."

"Did you tell him about the thefts? And that Yousif, you
had your heads together for a long time there."

"I did *not* tell them about the thefts, or anything else. Do
you really think I would—"

"Bob, you were there, did she say anything?"

Diehl stirred uneasily. "Uh—they were talking Arabic—"

"I did *not* say *anything* about that," she said. "That is internal need to know and I would *never* discuss it with anyone
off base. With *anyone*. If you don't believe that, sir, we'd
better have a private talk."

"No, no, forget it." He sat back.

She jerked the car around, almost sideswiping a taxi, so
mad she could spit. At both of them; Diehl hadn't even pretended to defend her. The security officer muttered something, some halfhearted apology, but by then she was taking

deep, even breaths, forcing it down, down. To where his instant assumption—that because she spoke Arabic, because she was Muslim, because she was black, she was not to be trusted—could not hurt her at all.

15

Off Jiddah, the Red Sea

Horn had her own little convoy for a few days. *Yazd* and a break-bulk cargo tramp *Georges Leygues* had caught smuggling nine hundred tons of Iraqi crude out of Jordan under a blanket of olive oil. The crude was heavier than the olive oil, but the French had sampled with a tube rather than a dip bottle and found it. The tanker was old and very slow. They slogged down to Jiddah, the principal Saudi port on the Red Sea, at the blazing pace of six knots when not actually hove to to fix breakdowns.

At Jiddah a patrol boat escorted *Yazd* and the break-bulk into the Royal Saudi Naval Facility. There the mysterious tubes would be pulled out of *Yadz*'s hold for examination by UN inspectors. Rashik had been packed off to purgatory with the State Department and Immigration and Naturalization. The Saudis would deliver the captured vessels to the custody area while the mill wheels of international enforcement ground their way to their disposition.

Horn, drawing too much water for the naval facility, lay that night alongside the mile-long container terminal, surrounded by ro-ro ships discharging hundreds of shiny Japanese SUVs and trucks. She had disgorged, too, four hundred bags of accumulated trash they hadn't been permitted to dump in the Red Sea. Since Jiddah was the pilgrimage port for Mecca, there was no liberty for non-Muslims. American crews were strictly limited to the pier, and the port captain advised Dan to have his women's faces covered even there, or else keep them on board.

He debated staying aboard himself, to show solidarity, but the prospect of a run uninterrupted by knee-knockers and fire hoses seduced him. He told Hotchkiss he was going ashore for an hour. Then suited up in shorts and a T-shirt from his last reunion and jogged down the brow.

The asphalt flatness, long as many football fields end to end, was dotted by ziggurats of containers, rail lines for the massive traveling cranes, and thousands of plastic-wrapped Hondas like pupating locusts. As he finished stretching and swung into a jog, sodium-vapor lamps detonated salmon-colored light into the Arabian dusk. The wind brought a fine dust that isolated him like fog. The buildings of the forbidden kingdom loomed indistinctly as a realm of ghosts across the moat that separated the pier from the town.

Gradually, as he ran, his mind recurred to where they might be going next. And where they might not.

They were due a week of port visit—actually, more like four days, since they'd used up part of it poking along with the slower vessels. But during the run down, Strong's inquiries on his location and estimated time of arrival had become more pointed. Dan wondered if he should warn the crew their long-anticipated liberty might not work out. The maritime intercept commander seemed to want them back on station as soon as possible. And just that morning a message from MIDEASTFOR had directed them to report the status of their Tomahawk loadout and daily systems checks, and communicate any degradation or casualty.

Isolated as they were, he was hard put to gauge what was going on. But the fleet news summary reported increased tensions with Iraq. The inspectors had probed too deeply, and sabers were rattling again.

If things lit up, *Horn* and *Laboon* might be called into the Gulf. But Strong was pulling them back north, to the head of the Red Sea. Contradictory? Or related to Commander, Mideast Force's sudden interest in their missile loadout? *San*

Jacinto, "San Jac," had fired Tomahawks from the Red Sea during the opening hours of the Gulf War.

After a couple of miles he found himself out of breath. You got out of shape quickly aboard ship. He slowed, then walked, looking at the distant lights of Arabia. Then forced himself back into motion, gasping in the gritty heat.

They finished loading food and fuel and cast off at 0800 into the same spectral, powdery-dust haze as the day before. The temperature was already over a hundred. It would rise as relentlessly as the sun. Dan was on the bridge, watching as they navigated the reef-strewn pass of Ras Quahaz, when Hotchkiss came up. He was getting used to her expression when she didn't have good news. Downturned lips, raised eyebrows, an indefinable way she tilted her head . . . He sighed and beckoned her in.

"Did you want to keep your head on the maneuvering, sir?"

"I can listen to you and watch the chart."

"I had an open-door visitor this morning. DK3 Hurst."

"Charmine Hurst," Dan said, getting a mental picture of a small, earnest black woman in her late twenties. The disbursing clerks were the navy's paymasters. "Good performer, her chief says. What's her problem?"

"Can we go outside for this?"

"We'll go back to my cabin," Dan told her. "It's too damned hot to be out there when we don't have to."

In the little stateroom behind the bridge he closed the door and motioned her to the settee. He took the chair and tented his fingers.

"She saw the corpsman. She's pregnant."

Dan grunted, his morning just ruined. The whole pregnancy issue was getting to him. He'd lost two sailors already this cruise. All young sailors weren't knuckleheads. But some were, and when you put nineteen-year-old male knuckleheads together with nineteen-year-old female knuckleheads . . . "And?"

"She says it's the DK1."

"Oh, swell."

"Uh-huh. They're in there in that little disbursing office all day. And of course with the cash, it's locked. Nobody can come in and surprise them. Apparently she didn't bother with birth control. Simple as it is. We give the pills out in sick bay."

Dan wondered why her gaze moved around his office. It struck him that it was a small, private compartment, too. She was leaning back, one coveralled arm thrown over the back of the settee. He could envision her nude . . . a small, slightly protruding belly, freckles down her thighs . . . he liked slim, fit women, and Hotchkiss spent as much time on the machines as he did.

The physical attraction was there. But even more alluring would be having someone he could just fucking *hold*. A skipper was alone as no one ever was ashore. Add the stark functional bareness of passageways, the comfortless machinery-humming desolation of air-conditioned spaces, and the thought of something warm and for yourself alone became worth risking very much for, indeed. He rubbed his lips, trying to concentrate on what she was saying, not the sway of breasts beneath blue cloth. And what did she mean by that reference to how easy birth control was?

"I told her policy doesn't require her to identify the father, but she wanted to. She's sorry she let the ship down."

"I guess we all wish being sorry made things better. Hurst's married, isn't she?"

"Unfortunately, they both are. Also unfortunately, DK1 Konow's wife is also the mother of his three children. And also the vice president—"

Dan closed his eyes. "Ouch. Vice president of the Military Wives' Association of Tidewater, Virginia."

"You see our problem."

"So what do we do? Take them to mast is my first thought."

"She came to me in confidence," Hotchkiss said. "I write her up, that finishes my open-door policy for the other girls."

"I see that, but it takes two to tango. Unless she's going to say it's rape, which is a whole different ball game. So to speak." He stopped, realizing by her incredulous stare he'd just made the kind of half-unconscious pun a guy might make to another guy, but that was most definitely non grata with Claudia H. Hotchkiss.

"You'd better get serious about this. It's flagrant fraternization. Not only that, it's adultery."

"You're right, sorry . . . but if it *was* consensual, the only way I see to play it fair is to take them both to mast. How far along is she? Is she planning to keep the baby? Did she share that with you?"

Hotchkiss told him, tone icier than it had been before his joke, "She's three months gone. But there isn't any choice. Navy medical care is prohibited by federal policy from terminating pregnancies. And she can't depend on a civilian facility out here."

"So we'll lose her regardless of what I decide."

"Lose her?" Hotchkiss seemed surprised. "Not necessarily. Not for several months yet, anyway."

"If she's pregnant, she can't do her job," Dan told her. "So I want her off the ship. Same as the first girl."

"Why? All she has to do is sit at a desk and work the pay program."

"We made this decision already, Claudia. We're running a warship, not a maternity ward. If a woman gets pregnant, we scrub her off the manning document pending a permanent relief. That's what we promised would happen, on the page thirteen entry and the fraternization briefings."

Hotchkiss said with ominous silkiness, "So let me get this straight: We fire the woman, and keep the guy who knocked her up."

"No—or at least not for the reason you're getting at. One, a pregnant woman waddling around can't do the shipboard damage control and firefighting job, whatever her day-to-day rate is. She can push a desk shoreside, but sea duty's tough even for a man in good shape. Two, she's not being 'fired,' we're sending her to a safer environment for an expectant mother. We may punish her for fraternization and adultery, but the pregnancy's a separate issue. We have a responsibility to both of them, mother and baby. And she's going to need family support intervention when she goes home, to explain this to her husband."

His phone went off. The comm messenger was trying to locate him. Dan told him he was in the sea cabin.

The message was from Strong. *Horn*'s liberty port was canceled, due to emergent operational commitments. They were to proceed north at best speed to a point off Duba. Due to a comms breakdown on the flagship, *Horn* was to stand by to receive the task group flag.

"What is it?"

"Port visit canceled. The commodore's coming aboard." He passed it to her.

"We aren't staff configured," Hotchkiss said, fingering the message doubtfully. "We don't have the space, and we sure don't have the comm suite."

Dan wasn't enthusiastic either, but he didn't see a way out. "Strong can go in my in-port cabin. Move the junior officers to overflow berthing."

"It's going to be crowded."

"Then maybe they won't stay long," Dan said. He caught her look. Yeah, in some ways having a female exec was a lot like being married. "I meant, this is probably just temporary, till another flag-configured ship comes available. Are we all clear now about this other thing?"

"I'm still not convinced Charmine deserves to get hammered. The man's a first class, she's a third. There's got to be an element of intimidation."

"She should have brought it up when he hit on her, then. I don't buy that, that the woman's always the victim."

"If one partner's twenty-four, the other's thirty-two?"

"Old enough to blow the whistle if her supervisor's coming on to her."

"If you're going to throw her off the ship anyway, why take her to mast?"

"We went through that," he told her. "Plus, so far all

we've got is her word he's the father. There'll be enough complications downstream. I don't want to pin this on Konow if it actually was somebody else. So he's got to have his say, too. Put together your evidence and start the process." He hesitated. "Actually we'll probably end up losing them both. There's that issue of trust when you're in there with the cash and the checks. And he's abused it. So let's get a message out to get some kind of quick fill body on their way so we can keep the people paid."

She tossed her foot nervously. Her coverall had ridden up and he saw fine blond hairs on her calf. "I don't agree. I don't think she should go to mast."

"Get them both ready," Dan told her. "And you're dismissed."

He sat listening to the echo of the slammed door, unable to shrug off that he'd just fantasized doing what he was bound to punish others for.

Ah, but he hadn't done it. Only thought about it.

Thought about it night after night, alone on that same settee. What she'd say. What they'd do. Just to have her hand gently fingering up and down his prick . . . and what that first long, irretrievable orgasm would feel like. Guilt and pleasure. The most explosive mix of all.

And if Lieutenant Commander Claudia Hotchkiss, USN, his executive officer, had gone to the door, and pushed in the button? Locking them in?

Fortunately, it couldn't happen. She was happily married. To a marine aviator she talked about with a lilt in her voice, her professional demeanor suddenly transforming with a sparkle, a smile.

Did Blair smile like that when she talked about him?

He drummed his fingers on his knee, head lowered in contemplation.

"New foxtrot corpen, relative wind will be three-two-zero, ten knots," said the speaker, the words echoing from the cavernous aluminum bulkheads and lofty overhead of the helo hangar.

Twenty-four hours later and two hundred and sixty miles to the north, on a hot morning backed by desert-blasted mountains. *Horn* was coming to a course to put the wind on her bow. Dan waited inside, watching the helo approach, then undogged the flight deck door as the rotors disengaged.

As tradition dictated, the senior disembarked first. Dan saluted a lean officer in a green flight suit. Strong handed him his cranial, fitting a pisscutter to a close-cropped head that was turning silver. The 1MC stated, "Red Sea Task group, arriving." Six bells, and the commodore's pennant broke at the masthead, rippling in the hot wind.

Horn was now the flagship, and Dan no longer senior aboard.

"This way, sir," he shouted over the engine howl. Strong eyed him, holding his salute. But Dan was uncovered. U.S. ships didn't permit headgear on the flight deck. Too much danger of them getting sucked into an engine and ruining a perfectly good aircraft. At last he returned a bareheaded salute. The blades were still turning, Strong's staff jumping out while a crewman tossed out luggage and tape-strapped cardboard boxes. They seemed to have a lot of gear.

The Australian glanced around the in-port cabin the same searching way he'd examined the flight deck. A carafe stood on the table. "Coffee, sir?" Dan asked him.

"No thanks. Comm arrangements?"

"My Comm-oh's already arranged that with yours. We'll have additional circuits on the bridge and in Combat for your staffers, and I'm putting an extra radioman on watch." He showed him the sleeping cabin behind the reception and work area, giving it just a word or two. Strong must have been aboard Spruances before and there wasn't anything remarkable about *Horn*. Other than the obvious.

As if Strong was thinking the same thing, he said, "I saw some sheilas back on the flight deck."

"We're an integrated ship. The first one, actually."

"Interesting. I rather doubt we'll ever go that way, but . . . How are they working out?"

"They're doing a good job."

"Friction?"

"There've been a couple of incidents."

"Such as?"

Dan told him the basics, neither emphasizing nor downgrading them. Just the facts. The commodore didn't seem interested in long explanations. Dan felt condescended to somehow, though that might be merely the man's manner, and had to take care not to be brusque back.

"Anything since this berthing fire?"

"No, sir, nothing since. I'm hoping whoever set it has either changed his mind or at least gotten scared off. Things are going better since I had that talk with the chiefs. Maybe they're getting used to them."

"The chiefs?" said Strong briskly.

"No, sir. The women," Dan said, wondering if he'd been listening.

A tap at the door, and the mess specialists began bringing in the commodore's gear. A much-abused duffel bag, boxes of records, a Toshiba notebook in a black case. Strong asked several questions about his Tomahawk loadout. As he talked, he opened the boxes with a pocketknife, one slice each, like a surgeon doing assembly line hernias. He cut open the bottom, not the top, so he could flip it over and all the files dropped into the open drawer at once. Dan gave him the password to the computer on his desk, and waited for him to write it down. Strong just nodded.

The commodore looked up, seemed to realize his discomfiture. "That'll be all. I'll come up to the bridge later," he said. He gave Dan a quick handshake and opened the door with the other.

In the passageway he watched the commodore's staff bustle past. They gave him quick neutral glances, as if he were a bollard or a piece of gear they might or might not use.

Strong had a U.S. officer attached. "A.J." Lambert was a commander, as was Dan. He wore the gold dolphins of a submariner. Lambert told him *Laboon* and *Horn* were headed back to Oparea Adelaide, while *Georges Leygues* took *Laboon*'s place inside the Gulf of Aqaba. The U.S. ships would be doing two missions now. One was the usual, maritime interdiction. The second was setting up for strike ops against Iraq.

"Saddam's resisting the inspection regime. The White House wants what they call an 'appropriate response.' Something that makes headlines but doesn't kill civilians. You know, like always, they want to have it both ways. What it bottlenecks down to is either an air force strike with smart bombs, or Tomahawk. They shoot a plane down, they've got a hostage. So we'll probably get the job."

Dan contemplated the flat area on his foredeck, the armored hatches. It was easy to overlook them at a glance, and they were so low maintenance he could all but forget about them day to day. But the Mark 41 Vertical Launch System was *Horn*'s main battery. His current loadout was sixty-one land-attack Tomahawks, with either conventional warheads or a thousand pounds of bomblets. They made *Horn* a strike destroyer, able to download data via satellite and destroy targets up to twelve hundred miles away.

A dependable weapon, but not a perfect one. As he knew from helping develop it. Sometimes you launched them and the engine didn't start and they went on over, falling out of the sky. Sometimes they missed. At best, they were only as good as the intelligence that selected their targets.

Which he had no input into. The team in Combat downloaded the strike package, programmed the missiles, and fired them as directed. Not only did they never see their target, there was no requirement they even know what it was.

Lambert lit a cigar. "Penny."

"We used to shell their forts when things didn't go like we wanted. Now we clobber them with missiles."

"Whatever. Get your guys ready to receive an updated package. When we're in position, the commodore'll want a rehearsal. He's interested in the strike concept, wants to bring it back to the Aussie navy."

Dan had never seem a non-U.S. officer in the chain of a strike command. "I thought Tomahawk was still NOFORN." No foreign nationals, U.S. personnel only.

"I'll show you the message appointing him launch area coordinator. So he'll need a red phone and a table, and connectivity to the strike commander and to *Laboon*."

"All right," Dan told him, though he was still uncomfortable with his own limited input. He'd always felt real weapons, meant to kill real people, needed human control all the way down. "We have all the taped missions loaded. The ones the theater commander thought we better have ready to fire. He can come down anytime we're at General Quarters Strike and we can walk him through a launch in training mode."

They discussed the patrol area and whether there was any air or missile threat. Lambert thought not, but had to admit there might be mines. "There's no reason one of these smugglers can't push a few over the fantail. It'd really screw up traffic coming down out of Suez."

"What do the Iranians think?" Dan asked him.

"Making hostile noises, as usual. But they lost half their navy the last time they tangled with us." He hesitated. "You were there, weren't you? Praying Mantis?"

"I was on *Van Zandt*," Dan told him, and watched the name trigger its usual effect. Like *Samuel B. Roberts* and *Stark*. Navy people had long memories for lost ships.

"But I don't think they're going to stick their hand in the meat grinder again. I don't think there's going to be much chance of anything on this side of the Sinai. But stay alert, that's all I can say."

"Commodore's on the bridge," Yerega sang out, and Dan turned.

Strong had shucked the flight suit for khaki shorts. He climbed up into what had been Dan's chair. Held out his hand, and a staff officer put a folder into it. He didn't say word one to anyone, and the other conversations on the bridge had gone silent. So had Lambert, so Dan went over to the nav table. The quartermaster had laid out their track. They'd reach their assigned operating area around 0300 the next day.

"Captain." It was Lin Porter. "Contact bearing zero-three-zero, fifteen thousand seven hundred yards, course zero-four-zero, speed fifteen. Seems to be outside the traffic separation scheme."

Dan went over to the Furuno. He liked the little radar in close quarters, because it showed course and speed arrows for each contact, which made it easier to prioritize when you had ten or fifteen on the screen. This blip jumped out at him. A big return, its course arrow aimed right down their throats. Still, it was a good distance away, and there'd be time to maneuver. The catch was, they were the stand-on vessel, bound not to change course or speed, but to wait for the other to change his. In fact, from what he recalled of the International Maritime Organization rules from the *Sailing Directions,* vessels outside the channels were doubly burdened.

"Get him on Channel Sixteen," Dan told her. "Ask his intentions."

Combat passed the word up that the contact they were calling Bravo Delta had a closest point of approach of less than a thousand yards in twelve minutes, and recommended coming right to course 000 to open. Dan went to get his glasses, found Strong using them. He borrowed the quartermaster's and tried to get them focused. At last he had it, a speck, but high enough to tell him what it was. An empty tanker out of Italy or France or Spain, bound south for another holdful of crude. Out of position for some reason. Still, it should be easy enough to sort matters out.

"No answer on Sixteen. Bravo Delta bears zero-three-zero, nine thousand yards and closing. Combat recommends coming right to zero-one-zero at this time."

Now the broad bow was clearly visible, and the bulge of green sea over a submerged stem-bulb before it broke in a churn of white.

"Captain? Come right."

He lifted his head, startled. Strong was still examining his traffic. Had he spoken? As he hesitated the commodore added, annoyed, "Did you hear me? I said, come right."

"We're the stand-on vessel, sir."

"I don't give a bloody damn who's got the right of way, get out of his path."

Dan snapped an order, then turned away, seething at being overruled so casually in front of his crew. He stood on the starboard wing with hands jammed into his pockets, trying to reason with himself. There were always frictions between the ship and the flag. Especially when the ship wasn't flag configured, which meant the staff didn't have separate spaces and comm facilities, usually even a separate bridge of their own.

Or . . . was it possible Niles was right, and Dan Lenson was projecting his ingrained distrust of authority? He remembered how unhappy he'd been, being a staff puke for Isaac Sundstrom. Yes, Sundstrom . . . Krazy Ike . . . so far, compared to that incompetent and self-centered clown, Strong rated up there with Nimitz or Spruance.

Over the next several days traffic was heavy. Both the Blue and Gold teams were called away several times a day. *Laboon* reported commerce as dense proceeding northbound.

Meanwhile the tasking message for the strike came through. Looking over the launch sequence plan when Kim McCall brought up *Horn*'s answering status report—line A, line B, reporting that the missions were executable—Dan saw the package included strikes from both the Red Sea, *Laboon* and *Horn,* and from the east, from the Gulf. When he plotted their targets, he got remote-looking locations in western Iraq.

The day after that, the mission data update and associated command information came down, revised missile flight data from Norfolk via a 9600-baud, secure, download-only satellite link. This updated the missions they'd brought with them on tape.

He had confidence in his team, but went down anyway and

watched as they rehearsed, from simulated engagement order to system warm-up, load, entry of ship position, launch direction, and prelandfall waypoints. A Red Sea launch would be tricky. They'd have to stay in a tightly circumscribed area to fire all the missions. He joined McCall and the first-class fire controlman at the chart table. "Strike, looks like the launch baskets can all be hit from . . . let me see . . . about here?"

The first class looked at him. "You done this before, sir."

Dan had to grin. The first class said it like an accusation, as if having a skipper who actually knew what he was doing wasn't playing fair. "You get a feel for where you ought to be. Kim, we need to make sure VLS is ready. Who's got the key?"

"Mr. Camill has one, sir. But if you want to be able to launch, he should have both Remote Launch Enable keys."

"We don't have an Indigo message yet." Of course, they couldn't launch without both fire-enable keys. Dan kept his locked in his safe . . . in his in-port cabin. He made a mental note to get it out, since that was Strong's space now.

They sent the missions to the launch control console and loaded data to twelve missiles, four for each of the three targets; then simulated the rest of the sequence in training mode.

Back in his elevated chair, it occurred to him that, theoretically, at least, Dan Lenson now had the power to kill any human being within a twelve hundred mile circle. He had the keys and sixty-one live missiles. The guys would launch on his word. Actually, since he also knew how to program the missiles, it wasn't just theoretical.

He tried to take his mind off it by looking at the large-screen display, the northern Red Sea and the Gulfs of Suez and Aqaba. But it only shifted his thoughts toward what exactly they were doing here.

Because he often wondered what exactly they *were* doing here. The forward-deployed U.S. fleet was supposed to be a stabilizing presence. The Mideast needed stability. But more and more, it seemed that the American presence was more of an irritant than anything that seemed to give the locals confidence, or fear, or anything else constructive.

But without them, who would deter Saddam and the expansionist Shi'ite fanatics of Iran? There were progressive tendencies in Islam. Regimes inching toward tolerance, circling around popular participation and limited forms of democracy. The United States had to back them up, not write all Muslims off as terrorists and dictators.

You couldn't be neutral toward change. You either welcomed it or feared it. When you feared it, you fought to keep things the way they were. Using whatever came to hand; the Qu'ran or the Bible, or slurs about combat effectiveness that seemed to him to have less and less justification the closer he watched his own crew approach the battle zone.

But what about his own doubts? His own ever-altering, changeable, always-questioning incertitude? Where did that place him?

He rubbed his face, features lit the hue of malachite by the flicker-running, never-constant imagery of the digital displays.

Off Ras Muhammad they intercepted the largest ship to date. The database said it was a thirty-thousand-ton motor containership, Indian registry, chartered to the Chinese, with a master from Singapore and crewed by the scrapings-up of three continents they'd gotten used to seeing on these trampers. So obviously they'd been boarded before. But this time MV *Royal Karnataka* did not heave to, even after repeated hails on the VHF.

On the bridge, Dan debated his courses of action, flipping through the UN and the USN ROEs, the rules of engagement. Blade Slinger was down for maintenance, so he didn't have the intimidation value of his air assets. The rules were vague when it came to what precisely an enforcing vessel could do. Finally he picked up the mike. "*Royal Karnataka,* this is U.S. Navy warship off your quarter. This is your final warning. Heave to now and permit boarding."

"This is Motor Vessel *Royal Karnataka.* We have nothing aboard from Iraq and do not need to be boarded."

"There a problem?" Strong swung up into the chair that

had now become the task group commander's exclusive possession. Coming up to find Dan in it the day before, he'd asked him rather brusquely to use the exec's, to port.

"They don't want to stop, Commodore."

"Then it's all the more evident you must stop them." Strong looked across to where the freighter was plowing stolidly along. "So do it, Captain."

Dan bit off a response and keyed the mike again. "*Royal Karnataka*, this is U.S. warship off your port quarter. I repeat, heave to at once or . . . I will fire." He said to the officer of the deck, whose eyes had popped wide, "Mount 51, train right, relative bearing zero-three-zero."

This was a bluff. He was pretty sure he didn't have the right to fire. The trouble was, it was hard to tell. Lawyers wrote the things, there were so many caveats and weasel phrases. Then he noted their interceptee's bow wave was decreasing. "She's slowing, sir," the officer of the deck said.

"Very well. Keep your relative position."

"Engines ahead one-third, set pitch for five knots."

"Away the boarding and search team. Which team's up?"

"Boatswain: away the boarding and search team, away, Team Gold."

He threw the dogs off the door and went out on the starboard wing. Every metal surface radiated like a microwave oven. He touched the leather of his wing chair and reflex jerked his fingers off before they burned. What wind there was, was from port; the RHIBs went down in the ship's lee; he couldn't see it go down but he figured it would be *Faith*. Some minutes later it came into view, playing ducks and drakes over the ruffled blue. He made out Cassidy and Marchetti, knees bent, clinging to the center console, nodding at each wave impact.

The officer of the deck put his head out. "Sir, contact's putting on speed again."

"You son of a bitch," Dan told the master opposite. He said to the petty officer beside him on the .50 mount, "All right, gunner. Lock and load." At the same time he was set-

ting the channel selector on the portable Saber radio they
used for bridge to boat. "*Faith,* this is Blade Runner."

"*Faith,* over. Hear you, Captain."

"Stand clear while we adjust this bozo's attitude."

Cassidy rogered. When Dan saw the RHIB's bow swinging clear, he told the gunner, "Give them a burst a hundred
yards ahead of the bow."

The sailor adjusted his helmet, cranked the charging handle, and swung the barrel. The OOD clanged the door shut.
Dan stepped back, clamping his ears, and the belt jerked and
six rounds went out *duh duh duh duh duh duh,* the smoking-
hot empty casings, thick as his thumb and twice as long, rattling into the gratings. The tracers arced out, hesitated, then
fell, pocking white gouts up across the blue sea.

Strong came out and stood in the angle of the splinter
shield. Dan tried to ignore him. Dan, as commanding officer
of *Horn,* was the on-scene commander here. Strong was the
sea combatant commander, in overall charge of maritime intercept ops for all the ships of the task force. So the commodore was both there, and not there, in one of those military
oxymorons, and Dan was both in charge, and not. Plus—he
knew it was childish—the asshole had taken his chair. It was
intensely irritating, and he snapped into the radio, "All right,
he's slowing. Get in there and get aboard before he changes
his mind again. And stay where we can see you."

Cassidy rogered, and both ships coasted to a halt on the
ruffled sea.

Time passed. *Horn* picked up the swing, rocking with a
heavy cadence that set something clanking back by the signal shelter. The sun was the upper element of a broiler
oven. The gunner, bored or heat exhausted, slumped
against the pyro locker, goggling at nothing. On the main
deck the crew of the chain gun sprawled like dead men
shot down where they'd stood. Dan waited for Strong to go
below. But the commodore, casual in white shorts and
short-sleeved shirt today, just stood smoking and looking
across the water.

After an hour he said, "Your boys are taking their time."

"Sir, they're experienced men. Our senior chief over there has done over a hundred boardings."

"Then he ought to be able to do them more quickly than this. Our team on *Torrens* have it down to half an hour."

"Blade Runner, *Faith*." Cassidy, on the radio.

"Blade Runner."

"Cargo data."

"Go," Dan said. He turned the volume up so Strong could hear, as a courtesy, though he didn't feel courteous. He felt like flinging him off the wing and letting the Aussie prick swim to Egypt.

"We've got a hell of a lot of dates here."

"Copy dates, is that right? Like what camels eat?"

"Two hundred containers of them. Packed with Syrian dates. The paper covers it."

"Okay, good work. Sign him off and come back."

"No, no, no," Strong said.

Dan said, "Wait one," into the handheld. To Strong he said, "I'm going to let this one go."

"No, you're not. Dates, you say? Out of Jordan? They're Iraqi."

"The documentation shows they're from Syria—"

"Fuck the documentation. They're Iraqi. They're famous for their dates. Which are contraband. They can't export anything without UN clearance, and the only thing they're cleared for is limited amounts under the oil for food program."

Dan held his finger on the button, looking doubtfully across two hundred yards of water at a *very* large ship.

"Blade Runner, *Faith*."

"Go, *Faith*."

"These guys are not being cooperative. They're shoving us aside and going back to the bridge and engine room."

"Oh, no, they're not. Keep them on the bow. If they give you trouble, cuff 'em."

"They're starting to play rough."

"Use the degree of force necessary to control the situation."

Strong cleared his throat, but didn't actually say anything. "Roger," Cassidy said, his voice muffled and distant.
Then a clatter, as if he'd dropped the radio.

Dan reached past the commodore and pressed buttons on
the 21MC. "OOD, Captain. Away the Blue Team, prepare to
assist Gold Team. Exec to the bridge. Secure repairs on Blade
Slinger and get it in the air." He keyed the radio again. But
Cassidy didn't answer. He grabbed the lookout's binoculars,
and after a struggle with the sling, which got caught on their
owner's neck, got them focused where tiny figures struggled.
As he watched, one broke away running. Another went after
it, then both disappeared behind the superstructure.

Hotchkiss undogged the door. "Leave it open," Dan told
her, and yelled past her, "Goose her ahead, get us in close.
We need the other team over there right away."

Cassidy came back on the handheld, breathing hard.
"Blade Runner, uh, boarding team had an incident . . . a runner, bound aft . . . got a man down."

"We've got the Blue Team on its way, Sean. Who's
down? One of ours?"

"Well, they're under control again now . . . Wait one.
Uh-oh."

The boarding officer clicked off. Then, seconds later, on
again. "We got a man overboard situation."

"What?"

"Machete had to uh . . . accidentally . . . We got a man
overboard. Off the starboard side. We're talking the RHIB
around to pick him up now."

"Machete or the crewman?"

"The crewman."

"Have you got him in sight? Keep him in sight."

Strong said disapprovingly, "Someone went overboard?"

Dan told Hotchkiss, "Get the leading corpman aft on the
double." He told the commodore, "Sir, let me get this sorted
out. I'll make a report after we have things under control."

"Captain? Master of the *Karnataka* on Channel Sixteen."

"I want to see the boarding officer myself, when he returns," Strong said. "It sounds to me like your men are a lit-

tle too John Wayne about this. I warned you, they have to know the ROE cold and act accordingly."

Dan thought violently that this was exactly what he needed at the moment, a lofty Anglic voice pontificating on what cowboys his men were. He switched his handheld to sixteen, catching an agitated voice speaking broken English in midsentence. "—filing a complaint on you," the voice said angrily. "Beating my men up. Injuring them. UN will hear of this. I will file complaint, swear to seeing this with my own eyes. Captain, is captain there?"

"This is the commanding officer of USS *Horn,*" Dan told him. He rubbed his fingers across his forehead, listening to a torrent of threats and vituperation as beside him Strong shook his head sadly. His hand came away dripping with sweat.

Both inflatables searched for three hours. It was not so rough they wouldn't have found someone if he was still afloat. But they came up empty-handed. Cuffed, the crewman had gone straight down into the blue-green sea. And never came back up.

At last Strong ordered him to let the ship proceed. The State Department would check out the provenance of the cargo. If necessary, the Saudis could board again before it passed through the Bab el Mendeb. As to the death, they'd deal with that through appropriate channels. He'd look forward to Dan's report at his earliest convenience.

Dan had Cassidy and Marchetti report to his sea cabin. They showed up sweaty and stained, still wearing pistol belts and float coats, boots dripping with the betadine-and-water footbath the boarding parties had to wade through coming back aboard. Otherwise, given the conditions of sanitation aboard the ships they inspected, *Horn* would be fighting bugs around the clock. He closed the door. "All right. What happened?"

"That was one uncooperative bunch of ragheads," Marchetti said.

"Let's hear it from the boarding officer first."

Cassidy said angrily that the crew had been restive and mouthing off from the moment they came aboard. The master did nothing to control them. They complained about being kept out on deck, in the sun, but that was the only place he could keep them in view. He'd ordered the most aggressive cuffed. At that the others started pushing their way aft. The security team pushed back. The bigger American sailors were winning when one of the restrained men broke into a run. Marchetti went after him. The crewman attacked Machete and the senior chief punched him out and somehow he went overboard.

"He physically attacked you?"

"Sure as shit," Marchetti said.

"I thought you said he was cuffed."

"He *was* cuffed. Son of a bitch butted me. Hard, too." He tilted his head back, and Dan saw blood bright on his tongue.

"You saw that happen?" Dan asked Cassidy. The ensign hesitated, then nodded. Dan asked him again and got a firmer affirmative.

"Okay, that's physical resistance. By the rules of engagement, we can respond to that with the degree of force necessary to control the situation." He looked at Marchetti. "But we're also responsible for the safety of people under our control. How did he go over the side?"

"All I did was hit him, to get him off me. The lifeline snapped and over he went." Marchetti spat blood into a paper towel from his coverall pocket. "He's in cuffs, he can't swim, he acts up, too fucking bad. Now he's snake food."

"That's hard, Senior," Cassidy said disapprovingly. Marchetti shrugged.

"The master said he was going to file a protest."

"He'll just have to file," Dan told them. "I'm not happy someone died, but I told you to use necessary force. This sounds like an accident, especially since the lifeline broke. If there's heat, that's what they pay me to take. Sean, I'll need a written report. Close of business today."

They stood glumly. He went on, fighting his own depression over things going so wrong, "Okay, new subject . . . we're taking a long time to do these boardings. I know you're not getting enough sleep, or much else done. Anyway, can we speed up the process? It's just taking too long considering how many ships we have to go through here."

"No, sir, not and do a thorough job," Marchetti told him.

"Sean?"

"Senior chief's right, sir."

"The commodore says the Aussies do this in half an hour," Dan told them.

"No fuckin' way they can search a ship like that in half an hour," Marchetti said. "These guys have containers three high on deck and just as tight below. It takes time to get up to them and cut the padlocks. Then you got to go through them, and put the seals back on."

Dan studied his shaven head as the senior chief went on to explain that particularly in the larger vessels, containerships and tankers, they had to check every space and every container. The only way to cut down on the workload would be to stand up a third boarding team.

"That might not be a bad idea," Dan told them. "Have you got anyone who could stand up as a boarding petty officer?"

Marchetti said he had a first-class sonar tech might have the leadership and judgment to take on the job. "A sonar tech?" Dan said, taken aback.

"Sir, Crack Man's not a weenie like the other ping jockeys. And they don't have squat to do up here, the water's so shallow. I'd shuffle the others around so you get a mix of raw and salty in each team. Blue, Gold, and . . . Green."

"All right," Dan said. They were glancing at the door when he added, "How are you going to man the new team?"

"We've got a waiting list, sir," Marchetti said.

"Is Wilson on it?"

"Wilson?"

"Commander Hotchkiss tells me she makes all the musters and workouts and familiarization fires. Think she deserves a shot?"

"I'd rather not, sir."

"Why not?"

"These ragheads hate Americans anyway. I'd hate to think what they'd say to a woman. You heard the stuff they say over the bridge to bridge, when one of the girls goes on."

"That the reason? Spare her feelings?" Dan asked him.

"No, sir."

"Okay, what's the real reason?"

"She's not going to be able to do the job."

Dan said, not wanting to order him to do this, wanting him to do it because he thought it was worth a try; to get him on the side of giving the girl a chance: "That's your opinion. Right?"

"An opinion based on a hundred and twenty-one boardings."

"Is it possible you could be wrong?"

"No, sir."

"Not even remotely?"

"No, sir."

"You're never wrong, is that it?"

"I didn't say that, sir," Marchetti said, face about as closed as it was possible for a rock-armed, slick-headed, tattooed senior chief's to get. "I said I couldn't be wrong about that."

"All right, I've heard enough. Put her on the team, Senior Chief," Dan said.

Marchetti snapped stiff. "Aye, aye, sir."

"You can cut the bullshit, too. I expect you to treat her like any other team member. That goes for you, too, Sean. If I hear she's not being treated with the respect due a shipmate, you'll explain why to me."

The Machete said aye, aye again. Dan let him stand at attention for a couple more seconds, then dismissed them both, telling Cassidy the commodore wanted to see him but that he probably had time for a quick shower first. Thinking as the scowling senior chief left that he wouldn't want to be in Wilson's boots over the next few days. But maybe it would work out.

Or maybe it wouldn't. But that was the whole point, wasn't it. To see.

He leaned back, staring blankly at his Compaq. Unless the environment in Washington meant they were going to be integrated even if it weakened fighting effectiveness. Blair didn't seem to think that was the case, and she was in the thick of it. He had to believe Congress had at least some modicum of responsibility.

Or did they? A conversation from when he'd been working in D.C. came back to him. With a staff aide to a congressman. What had Sandy said? Something about how the guy she'd worked for had tried to do the right thing once. And paid for it. That no one in government had any other goal than to keep their jobs.

He slicked his hair back, feeling the sweat and grit that coated it. He didn't think of himself as above that. But he'd decided a long time ago that if he couldn't do what struck him as right, he didn't need to stay in. Probably not an attitude that would get him to flag rank, but it let him keep some sort of relationship going with Dan Lenson.

He was thinking about that when the 1MC clicked into life. "General quarters. General quarters. Set condition Zebra throughout the ship. Class Bravo fire in main engine room number one. This is not a drill. Class Bravo fire, main space fire in main engine room number one. Repair Five provide."

16

Cobie was squatting on her boots beside the PLCC, working on her quals for the local control monitor, when she heard the explosion. It was the loudest thing she'd ever heard in her life. So deafening it paralyzed her for a second. She had no idea what had happened, only that her ears were ringing so loud all she could hear was a noise from the generator flat that sounded like a Tyrannosaurus sicking up a bad dinner. A hoarse, deafening ROWF, followed by a steadily decreasing *RRRRrrrrrrrr*. She didn't know what it was, only that sparks were flying through the gratings, and she tucked and rolled instinctively, balling herself tight under the heavy steel counter.

Suddenly the air was full of coffee-colored smoke and the stink of burning plastic. The lights went black, succeeded by faraway glows as the relays popped on the battle lanterns.

Sanders tore past, hauling ass up the ladder like a monkey in the zoo, somebody threw a firecracker in their cage. Somebody else rattled after him. Maybe Akhmeed but she wasn't sure. She started to follow, then hesitated, coughing as acrid smoke bit her throat. Shouldn't they try to do something? Pull out the little SEEDs, the emergency air canisters they had to carry in the space, and check things out?

To hell with it. She spun and ran after them, dropping her qualification book, boots ringing the deck plates. The smoke was getting thicker by the second. Now it burned like acid in her throat. She went to port and aft and up the vertical ladder. But at the top she caught something sharp with her head. Stars shot though her brain, and she staggered back, gripping her skull. But forced herself up again, coughing hard now, and turned around twice before she got her bearings and forced her numb legs to push her up the ladder to the IR flat.

This was it, the top of Main One. Only where was the door? Smoke and darkness, and somewhere outside the echoing bong of the general quarters alarm. She felt around and got her hands on the dogging bar. Closed tight. She almost screamed, but when she heaved the quick-acting lever whanged up and there were faces glowing in the emergency lighting and she stumbled through into Helm's arms, coughing and mopping blood off her forehead with the sleeve of her coveralls.

They stayed in the passageway for a while. Helm tried to make her go to sick bay to get her head taken care of, but she wouldn't. She let Akhmeed put on a dressing to stop the blood running down her forehead, though. She felt sick. Helm made her sit down with her head between her legs.

The lights were out in the p-way, probably all over the ship. It was hard to make out what people were saying, and she only gradually realized it wasn't them, it was her hearing. The petty officers were isolating the space, snapping off breakers and closing valves from the emergency control panel. The Porn King said he'd been back by the feedwater tank in the lower level when the big bang went off. It sounded like it was above him. Cobie said it was above her, too, from the PLCC. Helm said it smelled like an electrical fire, and whatever it was had dragged all the gens off line when it went.

"We don't have any power?" she yelled at him. "Anywhere?"

"You don't have to scream, I can hear you. Feel how we're rollin'? We're dead in the water. They're probably try-

ing to start number three back aft. They can do an emergency start with HP air from the Epsy."

She wasn't sure what the Epsy was although she'd heard
it mentioned. It was in Main Control, she knew that.

"Whassup?" The investigator, bulky in oxygen breathing
apparatus and mask and red hard hat. The rest of Repair
Five lurched and stumbled behind him. Helm told him
quickly—explosion, smoke—and pointed him down the
ladder. The guy looked at her. "She hurt? You need to evacuate her."

"She's okay. I need her to isolate the space."

The investigator shrugged and pulled the tab off his canister. He seated it, sealed his mask, and sucked. Smoke
curled behind the eyepieces. The oxygen candle lighting off.
The number-two man paid out line, and he disappeared into
the darkness.

Power came back, lights lit, the slam of breakers echoed
along the passageway. The ventilation whirred up the scale,
and the smoke started to clear, at least out here. "Are we
gonna go back down?" she asked Akhmeed.

"Sure. Unless it's actually on fire down there."

They hung there for fifteen minutes, listening to the repair party shouting and passing word. It was still dark in
there. You didn't deisolate the space until you knew what
went wrong. Then they started backing out, and she heard
the 1MC announce the fire was out and the reflash watch set,
and desmoking commenced by method A. The guys got up
and she did, too, getting ready to go back in.

Only she didn't want to. Her lungs still hurt. The black
oval of the door was a nightmare she didn't want to go back
into. She told Akhmeed she had to pee, she'd be right back.

She sat hunched in the stall, shivering, wiping her eyes
with toilet paper. What if she didn't go back down? They'd
put her on mess cranking till forever. Talk about her like she
couldn't take it. And they'd be right. Sure, you're scared, she
told herself. You just fucking got to go back down, that's all.
She thought about Kaitlyn. She had to do this. For her.

"Hey, Kasson! You in there?" Helm, cracking the door.

She screamed back to fucking close it. "I *said* I had to pee."

"Sorry. Just checking, in case you passed out or something."

When she got back, the Red Devils were roaring. The supply ventilators were on in Aux 1 and they were blowing the last of the smoke out of the escape scuttle. "Okay, let's get in there and see what we got," Helm announced. "Take it easy and watch where you walk. It's still isolated, but don't fucking touch anything looks like it might be hot. You stay with me, Sugar Mama."

"*Don't* fucking call me Sugar Mama, jackoff." The guys from the repair party sniggered, and she snapped her flashlight on and stalked past them into the dark.

The IR flat looked OK, but the boiler level was a mess. Stuff was tracked all over. Helm told them to get rubber gloves and foxtails and get it cleaned up, then they'd see what to do next. He and the captain and the exec and the chief engineer, "the whole fucking food chain," as Ricochet put it, were gathered around number-one GTG.

The first bad thing Cobie saw was the number-one switchboard. Still smoking, with a big hole down at shin level where the lower breaker panel had blown out. Bubbling chunks of brown plastic, blown-out wires. The disconnect bars, copper contacts big around as her thumb, were melted into shapeless globs of red metal. They were still sizzling as they burned their way into the deck matting. They picked everything up that was too big to sweep and carried it out in buckets. She tried to pull what was left of the breaker carrier out. It didn't move. Akhmeed couldn't get it out either. He said they'd have to get one of the hull techs to cut it out with a torch. She went down to tell Helm but, when she got to the gaggle around the generator, stopped to listen.

Lieutenant Porter, the chief engineer, was explaining to Captain Lenson that the labyrinth seal had blown on the generator. Not the turbine, but the part that made electricity. It had mineral oil in it to lubricate the bearings. When the seal blew, it sprayed the oil on the rotor. "That sent a high voltage, high amperage charge, just like a bolt of lightning, up the bus to the switchboard. That'd blow the 1SG breaker, the switchboard generator breaker. So that's what happened up there."

"Why'd the seal blow?" the skipper wanted to know.

"No reason I can tell you now, Captain. Could have been a manufacturing defect. Unfortunately, they're not a replaceable item."

"How about the LP compressor? What happened there?"

"Downstream effect. The breaker blew out of the switchboard and right through the 1SA section. It sheared the bus tiebreakers out of the board and shorted out all the power and tripped all the generators off the line."

Cobie thought, And we were just lucky none of us was standing in front of the switchboard. But Porter was saying that since the rotor was connected to the generator shaft it had made the shaft jump, and one of the blades inside the turbine had brushed the inside of the casing. Since it was going at thirteen thousand RPM, as soon as metal hit metal the blades came off.

Porter rounded suddenly on Cobie. "You were in the space when it went, right? Kasson?"

"Yessir. I mean, yes, ma'am."

"What'd it sound like?"

"A bang, superloud. Then a kind of rowfing sound . . . then a whirring, like everything was dying."

Mr. Osmani said, "That growl was the turbine eating itself. After the lightning bolt blew the generators off the line. Without power to the electronics the engines power down. They've got five minutes of fuel on the gravity tanks, but they shut down without the auto run signal."

Cobie kept looking at Porter. She sounded like she knew exactly what had happened and what to do. She didn't seem to be in awe of the captain or the exec. The captain wanted to know if they could fix the turbine. Porter said they weren't

allowed to and they didn't have parts kits. They'd have to re-
move and replace. Captain Lenson said to report the casualty, then, and asked how long would it take to put a new one
in once they got it. She said maybe a day. Then he asked
about the air compressor, if they could fix it. The chief engineer said they'd try, but they could run the plant, the pneu-
matic valves, and the rest of the system with the remaining
compressor. If that failed, they could bleed air down to operating pressure from the high pressure system, or run the
plant in manual if they had to, although they'd have to go to
two watch sections to do it. The skipper nodded. He told
Helm to tell the watch section they'd done the right things.
He was glad they'd all got out safe. Then he told Porter to
get on the repairs and ducked out the escape scuttle.

That afternoon everybody from the other sections, Punchy
and Drone and Ina and one of the hull techs they called Mr.
Blonde, after the Michael Madsen character in *Reservoir
Dogs,* came down. They stripped the switchboard and
cleaned it, and Mr. Blonde burned out the disconnect links
with the torch. After a while Patryce came down with root
beers, beaded cool cans they sucked gratefully, and the
scuttlebutt was they were headed for Jubail to meet their
new engine. She said she was off watch, she could stay and
help Cobie out. Cobie wasn't too sure about that, but what
the hell. They stripped the wiring out and got both switchboards disassembled and the electricians started putting it
back together, but that would take longer than taking it
apart. Then Chief Bendt put them on stripping down the
low-pressure compressor, but it was more fucked than it
looked. Some of the heads and blocks had to be replaced.
Helm wanted her to help him get the covers off the generator rotor. When they did, black water and shit came pouring
out of the casing, with chunks of burnt insulation. It stank,
big-time.

   She asked him, "Is this gonna be a big job, Mick? Replacing the GTG?"

   "You're gonna see it, Cober."

Cober? Well, it was better than Sugar Mama. "Ever done it before?"

"In Barcelona, in the yard. I don't think anybody's done it out here before."

Osmani came by as they were putting beam clamps in the overhead, setting up the chain falls. He asked how much the rotor weighed. Helm told him twelve tons.

"Twelve *tons?*"

"You'll see. This is a solid piece of copper wiring and stainless shaft as big as your desk in the log room."

Cobie was looking at Osmani, kind of admiring his eyebrows and his skin. He wasn't hairy, like a lot of the guys. He gave her a smile, and she switched her eyes away.

And found herself looking at Patryce. She'd come back down from the compressor where she'd been talking to the guys.

Maybe it was seeing Cobie looking at him. She didn't want to think that was it. But Patryce started to try for Osmani's attention. Cobie didn't notice at first. She just thought Wilson was acting silly. Then suddenly she realized what was going on.

Patryce was coming on to the Wiz. And, true, he was OK-looking, with that smooth brown skin and dark eyebrows and kind of twisted smile. But he was an O. Not only an O, but in their chain of command. But there Wilson was coiling herself around a stanchion like some hottie at the Full Moon A Go-Go. Asking him where he was from and how he got to be an officer. Then, God help her, she lay down on the deck and gazed up at him. Cobie couldn't believe her eyes. Even Helm was staring. "Wilson," he said, "don't you have something to do back in the Aux spaces?"

"I'm off watch. This is how you learn, working on the gear. Isn't that right, sir?"

"Definitely," Osmani said. Smiling down at her, like he didn't know what was going on. Or else did, and didn't mind. "You have to cross-train to get the big picture."

Cobie gritted her teeth, watching her play coy.

But eventually Osmani drifted out, like the Os did when

you were working and obviously didn't want to talk to them, and after that Patryce didn't want to help out as much, and finally left. Then the word came over the 1MC, early meal for watch reliefs. She asked if she could eat. Helm said yeah. She went back to the berthing space. Wilson wasn't in her rack, but she found her at the table in back reading an old *People*. She pulled out a chair. "Patryce, what were you doing with Osmani?"

She looked up, startled. "Me?"

"Coming on to him like that? Jeez."

" 'Zat a problem? If he's yours, I'll get off the bus."

"He's not *mine*. He's not *anybody's*. You can't fuck every guy on the ship!"

Her face set. "Sounds like fun to me. What's the fucking problem, Kasson? Can't you stay in your rate?"

She scratched her forehead, trying to think. But her fingers hit the bandage and her mind slid off whatever it was she was trying to put together. Then she had it again. "Look. We're going places we never could before. Like on this ship. Like, someday my daughter's going to be grown-up. When guys look at her, what are they going to see? Just another piece of ass? Or somebody who can do a job, too?"

"You are so weird," Wilson said, examining her like she'd grown horns and a tail. "Do you have any idea what you're talking about?"

"I'm talking about—Never mind. Look, you just can't hook up with everybody aboard who wants a quick lay. The whole ship's talking about it."

"I don't 'hook up with everybody.' Where the hell are you getting this shit?"

"All right, I'll tell you. You know, like in the helo with the helo crew? And the weight room, the guys you give massages to? Bartlett, from the ship's store? I saw that. At the Daiquiri Palace. You can't tell me I didn't see that."

"So I made some guy's day, so what."

"Guys don't keep secrets, Patryce."

"So what? Let them•talk."

The woman couldn't be serious. Cobie wondered for a

second if she'd have to turn her in. Then knew she couldn't.
But she was ruining it for all the girls. Once they got into
port, the guys would talk to the other crews, too. She knew
how this worked. She tried again. "Look, you're my friend.
But you've got to exercise some restraint. Keep it off the
ship, at least."

But Wilson's face had gone white. "Look, bitch, I've been
in the navy too long to have some fireman call me a slut."

"No, I just—"

"I like a guy, I show it. What their wives don't know
won't hurt them. They're having just as good a time at home.
And I don't need you telling me what to do. Not the way you
and Helm keep mooning at each other."

"We don't—"

"Just shut the fuck up, all right? You see this?" She
flicked her third-class insignia, the eagle above the stripe
they called a crow. "I tell you what to do, *Fireman* Kasson.
You don't tell me. So fuck the fuck off."

Cobie said, trying to keep her voice from shaking,
"That's how it is, huh?"

"That's how it fucking is. Yeah."

Wilson got up and went into the head. Leaving Cobie sitting at the table, looking after her. Wondering what she was
going to do now.

17

Marty could not fucking believe it. Now they had to take not just Cassidy on boardings, but a staff puke, too. An untrained fucking Down Under staff puke, to keep the rogue outlaw Gold Team from ass-raping the poor sono-fabitching smugglers. He could not believe it.

But that's how it was.

A piss-ass little Australian butterbars they called Booger. Actually his name was Berger, but they called him Booger when they were out of hearing of the other officers. It made him swell up like a toad, which meant it was the right nickname. Yeah. Booger fit.

Marchetti stood suited up by the stern, watching the ocher tint of boiling sand gradually turn the sun the color of dried blood. Waiting to go over on yet another boarding. He wasn't sure why, but things were getting tense aboard the old Blade Runner. Over sausage and grits in the chiefs' mess the quartermaster said the skipper and the commodore didn't talk anymore. They stayed at opposite ends of the bridge and sent notes back and forth. The fire in the engine room had blown the shit out of the plant, so they had to cut down on the electrical load. Which meant the forward half of the ship had to go without air-conditioning. In hundred-and-twenty-degree heat this did not make for happy campers. Bendt said they should be heading for Rota or Sigonella, to get a new generator. The chief radioman set them straight as to why they weren't: The new president was getting set to kick ass, and they had to stay on station till the word came down to shit or get off the pot.

Meanwhile it was same-same routine. Today was hazy, and that old-brick tint to eastward meant they'd be eating sand soon. He patted his coveralls, checking the extra bottles of water. He made the guys carry at least two liters when they boarded. Searching was hot work, and you didn't want to drink the water aboard these tramps.

This morning's objective rode between them and a dry-looking shore fringed with that reefish green. It had been slipping inshore on the Sudanese side, but the blip weenies had picked it out of the clutter. The skipper had run in and put the lights on it, the helo had circled it, and finally it had come reluctantly out into this burning dawn. Not large, couple hundred feet, with a rust-stained green hull and what looked to this Montana boy like tractor tires hung along the gunwales. A stumpy superstructure aft and two sawed-off masts. He'd heard its name, but forgotten it. Its running lights were still on, glowing like fireflies through the sandstorm dim. Funny, he thought, scuffing at the gritty deck. The wind was up, but it was still hot as hell.

Cassidy came out of the hangar, Berger trailing him. The Australian looked confused, like always. "Take extra water," Marty told him. Berger smiled foolishly, as if he didn't understand what he'd just been told.

They stood waiting for word. Marchetti kept glancing down. At the sea. As the square stern moved over the oily-looking surface it left a roiling road of bubbling jade wide as three lanes of traffic.

From nowhere at all he thought about how it'd be going down into it. Your hands zip-tied behind you. Maybe out cold already from somebody stroking you with a shotgun as you went back through the clapped-out lifeline. Hitting, and going down, and down . . . it was deep here . . . somehow the green water looked cold. Sweat was rolling off him. No wonder, with the float coat and coveralls, all the fucking gear. The green followed the stern for a hundred yards, then faded back into inky blue.

Fuck it. He was cool with it. Fucking raghead just had bad luck, that was all.

As the sky darkened he wondered why they called it the Red Sea. He'd never seen anything but that deep blue. And green, where it shallowed around the jazirats and reefs.

Drifting around down there, the sharks taking a taste. . . .

Cassidy's radio snapped, "Gold, in the boat and cast off. Sound off when you're on the deck opposite."

"Senior, you like the looks of this?" Lizard Man muttered. He pointed at the approaching bank of dust.

Marchetti ignored him. Sand, dust, fuck's the difference. "Let's go, go, go," he yelled. Sasquatch levered over the rail and dropped down the jacob's ladder. *Fear* rocked as he stepped into it. The coxswain yelled, "Next man," and Snack Cake let go. Marchetti looked around at the ship, then heard the yell from below. He hitched the Mossberg on its sling, grabbed with both hands, and swung his boots lightly over.

Dan sat in Combat, scanning the message again.

```
ZZZZ TTTT 9007WW--WUUUT-RHUALLQ-PZZZZ
Z 200010Z JUL 93
FM COMFIFTHFLT
TO COMIDEASTFOR
CTF 50
USS LABOON
USS HORN
USS PETERSON
USS CARON
USS OKLAHOMA CITY
USS DEYO
INFO USCINCENT MCDILL AFB TAMPA FLA//00/01/J3/J31/J32//
CINCUSEUCOM VAIHINGIN GE//J00/J01/J3/JFACC//
BT
T O P  - S E C R E T//FLAGWORD-DESERT SCORPION//
```

MSGID/A L E R T   O R D E R/FEB/001//
REF/A/NCA/DOC/31JAN93/NOTAL//
REF/B/USCC/ORDER/312345ZJUN93/NOTAL//
NARR/REF A IS EXECUTIVE ORDER 12349, DIRECTING CINC OPERATIONS
AGAINST NATION OF IRAQ. REF B IS USCINCENT ORDER DIRECT-
ING COMUSNAVCENT TO CONDUCT OPERATIONS.//
RMKS/1. (TS/FW-DS) NCA HAS DIRECTED ORIG TO CONDUCT
MILITARY OPERATIONS AGAINST THE NATION OF IRAQ, IN RE-
SPONSE TO ACTIONS OUTLINED REF A.
2. (TS/FW-DS) CINC AND NCA HAVE DIRECTED TLAM ATTACKS
AGAINST THE FOL TGTS:

TGT ID AND AIMPOINT	TGT NAME
AABN-1Y-02Y4-AB 236	RAS AL GHAZIR MUNITIONS DEPOT
AALR-4Z-06U7-AB	AL-NUHAYAB, COMMUNICATIONS FACILITY
ABQV-3D-04Z3-AA	SHALAT AL BAZIR INTELLIGENCE CTR

3. (TS/FW-DS) DESIRED TIME ON TOP IS NO LATER THAN
022300Z21JUL.
4. (TS/FW-DS) TAKES REF B FORAC.//
ENDAT
NNNN

He folded it and slipped it into his shirt pocket, glancing
angrily at the clock. Only two hours away. Not enough time
to finish the current boarding and reembark the team. The
launch window was critical for a simultaneous time on target. Ships in the Gulf would launch later than *Horn* and *Laboon*, since they were closer to Baghdad. He had to scoot
north to the launch basket. Why couldn't they stick to the
original plan? He told the tactical action officer to come
right and bring her up to flank three for the launch box.

"Sir, the MIO team's still over there. Shall I call them
back?"

He reflected. The seas were fairly calm; the sand in the air reduced visibility, but it wasn't a storm in the sense of high winds and seas. "No. Tell Cassidy what's going on. Tell him to board and start the search. We'll be back to pick him up as soon as we launch."

The original launch order and time and clearance had come in Top Secret just after midnight. Shaken awake by Kim McCall, Dan had passed the word for Condition One, Strike, then gone down to Combat. The mission was now in a control by negation mode, meaning they'd launch on time, unless told not to.

McCall had gotten her strike team together around the chart table. "Okay, this is a real-world contingency strike into Iraq. What we get paid for. Let's get busy."

The fire controlmen had rigged the top secret curtain and signs around the consoles. It was hot already in Combat, with the air-conditioning down, and it'd get hotter. McCall and the petty officer at the launch control console had begun entering the verification codes for the mission data already on the hard disk. As the system began retrieving landfall data—what the missiles had to know to cross the coast, so the operators could plan the overwater leg of the flight path—everybody had settled in for a hectic and busy several hours. Since then, he and McCall and the chief fire controlman had validated the launch order, number of missiles targeting, and salvo spacing.

Which was good, because with this new message everything had just been moved up. Launch was now set for 1510 local time. Giving the time of flight and the evasive pattern the missiles were programmed to fly, they'd reach their targets almost exactly at dusk. Arriving simultaneously with those fired from the Gulf, they should overwhelm and saturate the Iraqi antiair defenses.

He blinked in the dim coolness, sweat suddenly icy on his back as he remembered some of those defenses. Like the antiaircraft crew they'd had to crawl past on the banks of the Tigris, on their way to planting a flag on Saddam Hussein's ultimate deterrent.

That of course had been after he was tortured. He re-

garded the numbers scrolling across the panels to his left
with alternate flashes of fulfillment and horror. He told himself again that to have to resort to violence meant that someone, somewhere, had failed.

But faced with a lying and ruthless tyrant, maybe violence was the only answer. Litigation, friendship, trade, sua-
sion, threats, even war, all had failed with the man with the
mustache.

"Report from the Gold Team."

"What is it?"

"Completed the loop. They're alongside now."

"Alongside us, or—?"

"No, sir. Alongside the merchie."

"Did they get the message, where we're headed? That
they're on their own for a while?"

Camill said they had, and Dan let them go. He'd done all
he could. All that remained was to wait.

Two scruffy-looking dudes glared sullenly down from the
bow. Marty glimpsed another face at a bridge window.
Where they weren't supposed to be. If the bridge was
manned, the target could get under way, leaving the team
stranded aboard and the RHIB panting after.

Which might not be so cool at the moment. Cassidy had
just gotten off the radio with the Camel. They were going to
get left aboard for a couple of hours, while the ship went
north, shot, and then came back. Marty nodded, wondering
why the melonheads at the top couldn't do anything the way
it was planned. Anything to make it tougher for the dumb
snuffies who had to actually carry out the orders. He wasn't
worried, though. They'd just start the search while they
waited for the ship to come back. No problemo.

The first indication things weren't going to be that simple
came as *Fear* purred around the slowly rolling ship. As they
rounded the stern, he suddenly smelled something shithouse
horrible. Something rotting. But underneath that was another smell, a familiar one. One that made him look signifi-
cantly at Cassidy.

Oil. Just looking down he could see it welling up, weeping through the riveted plates, the waving sea moss. A sheen wavered on the clean sea.

The quarter looked like a junkpile. Rusty pipes, cables dangling over the side. "Barbwire," Crack Man said, pointing.

No shit, Marchetti thought. There it was, skanky-looking wire tangled along the handrails. No ladder, either. The rusty hull-steel looked shiny a few feet down from the deck. Leakage? The world was going dim. Something began stinging his face. Sand. The faces looking down did not respond until Deuce yelled up in Farsi.

"What'd they say, Barkhat?"

"You don't want to know, Senior."

"Tell them to clear that wire away from the rails. Then get the fuck up on the bow where they're supposed to be."

For answer they vanished, leaving the team bobbing below with no way of getting up on deck. Marty looked around at the rocking waves, the swiftly reddening light, the empty sea. Son of a bitch. Now he wished he'd piped up when Cassidy told him the ship was taking off. Well, they'd better get aboard. Even a shitty ship was safer than riding out a sandstorm in the RHIB. "Grapnel," Marchetti said.

"Wait, Senior Chief," said the staffie.

"What, Booger?"

"We're supposed to call the SEALS if it's an opposed boarding." The guy looked at the ship. "They've got anti-boarding measures in place. Isn't that resisting?"

"Fuck that. We're here." He said to the coxswain, "Give me your life jacket, melonhead."

"Fuck you, I need my jacket in the boat."

"Fuck *you*, give it here!"

Berger said, "The rules of engagement say we need backup."

Marchetti ignored him and he mumbled to a stop. Sasquatch had the grapnel out. He gave it a couple whirls, nearly taking the staffie's head off, and up it went.

It flew over the rail and caught. He threw the life jacket over his back, balanced on the soft gunwale, and stepped off, letting his weight come onto the line at the same time he jackknifed his boots up against the rusty rolling steel.

By main force, he walked himself up the vertical face till he got almost in reaching distance of the gunwale. Then his boots hit the shiny patch.

It was grease, black grease, and his steel-toes shot out from under him. He grunted as his biceps took two hundred pounds of fighting senior chief and forty more of weapons and gear. The tanker rolled and he went face to face with it, grinding his cheeks into greasy iron frosted with sand. Then it rolled back and his kicking boots swung clear above the sea.

Hanging there, he started to climb. Hand over hand. Fighting his way savagely up against gravity. When he got to the rail he let go with one arm, grunting, and pulled the life jacket off his back and threw it over the barbed wire.

A heave and just about the last of his strength, and he rolled over and his boots slammed down and he came up in a crouch, .45 cocked in front of him. The deck was empty except for a black litter of what looked like burnt wool. He yelled over his shoulder, "Clear on deck. Next man."

Dan watched the launch team work, heads down, intent on the screens. The fire controlman was entering the last of the verification codes. The chief was entering the required text data, which allowed him to determine when and how the missile would launch. He yelled to the database manager, asking if the picture was up to date.

Dan remembered when the Tomahawk Engagement Planning Exercise Evaluator had been a wonder of advanced technology. An HP9020 computer, state of the art. Now it was a kludge, and the men cursed it. This part would take awhile, to run the compensation program and get the adjusted launch time.

Strike handed them the go message. They compared the launch sequence plan and the Indigo and both nodded.

McCall turned to him across the space. "Captain? Permission to send TLAM make ready."

"Make ready" sent engagement plans, mission data, and

power to the Tomahawk land-attack missiles. Which would start powering up, performing their built-in tests. Slowly waking to their impending flight. Dan nodded. She bit her lip and turned back to the consoles.

"TLAM make ready, all plans sent."

"Missiles pair all plans."

He visualized the antique disk drives down in the control room pulling up the data requests from the Rolm 1666B computers. The size of refrigerators, they boasted a megabyte of random access memory and ran at the blinding speed of eight megahertz.

Strong came into Combat and stood pointedly by Dan's chair until he slid out of it. The commodore was in crisp white shorts. He wore a light tennis sweater, which he began working up over his head. He said through the weave, face concealed, "What's going on?"

"We're steaming Condition I on the way to our launch basket, sir. No contacts near us other than Skunk 16, which is a merchant . . . still trying to get a name on her, and some small craft that look like fishing boats. No air tracks, no electronic intelligence other than nav radars that equate to merchants."

"What about our close-in from this morning? The one who was trying to sneak past us?"

Dan explained how he'd sent the boarding team over, then had to leave them behind when the launch time had been moved up. Strong looked grave. "You left them there without backup?"

"I had no choice, Commodore. We can't put the helo up because of the ambient sand. We should only be gone about two hours."

"You couldn't retrieve them first?"

Dan explained he absolutely had to be in the basket on time. If he launched late, the time on target would fall out. Then the whole strike would be vulnerable, birds from *Laboon,* the others spinning up on the far side of the Sinai, too. "I agree it was a difficult decision, sir. I made it."

"Without consulting me."

Dan took a deep breath. "Well, sir—the strike's not a

maritime intercept matter. It's national. It didn't seem to me it was within your . . . purview."

Strong looked down at him for several seconds. Dan wasn't sure he was on firm ground, but he stood it. Finally the commodore said, "May I see the engagement order?"

Dan handed it to him. He ran his eyes down it, obviously checking the missions in the engagement order with those ready to fire. This raised Strong a notch in his estimation, at least professionally.

"Any coastal radars from the Sudan? Is your EW team alert?"

"No, sir, nothing but the merchant radars."

"So we're prepared to launch?"

"The strike team's been on station since midnight, sir. The move-up knocked us back a couple squares, but we'll be ready by the time we get to the launch point."

"The missiles are up?"

"The missions are updated, checked, and downloaded to the birds. We're spinning up the gyros now."

Strong nodded, but his expression didn't give Dan any idea what he felt.

Marty took a step, then blinked. The black wooly-looking material was moving. It was *crawling*. It lifted at one edge as he stepped forward, like the corner of a blanket turning itself upward.

His stomach turned as he realized it was flies. Millions of them. They rose from piles of stinking guts and entrails, milling in the hot dry wind. It carried thousands off, though they buzzed their best, but most settled again to their grisly meal. Gold Team stepped gingerly forward, trying to keep their soles clear of the biggest piles.

"God," Cassidy said. "What is this stuff?"

"Somebody had a bad day," Marchetti said. He saw a severed head looking back at him. It was a goat's head. He couldn't decide if that was a relief or even more horrible than what he'd thought there for a moment.

He turned and saw the others looking around shakily.

And yelled, "What's the fucking holdup? Sweep one, bridge. I saw one scumbag up there. Clear him, zip-tie him, and get him down to the bow. Two, secure the engine room. Three, follow me."

The Aussie was mumbling, but he ignored him. Cassidy had his pistol out, too, and was covering him as he went forward, zigging from behind the mast to a stack of the same tires that were slung over the side. The deck was empty. Except for the flies and the sand. The light was turning a deep bloody scarlet, like during an eclipse, and the greasy sand on the hull had grated his face down to hamburger. He wished he had a bandanna, or goggles. Damn, he should have thought of that.

His eyes noted something strange ahead. A line, or a wire. His conscious mind recognized it only as he was on his way to the deck, as the claymore went off above him with a crack and flash that cut through the hissing sand.

Twenty miles to the north, the clock clicked over. Dan and McCall and the chief had moved up to huddle as the first class called the information on the missions they were tasked to shoot. They were focused, in their team mode. Dan confirmed the time against his watch and felt in his shirt pocket for his key as the combat systems officer said tensely, "Initialization complete."

The Remote Launch Enable Panel was a holdover from the nuclear-capable days. Two keys had to be inserted to launch. Dan held his out. McCall took it, almost reverently, and matched it with her own. Her Waspish fine-boned face was flushed, hands trembling. She weighed them for a moment, then handed them to the chief.

"Load complete."

McCall blinked, cocked her head, coming out of whatever momentary state she'd experienced, and moved to stand behind the console operator.

"Start missile alignment."

"Watch the INS switchover. WSN-5 in manual switchover mode."

"Final review Plan One. Do not change course more than five degrees."

McCall repeated that to the others, then pressed the lever to inform the pilothouse. The bridge said they were about three minutes from the launch point at his current speed.

"Okay, when we're five hundred yards out, slow to just above steerageway."

Bridge rogered that, and McCall said, "Final review complete. Time until first launch—eight minutes."

"Now set material condition Zebra throughout the ship. I say again, set material condition Zebra throughout the ship. All personnel topside, lay within the skin of the ship. First launch, seven minutes."

The commodore said, "I understood you had to report in before launch—"

"Doing that now, sir." Dan had the red handset poised. "Terminator, Lone Gunman, this is Blade Runner. First launch seven mike. Over."

"Blade Runner, Terminator. Copy. Out."

"Lone Gunman, copy, out."

Terminator was the strike coordinator at COMFIFTHFLT headquarters in Bahrain. Lone Gunman was the Joint Task Force, Southwest Asia, in Riyadh. Any cancellation/hold fire message would come from them.

"Five mike."

"Roger."

The 21MC said, "Combat, bridge: booster drop zone clear to starboard."

The 1MC said, "First launch, five minutes."

But then it all went to shit. The launch controller cried, "Nav alignment failure. Mode regression plan two, missile F51."

"Backup plan," Dan said anxiously.

"There's no backup for that, sir."

McCall said, louder than he'd expect a woman who looked like her would, *"Shit!* Is that an overridable fault?"

"No, ma'am!"

"Captain, we have a problem. Plan two has a nav alignment failure and—"

Dan cut her off. He knew what was going on.

Somewhere in the missile nestled in cell F51 a relay had gotten hot, or a board had shorted. Its little brain wasn't agreeing with the location data the ship's computers were feeding it.

For the bird to get where it was going, it needed to know where it was starting from. And since Tomahawk had originally been designed as a nuclear-capable weapon, it had been written with a very restrictive code. If it wasn't sure it could navigate, it wouldn't launch. Once one missile in a salvo went, if another had a glitch, the computers would skip over it and fire the third. But as a double safety measure, if the first round in a salvo hung up, none of them would fire.

But at the same time something was tickling his thoughts. Something about nav alignments. What was it? "Okay, let's calm down and think this through. Lieutenant McCall. Which plan shoots first? How long to first launch, how far are we from the launch point?"

"Plan two shoots first. Four and a half minutes to launch, and about five hundred yards away."

His mind was racing. What was it, damn it, what was he trying to remember? Something about a serpentine maneuver . . . an S turn . . . How long did it take to go from steerageway to flank for a Spruance?

He reached over Strong and tabbed the 21MC. "Central, Captain. How many mains on line?"

Chief Bendt said they had all four engines on line. Dan told him to stand by for max turns, flank three, and told Camill rapidly, "Pass that over the sound-powered circuit to confirm. Tell them to disregard acceleration limitations and use the torque sensor cutout. I'm going to the bridge."

There might be one chance to make this happen. He wasn't sure it would work. He'd have to do it exactly right, the first time.

"Captain's on the bridge!"

He blinked in sudden rusty light. "I have the deck and the conn. Belay your reports. Nav, what's least water depth within five nautical miles from right here, right now?"

"No less than eight fathoms, Captain."

"All ahead flank three. Make turns for thirty-one knots. Right thirty degrees rudder."

The throttleman grinned and slammed the throttles all the way forward. "All ahead flank three, aye! Make turns for thirty-one knots, aye!"

"My rudder is thirty degrees right, no new course given."

Dan slapped the bitch box. "Combat, CO, mark our posit. Treat this like a man overboard. Keep passing bearing and range to the position I just had you mark."

Like a suddenly whipped stallion, *Horn* trembled and leapt forward. As the screw wash hit her hard-over rudders she heeled left as she skidded hard to starboard. A rumble began deep in her guts. On the bridge, pencils and binoculars slid and fell. The bridge team grabbed for handholds.

"Combat, CO . . . how long to launch?"

"Three minutes to launch." Camill's voice, breathless. No hesitation now, Dan noted.

The rumble grew louder. *Horn* leaned hard off her turn. Dan stood bracing himself against a repeater, staring at the sea but not seeing it.

"Bridge, Combat. Point X-ray bears two-zero-zero, range five hundred yards."

"Very well."

"Passing zero-four-five," the helmsman called.

The ship was plowing a furrow into the sea, skating hard around in the shuddering whining whoosh of eighty thousand all-out horsepower locked against the groaning protest of seven thousand tons of metal violently changing its inertia. Dan was balancing the bearing ring on the gyrocompass between the tips of his fingers and doing trigonometry in his head.

"Passing one-two-zero. No course given."

By now the missile's gyros should be steadying up. The oscillations that had been giving unstable alignment readings should dampen out. If he was right, it might be possible to make the missile's computer agree with the ship's again. How? By taking them back through the exact geographic point where the missile's guidance had first lost its grip on the situation.

"Point X-ray bears two-five-zero, range one thousand yards."

"Passing one-eight-zero."

When their bearing to the start point was 270 he snapped, "Rudder amidships. Ahead one-third. Make turns for five knots."

Horn reeled back upright. He staggered forward and cracked his head on the window as she decelerated, dropping from the whining full-ahead charge as she came back to her original course. Shading his eyes, he saw they were coming up on the green frothing water, the rocking foam of their own screw wash. Ahead lay the same spot on the planet's surface where he'd ordered the speed change two minutes before.

"One minute to launch," McCall shouted as he slid down the ladder back into Combat. "Captain, navigation aligned on F51! Request batteries released all plans."

He grabbed the red handset; caught his breath, pressed the transmit button. "Terminator, Blade Runner. Sixty seconds to launch."

"Terminator, roger, out."

"Confirm whip and fan antennas silent."

"Confirm blast exhaust doors open."

"Alignment complete."

"Time to launch: thirty seconds."

Strong watched without comment or guidance.

"Time to launch, ten seconds."

The chief plugged the keys in. Gave each a half turn, and the screen flickered.

"Skipper," he said softly.

Dan hesitated, thinking back in that second of responsibility over all the deaths he'd seen and been involved in. The men and women who looked back at him now didn't know what it meant. No reason they should. Maybe you had to look into a man's eyes as you killed him. Knowing, too, there was a chance innocents would die. But satisfied, this time, every alternative had been exhausted.

Was he sure of that? No. You could never be totally sure. But neither could you let yourself become nothing more than a tool, a conducting wire, an unthinking component of the machine. When you did, you opened the door wide for evil.

Sometimes he didn't think he was the right man for this job.

He hoped that doubt meant he really was.

Voice flat, he said, "Batteries released, all primary plans."

"Shoot," McCall said.

"Salvo firing commence," said the chief. The launch controller mashed the button.

A double slam, then a roar bellowed through *Horn*'s superstructure as the cell and uptake hatches whacked open and the booster ignited. Dan visioned what was happening forward. The missile bouncing up from its cell, then seeming to slow; teetering tail-down, balancing gooney-awkward on a cone of orange-white fire and bleached-out smoke. As it passed three hundred feet, the engine inlet popping open. Fuselage wing plug covers ejecting. Steering and stabilization fins switchblading out, followed by the wings. Then booster burnout, and the nose dropping. A heart-stopping moment as you waited, then the black smoke of engine start.

"Lookout reports, missile transitioned to cruise."

"Very well," Dan said softly. Holding the handset, listening to the roar of the second round going out. Of weapons on their way, hurled stone, loosed arrow, ball, bullet, and shell . . . the god of war bellowing, loosed again to insatiate frenzy.

When he heard it, Marty didn't recognize what it was. Then he did, and twisted. But he couldn't see.

A rusty haze stung his skin. It draped low over the waves, as if sanding their tops off. He shaded his eyes, looking for the birds. But couldn't see them. One after the other the distant thunder began, and peaked, and then moved off. Toward the east.

Then something plunged out of the murk, and he whipped back to where he was: alone on a hostile, booby-trapped deck, with an armed man coming at him.

He'd glimpsed the guy sneaking back toward the bow. Slipping between the piles of tires. Only now did he make out the rifle. The unmistakable long curved mag, like the lower jaw of a cartoon miser. Marchetti froze, another shadow in the sand-fog. The burnoosed figure ran past, disappeared. Just as he did, Marchetti caught two more AKs slung over his back.

The sound intensified, like an airfield with jetliners going out one after the other. Using the aural cover, as soon as the other was past he tucked the .45 and unslung the Mossberg. Jacked a round of buck into the chamber. Think fast, Machete. The boys were aft, out of touch. He grabbed Cassidy and breathed, "Tell them on the ship, Red Ball, armed resistance. We damn near got lit up by some kind of booby trap, a claymore or something like it."

"Armed?"

"I counted three AKs headed forward. If he comes back and I get a clear shot, I'll take him. But the ship better start hauling ass back here."

Booger whispered something about not shooting first. Marchetti told him to shut the fuck up and get ready to fight for his life. He looked startled, then fumbled at his holster. Marty faced front again, hoping he didn't get shot in the back.

The deck felt funny. The shadows, too . . . what the fuck was going on? Son of a bitch, she was moving. No. For a second he felt like on the Tilt-a-Whirl. Like the ship was sliding away under him. He blinked and shook his head.

Chattering raghead voices came from the fog. The after roar of the missiles going out was fading. So he could hear them now, clear, all talking at once. Coming aft. Armed, and the rest of the team didn't know it.

The lead one came out of the fog, Kalashnikov held down across his belly, and Marty put the bead on his chest and pulled the trigger. The gun bucked and the raghead went down, screaming, and he pumped and swung, searching for the other rifles. The guys behind him were scattering, but somebody cracked off a shot. The officers had their pistols out and were pointing them wildly around. As Berger's lined on his head Marchetti ducked away, then shouldered him back against the tire pile. "Get back to the boat, Booger."

"You shouldn't have shot him."

"Mister Cassidy? Take him back, sir. Now. I'll retrograde the team."

The ensign was nodding when the boom of running feet came from the starboard side and a burst hit around them, bullets whanging off the deck. They were sprinting, a stampede, a dozen going by while flame spat here and there from among them. Nobody seemed to be aiming, just spraying and praying. Marchetti got another round off into them but didn't think he hit anyone. The recoil thumped his shoulder, and he worked the slide, stuffed more shells in.

Cassidy was talking rapidly on the radio, vectoring the RHIB back in. Marty told him to belay that. As long as these guys were on the loose with AKs, they could lean over the side and hose out the boat. "We got to deal with these pricks first. Tell the ship we're taking fire. We need the helo, need help, we need some fucking backup here."

The boarding officer nodded. Marty poked the muzzle of the twelve-gauge around the tire pile. The deck was empty between him and the deckhouse. Just littered rotting flesh, the eddying fly-cloud, the stench, the sand. But something was different. It was like he was looking downhill. What the fuck?

All at once he realized what was going on. She was *going down*. The fucking crew had tried to scare them off, then tried to kill them. Neither had worked, and that was why they were stampeding aft. That was where the lifeboats were.

He jerked his head and yelled, "Follow me."

When he got the word about the Red Ball from the boarding team Dan was still in Combat, explaining to the strike team what he'd just done, how if everything went right and you got lucky, you could shock a recalcitrant bird into realigning itself. He stopped in midsentence and snapped the channel selector on his Saber to the boat frequency. He got Cassidy in midtransmission, saying they were in the lee of the bridge and Marchetti had gone below to get the sweep teams out on deck. "Do you copy that?"

"Runner Gold, copy that."

"Blade Runner, do you copy?"

"Gold, I copy, d'you copy my copy?"

Dan cut in. "Skipper here, Sean. What's the situation?"

"Sir, we took fire. This feels like a setup. They were ready for us. My feel is they've scuttled. This thing's starting to go. We need help here."

"We'll be right with you." Dan said to Camill, "Herb, get us back to Gold Team's position ASAP. Flank three. Secure from strike stations. Set surface action stations. Blue and Green boarding teams muster on the fantail."

Strong interrupted, wanting to know what was going on. Dan explained rapidly. He asked him to get whichever task group unit was nearest their position to start on its way, they might need help finding men in the water. For once the commodore didn't have questions, just wheeled away, shouting for his watch officer.

On the bridge the windows were scrubbed with dim ochre, a howling hiss filled his ears. The officer of the deck had pulled the lookouts and gunners inside the skin of the ship. Looking down, Dan couldn't see the bow. Just brown water scummy with floating sand. The missile hatches were still open. Drill was to leave them cracked for thirty minutes after launch, let the corrosive fumes of the boosters disperse. But sand would be even worse. He snapped at someone to close them, then went to the Furuno.

Sand return made a fuzzy blob at the center of the sweep. The intercepted vessel was ten miles off. The helmsman had the rudder over and the turbines were whining up. He leaned to the windows and saw sandblast already frosting the thick shatterproof glass. It was like peering into boiling tomato

soup. He did sums in his head and came up with twenty minutes to intercept. He made sure *Faith* would be ready to go in
the water and the boarders were ready. Unfortunately, he
couldn't launch Blade Slinger in a sandstorm. The danger of
pilot disorientation and engine damage was too great.

His mind went to the missiles, probably making landfall
by now. They'd wing their way for an hour across the empty
northwestern quarter of Saudi Arabia. Then dipping, seeking
the shelter of dry wadis to cross the Iraqi border near a place
he knew well. A place he'd once taken off from on his own
penetration of the dark republic where, like some unkillable
mustached specter dogging them through the end of the
twentieth century, the tyrant still reigned. From there they'd
execute evasive doglegs, till their lethal cargos reconverged
again to vanish in balls of explosive gas. If, that is, there
were no more of these killer sandstorms along their flight
path. Their simple electronic minds took no account of billions of shards of silicon slicing the desert air. They'd drill
on till their turbines froze. Till some wandering Bedouin,
huddled while the storm raged overhead, heard the deep
rock shiver to the boom of half a ton of wayward explosive.

If a Tomahawk exploded and no one heard it, had its
message been delivered?

At his waist his radio crackled. He lifted it and listened to
gunfire, miles away.

Marty stood in a deserted passageway, pointing the riot gun
down it. Someone was coming up the ladder at the far end.
In a moment his head would show. He put the bead on the
hatchway and took the slack out of the trigger.

Crack Man stuck his face up. Marchetti jerked down the
barrel and stage-whispered, "Get the fuck up here, dipshit.
Where's the rest of the team? What the fuck's going on
down there?"

"These scummers cracked the sea intakes. These fuckers
must all be Omanis, there's so much fucking kif weed down
there. She's going down, man, she's going down so fucking
fast." He looked past him at the open hatch with the expres-

sion of a man inside a sinking ship looking toward an open hatch. "Jesus. Is the boat coming?"

"You see any life preservers down there?" Marty asked him. "You see Turd Chaser? How about Amarillo?"

"They went down the engine room. I ain't seen them since we split up."

Lizard came up the ladder. His coverall legs were dripping. He didn't say anything, just pushed past. Marchetti grabbed him. "Amarillo? Turd Chaser?"

"Headed for the engine room, last I saw."

"Okay, get out. But stay forward of the deckhouse. The crew's aft, and they're armed. If they come forward, light 'em all up and let Allah sort 'em out."

"Roger that."

"Join up with Hopalong and Booger. Soon's we get everybody clear and I confirm the crew's out of range I'll call the RHIB in. All right, where's—"

Water came up the scuttle, racing toward him. Marchetti gaped at it for a second, it was that startling, it was moving that fast. Not only that, it wasn't water. Or not just water. It was black. Smelled like oil. When it got to his boots he saw, yeah, it was oil all right. He turned and headed out after the others.

The deck was definitely taking on a list. He walked uphill to where the officers were crouching behind cover, pistols out. They were learning. Cassidy was on the horn to the *Horn*. Lizard was doing a Columbus into the sandstorm, shading his eyes and coughing. Marty looked but couldn't see anything. He wondered if the coxswain was going to be able to find them in this murk. The ship had radar, but the RHIB didn't. Maybe the ship could talk them in, if they had them both on the scope. If the scope worked in a sandstorm. He didn't like the number of ifs that were building up. He touched the float coat, wishing it was a real life preserver. It had some flotation, but mainly it was to carry gear. If they had to go in, and there was a boat full of smugglers out there, he was going to hold on to the Mossberg. The .45 might go, though.

Kalashnikovs clattered in the Martian fog. "What are they shooting at?" Deuce wanted to know. "Oh. Shit. The RHIB."

"I hope not." But Marty figured it probably was. Which was not good news at all, at all. *Fear* was fast, they'd just drive away, but once away, that was it as far as coming back. Not in this muck.

The deck tilted more, and things started to fall inside the superstructure. Tires started to slide. Son of a bitch, he thought.

"Here she goes," Crack Man mumbled. "Just like the fucking *Titanic,* only we don't have a band."

"Anybody see Turd Chaser? Amarillo?"

Nobody answered. They were looking past him. He turned, to see the water rushing up from the stern. Took a few steps aft and peered round the deckhouse. The rear davits hung empty, lines trailing in the water. No lifeboats. No ragheads. No life jackets. Just a rising tide, and the gas-station stench of crude. It was geysering from vent pipes in the deck. They'd been hidden by the tires, so you couldn't see what looked like a junky worn-out freighter was actually a tanker. Oil smugglers, with orders to hold out if they were searched, and if they couldn't brazen it out, to suck the boarding party aboard and ambush them. Then open the sea cocks and scuttle. Trapping them. Cute.

Berger said brightly, "Anyway, the water's nice and warm."

Half an hour later Dan glanced over the side. The lookouts were double-teamed, each man searching the murky sea for the missing.

The smuggler had dropped off the scope. Its boats were beyond pursuit, lost among the islets and reefs of the Jazireh-Ye Khark. All that was left was a boil of rising crude, sweet and heavy all around them in the hot air. Hatch covers, wood, scores of old tires covered the water, all greased with a black paste. And it was still coming up, bubbling from be-low as the ruptured tanks gave up their integrity.

The Gold Team was back aboard. At least, most of it. Two souls missing. He hoped they were around here somewhere. If they weren't, they'd gone down with the ship. Trapped below as she slipped beneath the Red Sea.

He swallowed, thinking sickly that if he hadn't gone to the launch basket they'd probably be alive.

Strong came out onto the wing. "I recommended you not leave them here. Not with the escalating pattern of Iraqi smuggling."

"You said nothing about that, sir," Dan said.

"Indeed, I did. You'll have to explain yourself, Commander. First the dead Iranian. And now this."

Horn searched deep into the night. She found many things floating on that dark water, but none were her children.

PART THREE

AN ISLAND IN THE GULF

18

Strait of Hormuz

Quarters, quarters. All hands to quarters for muster, instructions, and inspection."

Early August, and the heat was even more intense east of
the Sinai than it had been to the west.

The day after the missile strike, and the disastrous boarding of the smuggler, Commander, Mideast Force had detached *Horn* from the Red Sea Task Force and directed
Strong to shift his flag to *Laboon*. After refueling and repro-
visioning at Jiddah, *Horn* had circled the Saudi peninsula.
Today she was transiting the Strait of Hormuz into the Persian Gulf, where she'd report to the U.S. Naval Support Activity, Manama, Bahrain, for replacement of her generator,
repairs to her switchboard, liberty for her crew, and an administrative hearing for her commanding officer before
Commander, Destroyer Squadron 50, the permanent Gulf
screen commander.

Dan sat with legs crossed and ball cap pulled low against
the brightness in what was once more the skipper's chair as
Horn steamed slowly past lace-bordered islets and emerald
green reefs. Past the sky-pricking needles of the great southern oil fields, as if the sea had grown steel hair. Saleh.
Mubarek. Fateh. Maybe the only reason the Middle East
mattered to the West at all. Those distant needles, and the
great tankers always in sight, high out of the water standing

in, sunk deep with crude plowing out. He sat watching them
pass, sink from sight, as they merged into the dusty obscu-
rity that was all too familiar to him. As the anonymous and
abusive kibitzer Americans called the "Filipino Monkey"
came over the radio, hearing McCall on the bridge to bridge.
"Fuck-a you, American bitch," and less quotable remarks.

He sat listening, letting her deal with it. Until his gaze
was suddenly riveted to a speck. A speck that grew as they
churned onward into a shape he knew.

The dread grew like ice around his heart. He'd forgotten,
till now. Pushed it back, not even consciously, as if his mind
itself didn't want to know it knew. Didn't want to go back
into this dark realm of pain and defeat.

The speck was Abu Musa Island, and this achingly beautiful sea was where *Turner Van Zandt* had gone down. Years
before. But the sky looked the same, the air smelled the
same—dry, dusty, with a hint of burning. Above all, the
lancing, penetrating blaze above them was the same.

His fingers turned the heavy ring. Feeling where they'd
soldered it back together, after sawing it off his sea-swollen
finger.

A hundred and forty-two men had gone over the side.
Two days later, after sea snakes, sharks, the bullets of Iranian patrols, and the endless, burning, remorseless sun, a
passing dhow had pulled a hundred and ten out of the water.

He was staring into the play of light when Lieutenant
Schaad, *Horn*'s combat systems officer, cleared his throat
beside him. He flinched back to the present. "Casey. What
you got?"

"Sir, wanted to check with you about security in port. XO
told me you wanted a boat in the water."

"Not just 'a boat in the water.' I want an armed perimeter
security patrol."

"Sir, I don't think we can do that."

"Why not?"

"Bahraini regulations specify national authorities—their
own—provide security in their waters. Foreign warships are

required to secure all weapons and lock down all ammunition. They permit handguns for brow security, but that's all."

He reflected on this. "What about the Naval Support Activity?"

"Well, I'd assume they have guards."

"You're an Academy guy, Casey. You know what the word 'assume' means."

As he might have expected, Schaad took it without the slightest grain of humor. "Yes, sir. Assume means, make an ass out of you, and an ass out of me."

"So let's not, okay? *Does* Naval Support Activity provide afloat security for visiting fleet units?"

"I don't see anything in the lessons learned database or the port descriptor."

"Then I want a boat in the water. Put them about two hundred yards off our berth, cruising back and forth. Random movements. No pattern. Chambers empty, but loaded magazines ready. That clear?"

Schaad looked doubtful. "That's not in accordance with port regs, captain. The weapons, I mean."

"Then we'll keep them under tarps," Dan told him. "But I'm not going to sit around naked. I may change that after I talk to the shore staff, but that's what we'll start with."

Schaad said aye, aye, and left. Dan raised his eyes again to the island, remembering the men whose very atoms had merged with the sea and air around him. They'd paid the price. For freedom? For democracy? Or just for those who jammed the nozzle into their tank and whistled idly as the numbers flickered?

While he still looked out over this deceptively calm blue. This time, in command.

At least, until they got to Bahrain. After that, someone else might be sitting in his seat.

He glanced again toward the distant land. And the black fear came on him, the one that squeezed cold sweat and made his breath patter rapid and shallow, spiraling his mind toward terror. He groped for control. Trying to talk himself

out of it. None of it was going to happen again . . . he
wouldn't be captured, tortured . . . *Horn* would not die as
Van Zandt had.

His fists clenched. Who was he kidding? This was the
Gulf. Anything could happen here. *Anything.*

Plodding along at ten knots, *Horn* passed slowly into the
most dangerous sea on the planet.

He spent that day strolling through the ship. He might not
get another chance to say farewell. So he made a point of
asking about each man and woman's family, finding something to praise about their work. They were still excited from
the strike. Delivering ordnance made a sailor's day. It wasn't
bloodthirstiness, though it might sound like it. More like
how a surgeon must feel washing up after an operation that
he felt went well.

When he went back up at 1430, a flattened darkness
loomed: the headland of Qatar. He sat musing as it passed
and Bahrain pushed over the horizon.

He'd been here before, too, during the Tanker War. He remembered Blair coming across the lobby of the Regency,
striding tall and cool and regal. Her hair shining, tumbling to
her shoulders. Then corrected himself. It hadn't been
Bahrain. Not the first time. That had been aboard a civilian
tanker *Van Zandt* was escorting. A sand-whipped deck, she
in slacks and goggles and cranial; he half asleep with a cold
Heineken in his hand. He'd barely noticed her, only recalled
the encounter when they met again.

"Make all preparations for entering port. Check the setting of modified condition Zebra. The ship expects to moor
starboard side to. Uniform for entering port will be service
dress white for officers and chiefs, dress whites for E-6 and
below."

The Bahraini pilot talked all through sea detail. Dan con-
tented himself with monosyllables as they moved without
fuss down the deepwater fairway. The land gradually closing
at both hands, low and blasted-looking. They passed the

Sitra terminal, a long causeway at the end of which lay two gigantic supertankers. The white domes of liquid natural gas tanks rose above their decks. Dan jiggled his foot as *Horn* passed a quarter mile away; each dome held the energy equivalent of a small nuclear bomb.

But then they turned and the city grew, the soaring office towers and hotels and futuristic minarets of the most modern and open Arab society in the Gulf and maybe anywhere. *Horn* glided past a dry dock, a shipyard. Claudia Hotchkiss stood behind the pilot as he slowed, maneuvered, and finally brought them safe alongside a half-mile-long concrete jetty jutting out from Minas Salman, the southern quarter of Man-ama City itself.

It was already crowded. There were no empty berths once *Horn* was fitted into hers, farthest from land on the western face. A dry-cargo vessel swung nets of sacked grain or rice down to trucks. A cruise ship flying the Italian flag lay oppo-site; passengers in suits and abayas regarded their new neighbor with noncommittal stares. Only one old man, in suit and tie despite the heat, raised his hand to Dan, who tipped his hat across a hundred yards of space. Another war-ship, too, a modern frigate-type that flew the Rising Sun.

"Now secure from sea and anchor except for line han-dling detail . . . secure from navigational detail. The officer of the deck has shifted his watch to the port quarterdeck. Set the normal in-port watch. On deck, watch section three."

Aisha had found a patch of shade on the west side of the customs office. A lieutenant in khakis nodded to her. She recognized him as the legal officer from DESRON 50. They agreed it was hot, then stood in silence as the destroyer came into sight past Sitra. Men on the Japanese warship stared at her.

When the shore party stood back from the brow, the lieu-tenant gestured for her to go first. She faced the flag, then the petty officer. He looked her up and down. Maybe it *was* cu-rious, she thought, seeing herself through his eyes: a black woman in a long pants suit and low heels, a beret on her

head and a hijab she was wearing at the moment down
around her neck like a scarf, a cell phone clipped to her
purse, and in it, although he couldn't see it, the nine-
millimeter. She held out the badge. "Aisha Ar-Rahim, NCIS.
I'm here for the threat briefing."

A woman stepped from beneath a shadowing awning.
"Ar-Rahim? Claudia Hotchkiss. The exec."

She must have looked startled, because Hotchkiss
laughed. "They didn't tell you? We're mixed gender. An
experiment."

"I wish they had. It will present—differences in how people here are going to react."

They shook hands, measuring each other. Hotchkiss was
attractive, in a hard-nosed way. She gave off an aura of cold
efficiency, but past that might be a friendly person. Aisha
thought her uniform distinctly unflattering to a woman's
shape, though.

"We're set up in the wardroom first, officers and chiefs.
Then we'd like you to present again on the mess decks, if
you'd care to do that. Or we can pass on what you give us."

"I'd like to talk to the crew, too. Things they need to know
before they go ashore. Especially with this—experiment."

Hotchkiss undogged the door and ushered her through.
Aisha braced herself for the chill, but inside it was little
cooler than out. "We have a generator problem," the exec
said. "Now we're on shore power, it should cool off, but we
had to secure the air-conditioning load."

The wardroom was like any other. The captain was tall,
with sandy hair. He shook her hand and told her he might
have to leave early, he had calls ashore, but the XO would
take care of her.

She was on. She shuffled her materials, trying to decide
what to change, what to add. Cleared her throat. "*Ahlan wa-
sahlan,*" she said. No one answered.

"That was 'welcome' in Arabic, the language of Bahrain.
I'm Aisha Ar-Rahim, Naval Criminal Investigative Service
Field Office, Bahrain. Welcome to the best liberty port in the
Gulf! You probably got an advance package from our morale

and rec office. Camel rides, tours, golf, beaches, diving. A lot of nightlife downtown. Great shopping. The people here are on the whole welcoming. Almost everybody knows some English. But as is true everywhere, there are things you need to bear in mind."

She shifted into automatic and went through the mores of moving through an Arab society. What not to do. Topics to avoid. A hand popped up. "Question?"

One of the women. "Will we have to cover up the way their women do?"

"No. Bahrain's not Saudi or Iran. You'll see the full-bodied cloaks, the black jilbab, but for you it's neither required nor expected." She touched her hijab. "A scarf's useful. When I go into a mosque, I veil."

"You're a Moslem?"

"I'm an observant Muslim. For the women aboard, I recommend the same guidelines we require on the base. No bare midriffs, no cleavage, no shorts. Pants or skirts below the knee are acceptable. Bare arms are OK on Western women, though you won't see Bahraini women in short sleeves. On the beach, conservative one-piece suits."

She went on to the security tips: be aware of your surroundings at all times; keep a low profile; stay low-key in dress, language, music, and actions. Be careful in telephone conversations.

"The island's relatively crime free, but don't walk alone at night. Stay in well-traveled, well-lighted areas. Don't park on the side roads or parking lots near the base.

"Before you leave the Activity, look at yourself. Can someone tell you're in the U.S. military? The locals wear brands like Gap and Nike, but leave your ship's ball caps, military belt buckles behind. Avoid large gatherings, especially near the mosques after evening prayers. Remember Friday's the equivalent of your Christian Sunday."

A tough-looking chief with a stubbled head wanted to know about unrest. She said most resentment was directed at the island's government, rather than Americans, but she still advised staying out of the Shi'a neighborhoods.

"Are you Shi'a?" someone else wanted to know. She parried that and went on to warn them about local drug dealers and how not to get ripped off when you bought a rug. She left her card, English on one side, Arabic on the other, with Hotchkiss, and told her to call her cell phone if they needed her.

Having a drink with the guys on the team was OK if he ran into them ashore, but Marchetti didn't want to actually go steaming with them. So he went down to the goat locker after the brief.

"There's only one place I want to go, and that's anyplace that's got a bar," somebody was saying as he came in.

"This guy in Jubail gave me a card, the carpets at this place will bug your eyes out. Persian. The good stuff. Tear the label off and there's no way Customs can tell."

He'd been here before and wasn't that excited about it, but a drink sounded good. He hadn't had one since Palma, and what he was hearing from the radio chief, Gerhardt, was that after they got their repairs done, they'd be heading up toward Iraq.

He went through into the berthing area and found Gerhardt and Andrews, the cryppie, getting dressed. They planned to start at Murphy's Pub, then hit the Ramada, then later on check in at Shwarma Alley. He showered and shaved, then lathered his head. At the mirror he pulled the razor over it with light careful strokes. Very gingerly; there was a place at the back where if he wasn't careful he'd cut the shit out of himself. He put on slate Dockers and a Harley buckle with glass jewels and a short-sleeved shirt with red and blue stripes and then his boots.

Dan slumped on the sofa in his in-port cabin, looking blankly at the equally blank television, drinking a diet Coke out of the fridge. Blair wasn't due in till five, at Bahrain International, on the far side of the city.

Someone from the staff should have been on the pier to meet them. Strange there hadn't been. He'd have to pay his calls, starting with the DESRON commander. He'd ask there if it'd be kosher to call on COMIDEASTFOR.

He was throwing his civvies and kit into an overnight bag when someone tapped at the door.

The lieutenant introduced himself in an apologetic manner as Palzkill. Dan found out why when he handed over the envelope. "Sorry to be the bearer of bad news, sir."

In accordance with Paragraph 4 of Part V, *Manual for Courts-Martial,* he was notified the command was considering imposing nonjudicial punishment on him. The alleged offenses were violation of the Uniform Code of Military Justice, Article 128, assault, and Article 134, conduct of a nature to bring discredit on the armed services. He had the right to refuse imposition of nonjudicial punishment. If he did, charges could be referred to trial by court-martial by summary, special, or general court-martial.

He looked up to see the lieutenant still standing, and waved at the settee. "Sit down. Want a soda? So, you're a JAG?"

A JAG was a navy lawyer, assigned to the Judge Advocate General's office. "Yessir," Palzkill mumbled, perching on the edge. "No, sir, nothing, thanks."

Dan turned it over and read the back. Nothing there he hadn't seen before, though it was unpleasant to read his name on it. "What exactly is this about?"

"I understand your boarding party killed a man on one ship. Two of your own sailors died on another."

"It's dangerous work."

"Yes, sir, evidently."

"And what have you got to tell me?"

"Well, Captain, you have to decide if you want to accept nonjudicial punishment, or go to a court-martial. Then you have to decide if you want to request a personal appearance before the commodore, or you can waive that—"

"I'll appear."

"Then you have the following rights: To be informed of your rights under Article 31(b), UCMJ; to be informed of the information against you relating to the offenses alleged; to be accompanied by a spokesperson. To be permitted to examine documents or physical objects against you; to present matters in defense or extenuation; to have witnesses attend the proceeding, if their statements will be relevant and they are reasonably available. A witness is not reasonably available if the witness requires reimbursement by the United States for any cost incurred in appearing, cannot appear without unduly delaying the proceedings, or, if a military witness, cannot be excused from other important duties. And to have the proceedings open to the public unless the commanding officer determines they should be closed for good cause."

"Okay," Dan said, taken aback at the rapid monotone in which this had been rattled off. "How about this. I don't want a lawyer; I accept nonjudicial punishment; and I want to appear in person. My witnesses are my exec and the men from the boarding and search party."

"Sure you don't want help with this, sir?"

"Do COs usually have counsel?"

"Well . . . not usually, sir."

"It's taken as a sign of guilt?"

"I can't comment on that one way or the other, sir."

"Then let's skip it. But thanks for offering." He signed the form. "When's the appearance?"

"The commodore's in Riyadh right now, but he wanted to get to this as soon as he gets back. I'd say two or three days."

"And how formal is it going to be?"

"I don't think it'll be too formal. He doesn't like that. If you don't want counsel, probably it'll just be like a sit-down meeting between you and him. Maybe with somebody from COMIDEASTFOR there. They're the ones who preferred the charges. He'll read the charges, you'll present your defense, he'll make his decision there and then."

Dan looked at the paper again, wanting to ask whether he was likely to be coming back to the ship afterward or not. Finally he just handed it back. "I guess I'll wait to hear from you when he wants to see me. Do you get a lot of these?"

"Article 128s, sir? No, sir. You're the first one on my watch."

That didn't sound good, but he resolved not to obsess about it. In fact, the prospect of some big Crime and Punishment scene didn't bother him as much as it would have years earlier. Either he was gaining some perspective, or else just getting jaded. "You say the commodore's in Riyadh. Anybody else I ought to check in with?"

Palzkill suggested the base commander, a Captain Fetrow, and maybe the CO of the Shore Intermediate Maintenance Activity, they'd be doing whatever repairs *Horn* had scheduled. Dan asked if he'd walk him over, and Palzkill said he'd be happy to.

Hotchkiss was on the midships quarterdeck when Dan got there toting his overnight. He'd asked her to stay aboard while he was gone, at least for the first day. He gave her the number of the Regency Intercontinental. Since that was where they'd met, he figured Blair couldn't fault it.

"We need some decisions before you vanish," Claudia said.

"Be with you in a minute," he said to Palzkill. "Shoot," he told Hotchkiss.

She led him away from earshot of the lawyer. "This boat you told Casey to get in the water."

"What about it?"

"He tells me it's a violation of Bahraini law to have weapons aboard. He said he advised you of that and you told him to hide them under a tarp."

"Correct. I also told him to keep bores clear but full mags handy." Dan looked around the sunny, shining water of the basin, at the Japanese can, at what looked like a ferry passing to the eastward.

"Don't you think that's a little . . . alarmist?"

"I'd call it being prepared. But I'll talk to the base staff, get their cut on it. What else?"

"The replacement generator."

"It's here, isn't it?"

"Lin called over as soon as the phone lines were connected. Yeah, it's here. The question is, how soon do you want it in? It'll take about eight hours to get the old one out and eight more to get the new one in."

Dan thought about installing the generator versus letting the snipes have the night off. But they could get orders to sea again anytime. He told her reluctantly to swap out and test it as soon as possible, then grant additional liberty for the work center concerned. "Anything else?"

"We had a policy overnight stays, hotels, required a special request chit."

"If you mean did I put in a chit to stay at the Regency—"

"No, sir, I didn't mean you." She unclipped a flimsy from her clipboard. "This is from Mr. Richardson and Ms. McCall."

Dan looked it over. The strike officer and one of the helo pilots wanted to get a room at the Sheza Tower together.

"You didn't want a no-dating policy. I went along with you. Then I got this."

Since Richardson was a pilot, he wasn't in Kim's chain of command. But he didn't feel comfortable with the idea of his officers . . . fucking each other, to use absolutely accurate language. Fornication wasn't an issue in the civilian world anymore, at least in legal terms, but he'd read about an air force general getting fired for it. And *Richardson?* The guy was such a twit. A narcissistic blowhard. Dan remembered how Kim had looked at him on the way to see Niles, how she'd gazed so worshipfully at *him*—

Hotchkiss was looking at him like she could see every picture in his mind. "What, they couldn't just get two rooms?" he said weakly.

"The frontiers of navy policy. Don't ask something if you don't want to know the answer."

"What's your call?"

"We should disapprove it."

"Because it would be officially condoning it?"

"Exactly," said Hotchkiss, compressing her lips in a subtle but extremely effective conveying of primness and contempt.

"I agree," Dan said. He put an X in the Disapproved box and signed it in the CO's space. "Okay, I'm out of here. I'll check at the hotel desk if we go out to dinner or shopping or whatever."

"Have a great time with your wife, sir," Hotchkiss said.

Dan wondered what *that* tone of voice meant. Trying to keep it light, he said, "Any chance Chip's going to make it out here, this cruise?"

She didn't answer, just shrugged. Which was unlike her. But he was thinking about Blair, so he just turned away and returned the petty officer's salute and ducked out from under the awning into brightness so intense he caught his breath. He went down the jetty with Palzkill, blinking, and showed his ID at the gate. The marine waved him into a crowded, heavily built up compound, past a movie theater playing *The Fugitive* and the Desert Dome lounge and a post office. The streets were full of dungarees and desert camo fatigues. At headquarters Palzkill mumbled to have a good day, and Dan went up the stairs.

Cobie hadn't figured on going ashore, even after the briefing from the black Arab woman or whatever she was. The rest of the crew got liberty, but not the engineers. The older guys, the ones who'd been on steam-powered ships, "teakettles" they called them, said it used to be that way in every port. You had to light off a week before you sailed, long before anyone else had to be back from leave. You had to keep the boilers lit in liberty ports, in case you needed to get under way in a hurry. They said she was lucky to be on a gas turbine ship. Fifteen minutes from cold iron to cast off. She didn't really care about how it used to be. She figured it was probably all about the same, and the most annoying things, like the whistles that went on and on till you were ready to scream, were what the navy liked most to keep around.

In the days since the seal failure and explosion M division had gotten the old turbine broken out and ready to move. They'd taken off the module walls, disconnected the hoses and piping, bleed air lines, and electronics leads, and unbolted and taken out the scatter shield. This was a four-piece steel assembly, each part an inch thick and upward of three hundred pounds, that was supposed to keep the turbine blades confined in case of explosive disassembly. Only Helm said they didn't fly out when they came apart, they went backward into the engine. Which seemed to be what they'd done in this case, so she didn't think they'd be putting the scatter shield back on. Especially since they'd lugged the pieces back aft that night and dropped them over the side. But that had been a bear, getting them unbolted and out of the module. There was zilch room to do this, and as the smallest, she'd done most of the inside work, S'd around the turbine with her boots sticking out.

She hadn't seen Patryce since their screaming argument. Or, yeah, they'd *seen* each other. You couldn't exactly miss someone, so many women in a space as small as the berthing compartment. Only now Cobie Kasson didn't register on Patryce Wilson's radar. Even when they came face to face in the head, the third class just pushed by, bulling her out of the way.

Or at least she'd *thought* she was off her radar. Till Ina had said, "I hear you and Helm got something going. That right?"

Cobie had said angrily that was an utter lie, where'd she heard that? But too late realized from the glances around her she shouldn't have reacted at all. Realized from Wilson's smirk as she went down the passageway—you weren't supposed to leave the compartment unless you were in full uniform, but Patryce went out in a bathrobe open down to her belly—she'd just been set up. Ina told her Patryce had said worse than that. She was passing all kinds of shit about her. Exactly the things Patryce did herself, she was accusing Cobie of.

It made a sick kind of sense, now she was starting to figure the woman out. It also made her so angry she could hardly talk. All she'd wanted was to do her job and send money home. Learn something she could use. Build up that reenlistment bonus. She didn't need this crap.

So now she didn't go back to the compartment, except to shower. She slept on a mat somebody had put in the IR flat to do sit-ups on. Let Patryce play her games. Fuck half the men in the crew and blame it on her. Pretty soon everybody else would see through her the same way she had.

So she hadn't expected anything different now, had figured they'd have to work all night and all day while everybody else went ashore. So when the chief came by with word the generator was going to be here in a couple of hours, they had to get the old turbine up on deck, it didn't surprise her.

For a ship that was designed to have the engines replaced instead of repaired, she was beginning to think somebody didn't do his job when he drew where to put things on the *Horn*. The generator had to go up the escape scuttle. Five decks, straight up. But before that, they had to get it out of the module, pivoted around, and headed aft. Then chain-fall it from point to point until it got to the scuttle entrance, then pivot it again until it pointed up.

"Ready to do this?" Helm said when she got down to the lower level. She cracked her knuckles and nodded.

Bahrain International was across a causeway on an island of its own. Dan waited at the lounge area reserved for U.S. military, reading back copies of the *Gulf Daily News* and trying not to keep looking at the clock.

Finally her plane glittered in the sunlight, a falling flake of silver, then slowly grew, landing lights like Venus in the evening sky. It flared out above the runway before slowly decelerating to pivot and trundle back toward the terminal.

They didn't kiss. Cold glances from waiting Arabs were no inducement to bill and coo. He just hugged her, wanting so much more but knowing he had to wait; then stood back. Her smile was like the sun on a winter day.

"God, you look tired," was the first thing she said.

"You look kind of travel-worn yourself."

She did look beat, as if too much had happened too fast to keep up her usual grooming standards. He touched her hair. "You got it cut."

"It was time for a change." She looked around. "Let's get my luggage before it disappears. Where are we staying? The Regency?"

"How did you know?"

"I know how your mind works. And I like it."

At the hotel she insisted on a shower first. Then they made love. He didn't think about anything while they were doing it. Just surrendered to his body, and to hers. Responding without necessity of thought, with the simple instinctual desire that had come long before thought.

Afterward they lay in the air-conditioning cool, her thigh thrown over his stomach, telling each other about what had happened to them. Except that he left out the part about the charges. If she didn't know, she couldn't help, and he didn't want her to help. She told him about her ongoing feud with the army three-star for personnel and how she was trying to get the military health-care system restructured. Then asked, as she always did, whether he'd heard from his daughter and his ex.

"A letter from Nan. Nothing from Susan."

"How's she doing? Nan?"

"Getting ready to pick a school. She's looking at Georgetown, I think. And American U."

"So that'd work out for you, if you got a Washington assignment."

"Yeah, I'd see her more than I do now."

"A girl needs her dad."

"A dad needs his girl. I miss her."

"Ever think about having another?"

"I always said, that was up to you," he told her.

"That's not what I asked. You jumped a step there."

"Just cutting to the chase."

"It's skipping a step," she said.

"Sorry."

"So do you miss having a kid?"

"Sometimes."

He thought she was heading for something, but instead

she let her hand rove over his chest. Rubbing it, tweaking a nipple and watching his response. "Enough talking? Is the commander ready for action again?"

"You're not hungry?"

"I'll just have a little *bite*," she said.

They had dinner atop the hotel, looking over the coastal highway, out into the darkening sapphire Gulf. Northward, he thought. So Iraq would be over that horizon. Dozens, scores of rusty-hulled dhows were putt-putting in. As they neared they fell into line ahead. Then slowed, threaded the entrance to the artificial harbor, and gunned forward and back, stacks jetting blue smoke, fitting themselves into the shelter of the eastern mole. It was exotic, magical in the ending light.

"How long can you stay?" he asked her.

"Three days. Maybe four. How about you?"

"We haven't gotten orders yet. I've got to do a generator swap, fuel, and do some—administrative stuff. Then we'll probably go north, to the interdiction line."

"We're putting a lot of effort into that. Isn't that what you were doing in the Red Sea?"

"Yeah, we put in a lot of hours. More than I thought we would."

"Is it working?"

He veered her away from that question. He wanted to forget about the navy, oil, *Horn,* about everything he'd been doing for months. He wanted to concentrate on having a fine dinner in the company of a beautiful woman who was also his wife.

"How are your women working out, Dan? We're very interested in that, on the committee."

"They're doing all right."

"Just 'all right?' "

"There are problems. I wouldn't say more than with male sailors. But . . . different."

"Pregnancies?"

"A few. Not enough to affect readiness. I guess if my XO

got knocked up it might, but it hasn't happened yet." He caught her glance. "I'm joking, okay?"

"Oh, yes . . . Claudia. Is she working out?"

"Yeah. She's good."

Blair sipped her wine. Said casually, "Have you thought about what you want to do after this tour?"

"Well, usually it's a shore billet after a command tour. Typically at one of the staffs."

"The Pentagon?"

"Could be."

"You don't have any preference?"

"Something to do with operations would be good," Dan told her. "Maybe joint operations, it seems like that's the way things are going."

"I want to get a house," she told him. "I'll probably be in the administration for a while. I don't see anyone taking this president's second term away, but there are figures who won't stay for a second term."

"So you could get a promotion?"

"We don't call it that, but that's what it'd be. If I do well where I'm at. And so far, I think I am. Oh, there's grumbling at having a woman, and a Democrat, and somebody who hasn't had any military service."

"I can see the point about lack of service," Dan said, "but the other shouldn't matter."

"Unfortunately, for some people they do. but they're just going to have to live with it." She shook her head. "Anyway, that'd put us both in town. I can start looking. If I find something I can send you pictures."

Dan felt uneasy, but he wasn't sure why. "Look, honey, don't take this wrong, but I don't want you setting up some special job for me. Understand? Just let the system work. I'll talk to my detailer and see if there's anything in the area."

She picked at her fish. Then said, "You don't like it when I bring this up. But what are you going to do after you get out of the navy?"

He tried to make a joke out of it. "Just being in takes all

my attention, Blair. I don't have time to think about anything else."

"You told me if you made commander, that'd be it. So now you're a commander."

"When did I say that?"

"In Philadelphia. When you were getting the *Gaddis* ready to turn over to the Pakistanis."

He was trying to recover the memory. Then had it: the garden of the art museum, the Schuylkill rushing by below, its cold breath coming up into their faces in the winter dark. "I didn't mean I'd get out when I was a commander. I meant I wouldn't make it to commander."

"And now you have, and you've got the Medal of Honor, and a graduate degree, and you're commanding a ship. Is this the old Dan Lenson I'm-doomed-before-I-start routine?"

"I don't know. Maybe." He had to grin, thinking she was probably right. He *did* tend to look on the dark side. On the other hand, that side had turned his way, often as not.

"You need me around to give you these pep talks once in a while. I don't think your career's over yet. If that's what you want."

"Can we talk about this some other time?"

"Sure. But think about it, okay? . . . Aren't those boats pretty?"

"Yeah, they're pretty," he said. Thinking only, as he looked out at their graceful shapes outlined against the declining light, that there sure were a lot of them, crowding in through the entrance to lie shoaled against each other as the nets of silvery gain came swinging ashore.

19

The coffee was rich and dark, the roll baked that morning. Doctor Fasil Tariq al-Ulam spread it with sweet butter and jam and ate it in small, leisurely bites in a street-front café across from the Gudaybiya Palace as cars and Japanese-made trucks roared past in the early rush.

Despite the traffic it was pleasant on Bani Otbah. Palms swept the far side of the palace wall, fronds swaying in a sea wind that down here, between the buildings, he could not feel. Across a wide avenue the glass stories of a new hotel flashed in the sun. Its angular façade contrasted oddly with the ornate domes and needling towers of the emir's palace. Younger men in Western suits, older men in spotless thobe and Western street shoes, children on their way to school walked rapidly past a gleaming new peach-colored Mercedes at the curb.

Young girls in a giggling line hugged books to incipient breasts. He watched their bare calves glowing in the sunlight. Smiling faintly, as he remembered how the fat Yemeni, bin Jun'ad, had looked away. To follow the path of jihad did not mean one lost sight of everything else.

Sometimes he found the cell's less-sophisticated recruits amusing. They had no life outside the mosque. Could not think outside the strictures of Qur'an. But what mattered was not that you'd memorized the Book. It was whether you had the courage to kill.

The girls swept by, and he looked after them. Youth and beauty . . .

Spoiling the moment came a picture of his own daughter, blind, mindless, and obese. Poor simple Badriyah. She'd be eighteen now; but she'd never been able to speak, or sing, or recognize her parents . . . Her only pleasure was to touch soft things, velvet and silk and fur. With them in her hands she was happy. He remembered her mindless croon.

He lit a cigarette with quick short motions, struggling with anger, regret. *Insha'allah.* The Will of God. But these beautiful schoolgirls were even more unfortunate, doomed and damned by the blindness of their parents. The Bahrainis were the most fallen of all the Arab states. The Saudis used the island, the British used it—as the Qari had said, the head of the Secret Intelligence Service was a Briton—for years now the Americans had made it their footstool. Bin Jun'ad said there were pious men in Bahrain, but he hadn't seen any yet. Other than the sectarians, the Shi'ites.

Too bad the Sheikh hated them. It was the furtive and brilliant Imad Mughniyeh, head of Hezbollah's secret service, who'd masterminded the suicide truck bombing that had driven the American marines out of Beirut.

Together what could we not do, al-Ulam thought. But the Sheikh loathed the "heretics," "apostates," as a wolf abominates a dog. So did Mullah Omar, who was killing thousands of Shi'a as the Taliban rolled across Afghanistan.

But there were enough volunteers. With each bulldozed house, the Jews made martyrs. With each arrogant, fumbling intervention America created more *shaheed.* The CIA had funded the Sheikh against the Communists. How surprised they'd be when they realized he hadn't conveniently gone away. Beneath the placid surface of the world the new and this time truly universal *umma* of the faithful was growing. Soon all Afghanistan would be under the control of Mullah Omar. Soon they'd strike in earnest at the land the Jews had stolen, then at the homeland of Shaitan itself.

As for himself . . . the final task . . . then, the fishing business . . . and perhaps then it would be time to marry again. Sudanese families would compete to provide a girl-child. Thirteen, fourteen, young enough to obey anything a husband might ask.

So, was that a plan, then? Marry again . . . perhaps have a normal child? Surely a son was not too much to ask of God, after his work for Him. He smoothed thinning hair. His skin prickled where powder and metal were still embedded. A blasting cap had gone off prematurely. Since then he'd seen the world half in darkness, only half in light. Fortunately, the cap had not yet been inserted into the main charge . . . It was growing warm, the sky rolling toward its noontime glare.

The fishing business was doing very well. Perhaps he could still become wealthy before he grew old. It was time for a younger man to do this sort of thing. Youssef, Ajaj, Mohammad Atta, several he'd helped train might serve.

But first he'd have to settle with the nervous-looking, silver-bearded Mamdouh Mahmud Salim. The Shiekh's ad-visor had told him any profit from the boats was the Organ-ization's. But he'd made that money, with hard work in the engine rooms of decaying dhows, endless arguing with crews and masters about staying out overnight rather than putting in each day. Salim would have to be put straight. One way or another.

He signaled for more coffee. Dusting crumbs to the ground for the pigeons who'd flocked the moment he sat down, he lit another cigarette and shook out the newspaper. Each day he read the Arabic-language journals, *Al-Quds al-Arabi* and *Al-Hayah,* and sometimes the French *Al-Watan al-Arabi;* then the *Gulf Daily News,* to keep up his English and pick up news that didn't make it into the Arabic press. He looked over the financials, then the soccer scores. Man-chester United had beaten Arsenal six to one in the Premier-ship. He looked carefully at the small notices that announced arrests. This might be the first warning of a secu-rity sweep. From time to time he raised his head slightly. But no one was taking any interest in a little man in a light gray summer suit drinking his morning coffee in a shaded court-yard. Taking his ease before strolling to the office.

Only God sees the heart.

He'd not seen Nair, Abdulrahman, Salman, or bin Jun'ad for days now. They had their tasks. Left alone, they'd carry them out. Salim had warned him the SIS was a dangerous opponent. He didn't think they suspected what he was planning. Nevertheless, the less often the members of the team met, the less chance of compromise. To become a *shaheed* in action was glorious; screwing up and getting caught was just amateurish.

As far as he could see, the weak link was Shawki, who worked on the American base. The one who'd taken the first team in and helped steal the plastic explosive. (Which was carefully hidden in a cool dry place at the boathouse.) He was taking an American paycheck, after all. And he was young. Their corrupt, permissive way of living, their sluttish, half-naked women could tempt a young man.

In which case he'd have to abandon the flat, the house, and the explosives and get out of the country. He kept the Mercedes fueled at all times. It was rented by the week on an American Express card. Once across the causeway to Saudi he'd be safe; the Center would pass him from hand to hand back to Sudan or Yemen or, as a last resort, Afghanistan. Until then, they were in danger on this side of the King Fahad causeway.

But he really didn't think anyone knew they were there.

He was letting his eye run more or less automatically down the columns of print when he noticed the picture of the ship.

A Japanese warship had come in a few days before. That photo, too, had attracted his attention. But this one was American. He snapped the paper open, adjusted his legs to a more comfortable position, and read on. Then frowned, pushing his sunglasses up.

A warship . . . *manned by women.* Only the Americans could conceive such a thing! A floating palace of fornication. No doubt with television cameras to record it all. He couldn't care less how the infidels defied God. There was room in hell for all of them. But why did they have to flaunt their dirtiness in the face of those who believed?

Because no one resisted. Because just as the Qari said, the puppet emir and his British advisors welcomed them.

The waiter, who'd been standing inside the door of the café, asked him in a Bahraini accent if he needed anything. Al-Ulam said yes, brother, another of these most excellent coffees. He brought it, fresh, steaming, and they stood watching the morning.

"Truly, God is great," the waiter said. "To give us this beautiful morning in this beautiful life."

"God is great indeed, *ya akhi*," al-Ulam said. "You have spoken in His praise with a grateful heart. May he bless you and myself as well."

The man nodded, dark-skinned, poor, by the ruined condition of his shoes under the apron, with great expressive eyes.

For a moment al-Ulam thought of asking what he thought of a ship of fornication violating the Lands of Faith. But even a waiter could work for the SIS. Or for the leftists, the secularists, Iranians, Hamas, Ba'athists, or the Hezbollah, any of which would be interested in a stranger who voiced opinions. The real Fasil al-Ulam was still working at his clinic in Abu Dhabi. And though he had another passport, if he was arrested, no document could save him. He'd left his fingerprints too many places where people had died suddenly.

His thoughts returned to the ship. He looked at the article again and realized it was not far away, indeed, within walking distance. He put on his sunglasses, tucked the paper under his arm, and left a couple of dinar notes on the table.

The jetty was an extension of the Al-Fatih Highway, jutting into the harbor. New but already dirty, paint-stained, chipped where something massive had run into it. The smell of rotting fish hung in the air. Within its concrete elbow a few shabby craft were tied up, but obviously most were absent. He'd noticed the fishing dhows, bound out early on their daily routine, returning at the setting of the sun. They reminded him of his own boats, in Sudan, and for a moment he wondered if the exhaust in Number Five was holding where he'd welded it . . . Workers in coveralls were repairing a piling below him. They ignored him after one glance. A trim, erect figure in gray suit and white shirt, looking across the water to the much larger jetty to the east.

The warship was huge and intimidating. Built for the deep sea. It looked very dangerous and very powerful. Its sides went up and up for many meters. To guns and antennas and electronic equipment. Figures stood on a stage, repainting the side. They wore hard hats and at this distance he could not tell if they were men or women, American or Arab.

He went to stand on the far side of a concrete building, placing it between him, and the workers, and the shore. Taking a camera out of his jacket, he snapped several photographs. Slipped it back, then stood watching for several more minutes.

He was about to leave when a small craft appeared from behind the jetty. He unfolded his paper. Looking down at it, then at his watch, as if waiting for someone, he observed the boat, a gray inflatable with three men in it, as it patrolled slowly around the ship. It turned in his direction, and he tensed. But then it turned away. It swept out a wide circle, accelerating, throwing up waves that rocked across the harbor and plashed on the rocky riprap at his feet. A few hundred meters out, it throttled back again. One of the men in it, in camouflage fatigues, was searching the surface with field glasses.

He folded the newspaper with a snap and walked briskly toward the shore. Turned right, and after a brisk march along the waterfront, detouring inland through narrow streets to avoid a repair dock, men chipping barnacles off the hulls of dhows, came out again onto the harbor front. He walked briskly down it, noting a cruise liner moored across from the warship.

"Excuse me, sir. Sir!"

"Yes?" He turned impatiently.

She was in a white uniform and a white cap. A pistol hung at her belt. A dark-haired woman no taller than he was. He was so startled and disgusted he did not at first react. Then he took off his sunglasses. Americans did not trust people in sunglasses. He said in his best English, "Good morning. I'm Doctor al-Ulam. I've been called to the cruise ship, there? May I pass, please?"

"Doctor?" She glanced at the white towering walls of the liner. Then back at him. "Where's your bag?"

He smiled. "I don't carry a bag, miss. The ship's well equipped. I'm a specialist."

He saw she didn't understand, but that she'd let him pass. "Well . . . I guess that's all right."

He thanked her and went on. Past the smaller warship, the one with the Rising Sun flag of the Japanese. Putting his dark glasses back on so he could examine the American without seeming to.

It grew larger as he neared. The bow was a great wedged blade of gray-painted steel. It was painted with strange ghostly numbers, as if meant to be invisible at a distance. Behind it the upper works mounted up, and up, till they terminated in spinning devices so high he could hardly make them out. The ship's voice came to him, a menacing hum of blowers and machinery. A crane idled, engine rumbling. Men in coveralls and uniforms stood back as it slowly lowered a long box to a flat area he recognized after a moment as a landing pad. A metal bridge led up to the deck. Uniformed guards glanced his way as he went by, then away.

The great machine looked armored and invulnerable. The Crusaders were proud in their strength. But so had the unbelievers been in the battle of Badr, the battle of the Trench, the battle of Yarmuk.

He walked on, noting with hate the flaunting of their gaudy flag. The only weapon he saw, however, was a cannon, and it did not seem large. There must be other weapons, hidden. He saw no sentries other than those at the metal bridge. And in the inflatable boat; but he didn't see it now.

He turned away, and climbed the steps into the hull of the cruise ship. He asked if the captain would be interested in hiring a well-qualified physician. After some time he was told the ship already had a doctor. He thanked them quietly, looking out over the bay from the lofty deck.

There was the inflatable, idling a hundred meters off. He saw no weapons, though.

Then he smiled. One man had a fishing rod in his hands. As he watched, he cast, then fixed the rod in a holder. The motor purred and the boat eased past, trailing a V-shaped wake.

Back on the jetty, he walked slowly past the destroyer again. Then, on impulse, turned and went up the gangway, the metal gridwork bouncing beneath his weight.

The sailors watched him without interest. As he stepped off, actually standing now on the deck—it was all steel, he saw, every bit of the ship was heavy, thick, welded steel, unlike the Vietnamese shrimpers, which were of thin metal, or his dhows, which were built of wood—one left the shade and sauntered over. He was large and pale, with a round face and blond hair under his white hat.

"Help you with somethin'?"

"Here's my card. I'm a doctor. I wished to offer my services, should any of your crew need medical attention."

The man had a southern, southwestern accent; al-Ulam guessed Texas. It brought back unpleasant memories. He trembled, keeping the hatred from his face. Smiling, an inoffensive, inquiring little man, trying to drum up a little business. Who glanced only for a moment at the empty machine-gun mount, at the padlock that secured the ammunition locker beside it.

"That's nice of you, buddy, but we got a corpsman aboard. And if it was something serious, we'd send 'em over to base medical." The sailor handed the card back and slapped him on the shoulder. "But thanks for stoppin' by, Doc."

At the head of the pier the same woman watched him approach. Another sailor stood with her now, a black man, large and imposing. The shape of his head and of his features looked Sudanese, though he was lighter than most Sudanese. Centuries before his ancestors had most likely been Muslims.

For just a moment he felt doubt. He remembered Americans who'd treated him well. The college friends he'd drunk and partied with. The tanned girls like the houris promised in Paradise.

Then he remembered those who'd thrown beer cans at him from pickup trucks. The humiliation on the beach. Their wars on Arabs. Their support of the Jews. And now their arrogant thrust into the heart of Islam.

Looking back at it, he realized the great gray machine was not a ship but the idol of a people so arrogant they had denied God.

What had the Qari said? "Bones must break and limbs must fly." The thought made him lick his lips, feel as if he'd just drunk several cups of coffee.

He'd attack neither the naval station, nor the apartment building.

He would destroy this monstrous *Horn*.

"You didn't take long," the woman guard said. She made no move to stop or detain him, though.

They trusted everyone. They were vulnerable, soft, and afraid. Weak inside their steel shells.

"They did not require me, after all," he said to her, a quiet, polite little man in a gray suit. "Unfortunately, it was the will of God that the sick man die."

20

The guys had stripped to bare chests, Cobie to a skivvy shirt. Even with shore power, the air-conditioning didn't work too good when you had an open access all the way up to the main deck.

Just getting the engine out of the module took two hours. Then it jammed athwartships. They had to slide it back in to free the beam clamp and shift it around a cable run. Then they reattached it and swung the inlet end out, took a strain, swung the aft end out, et cetera, et cetera. There was a lot of chain-hoist work. Manual hoists, not power ones. Pulling many yards of rattling greasy chain hand over hand before the turbine rose an inch. She was soaked through by the time they got it to the escape trunk.

Helm gave them a break there, and though she didn't smoke, she went up to the 01 level with those who did and stood looking out at the city. Across the water some guy was taking their picture from the end of a finger pier. She had absolutely no desire to go ashore. What had gotten into her, to sign up for four years of this? Kaitlyn would be ten by the time she got out. She'd have missed her kid's whole childhood. And for what? To float around the world with buttholes and turkeys, dipshit officers and asshole chiefs. She got so worked up she bummed one of the Porn King's Marlboros, and puffed angrily with her hands stuck into the back pockets of her dungarees.

When they went back down, Helm had gotten the Allison swung around until its intake duct was poking inside the scuttle hatch. He told her to take the seventy-foot chain fall up to the 01 level, to the scuttle in front of the data processing room, and rig it to the overhead and drop the fall down to him. And to make sure it was solid; he didn't want the engine coming back down on top of him. She smiled. He trusted her! She took Sanders and Akhmeed and went up to rig it.

They dropped the hook down seventy feet to where Helm caught it. She could bend over and look all the way straight down five decks to the terra-cotta bottom of Main One. She told the guys to stand well back when they got on the chain hoist.

It took more hours to rig the turbine up the escape scuttle. Hours of pulling on the chain hoist, bent over at the waist above the drop with the hot air from below coming up in her face. She couldn't do it for more than ten or eleven minutes, had to step back and let one of the guys take over. But finally the inlet end came up and Ina and Lourdes helped her rig another lifting point. Then Chief Bendt and the guys from the log room tailed on and they eased it on over and laid it down on a dolly and after that just rolled it down the p-way and out the starboard side of the ship.

It was much hotter outside now. She gasped at the heat and the dust. Gritty stuff you could feel scouring its way into your skin. Trails of it lifting from the streets. What a hellish fucking place. She went aft to the helo deck as a crane plucked a container off a beat-up truck and set it down next to her.

Standing there on the flight deck, Cobie looked down on a woman. At least she thought it was a woman. She was walking along the street where the pier ended. Completely in black. Completely covered. A meshwork mask so you couldn't even see her eyes. The woman saw her, though. Cobie could tell. She stood with her arms folded and her wet skivvy shirt cooling in the dry air, suddenly conscious of how much she was showing. Did she see Cobie as a threat?

A devil woman, come to seduce her men? Or as what her daughter might be someday, the way she thought sometimes about Kaitlyn? Cobie thought she probably couldn't even imagine what the woman was thinking. She wished she could go down and talk to her. It would be like meeting an alien from another planet.

The mess decks were empty, two duty sections being ashore. She shoved her tray along and got pork chops and mixed veggies and bread and carried them around the corner. Most of the girls sat on the port side forward. Cobie got one of the plastic tumblers you had to drink from—the ship didn't trust enlisted people with mugs—and filled it with weak coffee and got another glass of water to stay hydrated.

Patryce and two tough-looking cornrow-braided black girls were sitting at one of the four-man tables. Lourdes and two guys from Main Two were at the other one. The Mexican girl pointed to the empty chair, but Cobie put her tray down right across from Wilson. To her surprise Patryce said hi, like nothing had happened. Like she hadn't been spreading stories about her. She acted friendly, but now Cobie was wary. She didn't say any more than she had to, then went back and got pudding and ate it quick, standing up, turned her tray in at the scullery, and left.

Topside, Lieutenant Porter and Chief Bendt were looking at the documents that came with the new engine while Helm and the other guys were taking the leads and parts off their old one. Making sure they didn't ship anything out they'd need. She asked the chief about the new engine. He showed her the log that came with it. It was an Allison 501-K17 like the old one, serial ASP-1188. She asked if it was new, and Bendt said no, they came out of a rotating pool. This one had been on *Cowpens* and then on *Bunker Hill,* Ticonderoga-class cruisers, and rebuilt in Alameda and shipped around the world to meet them here. Their engine would go back to the factory in California and get refurbished for some other ship. She asked how long they lasted, and Bendt said forever, the navy operated them at one-seventh their max output ratings. *Horn*'s three GTGs could power the whole city of

Galveston, they put out that much juice for the combat systems and the rest of the ship. She asked what happened if the new one didn't work, and Bendt got a grim look on his grizzled old face and said it'd fucking work, all right. It might not start right away, they'd have to get the air lined up and wire it right, but it would run.

The replacement engine didn't look ten years old. It looked shiny and nice. All the new stainless bleed air valves and polished tubing. It'd be a pain in the ass getting it back down the scuttle, but after that she was looking forward to firing it up. Getting power for the ship, so everything ran.

Lieutenant Porter came over and asked her if she was getting along okay in the department. Cobie said she was.

"The guys treating you okay?"

"They treat me fine." She didn't add most of her troubles were with the girls, not the guys. Porter asked how she was doing on watch station qualification.

Then she threw her one Cobie wasn't expecting. "How'd you like to get out of Main One?"

"*Out,* ma'am? That's my work center. I work there."

"I know that. But I heard you asking questions. How would you feel about working in the engineering office? I need somebody who can keyboard and data process. Somebody who's got a curious mind and can figure things out."

She stood on the flight deck and thought for about two seconds. The air-conditioned log room, instead of the roasting engine room. Keyboarding instead of fixing shit. Not busting her nails and getting oil all over her hair. Helping the chief and the L-T, going to planning meetings and making up watch bills and helping with the department budget. It didn't take her long to decide which sounded better.

"Ma'am, I think I better finish my monitor quals. And I need to learn a lot more about the engines and switchboards an' shit. Is it okay if I just stay in the hole? I really think I'd rather work with the machinery than that other side of things."

Porter nodded a couple of times. She didn't seem pissed off, Cobie thought. She might even have looked pleased. "Sure. Sure. Up to you. Just thought I'd ask, Fireman Kasson. Just thought I'd ask."

Portal nodded a bounce of hopeful. She didn't seem pissed off, Gable thought. She might even have looked pleased. Blue, said, Up to you if you wanna. I'd say, Fitzhan's was someone thought a week.

21

"Take a seat," Aisha told Childers. "You can smoke if you want."

"I don't smoke." The storekeeper glanced at the brown paper bag she'd brought in with her, but didn't ask about it. He had a black toothbrush mustache and dimples in his cheeks. He wore the working uniform with the sleeves rolled, exposing forearms like slabs of baker's chocolate. A cough outside; Diehl was guarding the door. She'd persuaded him to let her try this one on her own. He hadn't wanted her to, but she'd pointed out the senior agent hadn't gotten anywhere with the suspect.

Aisha hoped she wouldn't end up looking foolish, and tried to keep her voice offhand. "Pepsi?"

He didn't want that, either. He sat in the folding chair in the break room of the armory, hands on his knees. She flashed on her classes in interrogation and interviewing. A classic posture of resistance. Often, of hiding something. Whatever it was, Diehl hadn't been able to get it out of him. The senior agent had had him back three times, along with the others with access to the explosives storage. Nothing. As far as these men knew, a Marvel Comics superhero might have walked through the concrete walls of the secure area, loaded up with weapons and explosives, and walked back out again.

She didn't think that's what had happened to it.

She arranged herself opposite him, pulling down the hem of her abaya. Normally at this point she'd read him his Article 31 rights. The military version of the Miranda warning: the right to remain silent, that anything he said could be used against him, the right to a lawyer, and so forth. But if she could pull this off, no lawyers would be necessary. So she told him in a friendly voice, "We need to talk about this shortage, Petty Officer Childers. It's really important we find out what happened to this missing stuff."

He just sat there. "I done told you and Diehl both already, I don't know anything about it."

She gave that a beat, pretending to consult her notes.

"Why do they call you Jaleel?"

"Childers was my slave name. I got papers in to change it, but they ain't gone through yet."

"Nation of Islam?"

"We don't make that distinction no more. They did once, but we been led back to the True Faith. Everyone who turns to Islam is the same. White, black, yellow, brown. There is no distinction in Islam."

"That's true. The whole earth is the *masjid*. Do they let you make salat here? Sometimes it's hard to slip away and do it in private. But Allah sees the heart. He blesses the effort, if we try sincerely."

Childers looked at her. "You putting me on?"

"I was raised Muslim."

"Where? Over here?"

"No. In Harlem."

Childers, or Jaleel, relaxed as she chatted about the trials of maintaining faith amid a community of unbelievers. His Arabic was out of a phrase book, but he tried to impress her with it. When she thought they had trust established, she said, "About these stolen pistols. Who would want guns like that, Brother Jaleel? If you had one to sell, who would you get in touch with?"

"Can't help you, Sister. Would if I could, I knew anything. But I don't." He turned stony again.

She opened the paper bag. Inside was a large plastic Ziploc, labeled with the date and place of discovery and an evidence log number, and an evidence tape with Peter Garfield's name over the seal. Clearly visible inside was a black Beretta. She left the custody document in the bag and laid the handgun on the table between them. His eyes narrowed.

She slid a sheet of paper toward him, forcing him to pick it up, to participate. "The serial number inventory of the weapons stored in this building. The missing serials are highlighted in yellow."

"What about it?"

She held it out, but didn't let him touch it. "Read the serial on the gun. Then compare it to the list."

He did, unwillingly. "Okay."

"Okay what?"

"It looks to be one of the ones was missing."

She sat back. His eyes flicked to her chest before he disciplined his gaze back to the tabletop.

"Know where I found this pistol?"

"No."

"I'm going to ask you to think about that answer again, Brother Jaleel. Because things are not looking too good for you right now. The navy's plan from here ends up with you behind bars for a long time. Have you heard of Fort Leavenworth?"

He mumbled something. "Excuse me?" she said. "I didn't hear that."

"Said, I heard of it."

"It's the federal penitentiary for service members convicted of major crimes of violence and theft. Leavenworth, Kansas. A long way from Detroit, Michigan." He nodded, swallowed. "Do you want me to keep going?" she asked again. Thinking, maybe this isn't so hard after all. Feeling some guilt, too, about using Islam to gain his confidence. But she was telling the truth: The only way he was going to save himself was by cooperating.

"All right, Brother. I'll tell you what they have. And what we have to do. It took a couple of days, but the senior agent got permission for a room search over in the BEQ. Not on your room. We figured it wouldn't be there. So we searched the rooms of some of the guys you hang with. And guess what. Palmer—you hang with Palmer?"

He murmured unwillingly, "I know Palmer. Yeah."

"Well, guess what he had under his mattress. A nine-millimeter Beretta 92F. Are you with me so far?"

Childers stared at the gun.

"Okay, we could send this weapon by air to Norfolk. To a forensic lab with certified fingerprint examiners. But we don't need your fingerprints on it. Because Seaman Palmer has given you up. Confronted with federal charges, he decided to help us solve the case. Two hundred dollars. That's what he paid you for it. Do you think that was enough?"

He didn't answer and she made a mistake; let her voice go. *"Was it enough?"*

He was shaking his head, she knew the tone was wrong even before the words were out of her mouth. The big Hershey-slab arms came up again and locked. "I ain't saying nothing. I ain't giving you nothing. I want a lawyer."

This was the worst possible moment for an interruption, so of course that was when Diehl chose to lean in. "Doing okay in here?" he said, glancing at the enlisted man. "Need a hand?"

She frowned at him. "We're doing just fine. Brother Jaleel's going to help us out."

"That's good," Diehl said, but his voice was saying, Is he really? Doesn't look like it. But he closed the door anyway. Aisha breathed out.

"All right," she told him. "You don't have to say anything. Just let me talk."

Over the next hour, as the room grew hotter, she showed Childers there was no way he could avoid being convicted of multiple charges of theft of explosives and small arms. The violation was UCMJ Article 108: Military property, property of the United States, sale, loss, damage, destruction, or wrongful disposition. He could also be charged under Article 121, larceny of property. The recommended sentences were dishonorable discharge, forfeiture of all pay and allowances, and confinement for ten years.

But it might be possible to overlook what he'd done. In fact, she had a paper with her that guaranteed that he would not go to prison. In black and white, signed by the base commander. The reason for their being willing to forego prosecution was that the navy wanted to recover the other pistols, the grenades, and most of all, the explosives, more than it wanted to fry Petty Officer Lyman S. Childers. He'd be discharged under "other than honorable" conditions. But he wouldn't have to stand trial or forfeit his pay. He'd go back to the States and be discharged there, a free man.

All he had to do was tell them where he'd disposed of the other materials, and who had them now.

She leaned back feeling sick, sweat trickling under her armpits. Now or never.

But Childers sat there without responding.

"What's the matter?" she asked at last. He still didn't say anything. But he was sweating now, too, beads prickling out on his forehead.

He cleared his throat, began to speak.

A tap at the door. The beefy red face of a white man who'd spent too much time in the sun. "Getting late. Read him his rights and let's get him over to the brig."

"Just one more minute, Bob." She was furious. Was he trying to be the bad cop, keeping the pressure on? Whatever he intended, it just made this guy upset, and when he got upset, he stopped cooperating. She said, "Will you excuse me a minute?"

"Huh? Oh, sure."

"Want anything? A soda or anything?" Childers-Jaleel didn't answer and she said, "I'll get you a Coke while I'm up," and let herself out into the corridor and closed the door.

Diehl stood there grinning. "Will you *go away* and *stop interrupting*," she hissed.

"Just wanted to let you know, it's quitting time. I think

you're right. If any of them know anything, he's the one. But he's not gonna give it up."

"I had him ready to sign twice."

"What happened?"

"You. Both times."

"Uh-huh. Well, you're on your own, then. I'm going back to the Dahab." That was the name of the apartment building where they both lived, where most of the Americans who didn't live in the bachelor quarters on base lived. It was outside the base, in Juffair, a new quarter being built on reclaimed land.

"You go on. I'm going to keep on a little longer."

He shrugged and went on down the corridor, rolling with that elephant-like gait he had, the combination of a seaman's walk and the lurch of a too-heavy old man whose joints were starting to give him trouble. Looking after him, she felt compassion. Still mixed, though, with her annoyance at his interference, at his jokes, his cigars, his sour looks when she wore hijab, his bad breath when he leaned close and explained in intimate and patronizing detail something she already knew.

When she went back in to Childers, he was standing by the window. Looking at the barbed wire outside.

"Brother Jaleel." She stepped up next to him. His eyes shifted away. "I'm worried you're going to really hurt yourself here. And not just you. Those grenades could end up getting thrown at your shipmates. Or some innocent tourist family. I know what you think, we're all one big family, it doesn't matter where we're from or what color we are. That's the way it's supposed to be, but not all Muslims think that way. There's enough C-4 and grenades missing from your inventory to kill a lot of people."

She waited, then went on when he didn't respond. "I don't know what these people told you. Maybe they said they were going to use it somewhere else. But where could they take it from here? We need to know who has it. You're the only one who can tell us."

She figured this for her last shot, she'd done everything she could think of, but he still sat unresponding. So she said, even quieter, "I know you must not feel good about how this is turning out. Do you know what *tauba* means?"

"No." He barely moved his lips.

"Tauba is sincere repentance. Do you want to know what I think? If you are really seeking God?" He shook his head, not looking at her.

"Brother Jaleel, al-Islam's not about stealing or lying. None of that has any place in our lives. I think you need to make sincere repentance and ask forgiveness for what you've done. You fell into error. But God has given you a great favor: a second chance, to do the right thing this time. Don't deny His blessing." She nodded to the paper. "*That's* the right thing. I didn't have an easy time getting them to give us that. If you won't help us, then it's a court-martial and prison."

He kept looking out the window. Not saying anything. And she'd pretty well accepted she'd lost, was turning away, when he grunted, "An honorable."

"What?"

"I put in six good years. I ought to get an honorable discharge."

She smiled. "Thank you, Brother Jaleel. I'll see what I can do."

The chief opened the locker and pulled out a wadded set of oil-smeared coveralls. Underneath them was a rusty toolbox. Aisha slid it out into the light. It was locked.

This presented a problem. Her search specified lockers, but not locked toolboxes. She couldn't open it without going back and getting another warrant. She shared her problem with the chief. Who said that was a bullshit rule, and he had a pry bar back in the shop.

It was nestled under the lift-out upper tray, wrapped in a rag. The olive-drab tangerine-sized sphere of an M67 fragmentation grenade.

Aisha straightened slowly from unwrapping it, suddenly tense, realizing she should have had the explosive ordnance disposal guys in on this search. Bob would have thought of that. But Bob wasn't here. Probably hunched over a martini recovering from his stressful day. Pete Garfield, the other agent, was coming in, though. But all this Shawki would have had to do was wire the lid to pull the pin when she opened it, and he'd have gotten both her and the chief in charge of the fuel pier.

But then, a lot had happened in the couple of hours since she'd left the armory. From a dead stop the case, as cases often did, had assumed velocity. When that happened there were a few golden hours where you were the only one who knew what was going on. You could take people by surprise. Then it turned from nine-to-five into twenty-four–seven. She had to keep pushing, before word got out and everyone on the other side clammed up or went underground. If she could get her hands on the guns and grenades and explosives, she could close the case. And maybe save some people from getting killed.

Childers, or Jaleel, had finally come out with it. Though not before seeing a lawyer. The office sent Palzkill over, the lieutenant she'd run into on the pier. He confirmed the revised letter of agreement would do everything Aisha said it would. Childers was free and clear, he'd get an honorable discharge and be exempt from prosecution.

Then, and only then, he'd started talking. As soon as he did, she'd called Pete in to help her.

Jaleel said he'd stolen the grenades and explosive at the urging of a Bahraini named Shawki. Shawki worked on base, in the fuel facility. Why did Shawki want this stuff, she'd asked him. Childers said he didn't know. He just wanted grenades and explosive and had asked him to help him get them. (This she didn't believe, but as long as he was naming names, she wasn't going to quiz him about his motivation.) He'd taken the pistols to make money on the side, there were always guys on base or the ships who'd pay for a

Beretta. He gave her the names of those he'd sold the others to, and told her where to look, in a rented locker at the base swimming pool, for the one he'd kept himself.

She'd called over immediately to Base Security and the fuel pier to have Shawki held, but they reported back he wasn't there. Shawki al-Dhoura had gone night shift the week before and was probably home in bed.

So she'd come right over and now, looking at the grenade, she told the chief, "I'll need to tag this as evidence. You're my witness. Is there anywhere else here he could have hidden things? Shawki?"

"This is the only locker that's personally his. I guess he could've hidden stuff anyplace, though. Want us to look around?"

"Let's hold off on that until I can make some calls. And another thing. Don't tell anybody I was here, or what I found. There might be others here who are in on what's going on. We're going to try to pick him up before he realizes he's under suspicion."

"What *is* going on?" the chief wanted to know.

"I can't tell you that. The investigation's in progress. Later. First we've got to find this Shawki. I'm going to send over an explosives team and I want you to let them do a search."

The chief said he would, but if there was a bomb, they had too damn much fuel around not to tell him about it. She agreed they'd keep him informed and looked at the box again. Remembering the grenade, how easily the man who left it there could have killed her.

She took a deep breath, and asked the chief where they could find Shawki on his off hours.

She pulled the Chevy over just past the National Museum, just before the causeway. Looking for Major Yousif. In the passenger seat, a semisnockered Diehl was blowing lint out of the barrel of his .357. Unholstering your weapon was a violation of NCIS policy, but she wasn't about to call an agent with twenty-two years of service on it. Garfield was in the

backseat, also armed. She and Pete were wearing the new issue Kevlar vests. Diehl couldn't get into his; it was still in
the trunk.

"There he is," Garfield said.

Yousif asked them to leave the Chevy, and climb into the
back of an anonymous-looking light green panel truck. The
address the chief had given them for Shawki al-Dhoura was
in Muharraq, the island the airport was built on.

It had taken a couple of hours to pull this together. She
couldn't just drive out and slap the cuffs on al-Dhoura. The
Bahrainis had to make the arrest. No American held any police powers off base. She wasn't clear on the mechanics of a
search warrant here, or if they needed one under Bahraini
law. But Yousif had pulled it together pretty quickly. What
was important now was getting their hands on this Shawki
before he got wind his friend had dropped the dime on him.

"I'd like to go in first, alone," she told Yousif. Who elevated his eyebrows, looking back at the squad of armed assault cops on the benches in the back of the truck.

"You?"

"Me."

"Alone?"

"They don't know me. They won't suspect a woman. And
I'll be armed. Block the back, like you planned. In case he
bails out. I'll leave my cell phone on, under my coat. You can
hear everything and be ready to come in."

"Bob?" Yousif inclined his head to the senior agent. "You
like that?"

Diehl looked sour, and she was glad she hadn't said anything about him taking out his gun in the car. Because what
she was proposing was out of line, too. But they had to find
those explosives.

"She broke the case. It's hers, far's I'm concerned."

The Bahraini smiled. "All right," he said.

A short woman in a housedress answered the door, the corner of a scarf drawn across her face. She peeped through the
crack as Aisha asked, in Arabic, if Mr. al-Dhouri was home.

"Who are you? What do you want?"

"I work on the base. I have some papers we need to have him sign, for his benefits."

"What kind of papers?" But the door opened a little more.

"Insurance papers. In case he's hurt. Are you his wife?"

"Oh. Yes. May I see them?" The door opened a little more, then all the way. Aisha stepped into a small front room.

"I'm sorry, these are for him. Is he here?"

"No, he's not here. He's probably out at the boathouse."

"The boathouse," Aisha repeated. "What boathouse? You mean, back on the base?"

"No—I don't know. I don't know where it is. That's all he calls it. He's doing some work there, after his regular job."

"All right." She felt like fishing. "Is Mohammed with him?"

"Who? I don't know. The only one of those people I know is Salman."

"Salman," she repeated, more for the cell phone than for the tired-looking woman before her. It was a common name.

She was turning to leave when the woman said, "Wait. I have the number there."

She tried not to sound eager. "At the boathouse?"

"Do you want me to try and call him?"

"Let's try. I've tried to get up with him on the base, but he's never there."

"He works nights now, that's why," the woman said. She took a phone off the wall. Punched in the numbers, then handed Aisha the handset.

There was an art, Diehl had told her, to phone calls. The most important thing was not to act too smart. There was, for example, a way to find out who else was in the room you were calling, along with the one actually on the line, which was often useful to know. So she started with, "Hello, who's this?"

"Hello?"

"Hello, can you hear me? Who's this?"

"This is the Qari. Who's this?"

"The Qari? Which Qari?"

"The Qari bin Jun'ad. Who else? Who did you think you were calling, woman?"

"I was calling the other one. Is he there?"

The voice grew irritated. "What other one? Who do you want? What do you want?"

She guessed that was enough. "Is Shawki there? Tell him his wife needs him at home."

But another voice broke in, one she recognized. The woman was on another extension, in the house. She screamed, "Shawki? *Shawki?* Tell him not to come home. The police are here. They're looking for him!"

Cursing, Aisha slammed the phone down, ran into the next room. Two of the Bahrainis had come in the back door. As she entered the kitchen they were wrestling the woman to the floor. The phone swung on its cord. Whoever was on the other end could hear them shouting at her. She bent, and clapped it to her ear. Hoping to find out what they wanted, at least. That might tell them what splinter group they belonged to. Accents. Background noises. Anything, because by the time they could trace the number and get out there, they'd be gone.

The line was already dead.

Diehl came in behind the police. He asked if she was all right. She didn't answer.

She nursed her black mood as the SIS led the handcuffed and screaming woman off, as the police ransacked the house. Wanting to chew them out for charging in while she was on the line with the very people they wanted. But knowing she couldn't. Till presently Yousif came over and without a word laid a plastic-covered slab the size and shape of a block of cream cheese on the breakfast counter. One end had been sliced open. Inside was a whitish substance.

"What is it?"

"What we're looking for."

"Where?"

"In the pantry."

She picked it up tentatively. Heavier than cheese, but not

that much heavier. She pressed her fingers into it. They made dents on the Mylar-covered surface. A demolition block. Probably enough to destroy the house they stood in.

"There's a lot more than this missing," Diehl said, dropping it into his pocket.

"Not here," Yousif said. He looked around the house, now littered and torn apart. The police were ripping up the carpet, to show bare plywood flooring.

She called that number back several times that afternoon and evening, but no one ever answered.

22

"Take in lines one through six."

"Fo'c'sle, midships, fantail report, all lines taken in."

"Rudder amidships . . . All engines back one-third."

Dan surveyed the receding jetty from the wing. *Horn*'s repairs were complete, and she had to vacate her berth for another paying customer. The wind had shifted to the north. The sky was turning a menacing saffron. A shamal, one of the infrequent summer sandstorms, was predicted. Yet still they had no orders, and he had no idea when he'd be called on the carpet. They were shifting to a mooring out in the harbor. They'd have to run liberty boats. But all sections had had a couple of days ashore. The first flush had worn off, and most of their disposable income had gone as well.

He'd left Blair at the Regency, saying he'd call when he knew what was going on, and when he could get ashore again.

The first day they'd stayed close to the hotel: investigated the gold souk, visited the Grand Mosque, shopped. They'd bought a rug, bargaining with a gimlet-eyed old Yemeni in Shwarma Alley. Blair had found crystal and rhodium jewelry sold by an Egyptian couple who spoke better English than they did. He bought her a tie-dyed abaya that looked terrific with her blond hair. On the second day they rented a car and drove out of the city to see the Tree of Life and the wildlife park, then to swim at Jazayer Beach.

The Tree was a disappointment—just a dry old mesquite surrounded by miles of nothingness—but he was impressed with the island. It was clean, livable, and the Bahrainis they met seemed to have nothing against foreigners. He told Blair he could see retiring here. She told him it wouldn't be as pleasant for a woman. At which point it became an argument, but Blair didn't hold grudges the way his ex-wife did. They knew they didn't have long. That made every kiss stolen in their rooms or in the car sweeter.

"Engines stop. Left full rudder."

"Navigator reports: nearest hazard to navigation bears two-two-zero, two hundred yards, shoal water. Navigator recommends continuing right to course zero-niner-zero; two hundred yards to the mooring buoy."

Horace Camill had the deck, Bart Danenhower the conn. The repair officer was doing well. Dan expected they'd be convening an OOD board for him in the not too distant future. Most all his wardroom was turning out well. He was less pleased with his chiefs. That jury was still out. On him, and on having women aboard. Well, Blair had said they were bickering upstairs on that issue, too.

Recalling his attention to what was going on, because it could be tricky, he sat up in his chair. There was the mooring buoy, a steel cylinder yawing in the blue-green chop. They were approaching it crosswind, which was the hard way, but he didn't have room to jog south and make an upwind approach. The buoy party was in the boat, life jackets and hard hats, running parallel to them and a little ahead, a hundred yards to port. The deck division stood ready with grapnels and shackles and pry bars. They'd unshackled the chain and flaked the heavy links out ready to go overboard. Dan thought about letting Danenhower do the approach. But considering how little maneuvering room they had, decided to take it himself. When they had the boat under the bow, and were lowering the buoy line and the messenger to the crew, he swung down from his chair.

"Captain has the conn," voices chorused. He went out on the wing and looked aft. The huge gas tankers looked too damn close. The end of the crowded jetty was no farther away. Directly ahead was the shipyard, and between it and them the steady procession of fishing craft nodding their way in to shelter. The whole sky was brown now with an ominous shadow, like a dropping cloak. He clicked his portable radio to the boat frequency. *"Faith, Horn."*

They rogered. He said, "We're going to have to do something like a flying moor. So move fast on this. Get going at five knots and I'll follow you."

They rogered, and he called the engine order into the pilothouse. Looking aft, he saw the stern was swinging; the wind grabbing the bow and forcing it to starboard. He used both engines and the rudder to twist back and nudged ahead, following the boat, to which he was now secured by a thread of wire rope and a two-inch messenger. This would depend on how fast the guys worked. If they didn't make it, he'd have to back off and try again. Above all, he didn't want anyone to get hurt.

He brought the ship to a halt fifty feet from the buoy. As it began to drift past, two men scrambled up on its heaving steel, boosted by the others in the RHIB. They had the wire line shackled in seconds and dropped back into the inflatable as the buoy spun and tilted, dragged sideways as the destroyer leaned on the wire. He kept jockeying the engines, keeping her bow in position as the line handlers on the forecastle hauled around on the messenger and paid out the anchor chain that would serve as the permanent pendant. The boat party caught the descending chain and made it fast, tripped the wire, and they were moored. A whistle blew. The underway flag came down. The jack and ensign fluttered up into the growing wind.

He shook the tension out of his shoulders and said quietly to secure the engines, secure the underway watch. He felt confined, though, penned in by shoals and jetties. They'd have to stay alert for changes in the weather and for passing traffic. More dhows were coming in, now, a long line pro-

ceeding in from seaward. Early, before their usual evening
return.

Hotchkiss, at his elbow. "What you got, Exec," he said,
looking down on the top of her head.

The wind kept rising through the afternoon, visibility dropping as sand filled the air. It kicked up a short, sharp chop
even in such confined waters. At 1300 he secured liberty. It
was getting too rough to run the boats. Hotchkiss asked did
that mean the security patrol as well, and he said yes.

He also grew concerned, as the bow rose and plunged,
that they had so little water underfoot. He and the navigator
went over charts and depths and the range of the tides. The
basin was dredged to at least nine and a half meters, but
Horn drew thirty-two feet forward, where the delicate bulb
of the sonar dome jutted down. Basin depth was calculated
on mean low water, and thus worst-case, but still there was
so little beneath the keel the fathometer gave random numbers instead of a true reading.

He considered getting under way. The up side: they'd get
some sea room. The down side: they'd have to pick their way
out in reduced visibility, through unfamiliar shoals, channels, and strong currents, especially at the entrance to the
Khawr al-Qulayah. There were abandoned oil platforms out
there, too. Some brilliant scrap-metal salvor had cut them
down flush with the level of the sea, and they didn't show on
radar.

If it got much worse, he'd try it. But there was one other
trick first. At 1400 he set the underway watch, started one
engine, and began steaming to the mooring. That seemed to
help the pitching, and the motion smoothed out.

The wind whistled. The windows showed only a sand-
colored darkness, with shipyard, tankers, the city, only distant outlines, without detail. The harbor creamed, lines of
spume lying the length of the wind. A dhow labored, making
for safety with agonizing slowness. Sand ground at the glass.
Ships returning from the Gulf routinely had their bridge
windshields replaced. The anemometer showed forty knots

gusting to sixty, to sixty-five. He stayed there for an hour. It didn't change. He left Hotchkiss in charge and went below.

He was in the in-port cabin going through the traffic that had accumulated over the past couple of days when Casey Schaad knocked. Looking across from his computer station, Dan saw Marchetti behind him, shaven dome unmistakable under the lights of the passageway.

"Yeah, Casey."

"Sir, Senior's got a concern about our security."

He tuned himself out of the CNO's training goals. "All right, talk to me."

They squatted on the settee. Marchetti said, "Sir, I don't like where we are. I brought it up to Weps here, and he said we ought to come up and let you know."

Dan wondered how difficult it had been to persuade Schaad to surface the issue. "In what sense, Senior?"

"Sitting here at anchor with our thumb up our ass."

"You don't like the location?"

Marchetti rubbed his skull, wondering how he could put it. He just had a bad feeling. "There's too much traffic. We're too close to the beach. All these dhows going by all the time. What if one of 'em decides to run into us and put some armed guys aboard? We don't have our deck weapons mounted, or ready ammo. We'd kick 'em off eventually, but it'd take us a long time. We could lose a lot of people."

Dan swiveled his chair, torn between his own doubts about their readiness and the local regulations that had been explained to him at the base commander's office. At last he said, "Casey, what's your take?"

"Well, sir, Machete's spent a lot more time in the Gulf than I have. This is my first time here."

Dan swiveled again, reminding himself when it groaned to get it greased. Nothing aboard was new. Everything needed attention. But if they'd given him a new ship, would anything be different? He didn't think so.

"I won't say you don't have a point, Senior. But when I asked Captain Fetrow about it he told me Bahrain's a safe locale. A low-threat area, and the authorities here want to keep the foreign profile low to keep from irritating the elements that don't like outsiders."

"Is that why they made us take the rifles out of the perimeter boat?"

"Correct. The COMIDEASTFOR ROEs prohibit loaded weapons or hostile display."

"Sir, that's bullshit."

"This isn't our country, Senior."

"You said that was U.S. regs, not Bahraini."

Dan had had enough. "It's not up to me, Chief. Headquarters knows the local conditions, they talk to the local security forces, the host government. We have to go by their call."

"Sir, I still think—"

"Thanks for coming in to see me, Senior Chief. Lieutenant."

Schaad got up, but Marchetti wasn't done. "Sir, that's just stupid, not being allowed to defend ourselves. Here's what we ought to be doing." He went on: boat patrols, the chain guns loaded and trained out, the .50s mounted and manned, antiswimmer precautions with the sonar, pinging intense bursts to disorient anyone approaching underwater.

Dan heard him out. Finally he said, "Tell you what, I think we're all right just now. The seas are too rough for anybody to board. But you've got a point about how long it'd take us to react, if something did happen. Casey."

"Sir."

"Look at the quick reaction team procedures again, how fast we can get weapons and ammo on deck. Meanwhile, I'm not sure we ought to be where we are, either. We could go out to the Sitra anchorage, but then it's a long haul for the liberty parties."

"A long haul for anybody trying to get at us, too, sir."

"I have to think about a lot of things, Senior. Security's just one part of it. Let me ask Port Control about an anchorage farther out."

"That would help, sir."

"If you actually see something suspicious, come back," Dan told him. "If it's a matter of security, force protection, come right to me or the exec, if I'm not aboard. Casey, same goes for you; if it's time-sensitive, skip the chain of command and come direct to me. But let's not get so focused on one piece of the puzzle we forget the rest, okay?"

They left. He tried to get back into the administrative minutiae, but failed. Finally he logged off and went topside.

The shamal seemed to be holding steady. He could imagine what this was doing to their paint . . . He picked up the phone to the local command net. The covered net got him the duty officer at COMIDEASTFOR. After discussing the storm—the staff officer said it would be brief, it would blow over before morning—he brought up his concerns about their location in the roadstead.

The staffie was surprised he didn't like where he was. They put visiting units there frequently and had had no complaints before. Dan asked about moving out to the Sitra basin. The staffie said it wasn't a good idea. There'd been a bad accident in Greece last year. A cruiser's launch had capsized, drowning eight sailors on their way back from liberty. Since then the Naval Safety Center had reminded commanders to moor or anchor as close as possible to the fleet landings.

Dan said he remembered that message. Well then, the watch officer said. Still, it was his call. Did he want to talk to somebody higher about it, maybe the J-3?

At last he said no. There were warriors, and there were worriers; he'd worked for both, and he didn't want to turn into another Ike Sundstrom, seeing disaster around every corner. The shrink, back in the States, had warned him inappropriate suspicions of danger were one of the symptoms of post-traumatic stress disorder. He said thanks and to have a good day, and was signing off when the watch officer said, "Wait a minute. Captain Lenson? There's something here on my desk about you. COMDESRON Fifty and the CO-MIDEASTFOR JAG want to see you at 1300 day after tomorrow. You're on the admiral's schedule at 1400. Got any idea what that's about? Over."

"Yeah, I know what it's about. Thanks," Dan said. "This is *Horn* actual, out."

The commodore's mast, of course, only now upgraded to an admiral's mast—not a good sign at all. He stewed about this while the wind droned on. At 1700 he called the beach again, on the marine telephone frequency. A credit card got him patched to the Regency. When Blair answered, he told her he wouldn't be able to get ashore that night, the weather was too rough.

"I'm afraid I've got some bad news, too," she said.

He could guess what it was. "They want you back."

"A plane went down with thirty-six troops from the Third Division aboard. The deputy secretary wants somebody in uniform and a civilian side appointee there. He picked the DCSPER and me. I leave at midnight on the MC-18 shuttle. That's Sigonella, Naples, Rota, Norfolk. The army'll have a plane there for me to go to Georgia."

"That's bad. About the troops . . . when will you get in?"

"I don't even know how to guess at that one, but we'll be in the air fifteen or sixteen hours just to the States. So if you can't make it tonight . . ."

"I really can't, honey. There's a nasty chop going. It should blow over tomorrow. But I guess that won't do much for us."

He listened to her breathing over the air, thinking how much of his family life had taken place over the telephone. "But at least we had time together."

"Yeah." He put his fingers to his eyes and squeezed. Jesus, what was happening to him, he didn't used to feel like this when somebody he loved had to go. "But now how am I going to do without you?"

"Are we getting sentimental in our old age?"

"I'm just going to miss you, that's all."

"You'll do fine, like you did before I got here. And I'll miss you, too . . . We'll both be busy . . . Think about that house. Don't just go from assignment to assignment like some mindless pawn. We'll talk about it. If you don't . . ."

"If I don't what?"

"I want a life," she told him. "Something more than work, and only being together when you're in port, or I can fly out to see you . . . I'm sorry. I want more . . . or something else."

He caught his breath as inside him something turned at bay. Not again. Not the same thing that had happened to his first marriage! "You didn't seem to think it was such a bad way to live," he said tightly. "I told you it would be this way. You said it'd work. But now, all of a sudden, it's not enough?"

"Let's not argue now," she said. "Look, it was the wrong time to say that. I was going to get to it, but we didn't have time. So we'll leave it. Okay? Do your job. Be the captain. I'll go do my job. And the next time we get together, we'll talk it out. Okay?"

It was not okay. Bitter words struggled in his breast. He didn't like postponing discussions. They only got worse if you did. But he could do nothing. He couldn't go to her. She had to leave. So they talked a little longer, conscious every word they said might be overheard; they did not even have privacy in their farewell. And at last, they said goodbye. After which he sat listening, alone, to the hiss of space in the earpiece echoing the storm outside.

23

All she had left to wear was the maroon sundress. Cobie cocked her head at it like it was an animal that might be playing dead. Well, at least it was feminine. When she got off the ship she wanted to look nice, in a skirt or a pretty ruffled blouse. Wear perfume, and have somebody give her flowers and compliments. Be somebody she couldn't be on board. Finally she shucked out of her coveralls, only realizing how bad they smelled when they were lying around her ankles and the stink came up. She padded toward the shower, turning sideways to butt-rub the other girls milling around the Mustang Ranch.

Today was the first day she'd get to go ashore, and all at once she was excited. Palma had been fun, but Bahrain was exotic. Ina, who'd gotten to go yesterday, had come back with glowing reports. She showered and got ready, pulling the dress over her head, and then padded back to the mirror in the head. She spent time on her face. Doing the things you didn't do down in the hole. When she came out, one of the gay girls gave a whistle.

"Some dress!"

"Where you goin' in that, homegirl? Them A-rab men going to be steppin' on they tongues."

She grinned and brushed out her hair. Feeling like she was in high school again and it was prom night. She was a mother, for godsake. Old enough to know better.

They'd gotten the new generator in and tested it and it didn't work. It was putting out some kind of irregularity in the sine wave, and for a while they were afraid they'd have to pull it out and do the job all over again. Which was a downer. They'd already spent two days working practically around the clock. But then Mick and Chief Bendt had figured it out. One of the cable connections for the computer controls was partially melted and had gotten plugged in backward. As soon as they replugged it, it smoothed out, but then the ship had to get under way because of the storm. She'd gone up to the main deck and cracked one of the doors, just to see it, so she could write home about it.

To Kaitlyn . . . her mom said she listened to every word, and asked her questions about the places the navy had sent her mom to, to keep them all safe. So she tried to see everything with a child's eyes, remember details she could write down later. The sand on the deck, fine, powdery tan, pale, pale, beige. Like . . . powdered sugar with a pinch of cinnamon. The ship was going up and down, she couldn't see much, just the tan air and the surface of the water. The shore was a pale washed outline. She could see building shapes and a low hill like a camel's hump and that was all.

She smoothed her dress, wishing her little girl could see her now. Would she think her mother was beautiful?

Someone punched her from behind, and she turned. Ina, in white shorts and a Hard Rock Café T-shirt. "Ready, luv?"

She bleated in horror. "Ina, not *shorts*. Weren't you at the briefing?"

"They'll have to live with me lush white thighs, love. All I have to wear. Lourdes is up on deck. Coming, then?"

When she came out who should she come face to face with but old Bendt. Who stopped dead, gaping at her. "What's wrong, Chief?" she said, stopping, too, wondering whether she'd got her liberty section wrong.

"*Kasson?*"

"That's right, Chief."

"Jeez, I didn't recognize—You sure as fuck don't look like no gas turbine tech."

It was probably his way of paying her a compliment, or as near as he could come. Going down the boat ladder, she thought of at least six things she could have said back. Smart, clever things. But a mysterious feminine smile had probably been as good a response as any.

The sun was blazing out of a clear sky but the ride was still bouncy. The breeze felt good. By noon it would be like a blowtorch, but this early it felt intensely real after the artificial environment of the ship. Spray flew into their faces, salty and cool, and they squealed like fourteen-year-olds. She felt like a fourteen-year-old, all of a sudden. Free from the ship, from the gray walls, from all the men around her, sealing her in like an audience. It was like a day off from school.

Lourdes had on a peasant skirt with little flashing mirrors sewn into it, and a white ruffled blouse, and a red-and-white embroidered kerchief around her head. She looked very Mexican. They were quite a trio, Cobie thought. Totally mismatched, but what the hell.

Fishing boats growled past as they maneuvered for the landing. A long line, rumbling past one after the other. One went by very close, smoke drifting from a slablike stern where a wash of wake bubbled. The upswept bow was extended by carved wood. Long poles were strapped fore and aft above a little white-painted pilothouse all the way aft. It looked like something from *Sinbad*. Dark-faced men in dirty white robes and small turbans like yarmulkes sat crosslegged, watching. They did not change their expressions, even when Ina waved gaily.

They took a taxi to the gold souk, marveling at the sparkling palaces. Bahrain reminded her of Disneyland. Everything was new and white and clean, at least on the boulevards. She could see alleys where things didn't look quite so bright, where black shapeless women, like clumsily wrapped fruit, toiled along carrying shopping bags or infants. But the taxi sped on, the driver touting this shop and that, handing back cards and brochures, telling them how cheaply they could buy. Gold, perfumes, dresses, rugs, brassware, art.

She slowly became aware thirty dollars wouldn't go very far. She'd had the rest of it sent home in her allotment. It wasn't a lot, but now she was in a combat zone it was tax free. The navy made a big deal out of the combat zone exclusion, it was like a fifteen percent pay raise, they told her.

The driver dropped them in a big parking lot surrounded on three sides by buildings and on the fourth by the highway, on the other side of which was the Gulf. Ina led them back between the buildings, most of which seemed to be banks, into shop-lined streets that quickly narrowed until they couldn't walk abreast. Insurance brokers, barbers, electronics stores, grocers, food booths with meat sizzling on skewers. The ground floors had the kind of pull-down security grating you saw in the States in bad neighborhoods. The air smelled like spices and hot grease and exhaust from the mopeds that kept racketing by.

She slowly realized they were the only women back here. The other pedestrians were all men. Small, fine-boned Arabs in robes who smiled at them as they slipped by. Others, darker, rougher-looking, in work clothes, turned to call out foreign phrases, or sometimes, pieces of movie English. "Wankers," Ina muttered. Lourdes looked scared. But Ina cruised ahead like a battleship, large and fair and with her big legs unabashedly bare in her shorts, and the men glared at her but edged aside.

They found an enclosed mall that was an Alpine-aired wonderland after the heat and exhaust of the alleys. It was almost like being in a nice mall at home, except the signs were in Arabic and French and Italian as well as English, and now they were surrounded by women. They bargained for perfume and clothes, and had tabbouleh and falafel with flat hot bread and jasmine tea at a noisy crowded restaurant.

She fingered ancient jewelry the shopgirl told her was
Bedouin. In the dress shops the Arab women laid their dark
cloaks aside. Exquisite lovely women, trying on expensive
European fashions, they eyed the Americans and slowly
turned away. Ina tried on dress after dress. She chattered like
a magpie. Lourdes kept complaining how expensive things
were. Cobie almost bought an Italian linen outfit but when
she went to pay found she'd mixed up dinars with dollars.
The price wasn't thirty dollars, it was almost a hundred. She
gave it back reluctantly to the girl, and one of the sleek
women said something in Arabic to the others, who giggled.
Then smiled sweetly at her, seeing she'd heard them.

"Come on, let's get out of here," she told Ina.

"Just a minute, I want to check out these scarves."

"We'll be outside. Come on, Lourdes."

When Ina came out, they walked along the waterfront
road, looking at the flower stands. They saw another mall,
but Cobie said, "I'm sick of shopping. I can't afford to buy
any of this crap anyway."

"All right, how about dinner?"

They agreed on what they wanted: a nice restaurant
where they could listen to music while they ate, where
somebody would wait on them. Somehow that last part was
important. That they wouldn't have to stand in line holding
fiberglass trays. Just the memory of it made her sick: the
grade B meat thick with fat and gristle, the watered-down
vegetables cooked to mushiness. Midrats, the leftover meat
from lunch or dinner, and hot dogs. Always hot dogs. Then
they'd find a nightclub, and have some fun.

The Gulf Gate was on the waterfront, with a pillared entrance, its name over it in blue light in English and Arabic.
Mercedes and Rollses and white limousines in front of it.
The doormen wore red uniforms and fezzes like in a movie.
They hovered outside till they got up enough courage to go
in. Then they sailed in together, talking loudly to cover their
nervousness. They followed Arabic music into a room deco-

rated like a seraglio. It was called the Scherezade Night
Club. "This is it," Ina said. "There should be some guys
from the ship here."

"Do we *want* to see the guys from the ship?"

The maitre d' led them to a table. Ina asked if there'd be a
band, and he said it was early; they could sit and have drinks
till it started. Ina ordered a Fosters and lime. Lourdes said
she'd have that, too. Cobie started to order a daiquiri, then
remembered how wrecked she'd gotten on them in Palma.
She changed her order to a vodka and orange juice, light on
the vodka.

They nursed them, figuring they were going to be expensive, and after a while the band started, a local combo called
Tweet Tweet. She thought they sounded like a garage band
back home.

Ina spotted other girls from the ship and waved and they
came over. They pulled their chairs apart to let them in. Then
some guys came in, too, but they sat on the other side of the
room. An Italian asked Lourdes to dance. She looked
alarmed and shook her head no. So then he asked Cobie. He
was a good dancer, but he started feeling her up while they
were walking back to the table, and she told him to get lost.

They started talking about what was going on aboard the
ship. Who was having a fling with who, from the one-night
stands to the deep friendships, from the innocent, fantasy
crushes to the full-blown affairs. About the rumors about the
CO and the XO. One girl said they were always together in
his stateroom with the door closed, and when Hotchkiss
came out, she looked rumpled and sweaty.

A girl from Operations said, "I hear there's this one girl
down in engineering, she's like the department whore. If she
finds out some other woman has a crush on one of the guys,
she goes after him. That's so pathetic ... Her name's
Cobie ... Do y'all know who I'm talking about?"

They must have guessed they'd said something wrong,
because not long after, they had to go. Cobie sat with her
teeth clenched. She'd always liked gossip as much as any-

body, but now she wondered how much was made up by evil
people. Sharpened like a dagger, and passed along till it
reached the person it was meant to kill. God damn Patryce.

"Ooh. Look over there," said Ina. Cobie followed her
gaze reluctantly, figuring she was trying to jolly her up, but
still sucked in her breath.

Settling at the table next to them were the two most stun-
ning women she'd ever seen. One brunette, the other blond.
Their heels were high, their posture aristocratic, their
makeup and hair professionally perfect, their bone structure
lovely, their dresses, as they pulled off sheer silk scarves, incredibly revealing of the slender yet curvaceous bodies beneath. Diamonds sparkled. They sat laughing, heads
together, as if they had not a care in the world.

"What language is that?" Lourdes whispered.

"I think it's Russian," Ina whispered back.

The Americans stared enviously. For a little while Cobie
had felt beautiful, as if life might hold someone who'd ap-
preciate her. Now she looked at her hands with sudden clar-
ity, as if these women had sharpened her vision.

Her nails were short and ragged, though she'd done what
she could with an emery board. The one on her little finger
was an ugly purple, it was coming off, she'd smashed it
grabbing for a handhold when the ship rolled and she nearly
went down a ladder backward. A burn mark was livid on her
left arm. She'd bumped an unlagged piece of starting bleed
air piping. It'd burned the shit out of her, she'd probably always have the scar. . . . She had calluses on her palms, and
under the polish on her nails she knew there was a black rim
of dirt and grease.

Suddenly she felt common and work-worn, dressed in
ugly cheap clothes. Her friends looked drab and intimidated.
They didn't belong in this sophisticated nightclub.

She was putting her hand on Lourdes's, about to suggest
they go, when the waiter bowed over their table, holding a
bottle wrapped in a white napkin. "From the gentlemen in
the corner," he said.

"Gentlemen?" said Ina hopefully.

The waiter twisted a teaspoonful into a glass and handed it to her. It was intensely sour. "It's delicious," she said, and he poured it all around and left the bottle on the table.

That must have been a signal, because other waiters brought more chairs, and suddenly three men were with them. Their business suits were dark gray or blue, it was hard to tell in the dim flickering. At first she thought they were Spanish. One sat with Lourdes, one with Ina. The man who pulled his chair up to hers was about forty, with light skin and a round face and mustache and a little beard. He looked as if he'd been drinking, but he wasn't drunk. The ones with Ina and Lourdes didn't seem to speak much English, but hers said, "So, where are you girls from?"

"We're from America."

"The United States? You don't look American."

"Well, we are, love," said Ina, in her best North London accent. He looked at her, at Lourdes; then grinned and snapped his fingers in the air. The waiters came running, and he rapped out orders. "My name's Hassan, but you can call me Harry," he said, turning back to her. "This is Ajeel. This big lug here, he's Jamaal."

She told him her name and Ina's and Lourdes's, and they all shook hands. "So, what brings you to sunny Bahrain?" he said.

"We're off a ship."

"The cruise ship?"

"No, the destroyer."

He looked confused again. "You're what, the wives of the crew?"

"We *are* the crew, love," Ina shouted at him. She got loud after she had a couple of drinks, but it was a happy, rollicking loud. "Part of it anyway. So what do you do to keep the money rolling in?"

Harry said they worked in one of the ministries over on the mainland. Ina asked why they were drinking scotch if they were from Saudi. They laughed. Harry said, "We drink for the benefits, not for the evil. No one's perfect. Are you perfect, Ina?"

"Lord love you, far from it."

"Allah, *subhanahu wa ta'ala*, does not expect perfection. He is forgiving and merciful. Tomorrow I will repent. As for now," he snapped his fingers and held up the empty bottle, "I will find the joy that life offers me. This is the wisdom of the poets, not the prophets." He added something long and rhythmic. The others listened, then raised their glasses. Poetry, Cobie assumed, and couldn't help being impressed even though she hadn't understood it. "So, what about you?" he asked her.

"What about me, what?"

"What do you do on this ship? It's a navy ship, you said?"

"That's right. I fix the engines." Might as well make it simple.

"Now, that's interesting. That's something I'd like to see, someone who looks like you fixing an engine. Are you married, Cobie? Do you have a boyfriend on the ship?"

She said she didn't, and this seemed to be the right answer as far as he was concerned. The food came, platters of sweet things, dates, cakes, pastries, chocolate. She caught the Russian women looking. Now *they* looked envious. Not of the men. Of the chocolate. "Do you know them?" she asked Harry.

"Who? Them? That is Masha and Viktoria. They're here every night."

"They live here? At the hotel?"

"Them? They're whores," he said, giving her a funny look, as if it was obvious. And looking again, maybe it was. But then what did that tell him about the three of them?

He asked if she wanted to dance. He was even better than the Italian, and she started to enjoy herself. The vodka and wine were getting to her, but she was having fun. He stepped back and did a whirling step like in *Fiddler on the Roof*. He wasn't actually bad-looking, with the dark hair and the black mustache and beard.

They danced until she had to quit, then sat close, panting, hot. He put his face next to hers, and for a moment she thought he was going to kiss her. She was turning her chin, trying to angle it so he could, when he muttered into her ear, "Shall I get a room?"

"Shall you what? I'm sorry—the band's so loud."

"Shall I get a room? For you, and your friends? I'll send a man to the desk."

She started guffawing. Ina squinted at her. "I don't think so," she said. Masha and Viktoria were leaving, two men helping them up to teeter off on those spiky heels.

"No? I thought you wouldn't."

"Thanks for the offer, but no thanks," she said, brushing her hair back. Whoa! The room was blurring at the edges. She rattled the ice and crunched some in her teeth. To cool off.

"Then let's go for a ride."

"A ride?"

"Sure. We'll go see the Bahrain fort. It's a knockout by moonlight. We can leave your friends here."

She said she didn't think she ought to go alone. He said great idea, why didn't they all go? And it didn't take much persuading. When they looked around for the waiter Harry said it was taken care of, they shouldn't worry about it.

She stopped dead when she saw the car. It was a block long, and glossy black. The driver was holding the door for them. She'd never been in a car like this. Ina muttered, "My Lord, he's a prince for sure." They looked at each other, and Ina pulled her in to whisper, "They've got guns."

"*What?*"

"I don't know about Harry, but I felt it dancing with Ajeel. He's either carrying a gun, or he's got a stiffie in a bloody weird place."

"A bodyguard?"

"I think they're both bodyguards."

"Then who is he? Really?"

Lourdes looked scared. They traded glances, daring each other. Finally they got in.

The night wasn't dark, it was wonderful. The highway lights blurred, and the lights of the city sank away as they sped along a coast road, then turned inland. The open fields were deserted under the rising moon. Ajeel and Jamaal didn't say much, but Harry talked a blue streak, telling them they should come here for the Friday bazaar, it was more colorful and truly Arabic than anything in Manama City. The girls fell silent, and Cobie felt a little scared: Where were they going? Why were the other guys so quiet? Were they a rich man's guards, or was there something going on she didn't know about? But just then, as she thought about asking who he really was, the limo slowed.

They turned in beneath a shadowy form that proved to be an immense mud-walled tower, dark except for accent lights around its base. Gardens spread around it, she could smell the flowers, and spray irrigation hissed. The silent men in the dark suits trailed them as they strolled. Harry told them the history of what he called the Qual'at al Bahrain. The eleventh century. The sixteenth century. Portuguese. Arabs. English. Seven distinct and separate foundations under it, dating back five thousand years.

In its shadow he pulled her into a niche he must have known was there. Because one moment they were walking in the moonlight and the next they were alone together in the sudden dark.

When he lifted his face from hers she could hardly breathe. From the moonlight, from his powerful hands, the scent of his skin. A lot of cologne, but it didn't seem effeminate. Quite the opposite . . . It was the first time she'd ever kissed a man with a beard. She shivered, both from fear and sudden desire.

"Let's go to my apartment," he said into her ear. "Let me show you how beautiful you are."

"It sounds great, Harry. You seem like a nice guy. . . ."

"All right, let's go."

"Cobie," Lourdes hissed warningly. *"Cobie!"*

She suddenly realized how vulnerable they were. It was romantic, but she had no idea where they were, other than that they were alone, with someone who seemed important but whom they really didn't know and two armed men who'd never said much at all.

Maybe he felt that, too—that they'd trusted him too far. Because he said lightly, "No dice? I'm striking out here?"

"She's right, we—have to get back to the ship." Not the exact truth, but everybody knew sailors had to get back to their ship.

"Well, then. Shall I just drive you back?"

"That would be nice," she said, exhaling. Feeling relieved. And at the same time, disappointed.

On the way back. Harry talked about how he had to be back in Riyadh in a day or two. She thought he was taking them back to the hotel. Maybe he had one more pass left in him. If he did, she didn't know what she'd say. His skin felt so good, so warm, rough and smooth at the same time. Soon she'd be back on the ship. Back with grouchy old Bendt and the Porn King and bitchy Patryce. Back in her too-hot bunk under the intake, with two dozen other women crammed around her.

She pulled his face down to hers. And felt his hand slide under the sundress. She buried her face in his neck, starting to lose it as his fingers burrowed inward, found sweetness and began to probe and stroke until she arched against the seat and drew a long shuddering breath.

The next time she looked out they were back at the base, slowing for the gate. When she sat up and told him the guard wouldn't let the car in without a sticker, he'd have to let them off here, he spoke to the driver and they stopped a few yards away. He waited as she pulled her dress down and got halfway put back together. Then bent forward and kissed her hand, then her cheek. "Good night, my sailor," he said.

For a minute she wavered. His bringing her back meant she could trust him. She almost got back into the car. She was shivering, her legs almost gave way as she stood. "Good night," she said, backing away.

The black car glided off. They stood looking after it until, after a little while, it blended with the night.

24

Aisha huddled, crushed among the bulks of armed men, nothing but her own sweat cooling her under the heavy thick Kevlar. She had the SIG in a holster today, and she was wearing black gear. Tactical gear, the harness and elbow pads and entry gloves that looked cool in movies but were heavy and hot in the close air of the truck. Unfortunately, the vest wouldn't stop anything with more energy than a pistol bullet. And the rest of it, or so she'd heard from other agents, might once have had some intimidation value, but now just marked you as a target.

Fortunately, she wouldn't be first through the door, or even, probably, twentieth. The three panel trucks sat with engines and lights off near the Makarqah Quarter, the oldest part of town, where a truck was too wide to go. Others were circling around from the south, creeping through the sleeping streets until they, too, would be in position. Together, they held thirty of the SIS's SWAT-equivalent Special Action Teams. The raid was timed for 0430. She tilted her wrist.

0415.

She shifted, trying to bump out room to breathe. Beside her she smelled Diehl's heavy cigar funk. Across from her, the shadowed outline of an observer from the embassy.

General Gough was in the command truck, with General Bucheery. It looked the same as the others, but the sides and top were fiberglass, not metal, so the comm gear would work without telltale antennas. He'd said a few dry words at the midnight briefing, about how essential it was to work together. Bucheery had praised the interrogation team that had developed the information on which the morning's raid was based. Parts of his remarks were in Arabic, about how unpleasant tasks had sometimes to be performed, to save life and maintain order.

She didn't like to think about what that meant. She was afraid the "unpleasant task" had involved the woman in Shawki's house. The NCIS couldn't get physical, but the host agencies they worked with were not always so concerned with the rules. The general went on to say that by "intense interrogation"—her mind flinched away again—of Shawki's wife, and working with what Aisha had caught on the phone, the SIS had taken one Rahimullah bin Jun'ad into custody.

Bucheery said bin Jun'ad, a would-be mullah with ties to radical groups in Egypt and Afghanistan, had been "persuaded" to give up the location of the stolen explosives, and other information about a plot to attack a United States installation in Bahrain. Bin Jun'ad had confessed to providing local recruits, but the actual leader was a shadowy figure he knew only as the Doctor. The Doctor was the primary goal of today's raid, along, of course, with the explosives and any weapons the group had managed to assemble or import.

Someone in the truck farted. The smell lay close and rank. She hated the idea of having to breathe in the actual molecules that had been in someone's lower gut a moment before. . . . She tilted her wrist again.

0420.

A few minutes later the word must have come through, because the back doors opened and the crush lessened as men jumped out. Quietly. No one spoke. She dropped to the dew-damp asphalt with them. Took position in line, and began jogging down the street, deeper into the ancient reticulation of the old city. No streetlights, just stars, straight up, a

narrow band of them between the tops of two- and three-
story buildings that lined the street with no setback whatso-
ever, in fact many with the upper floors levered out over the
frontages till they almost met. The muted crackle of a radio
ahead, and the scuff of boots. The distant sound of a television, on very early.

Sweating under the heavy vest, with someone treading on
her heels, she took deep breaths, trying to steady the accelerating hammer of her pulse. Tipping her wrist back, glancing
down at the luminescent hands.

0425.

Dan woke suddenly in pitch darkness. For a moment he
didn't know where he was. Where was the little red light that
marked the phone, the faintly illuminated circle of the
closed porthole. Then he remembered. He was in the in-port
stateroom, they were working on the toilet in his at-sea
cabin, and he'd shifted down here. He succeeded at last in
resolving the direction of the bathroom. Then groped his
way back to the too-short bed, wadded the pillow, lay back.

And stared into the darkness.

Blair had called from the States. A one-minute call from
an army base before taking off for the funerals. She didn't
sound as if she missed him. Didn't sound as if she was thinking about him at all, as if calling him was just another thing
she had to get done. He replayed the last conversation they'd
had. Then the days before it. Almost all of it, yeah, nice. For
a while they'd recaptured what had brought them together in
the beginning.

But the navy was tough on marriages. He could count on
the fingers of one hand the classmates who were still with
their June Week brides. Damn few . . . Claudia was having
trouble, too . . . and now he was starting to hear the same
lyrics from Blair. A house, settling down, building something. What, like she was building a career in the executive
branch? Compared with politics, the navy was as secure a
career as the post office. At least, since he'd made O-5, he
was guaranteed retirement, unless he really and truly

screwed the pooch. Which he'd almost done a couple of times already. . . . His thoughts spun on, a perpetual motion machine whirring in the dark.

He worried again about their exposed position, but not with the same intensity as when they'd first shifted out. What had the Senior called it? "Sitting here with our thumb up our ass." But nothing had happened. He wondered if he should knock off the boat patrols. It soaked up a lot of man-hours. At least Schaad had looked at the quick reaction team procedures again, and they'd streamlined the procedures for getting weapons and ammo on deck. The trouble was, the easier you made that sort of material to get to, the fewer safeguards you had against theft and misuse. They were both security issues, but heightening one meant lessening the other.

He didn't want to think about that. Or about Hotchkiss, or the crew, or any of the hundreds of other things that occupied his mind when he was vertical. God! Couldn't he just sleep! He rolled impatiently and socked the pillow. Tried to breathe slowly and think of some pleasant scene. Some pleasant scene . . .

He hadn't been able to spend much time with Nan when she was little. But now and then he'd read his daughter to sleep. Then lain with her head on his chest, her breathing deep and regular. And gradually his own slowed, and his thoughts began a slow spin into the freewheeling illogical vividness that preceded dream.

He was almost there when he remembered: Today was his admiral's mast.

His eyes popped open again as his brain surged back to battle speed. COMDESRON 50, Palzkill, the admiral, 1400. Why couldn't they at least make it early, why did it have to ruin his whole day? Would they actually relieve him? It was possible. CO's lost their ships every day. Well, not every day, but it happened. Christ, he couldn't worry about that. In fact, it might not be so bad, getting relieved. No, he didn't believe that. Christ, *why* couldn't he get to sleep!

0430. He lay totally awake, staring into the darkness with eyes wide open.

• • •

It looked to Aisha like all the others, a three-story building
on a street lined with darkened shop fronts, the steel knitting
of antitheft gratings. With the noiselessness of shadows, silhouettes disappeared one after the other into a door. The
translator said in a whisper they were headed for the third
floor. That was where the Qari bin Jun'ad said the cell met,
where they slept. The first floor was a shoemaker's.

The Americans stood next to one of the shops, trying to
stay inconspicuous, or as inconspicuous as you could get in
black gear. Aisha caught the twitch of a curtain above her,
barely visible dark eyes taking in the activity below. Then a
shade came down.

A thunder crack and flash shattered the darkness. The
third-floor windows illuminated again to another flash-bang
grenade. The embassy guy started forward, but the translator
got him in time. "Not yet, sir," he said, pressing him back.
Diehl had his big revolver out, holding it down along his leg.

High above, a window slid up. A black-suited figure she
only recognized as Major Yousif when he spoke called
down, sounding not pleased, and in English: "The area's
clear. Observers may come up."

The apartment was bare, as if no one had lived there for a
long time. It was small, low ceilings spotted with age.

And maybe they'd learned something at the house in
Muharraq, or maybe someone smarter was in charge, because they weren't tearing the place up. The entry squad was
filing out, submachine guns pointed at the ceiling. Evidence
technicians in coveralls and rubber gloves were taking their
places: opening the doors, closet and bathroom, starting to
take apart the air conditioner.

She stood looking around, trying to let her senses work,
if possible something beneath her senses, trying to kick-start
any intuition she might possess. She could still smell them.
Maybe from the old mattresses on the floor that showed
where bodies had pressed them not long before. Maybe

from the stale grease and sesame smell of cooking. She went into the bathroom. They didn't clean up after themselves, that was plain. Pubic hairs clumped in the bathtub drain. Yellow spots by the bowl. Sticky twists of food wrappers. But then, being a terrorist didn't indicate a high level of concern for others. And as traditional Muslim men, they'd be used to having someone, almost always a woman, to clean up after them.

One of the techs came in, glanced at her, saw the pubes, and began gathering them up, putting them into a plastic envelope. She thought he really ought to be using paper, for better evidence preservation, but he didn't work for her.

"They weren't coming back here," she said.

"So where are they?" Garfield said, behind her.

She shrugged. "That's a good question. Left the country, I hope."

"For where?"

She didn't know, so she didn't answer. She went back into the main room, to find it deserted. Then into the bedroom, and stopped, looking around.

Scraps of green-insulated wire, gray plastic wrap, hand tools, empty duct tape rolls littered a folding table. The techs were working their way through the wastebasket. On the floor: flyers and magazines. She picked one up. It was titled, in Arabic, *The Battlefield: The Safest Place on Earth*. There were other flyers, jihad material, some of it the same sort of thing she saw now and then in mosques back in the United States. And what looked like printouts, although she saw nothing like a printer or a computer.

She went slowly around the room, stepping around the techs, not touching anything. Phone. Copy machine. Fax machine. With a pencil, she lifted the flap of the copy machine. Sloppy people forgot things. Left originals in copiers, for example.

The glass was vacant, but she saw something behind the machine.

The paper had fallen between the copy tray, where it

came out, and the wall. It lay curled up just below where the
fax was plugged in. Above it the other outlet was occupied
by a square plastic box she recognized as a surge suppressor.
But nothing was plugged into it. There was a vacant space on
the tabletop beside the copy machine. A square space free of
the dust and trash and shed hair that covered every other surface in the apartment.

She glanced behind her, to make sure no one was looking, and reached down. Got the paper in her nails, and
tweezed it up into the light.

"Somebody's been at work here," Diehl said, behind her.
She nodded wordlessly, examining the paper. It didn't make
sense. Curving lines and straight lines. A little crude drawing of a ship, childlike, with pointed prow and matchstick
guns pointing up.

"That's the harbor," he said, looking over her shoulder.

"Our harbor?"

"Minas Salman. Right there—see? There's the inner harbor, where the fishing fleet docks. There's our pier, at the
ASU, I mean the NSA."

"And the ship?" she murmured.

It must have hit them both simultaneously, everything
coming together, the deserted apartment, the scraps of wire,
the missing explosives, the crude chart. Because she heard
him suck his breath in, too.

Dan was shaving when the rapid bong of the general quarters alarm echoed through the ship. At the same moment the
phone went off. He snatched it off the hook. "Captain."

"Sir, Hotchkiss. We just got a call there might be trouble
headed our way."

"What? Another storm?"

The 1MC was saying over her voice, "Security alert, security alert. Away the security alert team and backup alert
force."

"Maybe worse. A boat full of dynamite. Meet me on the
bridge."

The bridge was maybe not the best place to be communications-wise. But at least from there they could see. That went through his mind as he was pounding up ladders, tearing along passageways filled with others who when they saw him coming flattened against the bulkheads and yelled, "Captain coming through."

He burst into the pilothouse to find Hotchkiss issuing orders to heave around on the anchor, man up all deck weapons stations, and set Condition Zebra throughout the ship.

The first order of business was to verify the warning. He asked the man who'd taken the call exactly what he'd heard. Someone identifying himself as Petty Officer Rossetti of NCIS had called direct to the ship on Channel 16, warning them a small craft with a bomb aboard might be on its way out to them. One minute later substantially the same word came over the Harbor Control net. Dan was digesting this and searching the harbor surface when in the gray predawn the bow of a small boat appeared at the exit from the inner harbor, at the gap between the stone jetties that stretched out from Muharraq Island and Juffair.

"Bridge, forward lookout: dhow coming out of the harbor."

"Bridge, Mount 51: acquired visual on target."

"Mount 51, hold fire, and keep that breech clear," Dan said. The eastern suburbs were clearly visible beyond the emerging boat. He could not fire his main gun; any miss would ricochet over the inner harbor directly into those crowded houses. The missiles were useless, too. He was limited to the chain guns and .50s. He went for the 21MC. "TAO, Captain."

"TAO Camill here."

"Herb, I want weapons tight, all weapons tight for the moment. We're in very close quarters here. I want you working the net for more info on this threat." He let up on the lever and went on talking, to Hotchkiss this time. "Where's our patrol?"

A pointing arm. "Two hundred yards out toward the entrance."

"Pull him in here ASAP. M60s and small arms, flak jackets and helmets. Call away the Blue and Green Teams and get the other RHIB in the water as soon as possible."

Binoculars up again, he saw the boat had separated from the causeway, was headed in their direction. Movement was visible behind it, sticks and hulls . . .

With a sudden sense of doom he realized it was the fishing fleet. They were getting under way. As they did every morning. The lofty-prowed, colorful, slow-chugging flotilla that fed the island. That before first sight of sun left the sheltered inner harbor, plowing southward, past where *Horn* lay anchored, then wheeling to thread out into the Gulf and their day's work. As they had every workday morning for no doubt many centuries from an island that had once been the main source of pearls for the world. But now one might not be what it seemed. Detonated close in, partially under water, it wouldn't take much explosive to blow in a ship's bottom.

It was diabolical, and for a moment he grudgingly admired the cunning of the mind that had conceived it. Striking beneath the weapons and sensors of the superior technology. Using his own unwillingness to inflict collateral damage as a shield.

It was time to see how far that shield extended. "I need harbor control."

"Select five, sir."

Holding the handset, he forced himself to speak with deliberation. "Minas Salman Harbor control. This is *Horn* actual, over."

"Harbor control, over."

"I've received two warnings about an explosive-laden small craft bound for my location. We are at general quarters and am heaving around to short stay."

"Roger, copy that."

"Request permission to fire on any dhow that steers for this ship. Small arms and twenty-five-millimeter only."

He figured it would take them a moment or two, but when

there was no answer at all, he clicked transmit again. "Harbor Control, *Horn;* did you copy my last?"

"*Horn,* this is Harbor Control." Furious voices in the background; then "*Horn,* this is Harbor Control. We cannot give you permission to fire within the harbor."

"This is *Horn.* Intend to fire only on craft clearly making a hostile approach."

"This is Harbor Control. Sir, understand your situation, but we cannot clear you to fire within the harbor."

He savagely switched the selector to what he hoped was a direct circuit to the squadron. "Flash, flash. COMDESRON Fifty, COMDESRON Fifty, this is USS *Horn* in Minas Salman Harbor. Over."

"First dhow is making its approach."

"RHIB's alongside, transferring weapons."

"Who's talking to it?" Dan snapped. A talker stepped up, radio in hand, looking scared. Dan told him, "I want them between us and the dhow traffic. One hundred yards off the starboard side. Weapons loaded and *clearly visible.* Understand? Pass that at once."

"Sir, COMDESRON Fifty SDO on the horn."

A young voice, and he felt his heart sink. The SDO was the staff duty officer, not the commodore. Most likely some duty jaygee. Dan said rapidly, hoping to carry the guy with him before he had time to think, "This is CO *Horn.* NCIS and base ops warn me a small craft loaded with explosives is en route my posit. I suspect it may be one of the dhows in the fishing fleet. They are steaming in my direction now. If one swerves out of line, I need permission to fire, and I won't have time to ask for it when it happens."

A hesitation. "So what are you asking for, sir?"

"As per your rules of engagement, I'm requesting clearance to fire on any threatening contact."

"If it's threatening, sir, you don't need my approval."

"Yes, I do. It won't look any different from the other dhows. I'll have to take it out based on my best guess." He wished he hadn't used that word, tried again, "I mean, on the basis of my professional estimate of its level of threat based on its maneuvers, its apparent intent."

"Sir, I don't think I'm the one who can give you that."

"Is the commodore available?"

"No, sir. He's not here."

"Can you get him on the line? Or on a land line?"

"I'll try, sir." Clearly relieved at having a course of action pointed out to him, the voice signed off.

"I'm going to full self-protection," Dan told Hotchkiss. "How's that anchor coming?"

"It's up and down. But if we get under way, where are we going?"

He put his binoculars on the lead dhow again while he pondered that question. She was right, there was nowhere a ship the draft of a Spruance-class could go in these restricted, shallow roads except out to sea. And the path to seaward led through the same bottleneck channel the marching ant line was now bending toward. At least where they lay, an attacker would have to swing out of queue toward them. They'd have a few minutes to decide what to do as it crossed the three hundred some-odd yards of open water to where *Horn* swung to her shortened anchor. Not to ask permission. He'd given up on that. The rules of engagement would serve only to make sure his ass was the one to be fried if he decided wrong and shot up a boatload of confused, rudder-jammed, curious, or even just momentarily inattentive Bahraini fishermen.

"Where's the second boat?" he shouted. "I want *Fear* in the water. Right fucking *now!*"

In the hangar, Marchetti was suiting up as fast as he could yank gear on. The sling slipped off his shoulder, the Mossberg clattered to the deck. He grabbed it and reached for his life vest.

Ensign Cassidy came up from below, carrying the radio, and grabbed his .45 from the gunner's mate. Gold Team was suited and armed, as fast as they'd ever mustered. The gunner's mate handed Marty a handful of cartridges. He dumped them into a cargo pocket and swept a look down the line. Crack Man, Sasquatch, Lizard, Snack Cake, Deuce. The Old Gold. Amarillo and Turd Chaser were dead, lost on the Iraqi tanker. He had a new guy, Showboat, lanky and gangly, still learning the ropes. And . . . goddamn it . . . the supernumerary. Wilson. Spider Woman. There she fucking was.

"We set, Senior?"

"Yessir." All right, he didn't have the time to argue it. "Into the boat, you melonheads," he yelled, and ran, boots pounding, out onto the deck.

Dawn light, light wind. The boatswain was beckoning from the quarter, the bright orange plastic steps of the jacob's ladder already rigged. He grabbed the top rail, swung over, went down fast but careful and dropped into the bow. The bowhook grabbed him and pushed him aft and he yelled, "Next man."

The last guy dropped in, the engine gunned, and they moved out, rocking under the impulse of the prop.

Cassidy clambered over bodies back to where Marty clung by one arm, trying to keep the shotgun from sliding off with the other. "Here's the plan," he yelled. "They want the sixty in the bow. Everybody locked and loaded. Three hundred yards off the ship. One of these dhows swerves out of line, we fire a burst across his bow. If he keeps coming, they'll designate him to the twenty-five-millimeters. So we better be ready to haul balls out of the line of fire."

"Roger that," he said. The coxswain nodded, mouth hard, and reached down to pull his flak jacket out from under the console. Marty wiggled forward and got Crack Man and Sasquatch set up with the gun. Then went aft again, looking back at the ship for the other RHIB. He saw it alongside, saw another M60 being handed down. Good, they wouldn't be the only ones out here.

The Johnsons slowed, dropping to a ringing note like a free-running table saw. The boat coasted, then took up a slow pitch and tilt. He clung to the console and looked around the harbor, then back at the ship again.

Horn lay like a gray island, and behind her was the city,

and to either side the city. Her anchor chain straight up and down. What he didn't relish was that both the chain guns and the five-inch were pointed at him. The fifties were manned, too, heavy machine guns mounted high on the ship, one on the bridge wing, near the searchlight mount, the other on top of the helo hangar. Beside each gunner stood a phone talker with binoculars looking right at him.

He turned, to see the dhow approaching.

It came on unhurriedly, rusty dented prow parting the water into a modest ripple of foam. These were not high-speed boats. But with their swelling midships, their broad beams, they looked like good haulers. Of fish, or of less innocent cargo. Its hull was russet, as if painted with Rustoleum primer. A white prow extension, like the bow dragon on a Viking longboat, pointed in his direction. Under a stumpy mast amidships was a rack of very long, thick bamboo poles. Diesel exhaust blew downwind. Fucker was headed right for them. He went forward and knelt on the floorboards and dug his grip into Sasquatch's shoulder. "The first burst goes across his bow. Five seconds after that, he doesn't swing away, fire through the pilothouse windows, then sweep the rest of the deck."

"Roger that, Senior Chief."

"Riflemen, get ready to sweep the deck. Light up any melonhead who pops up. Okay, lock and load."

The rattle and clack of bolts and cartridges slamming home, then they steadied their sights on the oncoming prow. Only two hundred yards away now. It did not seem to have the slightest intent of going anywhere else than right over them. If anything, it was increasing speed, the putt-putting of the engine coming clearly across the harbor to the tensely waiting team in the rocking inflatable.

Aisha clung to the dash as the Chevy went faster and faster, finally hitting a hundred on the expressway leading toward the harbor. Ahead sirens warbled, lights flashed, Mercedeses and Toyotas pulled over as the convoy bore down. The trucks of security troops were going even faster than they were.

"You're sure you got through to the ship?" Diehl said anxiously, twisting around in the front seat. For some reason she didn't get to drive when it was a question of getting there fast. Garfield had grabbed the wheel without a word, Diehl slid in shotgun, leaving her in the back. They were mad she'd found the map, not them. That the newest agent, a colored girl at that, had managed to pick up the one piece of paper that told exactly what was going on.

"I didn't try to get through to the ship. I called Rossetti."

"Good call. Kinky knows what to do."

"They're calling their navy people, too, or coast guard, whatever they have," Garfield said, pulling around a cement truck, then stepping on the gas again. "One way or another, they'll get the word."

"Unless it's already too late," Diehl moaned. Aisha glanced at him. His cheeks were spotted pink and white. She hoped he wasn't going to have some kind of attack. He was staring through the windshield, a sheen of sweat where his hair must have been when he was young.

The trucks came to a straight stretch. The traffic police stood at the intersections, batons extended to block cross traffic. Buildings flashed by, avenues flashed by, startled faces on the sidewalks flashed by. The needle crept up again as Garfield floored it. Ninety-five. One hundred. One hundred and ten, the engine roaring, the wind tearing by. She leaned forward. "Tune the radio to four-forty."

"What's that?"

She couldn't believe he didn't know. "Their police frequency, Bob. If we want to know what's going on up ahead—"

"Yeah, but what's the use? We can't understand what they're—oh." He made a face. "I guess you could, though. Yeah. Four-forty?"

The voices overlay one another, cut into each other's transmissions. She gathered police were already in the dock area. Someone was asking if they could radio all the dhows, order them to turn back. Another man replying most of them didn't carry radios. Then a voice came through clear and strong.

"What's he saying there?" Bob wanted to know.

She said, slowly, "He says there's no way they can check all those boats. And anyway, they've already sailed."

Dan watched the leader come on, fingers tightening on the glasses. It did not slow or alter course. Beside him Hotchkiss said, "Twenty-fives and fifties manned, loaded, and tracking."

She sounded collected, and he was glad because he didn't feel that way himself. This had all the earmarks of a bad situation. He couldn't keep his attention both on the oncoming dhow and on *Horn.*

Nor, he suddenly remembered, did he need to. "XO, take over getting the engines started, take the conn!"

"This is Commander Hotchkiss, I have the conn!"

A chorus of acknowledgments from helm, quartermasters, boat-swain's mates, officers. As it died, the talker said, "Main control requests permission to start main engines."

Hotchkiss, crisply: "Start them ASAP. Verify ITC at 'stop.'"

"ITC verified at 'stop.' Engine room reports engines started, ready to respond to all bells."

"Very well."

"Rudder test complete: I have rudder control from the bridge. Bring in the anchor, Captain?"

Dan nodded. As desperately as he wanted to be under way, to have at least the option of choosing where an oncoming boat hit him, he hadn't dared to before he was sure he had power. Being adrift and out of control, possibly on fire, after an explosion close aboard could be much worse than being hit at anchor. He lifted his glasses again, returning his sight to where his attention had never left, the oncoming boat.

Which now, a bare hundred yards short of the waiting RHIB, suddenly put its rudder over. It heeled, tracking around, and steadied on course for the channel entrance, leaving a patch of whirling foam where it had turned.

He eased air out. So that wasn't it . . . then, almost immediately, held the next breath in his throat.

A second dhow had appeared behind it, replacing the first as if popped out of the same mold, like some hellish video game that kept feeding him the same image. The same upswept bow and stern and enclosed pilothouse. The only difference was a blue hull this time. Men stood on the deck, watching him curiously.

He focused, trying to get faces, expressions. If these were fanatical self-immolators, suicide bombers, wouldn't they be overjoyed on the long-awaited day of martyrdom? The bearded visages he scanned looked more like underfed toilers on their way to another exhausting day in the broiling sun. No jolly baseball-hatted guys with coolers of beer here, the kind of fishermen you passed in the channel out of Pascagoula or San Diego. Their clothes were ragged and dirty, their "turbans" rags wrapped around their heads.

Hotchkiss, at his side. "We're under way. Shall I head for the channel exit?"

"No! Back and fill. Just stand fast. Be alert for wind drift and don't get any closer to the shoals."

"Aye, aye."

"Have you got somebody working the radios?"

He meant, to their tactical superiors, the only ones, according to the rules of engagement, who could authorize him to fire on suspicion of attack. Of course, any ship had the right to fire in self-defense. But in U.S. usage, that meant returning rounds once the other side had started the firefight.

In its simplest terms, and as he well knew after their experiences in the Red Sea, ROE interpretation was anything but simple. *Horn* couldn't fire, in the absence of orders from her tactical superior, until a hostile act had been initiated. But what was a "hostile act"? How was making a run with an explosive-laden boat, steered by volunteers, different from launching a torpedo guided by an electronic guidance system?

He knew the answer, and it was unforgiving. Not an eye for an eye, but an even crueler resolution. An eye before he was mutilated himself; a tooth, before his own was knocked out; a life, before his own was taken.

Hotchkiss said, "I've got McCall on the net, trying to get somebody who's willing to make a decision."

"Carry on then. And keep an eye on the bow, the wind's pushing it around."

She said aye, aye, and put the port engine ahead. Giving him time to think next about exactly what he was going to do if one of those dhows marching out, a long line of them visible now behind the first two, *did* sheer out. Putting rounds into a suicide boat, especially the explosive chain-gun shells, might well set off whatever charge it carried. Explosives, the calls had warned, but not what type, or how much.

He discarded that problem with the realization that whatever the charge might be, it'd be better to have it go off a hundred yards away than alongside.

Because an explosion alongside could blow the hull plates in. He had to consider *Horn*'s own cargo, too—Tomahawk boosters, warheads, a magazine full of five-inch shells. If he had a choice, maybe take the explosion aft . . . It'd blow in the engine spaces, most likely sink them, but at least the magazines wouldn't go off.

He hoped. If they did, the navy'd be writing a lot of letters to dependents.

Fear was moving out now toward *Faith,* which bobbed inboard of the widening knuckle where the first dhow had turned. Where the second now approached, seemed to hesitate, then turned as well. Following in its wake, it, too, headed for the hazy, steadily brightening Gulf.

He couldn't just sit here, waiting for the one boat filled with desperate men and high explosive to putt-putt closer, judge their distance, and then, at their leisure and at close range, make their move. There just wasn't enough reaction time. He had to know sooner.

He clicked his channel selector to the boat frequency.

Marchetti was on the radio when the word came over to move on up the line. He saw instantly what the skipper was trying to do. *Fear* was coming out to take their place as goalie. He was sending *Faith* up toward the inner harbor. It would put them at risk, but also push the moment of target identification away from the ship. Which hovered now, stack venting a burble of gas, guns still pointed in his direction. He wondered why they didn't launch the helo, then decided since he was the man on the spot, he'd better stop second-guessing and get his ass in gear. "They want us to head on up this line and check out each dhow as we go by," he told Cassidy.

The boat officer hesitated. "Then what? If we find it?"

"I guess then we try to stop them."

The ensign looked doubtful, but nodded. Marchetti told the coxswain, "Goose her, Coxie. About ten knots, but slow way down as we pass each one."

The dual Johnsons were revving when Cassidy said, "And how about, when we get to that gap in the seawall, where they're coming out, we park ourselves there and cork the rest of them in the harbor? Till the local cops can check them out?"

"Now you're thinking, sir." It was good to see an officer using his head. Maybe he wasn't wasting his time with him. Then he noticed the rounded buttocks of one of the troops, and his eye puzzled for a second before he remembered: *she* was here, too. Well, fuck her . . . from what he was hearing in the goat locker, everybody else had . . . Who'd had the bright idea to put fucking girls on fucking ships anyway. What a boneheaded, melonheaded concept.

"Listen up, Golds. We're gonna run up this line of dinky dhows and check 'em out close range. Eye contact. Look 'em over good. See anything suspicious, weapons, people hiding, we'll haul them over and board. The first hostile move, shoot 'em. *Capisce?* You see a weapon, you shoot first."

The coxswain twisted the wheel, the engines roared, the boat rocked as the wake from dhow number two hit it. Three was coming on, something vaguely cowlike about it as it plodded on its day's routine. Shit, he didn't think ragheads even ate fish. Goat and rice, but not fish. There sure were a lot of boats . . . He pushed speculation away as the coxswain steered in, in, till it looked like they were going to ram the bitch head-on. The oncoming prow wavered, then steadied, obviously deciding to let the smaller RHIB do the dancing. He grabbed the sailor's shoulder. "Don't fucking run us under his bow, Coxie."

"Spitting distance off his starboard side. That close enough?"

"Okay, but no fucking closer, okay?" He pulled sweat off his eyes with his sleeve. The sunlight was burning, bouncing off the flat harbor water. Christ, he should have brought grenades. No, you didn't want to drop a grenade into a boat full of explosive. Pistol and shotgun, hope you cut them down before they got to whatever they used for a trigger. The hull, this one the dull red again, grew, became an iron wall stained with what looked like decades of fish guts and scrapes from the dangling gear. What were those poles for? He blinked sweat away again, cradling the Mossberg in the crook of his arm.

Faith roared slowly closer to the oncoming fisherman, then, throttling back as its bow came abreast, passed it so close aboard spray coned up between the passing hulls and soaked everyone in the RHIB. Arabs yelled angrily down at them. They ignored them, swept past. The coxswain glanced over with a question in his eyes. Marchetti shook his head, pointed ahead. Three boats yet till they reached the seawall. This next looked different. Somehow . . . a dark green hull, white trim, it looked better cared for than the others. He yelled to Cassidy, "This guy's on a better budget."

"Must catch more fish."

"Or just be new," Snack Cake yelled from where he swayed, one arm hooked around a grip rail, other hand clenching the loaded M-14. The flash suppressor swayed over the sea.

The green dhow went by. Marchetti saw nothing suspicious other than the new paint job, the new-looking gear.

The ragheads didn't spend much on their clothes, that was clear. He realized he could smell each boat as it went by, a rancid odor like the cod liver oil capsules he'd had to take when he was a kid. He'd cut one open once and the same stink had welled up.

The next dhow was red again. Must have had a special on red paint. Or else they just slapped primer on and didn't bother with the finish coat. He wondered if he should be putting guys aboard each one as it went by, check them out belowdecks, then get off when they got to *Fear*. No. He didn't have enough men for that, and the following boats would just sheer out around the one he stopped and crank on by.

Red hull checked out, bearded dudes gaping at them as they purred past, passed the smell check, too.

He shook his arms out, realizing his skivvies were sopping with the heat and tension and spray from going right under the boats' counters. Their props kicked up a shower at the stern that douched them as they went by. It felt cool, good. Not so hot getting saltwater in the small arms, but at least his shotgun was marinized. He forced his attention back on the next boat. He had to stay sharp. The guys were depending on him.

"Almost there," Cassidy yelled.

Yeah, they were nearly to the seawall. Waves broke on the tumbled rocks. Another dhow percolated by. He returned the captain's wave, older guy with a gray beard and a cleaner shirt than the rest, with a curt nod.

The throbbing beat of a chopper. An insectile pinpoint coming in from cityward. Not the ship's. Probably the local cops. He twisted his head, made sure the flag was visible on their stern. He didn't want to get taken for the bad guy.

Low decks, scraggly messes of lines, yeah, there were some nets, this boat had a lower freeboard, he just wasn't seeing them before. These guys were scowling back but he didn't think scowls counted. The real bad guys would probably have shit-eating grins. He waved them on, and suddenly they were shit in the middle of the channel entrance, and now he could see them all, *ay, caramba,* dozens of 'em backing and maneuvering, circling, coming for him. The whole fucking fleet was on its way out. Cassidy looked at him, that questioning, open-eyed "hey, what now?" look you got used to from young zeroes. Marchetti yelled, "Coxie, put her broadside and hold her there. Right across the exit. We're the cork, got it?"

Only it didn't work out quite that way.

The Chevy skidded to a halt, just missing a spike barrier the Bahrainis had set up, apparently to protect their own operations from truck bombs. Nice work, she thought . . . except they could have waited for us. The doors slammed open, and the agents were out, guns carefully not drawn. They jogged toward the harbor, holding up their shields and the local IDs General Bucheery had ordered they be issued. They came out on the waterfront, and she found herself face to face with General Gough. Who saluted with the same mix of light-hearted condescension and ironic disdain he always seemed to affect with her. "Sister Aisha. *Sabaah el-khair.* Thanks be to God, you are well and with us."

"The morning is good," she said shortly, then reverted to English for Peter and Bob. "What have you got?"

"I have 'got' three teams going through those dhows which have not yet cast off. And the Harbor Police pursuing those which have already left." Gough waved at the basin. It was filled with a restless throng of small craft, like a bowl of cereal stirred and only slowly coming to rest. Some were still moored, in rafts two and three deep out from the stone and concrete wharf front; others drifted or circled as motorboats with the Arabic lettering شرطة and below it the word POLICE moved among them, constabulary officers with bullhorns shepherding them back to their moorings. Others were already under way, standing toward the distant horizon of the sea. Beyond the mole she glimpsed the gray upper works of the destroyer.

Diehl shouldered forward. "General. Anything can we do?"

"Have you radio communication with your ship?"

"Not directly, but we can get word out to her."

"I should very much like to be able to speak directly with her. If you can—" He was interrupted by an officer who came up with a handheld radio. "—Just a moment, we may have that problem solved. Yes? And her name, or call sign, or whatever they use?"

"They'll answer to USS *Horn,*" Diehl told him. Gough nodded and lifted the radio.

At that moment a series of cracks came flatly over the water. Then, rising to a fusillade, the rattle of small arms firing at full automatic.

Marty saw the dude first. He was standing where the bow rose to the upswept prow. The first thing he noticed was that he wasn't dressed like the others. He wasn't in rolled-up pants and bare chest, or tatty torn undershirt, or stained robes. He wore regular clothes, a sport shirt and slacks. The second thing he noticed was that he was shouting back toward the enclosed cockpit they steered these things from.

Things happened fast after that. The dhow was still on its way out; *Faith* was still on its way in. Police boats with black hulls were trying to hold back the other fishermen. Arabic came from loud hailers. But these boys weren't making any move to stop. They were cranking it up, still headed for the gap in the seawall that led out.

The only trouble was, Team Gold was between them and it. And the dhow was about eighty times the displacement of the inflatable, and didn't look like it intended to lose this game of chicken.

"That them?" the coxswain yelled. "Want me to head for 'em?"

He was opening his mouth to give him the order when the fellow in the sport shirt bent down and picked up what looked like an AK, but with a longer barrel. And before Marty could reorient his brain to say something else, he started firing.

The bursts blew water into the air between the two boats, then, as the firer corrected, all around them. Then Marty was yelling. Cassidy was screaming, the coxswain was twisting the wheel into a tight turn away.

Lizard got the first burst off. Then the others, Crack Man, Snack Cake, Deuce jumped in with deafening cracks that blended into a roar as somebody else opened up from the dhow. The M-14s weren't so great in the confined spaces of a boarded trawler, but over the fifty yards that separated them from the dhow their heavy, high-velocity bullets hit hard. The windows of the dhow opened up with flashes, and two more guys popped up at the stern and began firing, too.

Then Sasquatch opened up with the M-60 and brass really started flying. He got on the pilothouse and shot out all the windows, took one of the stern guys out as he straightened, started to aim, instead caught a burst in the chest and tumbled backward. Then the big seaman started stitching fire into the engine area, below the empty windows where now they couldn't see any flashes, any activity at all.

Which was good, except the dhow was still coming on. Still headed for the channel and the ship. He couldn't see anybody at the helm, but the inside of the pilothouse was a black hole.

The helicopter had come back, skating around above them like the sky was blue ice. It kept moving, which he guessed was a survival tactic. He wouldn't want to come in at a hover above guys with whatever it was the man in the blue shirt had been firing.

Meanwhile the coxswain had come back around and they were headed right back toward the oncoming prow. So that all Marty had to do was lean over and say, pointing, "Put her right there."

"Right there?"

"The bow. Right there." He told Cassidy what he was going to do. The ensign nodded. He was gripping the roll bar on the center console with one hand, his pistol with the other. He hadn't fired yet, though everyone else had.

Marchetti switched his attention back to the swiftly closing hull. It was rippling along through the green water, still on its steady course. He couldn't scrub from his mind the thought that any moment now he'd see a flash and the next number would be the singing angels. He unslung the twelve-gauge, jacked a round, and put the bead on the gunwale. Which grew quickly, loomed over them. He squatted suddenly and braced just as the coxswain ran the blunt air-padded bow full into the side of the dhow at about ten knots.

It staggered everyone in the boat. The motors roared as they rebounded, like throwing a basketball against a concrete wall, but the coxswain kept her aimed where Marchetti had pointed and drove right back in again. She snarled ahead, pressing with all the power of his steadily advanced throttles against the dhow's bow. Like a little rubber tugboat, crowded up against the paint and rust and caked salt in a meat-grinder snarl of hard rubber and plastic against steel. He leaned back, trying to keep the bead where anybody leaning over the side to shoot down would first appear. But they didn't, and the Johnsons howled, and Crack Man reared back and the grapnel went sailing up, line uncoiling behind it.

They went up hand over hand, stepping first on the inflatable's nose as it rode up, then either jumping up to grab the deck edge and haul themselves up and over bodily or else walking up the line from the grapnel. The deck was only about ten feet above the water, but it took muscle to pull yourself straight up burdened with weapon and gear and ammunition and wet clothes and boots and, of course, the damn flotation vests they didn't dare leave behind. He rolled into the shelter of a cathead, whipped the barrel around, and scanned the afterdeck. Through the missing windows a chromed wheel in the empty pilothouse rotated slowly.

Crack Man jumped out and fired a full clip down into it, from the hip. From the far side Cassidy, recovered, it seemed, was firing into the far window, both angling down, so they wouldn't shoot each other.

Marchetti rolled over and lurched up, sprinting as hard as he could down the port side. One of the crew lay there, blood running into the scuppers, a smashed Kalashnikov beside him. Marty vaulted over him and fetched up beside the pilot-house. He and Cassidy looked down the glass-littered stairs.

The ensign started to move, but Marty had him by a quarter second and went down first, blasting blind ahead of him as he went, the shells chucking out as he worked the pump.

The wheelhouse smelled of paint and fish and diesel oil. There was nobody there. He was about to take another ladder down when a horn began. The RHIB's horn. One, two, three stuttering blasts.

He glanced out to see the seawall looming.

They hit with a crashing crunching impact into solid concrete and stone. Every piece of glass still in the frames shattered and fell. Horrible sounds came from below, as if heavy machinery was rotating fast while winding steel cable around itself. Shrieking and complaining, tearing itself into pieces.

Heads came into view over the bow and he jerked the Mossy up, almost blasting them through the empty windows before he realized they wore black assault gear and black helmets and carried submachine guns.

As lines rattled across, he wanted to pull his head into his shoulders and his dick into his groin, waiting for the explosion. They'd run full tilt into the seawall and were probably going down. Any sane man would get off before whatever was down there sent them all to Cloud Nine.

Instead, he grabbed the overhead and swung down the steps, boots crunching glass and slipping on cartridges, most empty but some still bulleted, still live. But he just kept going, and as his eyes adapted he made out an opening leading down and forward. The engine-eating-itself sound was coming from there, and he followed it, but had to reverse himself first and back down a ladder. His hand went for his flashlight and grabbed air, a lanyard keeper dangling with nothing at the end of it. He didn't know when he'd lost the Maglite, but he wished he hadn't. The interior was black.

A shot sledgehammered steel by his head. He twisted and fired into the dark. Something hit his chest, hard, like an iron ram with a sharp point swung abruptly into his breastbone. He saw stars and flashes, but kept pumping and firing and someone was firing back and he pumped and fired till the striker clicked empty but the answering flashes stopped and he heard someone scrambling away on hands and knees, crying or praying in a foreign-sounding whine.

Someone came down the ladder with a light, and he reloaded, thumbing shells into the mag, keeping his eyes where the muttering whimper had disappeared. Then grabbed the Maglite out of whoever's hands and went forward, feeling like it was blood or semen instant after instant of time itself being squeezed out of him.

The beam lit up a cavernous hold, bigger than he'd have thought, seeing the dhow from outside. One side was bagged solid with heavy-looking sacks. The air was thick with the lime smell of wet concrete and old fish and the sharp coppery tang of blood. On the other side, blue polyethylene drums like the ones chemicals came in. He reached out to thump one, then thought better of that. He was used to seeing holds loaded symmetrically, with careful dunnage between cargo. There was none here, as if this voyage would only be a little distance in calm water.

He slid among them hastily but quietly, following the flash beam with his shotgun. Left hand clamped to the fore end, beam aligned with the bore. The flutter-roar of the helicopter from the far side of metal, the metallic tone of a bullhorn, the scrape and lurch and boom of a rock incisor gnawing along the outer hull.

The spotlight wavered on a square case with green wires coming out of it. He caught his breath. Each step took an age.

He was almost to it when someone stepped out of the dark and slugged him in the back with what felt like a two-by-four. The flash tumbled away. The Mossberg blasted a red tongue of flame. Then he was on his knees, scrabbling to get up again as the board or bat or whatever it was slammed into his ass, then boomed hollowly, missing him and hitting steel.

Five sharp explosions loud as close lightning filled the hold with sound and light and powder smoke. In their intermittent flash he saw a boy in a white shirt jerking his hands up to grab his chest.

Marchetti got his hands on the Maglite again and pointed it to find the guy on the deck, crawling for the box. The pistol cracked again and the kid sank down, hand stretched out. His legs kicked.

Wilson came out of the black, pistol extended, ready to fire again. Her extended arms were locked, shaking. Marchetti spoke softly to her. Took the pistol away and let the hammer down. Held her for a few seconds, feeling her shudder and breathe, shudder and breathe.

To his surprise, she didn't show the first sign of wanting to cry.

Aisha finally got aboard hours later, after the local bomb squad had removed the detonators and made sure what was left was safe. The dhow lay tied up to the outer seawall, far from other craft, apparently sitting on the shallow bottom there. An assault trooper guarded the gangplank.

Yousif was standing on top of the pilothouse as she and Pete and Bob came aboard. He welcomed them with a nod, gestured them on; she took it they were free to look around, to go below.

The place was littered with glass and cartridge cases and footprinted all over with bloody boot marks. The bodies were still in place, being photographed and searched. She hesitated over one in a blue shirt. Its arm dangled over the gunwale. Techs were picking up the weapons, bagging them and carrying them ashore. She hesitated, looking at the body. Then followed Diehl below, stepping cautiously on glass-strewn ladder treads.

Work lights illuminated the hold like a stage. A chalked square showed where the explosive had been. Beside it, hand extended as if pointing, lay the crumpled body of a small dark man of about twenty.

A crunch behind them. She turned to see Yousif bend, straighten. Wait.

"Identify any of them?" Diehl asked him.

"They're all ours, Bob."

"Bahraini nationals?"

"Right. But the guns, of course, not from here. Russian manufacture, but they've passed through many hands. The grenades are yours. The plastic's yours. The blocks are still in the original wrapping. We will make some arrangement presently to return it, with the proper paperwork of course."

"And this stuff?" Diehl thumbed the blue drums.

"The main charge. Fertilizer and diesel oil. We were lucky today."

Aisha said, "What about this doctor? The one bin Jun'ad mentioned. The foreigner. Where's he?"

Yousif shrugged, looking as if someone else had asked him that recently, and hadn't liked his answer. They looked at the body, as if the brightness that spotlighted it meant it was worthy of their attention. But she didn't see anything else. Men carrying a stretcher worked their way between the drums. They glanced at Yousif, and when he nodded, began rolling the corpse onto the stretcher, to take it away.

25

The King Fahad Causeway

The peach-colored Mercedes could make two hundred and forty kilometers an hour. But the man with the drooping eyelid lifted the toe of his polished oxford from the accelerator when it reached a hundred. To drive at less, on this long stretch of perfectly straight causeway, would attract attention.

Above all he didn't want to do that. Though, as always, his paperwork was in order. The passport and visa he'd used to enter Bahrain were now only stirrings of powdery ash in the tide. First shredded, then burned, then scattered into the harbor while the third team, the local boys, finished their preparations for today's action.

Doctor Fasil Tariq al-Ulam no longer existed.

He watched the sparkling towers dwindle to distant white specks in the rearview mirror. Watched another coastline push up ahead, though its outlines were flat and undetailed through miles of dusty air. A taupe horizon toward which the highway arrowed, propped above the shining sea on concrete pilings that went on and on, rising only once, in a graceful arching stride, to let ships pass beneath.

The King Fahad Causeway linked Bahrain to the mainland of Saudi Arabia. The dun distance was Al-Khubar, in Saudi's Eastern Province. But before he got there, in not too many minutes at the speed he was making, he'd have to stop.

A basement of riprap, a verdant icing of foliage; then,

soaring, what looked like spaceships impaled on bayonets. The artificial island lay midway between the two countries. He'd have to go through immigration. That didn't worry him. His new papers weren't forgeries. They were real, with the proper stamps and clearances. He was a reporter with a new Internet news agency.

But before that, before his next identity and the long-awaited and long-prepared mission to the north, one thing remained. A treat, of a sort, that he allowed himself with each outing.

He pulled off into a pleasantly landscaped parking area that overlooked an artificial beach. Families had spread cloths on picnic tables. Children ran shrieking through friendly waves. He pulled the car around until he was looking back in the direction he'd come from.

He glanced at his watch. Then turned on the radio, got out, and climbed up to sit on the hood and light a cigarette.

He sat there for a long time in the sunlight and sea wind, watching the children and listening to the radio. His fingertips stroked the gleaming surface of the hood. Waiting for the distant plume of smoke—yes, he should be able to see it from here—listening for the terrified, shocked words announcing another disaster.

But they didn't come. A traffic reporter said flow was interrupted on Avenue 40, on the way to Juffair, due to a police barricade. At that he turned the volume up. But the announcer said nothing more, until some time later he said the delays were now lifted and morning traffic was flowing normally.

Something had gone wrong. It hadn't come off. Even now the local talent might be undergoing interrogation.

He took out his new passport and flicked the lighter beneath it. Held it away from his suit as it writhed, blackened, became a wisp of char that he carried, still burning, to a trash container and rubbed into powder between his palms. He took a third set of documents from a slit cut into the leather of the rear seat, cunningly concealed by the seam. Now he could not be stopped, searched, photographed, or fingerprinted. This was a diplomatic passport. On its cover gold gleamed: a deeply embossed seal of crossed swords beneath a palm tree.

The official seal of the Kingdom of Saudi Arabia. Holding it up, he'd be waved past the businessmen and tourists waiting for access to the Land of the Two Holy Places.

He looked again, hoping still to see smoke. But still the sky hovered clear, pale, innocent of the sign and evidence of destruction. Behind the sunglasses his eyes narrowed. He did not like to fail.

Then his chin lifted again. The road which makes our feet bleed is the path which leads upward. To topple the colossus would take many blows. Much sacrifice and pain.

Or perhaps—his mind moved ahead—one great blow. Greater than any that had ever been struck before.

The heavy car accelerated again, heading west.

PART FOUR

THE MED

26

The Eastern Mediterranean

The darkened bridge was quiet, but not relaxed. It was the calm of those who didn't need to cover uncertainty with talk. Who in months at sea together had worn through idle conversation. So that words were scarce now, consisting of the chanted antiphon of the phone talker, the helm's terse reports, the murmur of the conning officer keeping them on station a thousand yards astern of the deck-edge lights of USS *Theodore Roosevelt*, CVN-71.

Dan sat with legs crossed and shoes kicked off in the dark. He'd started chewing gum. It seemed to help. Working out helped, too. Running was out, at least temporarily; Blade Slinger 191 had operated practically round the clock since they'd rejoined the battle group. Even during down time, hauled inside with the maintenance crews working her over, the deck had to stay clear in case another aircraft needed a dry spot. He tried to get to the weight room every day. Around 0400 seemed to work best. A hard hour on the machines, then a shower before his self-imposed date with the rising sun.

Around him the Battle Force Sixth Fleet, carrier, cruisers, destroyers, frigates, combat support, drove massively through the night. It had been here since 1949. Nearly every sailor who'd served in the navy since had been part of it at one time or another. Along with its associated amphibious ready group, two hundred miles to the south at the moment, it could react to anything from a humanitarian crisis to all-out war. It could move seven hundred miles in a day, refuel, rearm, and strike without the permission of tacit enemies, doubtful neutrals, or reluctant allies.

They'd departed the island emirate two weeks ago, three days after the dhow incident. But not for the upper Gulf. Instead, with no explanation, they'd been traded to the Med. Out Hormuz and through the Red Sea again, the passage familiar now. Past the low coast where navy men had died aboard a sinking tanker. They'd never laid hands on the smugglers, never heard another word about them. Like they'd never found out who was behind the dhow attack. Boxing with shadows . . . Through the Canal again, the usual frenzy when they couldn't find the certificate. *Horn* dogged *Roosevelt* tonight at the triple crossing of lines drawn south from Turkey, west from Cyprus, and north from Egypt. Where the stars arched over the sea like diamonds set in the roof of an immense cave. Waiting for whatever came next.

He scratched between his stockinged toes, remembering Riyadh.

They'd crossed the causeway under heightened security in the wake of the attack on *Horn.* Dan had ridden with a four-striper from COMIDEASTFOR in the second unmarked white Suburban. A convoy of SUVs didn't seem the least conspicuous way to travel, nor was the requirement they wear body armor exactly reassuring. It weighed on him like the lead aprons they give you before the X-ray.

They sped at seventy miles an hour toward the capital of Saudi Arabia, four hundred kilometers to the west. The highway was perfectly flat, perfectly new. Once they left Al-Khubar behind, a city that looked like it had been built the night before, the broad, exquisitely planed lanes were empty. All there was to look at was rock, sand, and, set well back from the highway, new, huge, seemingly deserted mosques. Or at least the buildings had minarets. The heat penetrated the glass and steel around them despite the roaring air conditioner, made the Americans suck on their plastic bottles of water. It made everything shimmer and run together, as if shape were only a fleeting attribute of reality. He was beginning to suspect that nothing he saw in this quarter of the world was what it seemed. A gaunt hunted-looking dog shied as they sped past.

Today's meeting was with Admiral Curtis D. Kornack, Commander, U.S. Naval Forces, Central Command. Kornack's flag was in Bahrain, but the admiral himself was in Riyadh. Dan's disciplinary mast had been postponed. Or maybe OBE—overtaken by events—more accurately described what had happened to the accusation of excessive force while boarding, in the aftermath of the attempted bombing of the *Horn*. He'd stayed aboard, of course, through the day. No one knew if the dhow was the main event or a diversion. Hotchkiss drafted an OPREP-3, a terrorist incident report. They stood to into the night, with *Fear* and *Faith* circling, manned and armed. At any rate, no one had mentioned that investigation since. And he wasn't about to bring it up.

They reached Riyadh as the sun hit zenith. The roundabouts and flyovers were deserted, as if scanned by some futuristic ray that destroyed everything but architecture. The Ministry of Defence was, no surprise, white, modern, and brand-new. They parked in an underground garage, left the armor in the vehicles, and checked in with a sergeant in battle dress. He led them down concrete stairs as the air grew colder and took on a subterranean smell. A large room with acoustic tile ceilings and many Americans at terminals. Past that, more corridors terminated at a windowless briefing room where carafes of coffee and bottles of mineral water and soggy date pastries on plastic plates waited. He saw a face he thought he remembered. As he focused the other, large, rumpled, stepped forward and stuck out a hand. "Been a while, Commander."

"The NIS officer. From Gitmo."

"That's right. Bob Diehl. Only it's NCIS now." The agent winked and raised his paper cup. "Yeah, awhile since we had our last chat. And this is better coffee than you gave me then."

"You on this, too? I thought Ms. Rahim was the agent in charge." He smiled at her; she nodded back, but without smiling, her dark face giving him nothing but wariness and distance.

"*Ar*-Rahim. She works for me. But you know you'll always get a fair hearing from me."

"Like the one I got last time?"

Years before, a seaman from his department had gone overboard one night off Cuba. Dan had helped inventory the dead man's personal effects. After reading Sanderling's diary, he'd wrapped it in copper cable and deep-sixed it over the stern. Which had led to Diehl's accusing him of being Sanderling's lover, if not his murderer.

The agent laughed soundlessly as the admiral came in.

Karnack had an air force colonel with him, and a civilian in a sport coat and dark slacks whom he introduced as his "political advisor"—which Dan figured was spelled CIA. They sat on one side of the table, leaving the delegation from Bahrain to take the other. Dan added that up: the intelligence-side captain who'd accompanied him from CO-MIDEASTFOR; a Commander Hooker, the base security guy; Diehl, Ar-Rahim, and himself.

Karnack opened a file folder the colonel gave him. "You're Lenson?"

"Yes, sir."

"I respect any man who wears the Congressional, but I'm not happy about what happened in Manama. It took too long to get your security force in the water, and you weren't ready to repel a waterborne attack. Nor were you maintaining proper lookouts."

"I don't know who gave you that information, sir, but none of those assertions are correct," Dan told him. "Did you read our OPREP?"

"And the other reports. You were lucky the Bahrainis took out that dhow before it got close enough to do some serious damage."

Dan controlled himself. Karnack was still listening; if

Dan got emotional he wouldn't be. "I'd like to respond to those points, sir?"

"You'll have your chance. The CINC told me this incident's going to be the subject of a congressional investigation."

"Congressional," the captain from COMIDEASTFOR repeated. "I can see a JAG Manual investigation. But bleeding Christ, sir, why *congressional?* There was no loss of life, no property damage—"

The civilian said, "Same reason we investigated the Khobar Towers bombing. To find our security holes and fix them."

Dan said the major security hole was that he hadn't been permitted to be ready to defend himself. The colonel started to interrupt, but Karnack gestured for him to speak.

Dan recounted his initial arming of his patrols and the subsequent orders to pull the weapons off the boats. He'd also requested more security on the pier, but had been told that was a national, meaning local, responsibility. Finally, he recounted how when he got the call warning him a situation was developing, he'd requested permission to respond preemptively but couldn't get it through the chain of command. "I called away my security teams, armed the boats, and stationed one off my beam as a sanitizer. I sent the other one into the inner harbor under my inherent right of self-defense. As for the Bahrainis stopping the dhow—it was my men who identified it, neutralized it with fire, boarded, and prevented the last of the terrorists left alive from triggering it in the middle of the fishing fleet. And so far I haven't heard any objection. If there hadn't been a bomb aboard, though, I'd be hanging by my thumbs. Right?"

"We're guests in Bahrain," the colonel said. "We're guests here in Saudi, too. Arabs are very sensitive about their sovereignty. Don't ever forget that."

"Even guests have the right to defend themselves. Especially if we're here to protect the regimes hosting us."

"This is a bigger issue than you and your ship, Commander."

"I understand that, sir," Dan said. "And I agree, I acted wrongly. What I should have done, in retrospect, was to refuse to stay in a port where the authorities knew a possibility of attack existed, without being permitted reasonable means of protecting my men and women."

The unspoken point being that Karnack had been responsible for those rules of engagement. From their expressions, he saw they understood, and didn't like, what he was saying, spoken aloud or not.

Karnack drew an invisible triangle on the tabletop with his fingernail. "Okay, we've cleared the air on that issue. Let's move on. What I want to know is, is there anything new on the dhow's crew, the weapons, who built the bomb? Who's behind it, and who they're linked to?"

Hooker started to outline what they had, but Karnack cut him off with a shake of his head. "What I'm really interested in is this doctor figure. He sounds like the traveling mastermind, the outside expertise."

"He designs a hell of an interesting bomb," the civilian said.

"We'd like to know more about him, too," Diehl said. He was the only person there who didn't seem intimidated by three stars. He patted his paunch like an old dog. "Unfortunately, he's disappeared. None of the captured plotters know who he is or where he went. At least, according to the SIS."

The civilian in the sport coat said, "We think he's Egyptian, but currently based out of Sudan. He may be with the Egyptian Islamic Jihad, the group that assassinated Sadat. So he's probably been at this a while. He escaped across the causeway to Saudi in a light-colored 1992 Mercedes S-class."

"So that's the Sudanese connection," the captain said, looking enlightened.

"How do you know that?" Hooker demanded. "The Bahrainis don't know any of that, do they? Because they sure as hell didn't tell us."

"He was traveling on a diplomatic passport."

"How do we know—"

The civilian advisor drawled, "Don't keep asking *how* we know. Ask *what* we know, then what it means. One last detail: it was a Saudi diplomatic passport."

Diehl whistled.

The captain said, "If I could forge a diplomatic passport, I'd do it for someplace obscure, where no one could check on whether it was genuine—like, Sierra Leone."

"That's right. Therefore, I don't think it was forged," the CIA man said.

Diehl said, "You mean the Saudis are playing us both ways? Hosting us, but helping these guys attack us? Aisha—what do you think? Does the Moslem mind work that way? Mine sure doesn't."

The black woman said coolly, as if, Dan thought, he hadn't just insulted her whole religious community, "I would regard it as more likely that it was forged. We know this organization, whatever it is, has sophisticated capabilities."

Karnack got up. The military members bolted to their feet; the civilians simply looked up. The admiral said, "I've got to move on. But before I do, I'd like to get certain things clear with Captain Lenson here."

"Yes, sir," Dan said.

"People tell me you have a rep for taking independent action. Pending the results of the investigation, you're forbidden to move *Horn* inside Saudi territorial waters. Nor will you approach the Saudis or the Bahrainis in any way outside of official channels."

"I had no intention of—"

"Don't tell me your intentions. Listen to my orders. Any unauthorized action on your part will result in your instant relief. So you won't take any. Am I crystal clear, Commander?"

"Yes, sir, Admiral, you are."

"That goes for the Bahrainis, too," Karnack said to Diehl.

The civilian advisor said, "He's saying the crime, the attempted crime, took place in their waters. The attack was launched from their streets. None of you—that goes for you NIS clowns, too—are going to try to solve it yourself."

With that the meeting seemed to be closed, or at least
Karnack, the colonel, and the advisor left. Those who
remained looked at each other, then, as one, began stowing
away what cold water was left for the trip back.

On which, he found himself with Ar-Rahim and the intel
captain in the second Suburban. They didn't start the conversation. So he had to, or sit in silence all the way back to
Manama. "You work with the Bahraini cops, don't you? Ms.
Ar-Rahim?"

"To some extent."

"I heard the guys who actually ran the dhows were all
Bahrainis."

"That's right."

"No outsiders?"

"All Bahrainis."

"So the only outsider was this doctor guy. I'm wondering
what if anything's going to get done about him."

"We're continuing the investigation," Ar-Rahim said.

The captain said, "That's the official answer. The unofficial one is: Probably not much, if he's actually Saudi-
sponsored."

"You think that's possible?"

"You heard everything I just heard. As to doing anything
about it, that gets decided at a lot higher level. This administration doesn't like to strike back without a clearly identified
guilty party. You were on that last launch from the Red Sea,
weren't you?"

Dan nodded, remembering the missiles roaring away into
the sandstorm. The captain said, "We already proposed a
punitive strike against the Sudan. With *Horn* participating,
for the public relations aspect. The ship they tried to blow
up, striking back."

"My guys'll be happy to smoke whoever tried to take us
out."

"No they won't, because it got turned down. It might lose
us basing rights for the Southern Watch overflights."

"So we do—what?"

"At most, they'll try to get the Saudis, and maybe the Sudanese, though we don't seem to have much leverage there, to cough this guy up. Which they probably won't, based on their performance to date."

"There've been other bombings like this, haven't there?" Ar-Rahim said.

"Let's talk about that in a secure location," the captain said, and Dan figured what he meant was, not in front of Dan Lenson and the enlisted driver, since he couldn't think of a more secure location to talk than in a huge SUV tearing across the desert at eighty miles an hour.

But he was just the dumb ship driver who wanted to shoot first and ask questions later. But from now on, he was going to pay a lot more attention to security. Marchetti had been right. If the Machete hadn't trained the boarding team and personally led them aboard the dhow, they might all be dust motes floating over the Arabian Peninsula now.

He looked out the window and there was the dog again, or maybe not the same one, just another gaunt-ribbed starving-eyed pariah mutt. If you had to be a dog, Saudi Arabia was probably the worst place in the world to live.

When they'd gotten back to Bahrain, and he was getting out, back inside the compound, the captain had leaned out and put his hand on his arm. "Karnack wasn't joking," he said.

"I didn't think he was."

"No independent action. You'll get sailing orders tomorrow. Out of the Gulf, is my guess. You just go play destroyer captain and let us handle the downstream effects. Copy?"

"Yes, sir," Dan said, although being told again annoyed him. What did they expect him to do? Shell the Saudi coast? Launch a Tomahawk zeroed on the Kaaba?

He was interrupted by Porter with a message responding to Naval Sea Systems Command's request for a shipboard evaluation of the condition of the BLISS. BLISS—he'd forgotten what the acronym stood for—was the water spray system at the top of the stacks that cooled the exhaust plume to where an infrared seeker wouldn't be able to home in on it.

Or that was the theory. The reality was that spraying salt water on steel at eight hundred degrees resulted in such horren-
dous corrosion no one ever turned it on. He signed it and she
went away. He sat alone again.

But not for long, because the radio crackled, putting out
the new foxtrot corpen, the carrier's new flight course. The
very first ship he'd ever served in had been run down and
sunk by a carrier on a dark night not unlike this one. He
didn't want to repeat that experience. So he kept close tabs
on the bigger ship's relative motion.

He was trudging out to make certain they'd pass clear
when the radioman chief intercepted him. Dan read the message, then undogged the wing door. He thought about it
when he was out there, watching the carrier's sidelights and
the pretty deck edge lights, which looked festive but actually
filled him with dread, move slowly from starboard to port,
then wink out as *Horn* followed her around.

This time around, he'd be in tactical command. That was
interesting.

The message said *Horn* and *Moosbrugger* were detached
effective 0200. *Horn* would be replaced on plane guard by
Underwood. The two destroyers, now constituting a surface
action group called Task Element 60.1.1, under command of
CO *Horn,* would detach and proceed to an area bounded by
the lines of 32 and 33 degrees north latitude, and the lines of
32 degrees and 32 degrees 30 minutes east longitude.

The latitude figures told him the center of that area would
be about a hundred and forty miles south of their current location. He looked out the window to see that the carrier was
still where she'd said she'd be, then checked the big chart of
the East Med, Gulf of Sollum to Iskenderun, that was pinned
down under a dim red light.

The rectangle started about forty-five nautical miles off
the Egyptian coast, roughly off Port Said, and extended sixty
nautical miles northward. It was a strange shape for an operating area. Usually they were constrained by geography, or
by depth, if the intent was antisubmarine work. But this one

was a simple rectangle, and the boundaries were whole and half degrees.

"What's this about, Chief?" he asked the radioman.

"No idea, sir."

"Do we have these references?"

"On the clipboard, sir. The ones we got—Ref C's NO-TAL."

References, A and B were both boilerplate and left him no wiser than before he read them. He looked for Ref C but then remembered, as Gerhardt had just told him, it hadn't been addressed to him—that was what NOTAL meant. So everything was as clear as shit, but that didn't matter. His orders were clear: Take charge of *Moosbrugger* and get both destroyers down there. He signed to acknowledge and asked the chief to tell Lieutenant Camill to give him a call on the bridge after he'd read it. He told the officer of the deck what was going on and told the quartermaster to let the chief QM know.

At 0100 he called the screen commander and requested permission to depart on duty assigned. *Horn* accelerated smoothly out of station into her southward turn. Dan noted the lights of a Perry-class frigate crossing from port to starboard miles astern. *Underwood,* taking the plane bitch slot. At the same time *Moosbrugger*'s CO came up on the horn, reporting in. His name was Bill Brinegar. Dan didn't know much about him; The Moose was based out of Charleston. He made sure Brinegar was on the same sheet of music and gave him a course of 165 and a speed of twenty-two knots. And gradually the other lights faded into the darkness of the night sea.

27

Ministry of Justice and Islamic Affairs, Bahrain

She could barely sit still. The briefing was unbelievable . . . and all too familiar. Rival agencies fighting over credit for frustrating the attack in the harbor. The Americans, so sure they'd performed miracles for the incompetent locals. The Bahraini police, pointing out their helicopter-borne team had been in position for an assault that wouldn't have put every innocent fisherman in Manama in danger. The SIS, pushing their counterintelligence work as the key to frustrating the plot. Each hungry for credit, and through it, appropriations and promotions and power. It was disgusting.

Still, it was instructive. Maybe she should just look at it that way. As Allah's will she should be enlightened as to how things actually went behind the scenes of smiling diplomats and smoothly worded joint communiqués.

As if He were answering her thought of Him, Aisha heard the *adhan* from outside, the call to prayer. It was time for *asr*. She said "Excuse me," to Hooker and Diehl, who looked surprised, and followed the other Muslims out of the room.

Down a hallway, past a bearded cleaning man shutting off his buffer to follow them into a large empty room with rugs thrown over the polished parquet. The Arabs glanced at her in surprise. Some frowned. Others, observing her pulling hijab over her hair, murmured a welcome. Since she was the only woman, she separated herself from the men, choosing a corner where she could pray with them, but not as one of them.

The general didn't lead the prayers, but rather the bearded older fellow who'd been running the floor buffer a moment before. He stared at her, seemed about to say something; glanced at the general; then smiled. Then they all did the ritual ablution and began murmuring through the *raka*s. Like most African-American Muslims she knew the prayers in both English and Arabic, so joining in wasn't a problem, now or anytime she'd gone to *masjid* here on the island.

"God is greater than all else."

"God is greater than all else," they repeated, generals, colonels, civilians, waiters, all together facing God and setting aside the world and its temptations.

"Praise be to Allah, Lord of the universe. The Compassionate, the Merciful, Master of the Day of Judgment. Only You do we worship. Only to You do we cry for help. Guide us to the straight path. The path of those on whom You have bestowed Your grace, whose lot is not anger, and who go not astray."

She emptied her mind, going through the bows and prostrations. Feeling her heart empty of the resentment she'd felt moments before.

You couldn't expect perfection from human beings. The only perfection was in God. She added her own prayers and intentions: for her mother; her father. That she herself might act in the cause of justice against those who intended evil. And further, act with modesty and without thought of praise or reward. They ended in the sitting position, with the central affirmation of Islam, the *shahada*.

None has the right to be worshiped but God, and Muhammad is His Messenger.

The day after the raid, Diehl had put her on a flight to the States, to report to Washington about the attack on the *Horn*, how they'd averted it, and to present a threat assessment as far as the possibilities of other attacks on units and personnel in Central Command. There'd been high-level interest, he said.

But by the time she got to the new NCIS building in the navy yard, it seemed to have dissipated. She saw the new director, but only for five minutes. He said he'd read her report on the dhow bombing, complimented her on their work, and asked her to "share her expertise" with the agent who ran the Antiterrorist Alert Center.

Who, when she sat down with him after a quick tour of the ATAC, asked her several pointed questions: how they'd gotten their initial warning, what the relationship was with the local police. He seemed more interested in base security than obscure Islamic religious groups. He didn't know anything about an Egyptian doctor who specialized in bombings.

When they were done, he'd shaken her hand and asked if at some point she might be interested in a double agent operation. She'd almost laughed in his face. It was hard enough being a female, Muslim, and African-American, without setting loose the rumor she was working for the other side. She said politely she was still new in the counterintelligence world; she'd better not get involved in anything like that until she had more experience.

When she got back to Bahrain, Diehl put her in charge of the Antonia case. "Antonia" was their name for an unknown infant found in a Dumpster at NSA. The worst part of it was no one had noticed the baby until the outside contractor had been about to dump the container. Fortunately she was still alive, if dehydrated, and while the little girl recovered at Ibn Sina Medical Center, Aisha was supposed to find out who'd carried her for nine months and then gotten rid of her the day she was born. Bob also wanted to push hard on the drug front before the next ship arrived. She spent a lot of hours sitting in her car outside the stables. A good location for hashish dealing; sailors and marines headed there to ride a "real Arabian horse" after they'd done their bar crawling and bought their rug. And of course there was the usual caseload of thefts and bad checks.

That was what she was doing during the day. In her off

hours, she'd decided she needed to find out more about the stranger who'd brought enough hatred to Bahrain to turn four young men into suiciders. Because—surprise—she wasn't hearing anything back from Major Yousif. Except for today's showcase briefing, which had left them all knowing nothing they hadn't known before.

She'd started by just walking around the Makarqah. Like all neighborhoods, she figured, everything depended on who knew you. Families lived above their stores. Grandparents lived with the family. These people were Shi'a, the despised majority in the Gulf Arab states. The ruling families—the al-Sabahs and al-Sauds—considered them superstitious, lazy, and, like as not, disloyal. They were also suspicious of outsiders. She'd shown Dr. X's photo to a few people he might have come in contact with: the local grocer, the barber, the shoe repair shop. Unfortunately, all she had was a visa photo, too small to show detail. It could have been any middle-aged Arab male with a tired look, a sagging eyelid, mustache, and glasses.

Tonight she hoped to make a little more progress.

By the time she got out to the Makarqah it was dark. It was also Friday evening. Bahrainis weren't the most pious people she'd ever seen, but they kept the sabbath. Along the King Faisal the hotels were sparkling, beacons of the nightlife the foreigners went to.

She smiled to herself, realizing she'd thought just that: *the foreigners.* As if she, herself, was one of the islanders. But that was how she saw herself sometimes, in this strange inverting mirror of a country. Where sometimes she felt more at home than with her own countrymen.

But that didn't mean she felt any sympathy with those who used Al-Islam as an excuse to kill. She parked between the Regency and the Heritage Center and joined the throngs drifting to and fro under the streetlights that lined the corniche. Out here it didn't look all that different from Ocean City or St. Augustine. But as she threaded into the alleys, the light fell away. Here tea shops were filled with men. The murmur of televisions, of women singing came from open windows on upper floors. Men turned as she passed, and she realized this was the first time she'd gone into the Shi'a quarter after dark. And that no other women were out, even in their black burqas.

She shifted her purse, feeling the mass of the loaded pistol. She wasn't afraid. But there were a lot of men out. Some looked like they'd been there all day. Like the brothers in Harlem hanging in front of the stores. She caught the smell of hashish. The gleam of a lifted bottle.

If she'd worn a burqa, she thought, they wouldn't even see her. If she'd been white and blond, they'd follow her with their gazes, but she didn't think they'd actually do anything. But now an older man called out, "Where are you going, whore?" and her hand tightened on her purse strap. She pretended she didn't hear, pretended she didn't understand the slurred Arabic.

So these were the followers of Ali. Those who flogged themselves bloody. Their strange festivals and traditions, like Mazzam and Hazara. Their superstitious veneration of their infallible imams. She debated turning back, but the next moment steadied herself. Some jerk had called her a name. That was all. And there was the street she wanted.

Then she remembered. She *had* been here at night: in the back of a truck, in black gear. Then these shops had been shuttered cages. Now they were thronged with men. Their eyes went past her, then jerked back. They gathered at doorways, scowling. She was glad to see the shoemaker's shop. Above it the windows of the apartment were . . . *lit*.

She blinked. Someone was up there.

She stood clutching her purse, wondering what was going on. Could it have been rented again, in the two weeks since the raid? Space *was* at a premium here. Crossing the street, she pushed open the door.

In the heat of the day, businesses often closed; then stayed open into the evening. Especially during Ramadan, but to some extent through the hot season. After a moment someone coughed in back.

The woman was swathed from head to toe in the black folds of her abaya. Dark eyes examined her. Aisha had spoken to a man before, the cobbler. This might be his wife, his mother, his sister—it was hard to tell from the eyes alone. She spoke first, hastily, in Arabic. "*Kaaf haalik*, how are you?"

"Praise be to God, I am well, welcome."

"I spoke to your . . . husband before, perhaps he mentioned it to you. I work with the American police, on the naval base. Can you tell me—have you ever seen this man?"

The woman took the photo unwillingly. Glanced at it, then back into the recesses of the store. Returned it, saying nothing.

"I see you have new tenants upstairs."

"They're from the neighborhood." The woman glanced over her shoulder again.

The cobbler came from the back, wiping his hands on a rag. "Hello again," he said, in English. "American policewoman. My wife has not seen this man you look for. Why you come back?"

"I see you have new tenants."

"Family. No more I rent to strangers."

"I just thought you might have remembered something else."

He just looked at her, and she understood that if she hadn't told him she was with the police he might have told her more. "Well, excuse me, then."

She was at the door when the woman said something, too low for her to hear. And the owner said, "Wait. Wait. You are here alone?"

She turned, surprised and a little suspicious. "Yes. Why?"

"You should not be alone," the woman said, still in Arabic. Clear classical speech, too, as good as Yousif's or Bucheery's. "Wait for me. I'll take you back to the souk. And I have something for you to put on. That we may go safely in the night."

The world looked different from behind a veil. Now none of the men looked twice. She and her companion moved through the descending night as if invisible. She'd become one of the shadows. Unseen, but also undisturbed.

She made as if to turn the corner, but the woman took her arm. "Not that way. This."

"*Shukraan.* I was turned around."

The narrow streets twisted and turned. She realized she was lost. The woman glided like a cat down alleys no broader than their outstretched hands. They smelled of dust and piss. Around her throbbed the intimate sounds of close-lived lives, babies crying, radios, the rhythmic thump of someone beating out dough or laundry. She was walking very fast ahead through a particularly close warren of passages. Then Aisha lost sight of her, black cloth vanishing into black night, and she ran to catch up, suddenly scared.

She ran full length into the men who stepped from the shadows. They smelled of cheap cologne and sweat and cigarettes. They weren't much bigger than she was, but they were much stronger. Three, maybe four of them, and before she could scream they had her hands twisted behind her, her mouth sealed by a rough palm, and she was being dragged backward. She heard the rasp of a wooden door, the squeal of unoiled iron. The ground dropped away in worn, rounded steps, and she smelled old spices, cool stale air, stale breath.

Hands at her face, stripping off the veil. Then binding the black cloth, twisted, over her eyes.

A light clicked on. She couldn't see what it illuminated. She felt a corner against the back of her knees. "Sit down," a voice growled.

She obeyed, trying to find a seat behind her with her bound hands before she trusted her weight to it. She couldn't stop panting. Her heart was going very fast, and she wanted to pee.

"Allah is great," she said tentatively, into the waiting silence.

"Indeed He is, blessed be His name. You are truly Muslim?"

"And have been since birth."

"Yet you work for the Americans."

"I *am* an American. There are many American Muslims."

This seemed to be news to her captors. She listened hard to the whispering. She couldn't tell how many were in the cellar with her. She fought for control, trying not to dwell on being alone, trying to tell herself they couldn't just cut her throat and bury her beneath this dusty basement earth that her shoeless foot kneaded gritty beneath her toes.

Obviously the cobbler had picked up the phone as they'd left. But who *were* these people? Her first fear had been Egyptian Jihad, like the suicide boaters. But the Jihad was Sunni. Not likely they'd have adherents among the despised Shi'a.

"Why are you asking questions in the Makarqah?" A different voice from the first.

"I'm trying to find out more about the man who attacked our warship a few weeks ago. He called himself Doctor Fasil Tariq al-Ulam. I have a photograph."

"We know who you mean. He was working with bin Jun'ad."

"With . . . That's right." Interesting, because as far as she'd seen in the local press, not one word had been released about local involvement in the incident. She took a deep breath. "And who are you?"

"You don't need to know that. All you need to know is what we're going to tell you."

"Then I'm listening." She bent her head, both to show submission and to glimpse something over the blindfold if she could. But the black cloth was impenetrable.

"Tonight you will go to the new madrassa east of the Japanese embassy. Across from the Salmaniya Gardens. Do you know where that is?"

"I know where the Gardens are. At the roundabout."

"Near the Old Palace, *eiwa*. The street door will be open. In classroom number eight, you will find something that will interest you."

Madrassas were Islamic schools. She didn't understand

what was going on, but if it meant they were letting her out
of this basement alive, she'd agree to anything. She was beginning to guess who these rough-speaking men were: local
militants and sympathizers orbiting the Party of God. The
Hezbollah were certified terrorists. Iranian-backed. But according to the Defense Intelligence threat updates, it had
been some years since they'd carried out a verifiable action.
There was speculation Iran was tapering off its support.

All that was conjecture, though, and it left her head the
instant she was jerked upright and the light snapped off.
"Step up," the rough voice commanded, and she stumbled
over invisible stairs back up into the alley. Where she was
told to wait for ten minutes before taking her blindfold off.

When she finally dared to reach up and unfasten it, she
was alone. Her purse lay at her feet. The good news was her
badge was still there. The bad, that the SIG was gone.

By the time she got back to her car her tears were crumbs
of salt on her cheeks. She rubbed them off, threw the chador
in the backseat, and drove straight to the roundabout in the
center of the city.

The madrassa was the same futuristic, kitschy, Saudi-
financed white concrete she was beginning to really dislike. A
figure stepped from the entrance as she approached, trotting
off into the night. When she tried the handle, it was unlocked.

She hesitated in the entryway. Fighting the urge to go
back to her apartment and chain the door forever. Then
sucked air past a self-mocking smile. Her job was too bor-
ing? She never got to do any real counterterrorism?

She took a breath and eased the door open. An empty
hallway. She tiptoed down it, easing her feet down on the
carpet, until she came to the door with the number eight on
it. Looked inside, warily, then switched the light on.

Just a classroom. No pictures on the walls. Only a table
of the elements. She slid the drawer of the teacher's desk
out. Chalk. Pencils. A photocopied sheaf that turned out to
be the answer key for a chemistry final. Yeah, there were

probably people who'd kill for this. But they were all in high school.

Then her gaze steadied. Remembering a surge suppressor in a wall socket, a blank space on a tabletop.

A Sanyo desktop, not new, not old, plastic case slightly yellowed. It was set up with a battered-looking monitor. She looked underneath. It was plugged in.

Using the eraser end of one of the pencils, she turned the monitor on, then the computer. It powered up, but froze on the Sanyo screen. Which meant the boot sector on the hard drive was erased or inoperative.

Which in turn meant either that it was broken or that whoever had sat at it last had reformatted it.

Suddenly she wished she still had her gun. She didn't want to be found here. She almost took the computer, but remembered: chain of custody. She turned the light off, closed the door, and went quietly out and down the corridor and out into the street.

Her shaking fingers groped in her purse for a coin. There it was. A pay phone. Diehl, answering. "Yeah? Aisha, that you?"

"It's me," she said. "And I think we just got a break."

28

The Southeastern Med

A *Horn* mile was five times around the main deck, through the starboard breaker, the forecastle, down the side. Each time he went through the port breaker the smokers flattened themselves against the fire station. Marchetti and Hotchkiss were running, too. Nothing prearranged, they just happened to be out here. He only saw the senior chief occasionally, which meant they were doing about the same pace. He lapped the exec every couple of circuits, though.

Horn cut with a steady pitching whine through a sea that glowed like the green phosphorescent fluid that filled light wands. They were out of sight of land, had not glimpsed it all through the last week. Though once, to the south, distant clouds had hovered over what might have been land. That way lay the Egyptian coast, and Port Said, the by-now-familiar entrance to what navy men called the Ditch. To the west lay Alexandria. But both cities lay over the horizon, though identifiable on the surface search radar.

Nor had they seen *Moosbrugger* all week. Dan had placed her in the northern half of the box. The two destroyers maintained a close radar watch and kept their electronic surveillance and signals intelligence stacks manned. They were looking for a motor vessel, no name available as yet, nor even any description, that was suspected of preparing to get under way from somewhere in the eastern Med. Nothing further was available, neither its destination, its intended course, its cargo, or its nationality, and "somewhere in the eastern Med" covered a lot of territory. But those were his orders. So he put aircraft up early each morning and just before dusk, to sweep the approaches and visually identify any suspicious contacts. All in all, it was a lot less stressful than steaming in close company with the task force, and he'd let the crew relax. Five section steaming watches. A cookout on the fantail. Early movies on the ship's closed circuit TV.

He came up on Marchetti, who was starting to lumber, and after a couple of false starts—the senior chief kept blocking him—took him going around the Sparrow launcher. Back here the wind was fresh, and the soar and drop of the deck made him stagger.

This time Hotchkiss heard him coming as he closed on her. She speeded up, and he tailed her for a while, dodging knee-knockers and scuttle coamings, enjoying the perky bounce of tight little cheeks in skimpy green nylon running shorts. She had shorty socks with the little red balls at the back and white Adidas, and a light top that didn't leave a lot to the imagination either. Her hair was a tight bun above a terry sweatband, and as he gained on her, his eyes moved from it to the sweat shining on her neck, darkening the back of her sports bra, and down to a damp patch on green nylon. Right there at the cleft . . . He jerked his gaze away and grunted, "On your right."

Barked it more harshly than he'd meant to, and she flinched away and stumbled into a ventilation tube sticking up from the deck. Then she was down on one knee, cursing a blue streak. "Sorry," he said, stopping.

"I was showboating. Trying to stay ahead of you."

"You okay? I can help you down to sick bay."

Marchetti came pounding around the corner. As he neared, Dan saw his expression, and realized what it must look like, with his arm around the exec. Glancing up he saw the lookout watching, too, finger on the button of his mouthpiece. Fucking great, it'd be all over the ship in seconds.

"She cracked her shin on one of the vents," he told the Machete. Hotchkiss fended them both off, undogged a weather hatch, and limped inside.

Dan started to jog again, then stopped and went back to the quarterdeck phone and punched in the sick bay number. He told the duty corpsman the XO had hurt her leg running. She was probably in her stateroom, would he mind taking a look at her. Then immediately felt disgusted at such a cover-your-ass thought. That he'd actually worried about documenting he hadn't been groping her on the main deck. With time, did it become second nature?

Wiping sweat from his eyes, he started on his fourth mile.

That afternoon, in Combat. Kim McCall, the on-watch TAO; Hotchkiss, limping; Casey Schaad, Lieutenant Sanduskie from the intel det, the Camel, Marchetti, and Dan. The ops officer chaired. He still spoke deliberately, but the others had gotten so used to it they spent the time between words thinking about other things.

As Camill reviewed the day's contacts, Dan wondered again what they were doing out here. His private theory, based mainly on a month-old *Time* magazine someone had gotten in the mail from home, was that they were looking for someone smuggling Scud boosters to Iraq. But he hadn't seen any reference to Scuds in the message traffic or any indication whatever they were looking for would actually transit their area. It was all so vague he doubted they'd be out here much longer. And the deployment was drawing toward an end. Then a little time at home, and he'd have to think seriously about what next. Like Blair's proposal. A nine-to-five shore billet, a house in Alexandria or Arlington or maybe a little farther out, Falls Church or Reston.

Looking at the absorbed expressions around him, listening to the hum of the blowers and the monotone of the controller talking Blade Slinger down for a hot refuel after searching a hundred miles to the east, he realized he'd never be as happy in any other job. Commanding USS *Horn* was probably going to be the high point of his career. He'd done

well, considering its . . . checkered nature. That was probably the right word. A red square, then a black. In the navy's
good graces, then, most decidedly, out.

He tuned back in to hear Marchetti say, "If we do have to
board anybody out here, I want the Gold Team."

"Despite Petty Officer Wilson?" Hotchkiss said, only the
faintest edge cutting through the sweetness of her tone, like
a blade that has to be oiled to penetrate a tough alloy.

Marchetti just shrugged, not giving it away. Which, Dan
thought, was being a little rough on somebody who'd saved
his bacon.

He got the phone on the second buzz. "Captain," he muttered, trying to snap himself into something resembling
awareness.

"Sir, TAO here. EW reports warship type radars between
sixty and a hundred miles northeast of us, based on bearing
drift over the last twenty minutes."

He blinked into the slanting darkness. The wind was
rushing outside. It had been rising at dusk. "Any idea what
type, what class?"

"It might be a Kashin."

He sat up. A Kashin-class destroyer displaced less than a
Spruance, but in terms of weaponry they could be considered evenly matched. The next moment he shook his head.
This was what Nick Niles had accused him of. Reacting too
fast. Assuming the worst. What Fetrow hadn't liked about
his arming his boats in Bahrain. "Have we got them on
JOTS?"

"Coming up now."

Dan was reflecting how once, and not that long ago either, detection of a Soviet destroyer would have sent a U.S.
warship to general quarters. For his entire career, the Soviet
navy had been the U.S. surface fleet's number-one enemy.
Now Yeltsin's newly downsized Commonwealth of Fewer
and Fewer Independent States was trying hard to impress the
West with how great an investment opportunity they were.

Yeah, everybody was friends now. The Russians. The

Chinese. The Wall was down. The Cold War, over. The vortex that had sucked down blood and treasure for fifty years.
Could it possibly be everyone had learned to play together in
the same sandbox at last? He told Camill, "If it's on JOTS,
the world knows about it, but let's make a satellite voice report anyway. Just to reassure 'em we're on the beat down
here."

He thought about getting Camill to plan an attack, just for
drill, but didn't. He hung up and lay back in the dark.

Then he couldn't sleep. His mind was just jumping
around. Thinking about this and that. Once they got back,
they'd spend the next year more or less in port. Maybe some
counterdrug ops in the Caribbean. About the time *Horn*
started gearing up for her next deployment, he'd be briefing
his relief. And maybe thinking about a civilian career. Except . . . he couldn't think of a job that'd give him a tenth the
satisfaction that welding this crew together had.

Yeah, they'd come through a lot: overcoming the divi-
siveness Ross had left, fixing the engineering and combat
systems problems, getting the women accepted. It'd be
tough to see them go. Especially since they'd added their little footnote to history.

But it happened to every crew. They'd transfer, ship out,
get out, retire. And in later years they'd think fondly of their
old ship, and whenever they met someone from her, they'd
talk about this character and that; and maybe someday
there'd be a notice in the *Navy Times* about a reunion. He'd
heard the way former skippers talked about old crews and
ships that were gone, heard the regret and homesickness in
it, as if for a little while they'd actually tasted what life had
promised when they were young.

The phone. "Skipper? Just got off the horn with CTF 60.
They said they know about the Russian. Not an object of
concern."

Dan asked if there were any other contacts, and he said
no. A second later the phone was back on the hook.

He was almost asleep again when someone tapped on
his door.

. . .

"Who is it?" He kept his door locked when he slept, something he felt equivocal about but couldn't neglect. Not in the navy of the 1990s, and maybe, thinking about the *Bounty* and the *Globe* and a lot of other infamous incidents over the years, maybe never. He leaned against the jamb, waiting.

"It's me."

Hotchkiss. He opened at once, and there she was in the dim red light of the passageway. He heard the ever present hum from the nav shack, the creak of steel around them. Not a heavy roll. Just a light, comfortable sway that told him they were taking the prevailing seas on the port beam. "What you got, Exec?"

"Can I come in?"

"Yeah." He turned the stateroom light on as she came in, snapping the switch to red. Giving her visibility to navigate, but not so much he'd be dazzled if he was called to the bridge. She was limping and he took her arm. "How's the knee?"

"Not so bad. Nothing broken."

"That's good." They were face to face in the dim light. When she said nothing, he shifted his gaze and cleared his throat. "Well, what you got?" he said again.

"I'm afraid it's about you," she said.

He cleared his throat, trying to reorient even as his body, understanding more swiftly than his torpid sleepy mind, began to respond. In the red light her lips looked softer even than he'd dreamed. He stood riveted, unable, in that moment he'd fantasized so often, to move or act.

She looked around the stateroom she'd been in so often before. He saw it suddenly through her eyes. The rumpled blanket on the settee, the coffee cups racked over the desk. The hum of the computer. The sigh of the wind. The creak and sway around them loud enough, the devil in his heart proposed, to cover any noise they might make.

Finally she said, "Can I sit down?"

"Sure. Sure." He waved to the chair, but she perched on the settee, almost primly, knees together. Looking closely he saw perspiration gleaming on her upper lip. He lowered himself beside her. Conscious suddenly he was in skivvy shorts and T-shirt, neither exactly fresh.

"Thanks for helping me today," she said.

"All I did was help you up."

"With your arm around me. You know what they'll be saying now."

"I guess so. Yeah."

He was so used to seeing Claudia Hotchkiss in control that seeing her nervous was almost frightening. Seeing her pressing her fingers together to keep her hands from shaking.

"We're not going to be together much longer."

"We'll have to take her through the yard together. Then postdeployment training. No," he tried to joke it away, "I wouldn't let go of the best exec I've ever had."

"I've decided to put in for a transfer. As soon as we get back."

That was when he noticed she wasn't calling him 'sir' or 'skipper.' In fact, she wasn't calling him anything. Just talking directly, in an obviously stressed tone. Maybe he was wrong about what was going on here. He'd assumed . . . the obvious, but maybe he was wrong.

"This isn't about Chip, is it? Are you still having problems?"

"He's met someone else. Someone who . . . fulfills his needs. He told me when I get back, he's filing for divorce."

"Oh, Claudia. I'm sorry."

He didn't ask her if there was anything he could do, because he knew there wasn't. No one could do anything for another in that stark time when the one you loved told you it was over, when you realized your plans and dreams were a mug's game. But he put a hand on her shoulder, to give her a human touch in her pain.

Without saying anything she pulled his head down to hers. So hard and fast their teeth slammed together, and the sea taste of blood mingled with the kiss.

"I've wanted to do that for a long time," she whispered.

"Don't worry. I know you're married. I'm not the clinging kind."

He took a deep breath, trying to get past wanting to lay her down and let go all the tension and stress and lust he'd buttoned up for months. "I wanted it, too. And I can't say I don't want to now. But we can't. You know that."

"I guess I do. But, oh, shit, I just needed that kiss so much. I didn't really think past it when I stopped and knocked. Actually, I was going to the nav shack." She laughed shakily, almost crazily, and he caught a glimpse of a far less controlled and hardheaded Claudia Hotchkiss than anyone had ever seen aboard *Horn*. "That's why I want off. Going to sea with you and having to deal with you and work with you. Talk about living hell!"

"You can take it, Commander. Or else do a damn good imitation."

"That's all it is. A fucking imitation." She laughed again, shakily. Her hair had come undone and hung over her cheek. "See, I know you don't want to hear this, but—"

He put a finger over her lips. "Don't say it, Claudia."

"You know what I'm going to say?"

"I've got a good idea."

They were whispering, of course. He could smell her breath. Clean, like balsam, or pine scent. An inane voice in his head prattled about pheromones and chemical receptors. He got a breath in and out, but couldn't look away. In the red light, flushed, eyes wide, with her shirt coming undone, she was as desirable as it was possible for a woman to be. All he had to do was reach out and she was his. And his prick kept popping up out of the buttonless fly of his Uniform Shop yellow-label boxers. Making him fear that any moment she'd bend over and very slowly and delicately slide those parted warm lips down over it.

In which case, he'd be well and truly lost, because his inhibitions were holding forty million years of heartily copulating primates back now only by the barest fingernail.

He cleared his throat again. "Don't go there, Claudia. We

wouldn't give McCall and Richardson the seal of approval. Or Konow and Hurst, in the paymaster's office. So how's it look if we do what we punished them for?"

She didn't say anything, just adjusted something under her shirt and looked away from him. He felt uneasy, like he always did when women didn't speak.

"You're probably right," she said, almost listlessly. "Anyway, thanks for listening."

"I'll take it as a compliment."

"Not as a lapse of professional conduct?"

"Maybe a misstep," he said. "But I'm guilty, too. Whatever you want, Claudia, I want, too. And I might have communicated that on some subverbal level. But let's get one thing straight. You're finishing your tour, and you're going on to screen for command and get your own ship and have a sterling career. Is that clear?"

"Aye, aye, sir," she said, and he honestly couldn't tell what her tone was actually saying.

She was at the door when he remembered and got up quickly. "Wait a minute."

"What?"

"Let me look first."

She stood back as he cracked it, peering out, feeling the insane weirdness of having to check the passageway. But they couldn't let somebody spot her going out at this time of night. Perceptions mattered, sometimes more than what really happened.

Which had been nothing. Right?

The passageway lay empty, a disturbing scarlet-lit vacancy that always seemed to him like some midnight knife-murderer should be prowling it. "The coast is clear," he whispered back, feeling like a teenager getting his girlfriend out of the house before his parents heard them.

She was about to go when she turned back. "I guess I'll read about this, right?"

She meant, on her fitness report. And he saw again her keen hard ambition, and knew this moment would vanish

soon enough from her memory. Or maybe that was cruel.
But he knew what she meant.

"I already addressed that issue, Claudia. We're all feeling
our way through this thing. Let's call this a free throw. If it
doesn't happen again."

She chuckled. "I don't think you have to worry about
that."

At that moment they both heard a watertight door scrape
and bang open. Someone coughed at the bottom of the ladder. He let go her hand just as, inside his stateroom, the
buzzer went off.

"Shit," he muttered, and closed the door as her steps
faded. "Captain," he said into the phone, tucking his still ob-
streperous member back with his other hand.

"Sir, Lieutenant McCall. I took over TAO from Mr.
Camill."

"What you got, Kim?"

"Flash traffic from COMSIXTHFLT. The radioman's
gonna be knocking on your door about now, but I thought I'd
have the figures ready."

Dan opened the door, revealing the radioman with fist in
the air ready to knock. He looked surprised. Not as surprised, Dan thought, as you'd have been if you'd come up
that ladder sixty seconds earlier. "Flash message, sir," he
said, holding the board out and looking away from his commanding officer's hard-on.

He scanned it, cradling the phone in one shrugged-up
shoulder as McCall filled him in with short staccato statements. He heard her out. Then gave the word to come up to
flank speed.

29

Domiat, Egypt

Shifting the heavy, clinking bag from hand to hand as he made his way down to the waterfront, the man in the loose-woven dishdasha thought this was not the most remote cranny of the world he'd ever seen. At least it had trees. Stores with refrigerators, though the flyblown goods smelled of dust and kerosene. It had mosques—true ones, not the elaborate and idolatrous Shi'a mockeries.

And turning the familiar corner he saw again through the eyes of a gangly boy running these dusty alleys, shouting to passing captains to take him on as a hand.

Because this rundown village of adobe mud was where he'd grown up.

Now, thirty years on, he walked the same narrow shaded alleys, mind weaving strangeness with familiarity into a loose fabric of past and present through which the incandescent sun burned with unvarying ferocity. Now he called himself Mahmoud. With his new identity he'd put on once more the voluminous cotton country Egyptians wore about their business. In the heat and light and sea wind its fluttering caress surrounded him like a cool flame as he neared a wooden pier that stretched out into the Nile.

Domiat, or Damietta, was eight miles upriver from the sea. This eastern branch of the great river was the poor relation. It met the Mediterranean through a tortuous, shallow way, almost choked at times by a shifting bar of sand. To the east lay Port Said. Far to the west, Al-Iskandariya. The land between slumbered in broiling heat, a sandy coast given over to dates and figs, goats, donkeys, and water buffaloes.

Even in his boyhood, though, it had based an intensive sardine fishery. Along the English-era stone quay, along the piers that groped out into the scum-flecked stream oozing at this low season at barely a walking pace, rode scores of the nondescript, tough little craft that grazed the southern Mediterranean for the tiny fish that served not just as food but as fertilizer for the sandy fields.

And breathing in the river smell, the rich after odor of the fishery, he closed his eyes, behind gold-rimmed sunglasses such as a liberal cleric might wear, and for a moment was also in Cameron, in Calcasieu, in Cypremort and Grand Chenier and Bayou la Batre, listening to the chatter of Vietnamese. And the whine from a distant radio became the strange atonal music Vinh and Nguyen had played in the land of their exile.

And at the same time, a barefoot child squatted outside the coffeehouse, brushing flies from his lids as he hung openmouthed on the tales of graybearded seamen.

And at the same time his own fleet would be far out from Bir Sudan by this time of the morning; out where the water lay flat and lightless as oiled steel and the sky shifted with a pulsing ruddy haze, and the radios lilted with Mohammed Mounir and Ahabaan Abdul Rahim.

Was this, he wondered, what growing old meant? That you lived not just in the present, but in all the moments you'd inhabited? He'd heard once that the Sufis, may they be cursed, said man was only a thought in God's mind.

Yet even Damietta, remote as it was, bore the marks of the ceaseless struggle between Islam and the West. The ruined forts at the entrance testified to that. The Franks had controlled all this stretch of coast during the Crusades. Till Salah-ad-Din, the great prince of Islam, had thrown back the Westerners eight hundred years before. He stroked his newly grown beard, pondering that struggle. Which had never ended and never would until the last soul on earth bowed in submission to God.

But no man could fight forever.

He waved flies off his face, frowning. Unfortunately, he still had to settle with Salim. Where the Sheikh gave with open hand, his querulous advisor doubted and misered. No better than a Jew. But surely such an action as he was about to carry out would close his career with honor. Surely after it a tired, no-longer-young man with only one eye could retire to his boats, his company, his private devotions. To a quiet life in the Sudan.

When he called out, several men emerged into the sunlight, wiping their hands on cotton waste. He acknowledged their greetings with a smile. Went down a rickety gangplank, clutching the bag to his chest, feeling the cool sweating roundnesses within with anticipation.

The boat smelled of years at sea. Its deck was patched with the paint the villagers had compounded of the oily fish from time out of mind. It was a hundred feet long, with a midships deckhouse and a stumpy pole mast to which the outrigger nets were hinged. Moored by a line to the stern, a smaller craft lay on the sluggish river: a beaten-up fiberglass-hulled sport fisherman with a tilted-up Yamaha outboard.

The first team, in this same boat, had sailed from Domiat the month before, made the round trip to their target area, and returned. They'd been boarded and searched a few miles from their destination, but of course there'd been nothing in the hold but sardines.

The second group had been here a week. They'd overhauled the engines and installed steel plates shielding the wheel and the fuel tanks. They'd installed another bank of batteries, a second generator, and two more bilge pumps, and had scrubbed down, decked in, and run lighting to the hold. They'd bought bottled water, new mattresses, a butane stove, rice, couscous, dates, tea, coffee, chocolate, and canned meat.

Then, the night before, they'd driven the truck in from the

warehouse in Port Said. Under cover of darkness, they'd swayed the heavy crated package down into the hold. Where it rested now beneath closed hatches, snuggled into its cocoon of the other material.

He spoke briefly with them, saying all would be as God willed, but he had hopes of success and victory. Then stood watching as they filed up the gangplank. From the pier, one of them—the Sheikh was very media-savvy—held up a video camera. Shielding his face with his sleeve, he bowed deeply to all those who would see and thus be moved to follow in the path. The cameraman panned over the boat, then out toward where the river met the sea. Then the red light went out, and they waved, and he waved back to them.

Then he was alone.

The third crew, the final crew, would not board for a few hours yet. He went below and checked the hold again. Running his hands over the sacks stacked close against the bomb, their contents slowly warming in the dim heat of the hold.

The bomb itself was not so much. A small charge, as such things went. It was the heavy plastic-covered sacks stacked around it that made him smile. They were covered with writing in many languages. Most also bore colorful pictures of healthy, robust sheep and goats, for the benefit of purchasers who couldn't read. Products of India, for the most part, though some came from China and other countries as well. The Sheikh's men had purchased the material in small lots here and there throughout the Middle East, from various agricultural suppliers and commercial growers.

Sheep grazed on pastures without trace amounts of certain rare elements lost their appetite. Their skin grew scaly. They became anemic, and the lambs did not thrive or grow. Most of the sacks contained cobalt sulphate, a heavy sand the color of dried blood. Others contained cobalt chloride. A few contained cobalt carbonate, which potters used in blue glazes, but as this was the most expensive form of the element, they numbered only a few.

He snapped a padlock behind him, then looked into the

engine room. Humming quietly, he checked the battery charge, fuel level, oil level, through-hull fittings. All secure. He went topside again and looked across at the dusty streets.

Almost against his will, he went slowly up the gangplank. Checked the lines.

He hesitated there for a moment, a white-clad figure alone in the burning sun, on the hot stone of the quay. Then began walking, with firm, steady steps, on into town.

She was heavier than he remembered; shorter than he recalled. She stared at his shoes from the barely opened door with no sign of recognition, a fold of cloth drawn across all but her eyes.

"Haleemah?" he asked, not even sure it was her.

"Who . . . You are not him. Who are you? Who sent you here?"

Did she know him? Had he, too, changed so much? Or did her dull tired gaze no longer see? He remembered her beside a fountain, the day they were married. The radiance of her smile, her slender body in the night . . . "It's me. Your husband."

Her eyes came up, flickered on his face. Recognition came. And with it, something that looked like shame. "Ahmed. You didn't write me you were coming."

"I'm here on business. Let me in." He glanced down the narrow, stinking hallway. A state apartment, built not long before but already its concrete flaking, the halls smelling of urine.

Unwillingly, it seemed, she opened the door. Closed it immediately, and stood wringing her hands as he looked around.

"You have been well?"

"Well, well . . . God has given us health . . . but this is not a very big place," she murmured tensely. He noticed her front teeth were blackened, rotten. Furrows of worry had engraved her face. "The government lets me stay here because of Badriyah. But they only give us twenty-five piasters a month to live on, and the *baladi* keeps getting smaller, and it's five piasters now—there's no fish or rice anymore on the green card—and I can't go out, I can't leave her here—it's been five years! Five years!"

He patted her shoulder. She was weeping, clawing her face. He said, "Things will be better now."

"What do you mean?"

"We're going to Sudan. I have a business. A fishing business."

She said wonderingly, "You always loved boats."

"I have eight. Every day they go out. Fifty men work for me. You will both live in my house."

"House?" she said, like a child repeating a word it has never heard before.

"I have a house on the Red Sea, in a place called Bir Sudan. I'll take another wife. But you'll still be my senior wife."

"Your senior wife," Haleemah mumbled. "But what of the girl—"

"We'll hire a Sudanese woman to help you take care of—" He nodded toward the other room, assuming she was in there, though he didn't hear her. He remembered her as never silent. That mindless crooning, wordless, endless, not disturbing, unless you were disturbed by the wind in the desert or the mindless tinkle of a fountain.

His wife trembled. Her eyes burned. She clutched his hand and began kissing it feverishly again and again, mumbling rapidly "God be praised, God is great, God be praised." He caught her smell, close, rotten, the stink of a woman who has not bathed in months. There was no air-conditioning or even ventilation in this concrete tomb. The glassless windows were shrouded with dark cloth. She was muttering rapidly now about houses and maids and money, interspersing it with pious *du'a* and praise of her husband's generosity.

And something within him moved away from her. She was so intent on her comforts, on the outward things that meant nothing. Her breath stank. He shook her hand from his sleeve. "Where is she? I will see her now. Then I must go."

"Oh—she's—in her room." She grabbed his sleeve again, then, as she grasped what he'd just said. "Go? Wait. Coffee—I don't have any—a bad wife—not ready—so expensive—I'll go across the hallway. Sit down, wait, sit down—"

"Don't disturb yourself. Be calm. All things in good time," he said, trying to make his voice reassuring. He pressed her hand again, felt its roughness. She was old. Old.

He went into the next room. Pushed aside a sheet hanging in the doorway, realizing too late it was damp, hung there to dry.

He stopped, breath catching in his throat.

Small bowls of lentils and couscous, half eaten, half decayed, covered the floor. The stench of feces hung where flies swarmed above an uncovered pot. Cloths stained with brown dangled from a line.

A black bundle lay on the truckle bed. The room was very hot. The windows were sealed. He moved carefully among the pots of food and ordure until he could bend over, then sit, carefully, twitching aside the blanket.

His daughter's cheekbones stood out like those of a corpse. She breathed rapidly and shallowly, as if she'd just been running, and red spots flamed on her cheeks. Her eyes were closed. He touched them gently, the blind eyes that had been so beautiful when she was little. Her skin was puffy and unnaturally pale, save for that flush. A smell welled from beneath the blanket. He touched her cheek, but she did not open her eyes or move. He shook her shoulder, so thin he felt bone; nothing altered. Indeed, now that he looked close, he could hardly recognize her.

He glanced back, becoming angry. "Why's she asleep?"

"She's like that all the time now."

"What do you mean? Doesn't she sing?"

"She hasn't done that since you went away."

"She opens her eyes?"

"She no longer opens her eyes. She no longer sings. There is no money for doctors."

He grew angrier, rage grew monstrously within him.

"Where are the things I sent?" he shouted. "The silk? The furs? For her to touch, and stroke?"

"No, no! Don't shout at me!" His wife covered her ears, cringing. "I had to sell them."

The bowls shattered as he kicked them aside. He shouted, "You sold them? She loved to touch them. That was her only pleasure! You have not taken proper care of her!"

"There's no money—no help—I can't do everything—"

"What have you done to her? Who were you expecting to see when you came to the door? Bitch! Whore! I will not take you to Sudan. You would shame me before my friends. You are no longer my wife. This is a sty."

He kicked over the chamberpot, then jumped back as a flood of shit poured across the floor. His wife screamed and fell to her knees in it. She screamed, throwing her abaya over her head, pleading for forgiveness, for God's mercy to enter him, for him not to leave them again, for him to stay.

He strode down the hall, filled with disgust. The sound of her wailing followed him. But he did not look back.

He stopped at the store again for more soft drinks and *baladi* bread on the way back to the harbor. The old storekeeper served him with unspoken questions in his gaze. He didn't greet the man, or ask his name, though his face was obscurely familiar. The boy who'd grown up here was long buried beneath other identities, other experiences. His daughter would die soon. He accepted that. It was the will of God, like her blindness, her retardation. Written in the Book before the ages had begun.

All was the will of God, and no man or devil or might of empire could change the smallest jot of what He had written.

The quay, the trawler, the burning sky were the same. The only difference was a battered pickup ticking over in the gritty heat, and in it three dark-haired, dark-skinned young men abiding with the eternal patience of Egypt.

He greeted them courteously, shaking each's hand for a long time, holding it as the dust from the departing truck sifted out of the dry air. Three. Not overmany to crew a hundred-footer. But enough, if they were willing. They'd not need to work the nets, after all.

They squatted in the skimpy shade of the deckhouse and he shared out icy colas they accepted with childlike pleasure and nervous reserve. Their names were Ali, Antar, and Rasheed. He did not know what they'd been told about him, but they seemed respectful, even afraid. He uncapped a bottle for himself and sat questioning them, asking how long they'd spent at sea, what experience they had with engines, whether they could steer and read a chart. As he'd expected, they were quite young. Older men did not want to sacrifice. Too much bound them to this world. Antar seemed to know enough about diesels that he felt confident appointing him to their care. The others were deckhands, no more, though they swore they could steer. Not a great deficiency. It was only a hundred and forty sea miles to their destination. He could train them well enough on the way that they could make the last few miles on their own.

They sat together for some hours as the sun descended, and prayed together, when the call rang out to *asr*. The volunteers gradually relaxed. They spoke of their families, and what had driven them to oppose the enemies of Islam. They had no children. They were filled with hate and recklessness. This was good, he thought. The network had chosen well. These men would not even miss themselves.

For all of them, maybe even for himself, he thought with sudden insight in that drowsing heat of oncoming evening, that was the Sheikh's wisdom: to find such hollow vessels and show them how God fit the void within them so perfectly none could doubt he had been fashioned to fulfill a greater cause. Sometimes a tool was broken. Sometimes it was lost. And sometimes left behind, when others were more suitable. When the task was truly understood, the fate of the tools did not matter.

"Teacher," Rasheed said at last, "you will become a *shaheed* with us?"

"I will accompany you. But it is not written that I am to die with you."

"You'll sail with us? We don't know the way."

"I will go with you even to the gates of Paradise. From there on, you will be far above me in honor. You will be the truly firstborn sons of God. His beloved soldiers, who will purify the earth of the Zionists and restore His golden land to the Faithful. *Insh'allah,* and your names will be inscribed forever in the Book of Life."

"*Insh'allah,*" they murmured, shyly. May it be the will of God.

"I bow down to you, and wish you the tranquility that comes before battle. I only wish I could join you at the end. But perhaps one day I will."

This last, he thought, was not perfectly accurate. He yearned for a cool house and a young wife more than martyrdom. This would be his last work for the Sheikh. But these were young and filled with zeal, and he turned his face away that they might not see his thoughts. Might not see his contempt for them . . . The sun was declining. It would be best to be at sea before the night was complete.

"First we'll pray," he told them. Then Antar will go below and start his engines. I'll take Ali on the wheel for the first watch. Rasheed, eat of the food below, then sleep against my waking you. And then we will see what God has written."

30

Base Security, U.S. Naval Support Activity, Bahrain

Hi. Hi." The FBI agent smiled shyly as Diehl introduced him around the table. To Aisha, Major Yousif, Commander Hooker, and a somber-suited, light-skinned Arab who had been introduced only as Mr. Hassan.

Arnold Nimmerich was a computer forensic examiner. The first one Aisha had ever seen, though she'd read about them in the criminal justice journals. He was her age, but his blond hair, long in back, was already receding in front.

Presently everybody in the agents-only meeting upstairs in the base security building took seats. At last, as if bringing forth crown jewels, Major Yousif unlocked a briefcase, unwrapped several layers of bubble wrap, and gently placed on the table the drive a joint SIS/NCIS evidentiary team had seized from the Salmaniya Avenue madrassa.

Diehl asked whether they'd dusted it. Yousif said dusted and photographed, but the only prints on it were old, from when it had been assembled. Which meant they didn't need to do the usual rubber-gloves routine.

Nimmerich picked it up and turned it over. Studied the label pasted to the bottom, then rattled it, like a kid with a present. He put it back on the bubble wrap and said, addressing nobody in particular, "So, is this particularly time sensitive?"

"We think it might be," Hooker said.

"Ey-yup. Well, sometimes these things take awhile. Just

to let you know. Was the computer running when it was taken into custody?"

"No."

"If you take one running, dump the RAM to a disk before you pull the plug. That'll give you passwords resident in memory, any decrypt process that's running, stuff that makes my job easier. If there are usable files on this one I can probably get you some degree of recovery, unless whoever used it last knew how to do a disk wipe. Was there a modem on the source machine?"

"Yes," Aisha said, since no one else looked like they knew what he was saying.

"Then there are probably e-mail files. They can lead to other connections and potential suspects."

She said, "He could have used a Web-based e-mail, like Yahoo or Hotmail. Then the files wouldn't be resident on his computer."

Nimmerich looked at her and said, rather unwillingly, she felt, "Correct, but you can find traces and sometimes parts of messages in the unallocated clusters. I can do string searches to bring up hidden information like that. But again, it'll take time."

"What do you need from us?" said Hooker.

"Well, I brought the software I think I'll need, and some blank, formatted hard drives and cables, but I'll need two machines. One like the one this came out of. The other, the fastest IBM compatible you have, with a dual processor and a high-capacity tape drive. A phone line, back to Quantico. And a secure place to work."

He looked around uncertainly, not meeting her eyes, obviously wondering who was in charge. He picked Diehl to address, probably because he was the oldest white man. "Where will that be? Someplace I can plant myself for a couple of days?"

"Major?" Diehl deferred to Yousif.

The SIS man cocked his head. Running out the various angles, she thought. At SIS headquarters, where his men could learn from the visiting American computer expert?

But also where the American could see how well or how
badly they were equipped and trained. Here at the base?
Where he might lose control of whatever they managed to
extract. Aisha caught the flicker of a glance between him and
the Arab. 'Mr. Hassan'—it was like introducing someone as
Mister Jones in the States. A pointed little beard, and
hooded, watchful eyes over a too-ready smile. He'd spoken
only a few words, in Arabic. But she'd gotten to talk to some
Saudi sisters in her souk roaming. He had their accent.

"We'll do it at the ministry," Yousif said. "In a special
room, separate from our regular offices. We'll have to re-
strict access. I'm sure everyone understands how sensitive
this information may be."

"I don't," said Diehl. He'd hauled out one of his El
Stinkos, was chewing it, and seemed, despite annoyed
glances from around the table, about to light it. "We'll close-
hold it, but this is a criminal investigation of a very nearly
successful attack on one of our ships. We led you to the evidence. We want access to the result."

Yousif said, "Mr. Nimmerich will be your access, Bob.
What more can you want? He is, after all, an agent of the
FBI."

Diehl asked Nimmerich, "You read Arabic, Arnold?"

"No."

"You a Moslem?"

"I'm a Mormon."

"A what?" said Yousif. No one answered, and he frowned
and made a note on his pad.

"Well, Aisha does, and Aisha is. So she goes, too," Diehl
said. "She's got a top-secret clearance. She knows the background of the case. She's hot stuff on the computer, too."

She reflected bitterly that now she "knew the background." Somehow the senior agent had conveniently forgotten she'd actually *broken* the case, getting a confession from
Childers-Jaleel, tracking down the missing explosive, finding the computer. Yes, a woman needed all the modesty God
could give her. Not to mention a hide like a rhinoceros.

And here was "Mr. Hassan" pursing his lips, shaking his

head. And Yousif taking his cues from him, saying lightly, "No, no, that won't be necessary." Who *was* this guy? The only guess she came up with was one she didn't like to contemplate. The Al-Mabahith al-Amma, "General Intelligence," the Kingdom of Saudi Arabia's shadowy and ruthless secret police.

Nimmerich said, obviously trying to be helpful in a situation he didn't understand, "She could help evaluate the files, if I can recover any. If they'll be in Arabic."

"We'll provide any language expertise necessary."

"Forget it, Major. Nimmerich's not gonna have any idea what he's looking at. So without her, no deal," Diehl said. He got up. "Come on, Arnie, we're booking you back to D.C."

Nimmerich looked up, surprised and not pleased. Or, she thought, he didn't like being called Arnie. Yousif said disapprovingly, "You're not cooperating, Bob."

"*You're* not cooperating, Major. A joint investigation means both sides get the results of all the forensics. That means both sides are *at* the forensics. But either you don't trust us to turn over everything Arnie here gets off that drive. Or else . . . Could there be something on it you don't want us to see?"

He didn't look at Hassan when he said this, but Aisha smiled. The senior agent might not know the local language, or the latest technology, but he'd smelled the same rat she had.

"Ridiculous. Of course we'd share everything, Bob." Yousif motioned like he was smoothing out a rumpled cloth, but he was showing the strain. She had noticed that he gnawed at his mustache when the pressure was on. He kept looking from Diehl to Hassan, as if caught between irreconcilable responsibilities. "Sit down, please. Commander Hooker, talk sense into him. We're all friends here. We've always been open with you, haven't we? Always shared everything? Well, well . . . if you want her there, she's welcome. Aisha? We'll issue you the appropriate passes and so forth as soon as we break."

But the Saudi didn't like it. Aisha didn't miss how he

stayed in his seat as the others rose. The flash of distrust, dislike, maybe even hatred, as their gazes clashed, just for a moment, then turned aside.

The room was on the third floor of the ministry, in a lofty-ceilinged work space that bore all the hallmarks of being hastily converted to its new use, like folding tables and lots of extension cords. Four computers were set up around the walls. Two Pentium Gateways, the Sanyo from the madrassa, and an Apple. The last was the only one with a modem, set up with an encryption program for Nimmerich when he had a question for the guys back at Quantico. A laser printer, too, a hulking cream-colored Hewlett-Packard the size of a small refrigerator.

Nimmerich began by examining the hard drive again, making notes in a fresh spiral notebook. "So how do we proceed?" Yousif asked. He'd attached himself to them, and it didn't look like he was going to leave.

Nimmerich said, slightly pompously, she thought, pointing to the nearest Pentium, "First I'm going to convert this into a forensic workstation. Then I'll explain as I go, all right? If you're interested."

"I'm interested," she said. While Yousif sat back, making it plain as he could without saying so that the actual work of recovering the data was beneath him.

"Most girls don't know much about computers. Or care."

"I'm probably not like the other girls you know," she said.

Nimmerich pursed his lips, but didn't follow that one up. In fact he reddened and buried himself in his work.

Using screwdrivers from a kit in his briefcase, grounding each on a conductive pad, he took off the side panels to access the interior of the computer. He pulled off cables, slid out the hard drive, and replaced it with the evidence hard drive.

He said, not meeting her eyes, "Okay. I'm going to configure the evidence as the master, and this second drive as the slave." He installed one of the blank, formatted drives he'd brought in the lower bay. "Now we're gonna copy it to this new drive, make what we call a forensic image. That means everything: active files, deleted files, hidden files, password-protected stuff, everything. Then we'll take the evidence out and bag it again. Protect it from viruses or data corruption, and any accusation from the defense we added files that weren't there."

When he had the machine buttoned up again, he put a 3.5-inch minidisk in the A drive and turned the power on. As it whirred and images flickered across the screen she said, "What was that? A boot disk?"

"Uh-huh."

"Why don't you boot from the hard drive, like usual?"

"So we don't accidentally write to the original evidence. I just took a normal boot disk and neutered it—made all the pointers look at the floppy disk, and not the hard drive. That's also got the SafeBack software, the utility I'm going to use to make the image."

Aisha kept watching, a little surprised this wasn't black magic. She was following everything so far.

The FBI tech finished the boot and in DOS, not Windows, typed in the command to make the forensic image. The little lights that showed hard drive activity started to flicker, the machine making an intermittent chirruping that reminded her of a cricket.

He got up. "Okay, where do we eat?"

"You're hungry? It's only ten o'clock."

"Jet lag. It's dinnertime for me—at least, I think that's right."

"What about this? You're not going to just stop. We need access to whatever's on this drive. It's urgent."

"Really urgent? Or just department urgent?"

She looked at Yousif, who hesitated, then nodded. She told Nimmerich, "Really urgent. You know someone tried to bomb one of our ships."

"They told me that. Yeah. A navy ship, right?"

"USS *Horn,* here in Manama harbor. This belonged to the

perp. We missed him just by minutes, the day of the attempt. We think he's on his way to do the same thing, or something like it, somewhere else."

"You mean, another bomb?"

"Based on the MO, we think he's done this before. It'd be nice if we could catch him before the next one." She glanced at the flickering lights. "So if you can do that for us—"

Nimmerich checked his watch. "Okay, I'm motivated, but it's still gonna take awhile. What it's doing now, it's actually checking each bit on the disk and copying it and checking to make sure it copied it right. Then it goes on to the next one. It's going to do that even for the overwritten parts, even for the parts on the drive that were never used.

"After that we're gonna try our recovery procedures, sector by sector. I'll look for hidden files, then any temporary or swap files used by applications or the operating system. I'll go through the unallocated spaces and any slack space. Then we go after password-protected or encrypted files. I'll go as fast as I can. But we still have to analyze the system as we go, list all the files of interest and any data we discover. That's evidence, too—file structures, authorship information, any efforts to hide or delete or encrypt data. Okay? You following all this?"

"Actually I was."

"Good," he said. "So. Where are you taking me to eat?"

The image took four hours to make. When the screen showed OPERATION COMPLETED, Nimmerich powered down the computer, took the side panel off again, and slid the evidence drive out. Yousif immediately held out his hand. The SIS man locked it in the briefcase and left. While he was gone Nimmerich fitted a second blank hard drive in the upper bay. Then, using the SafeBack disk again, he recopied the image to the second blank hard drive.

Meanwhile she drove back to the base and caught up on her e-mail and phone messages. Four hours later she was back at the ministry to find Nimmerich blinking sleepily and drinking coffee with Yousif. Which she hadn't thought Mor-

mons were supposed to do, but she didn't ask, didn't want to
bring up religion in any way, shape, or form.

Nimmerich had put the computer's original hard drive
back in and loaded Norton Utilities for the analysis. He explained what he was doing as he used the diskedit feature to
recover files.

"Hmm. He reformatted it."

She said, "I thought so, when I found it wouldn't boot.
When we discovered it. That wipes everything, right?"

"Not exactly, but it makes it harder."

Yousif said, "These are all erased files, right?"

"Erased, right, but also reformatted. You probably know
this—Aisha?"

"Right."

"But what DOS actually does when you erase something,
it just reclassifies that file sector from 'used' to 'available.'
That's easy to recover, especially the last things they deleted
before they left, that's all gonna be there. But this guy's
wise to that, he actually reformatted. Then it gets tricky. But
fortunately he didn't have the software for an actual wipe.
That overwrites every physical byte on the disk." He
worked on for some minutes. Then he clicked his tongue as
a list of files came up. She saw some titles were in Arabic,
others in English, a few in a character set she didn't even
recognize.

"Here's something. Can you read this?"

Yousif leaned forward, too, as she went down it, reading
the titles and translating. Nimmerich clicked his tongue
again. "Here's his system. The stuff in English is unpro-
tected. Everything else is password-protected. I'm gonna assume the passwords are in the same character set as the file
name. I got one program that just runs through all the possible combinations that you give it. A five-character password,
that's not gonna take it too long to . . . How many letters are
there in Arabic?"

"Twenty-nine," Yousif said.

"Well, we'll try that first."

It took him awhile to set up the program, but after twenty

minutes' run time it opened the first file. "Uh-huh. Uh-huh."
Nimmerich made another note in his spiral-bound, then
went back to keyboard and screen. "Okay, this looks like a
graphic of some kind . . . reach into my bag of tricks . . .
we'll try QView Plus . . . Anybody recognize this?"

Yousif leaned close over her shoulder. She could smell
the coffee on his breath, the musky scent of his body. He was
gradually moving his stool forward, crowding her. Bob and
Kinky had done that. Gotten in real close, in the office, till
they were all but touching her. After asking them a couple of
times to back off, and seeing their confused reaction, she'd
realized it wasn't intentional; they were just both ex-
submariners. But Yousif had no such excuse. She edged her
chair away.

The major said, "It's our harbor. Manama Harbor."

"Ey-yup. You want a hard copy of that?"

They said they did. Keys clicked, and the printer started
to hum.

"This?"

They studied the next image for a long time before
Yousif suggested it might show the layout of the explosives
in the dhow.

"So you want that one, right? Printing. Another graphics
file . . . map here, I'd say . . . how about it? What's that look
like to you?"

Aisha said, "It looks like . . . Israel?"

"Palestine," Yousif muttered, correcting her.

Aisha furrowed her brow. This was something she
hadn't expected. In the upper right corner was a scale in
kilometers. In the lower right corner, a feathered arrow that
after a moment she recognized as showing the prevailing
wind direction.

"Print it?" Nimmerich asked, into the sudden puzzled
stillness.

Yousif said casually he guessed not. Aisha cocked her
head, still trying to figure what this was doing here, but when
the FBI man looked at her, she did not object.

He went on. Plowed through more files, muttering to himself, while she tried to work out why a map of Israel might have resided on a hard drive in Bahrain.

Meanwhile Nimmerich came on the .exe file for an e-mail program. "Which means there should be address files and some in and out mailboxes here somewhere, too. I'm glad they didn't wipe. Then you've got to take the drive apart and put it on this special machine that detects like really minute remaining magnetic charges, try to recover data from that . . . and . . . uh-oh."

She said, trying to push away what she'd been thinking, "That doesn't sound good."

He pointed at the screen. "I was cruising around while I was talking. . . . This is Windows Explorer, the attributes window. Look at that."

"What is it?"

"That's an encrypted file, guys."

"Encrypted," said Yousif, leaning forward to see. Suddenly going tense, as if this was what he'd been waiting for.

"Huh. He's got encrypted files in nonencrypted folders. Cute."

So far Nimmerich had seemed relaxed, more so than when he'd been talking to her, but now he went into a focused mode. "Might be harder than I thought. This looks like PGP Disk, or . . . no, it's not, but something like it . . . uh-oh. Seven-digit key. *Not* that Indian thing!"

"What Indian thing?"

"It's an encryption program that has this extra wrinkle. You bring up the file, it prompts you for a key. If you don't have that, or the god mode, all you see's garbage."

She didn't like the sound of that. "The what mode?"

"God mode—the master key that gets you into any of the files. Oh, I don't even want to get into public-key encryption. Factorials and all that crap . . . but you can understand every file getting its own individual key. As it's being created."

"Sure."

"But only the master administrator has the god key. Him and maybe a deputy, for backup. He can read everybody's files. They can only read their own."

"Okay, so this program—"

"Just wait a minute. Regular encryption programs, the file comes up, you don't put in the right key, you just don't get in. It just sits and waits. But this one—Shiva. That's what it's called. If you don't put the key in right the first time, type the whole ten digits exactly right, it overwrites everything in the file. Self destructs, like in *Mission Impossible*." He clucked his tongue. "Somebody was serious."

Yousif said, "But you have a copy. This whole drive you're working on is a copy. Right? So do like you did with the other passwords. Try a key, and if it doesn't work—"

"Make another copy of the drive, and try again." Nimmerich nodded. "Sure, theoretically. But that's not a process we can computerize. At least, not here; National Security Agency might be able to do something like that as a virtual machine . . . but here, it'd be a physical process. A seven-digit key, twenty-nine letters each, it'd take . . . centuries."

"Centuries?"

"Ey-yup. Look, I understand, like you said, this is high priority. But this is solid encryption."

Yousif muttered to himself. Words she'd never learned at Defense Language School. Then said aloud, "This is a good place to stop."

"Stop? Why?" Nimmerich's head snapped around. "Isn't this why you wanted me?"

"No. Your job was to recover the data. *We*'ll interpret it."

"Major," Aisha said warningly.

But Nimmerich was still talking, oblivious to the security people eyeing each other. "Well, you're not going to do much interpreting on this. But like I said, somebody back in D.C. might have some magic wand they can wave over it. If I could take this copy with me, fly it back, we might get them to take a look at it. . . . Want to give it a try?"

"I don't think so," Yousif said. He got up. "In fact, it's time to wrap this effort up."

"Why not?" she asked him. "We might find something interesting."

"I don't think there's anything interesting here."

Aisha ignored him. "Mr. Nimmerich. You said you needed the key?"

Nimmerich said, still eyeing the screen, still oblivious, "Hey, if you got any brainstorms, now's the time to try 'em."

"Then get ready to copy what comes up. Because I think I might know the . . . the god key you need."

From his right she leaned, eyeing the screen. He was still in the Arabic character set. She began to key in the characters, carefully, one at a time, making absolutely sure she hit the right keys.

Remembering a crushed bicycle, the smells of blood and feces.

How she herself always had to write down her password, so she wouldn't forget it.

A smear of ballpoint on a dead man's wrist.

As she was halfway through entering it, Yousif reached across to block the keyboard. But Nimmerich must have had a brother and grown up playing computer games; he caught the motion from the corner of his eye and blocked it so fast with his shoulder it must have been reflex. She'd never seen him move as fast and sure as that before. "What's that say?" he snapped.

"It says . . . *Imaamah.*"

"Is that a word? What's it mean?"

From behind them Yousif said, "It means . . . ruling over someone. We would say, The emir has *imaamah* over Bahrain."

"What is it? A code name?"

"It doesn't mean anything," Yousif said. "Shut it down now. That's enough."

Aisha took a stretch, looking back casually as she did so. The SIS officer returned her glance with an angry scowl.

He'd never forwarded her the autopsy report on the dead man outside the base gate, though he'd promised to. Now the word scrawled on his wrist that had unlocked a secret file didn't mean anything?

When she looked back, the screen had changed. To a list of files and documents and graphics. They were only on the

screen for seconds, the three of them staring at them, before
Yousif reached again, taking Nimmerich by surprise, and
stabbed the power button on the computer. The screen wavered, faded, went to black. "Hey!" Nimmerich yelled.

"Don't turn it back on again."

"What'd you do that for?"

"Miss Ar-Rahim, Mr. Nimmerich. I'll call a car to take
you both back to the base."

He reached behind them, pulled the plug out of the wall,
and left. Hastily, as if, she thought, he had to report to someone. Leaving them alone with the computer, at least for the
moment. The hard drive still whined inside the case, slowing, powering down toward silence.

Nimmerich looked astonished. "What's with him? Did I
say something wrong?"

"I think we saw something we weren't supposed to see."

"Like what?"

"Like the plans for the Doctor's next attack."

He blinked at the blank screen. "Is that what it was? Say,
what's going on here?"

"They don't want us to read this drive. The e-mails. The
addressees. The messages."

"Course they didn't. That's why the perp erased them."

"I mean someone here, Agent Nimmerich," Aisha told
him. "And we're not going to see this data again. It's going
to disappear."

"Uh-huh. Well." Nimmerich cleared his throat. "Is that
right? One of those local sensitivity things. So, I guess that's
it, huh?"

Aisha took a deep breath then. Knowing that what she
was about to do would go against host country orders.
Would make her persona non grata in Bahrain, and maybe
other places, too. Might even be seen as betrayal by other
Muslims.

But what someone was protecting here wasn't the way.
No one had the right to take innocent life, women and children and the aged and ill. The Prophet, *sullallahu alayhe*

wa-sallam, had made that plain, no matter how men seduced by Satan twisted God's word to mean something else.

She put her head down next to Nimmerich's. Watched his ears redden as she breathed into them. Whispering, in case the upstairs conference room of the Ministry of Justice and Islamic Affairs happened to be wired: "Pull the hard drive. Right now. No arguments. Hand it to me. Turn around, don't look."

They hurried down the stairs. The hard corners of the copied drive poked into her belly under the abaya. Her heart was hammering. The main corridor. The door. The big clumsy Suburban seemed to take forever to start, to get backed out of the parking space, to get lined up for the gate.

Yousif burst out of the door, screaming for her to stop, screaming at the sentry to close the gates. By then she was already pulling through, hitting the accelerator. A truck was looming over them, Nimmerich was making strangled noises and flailing for his seat belt, and she was merged, she was in the roundabout, she was gone.

31

The Southeastern Med:
Oparea "Blockbuster M"

HORN rode alone, yet not alone, beneath a clear blue sky shading toward dusk. The wind and seas had kicked up over the last couple of days, with a fresh northeasterly breeze. The ride was still comfortable, but the ship felt alive. The weather-deck doors had been open all day, letting in a welcome coolness after the months in the Red Sea and Gulf.

Dan had his feet up in his captain's chair, on the bridge. He'd just come up from ten straight hours in Combat. Would probably spend the night there, too. But he needed a break from the endless crackle of data. He yawned between the last forkfuls off the tray the mess attendant had brought up. Then filed his cleaned plate against the window and leaned back, listening to the drone from the helm as the helmsman corrected to a course of 090, speed ten knots, the chatter over the VHF as, miles to the northwest, an Italian frigate interrogated the master of an Indian bulk-cargo carrier.

The Camel broke his reverie. He had the draft OPREP-5 feeder report, and Dan went down it quickly, checking only here and there because he'd never caught the Ops boss in a mistake yet. "Lin give you this, about the evaporator?"

"Yes, sir." Past Camill's skull, no longer shaven—with the onset of cooler weather he was letting his hair grow back— Dan saw Hotchkiss come on the bridge. Once again composed, clipboard under her arm, she met his glance across the pilothouse. He initialed the message and Camill left.

"Evening, sir," she said. Dan nodded, waited, but the exec didn't seem to have anything more. Just stood by his chair, looking past him at the sea.

"Nice night," he said at last.

"Yes, sir. Sure is."

"I know I've been tied down all day. Have you got something for me?"

"I just wanted to say that . . . last night's not going to happen again."

"I already told you, ancient history. Okay?"

She nodded, but didn't look convinced. He saw now there were circles under her eyes, as if she hadn't slept. Well, since the flash message sending them east, few aboard had. He started to say something reassuring, but was interrupted by the 21MC calling him back to Combat.

The screens showed the southeastern Mediterranean off Israel, where *Horn* had moved during the previous night, as a blue field overlaid with yellow squares and circles. The squares marked operating areas. Over the last eighteen hours they'd filled with most of the U.S. destroyer-types in Task Force 60, two British frigates, *Active* and *Scylla,* two more each of French and Italians, and even a Turkish frigate. Closer inshore, smaller rectangles marked a second barrier pattern off Gaza, Ashqelon, Ashdod, Tel Aviv, Netanya, and Haifa. The squares alternated in a slipped checkerboard, so any intruder snaking between two of the first-line defenders would go straight through the center sector of the next.

He settled into his chair, fitting his spine into the familiar indentations like some piece of expensive and delicate equipment into a form-fitting case. The dim blue light haloed profiles at the surface weapons console, the Harpoon engagement planning console, the Tomahawk data console. Beyond that, men and women sat intent at the EW stack, the gunnery control station, the fire control radar consoles. The horizon rolled slowly on a monitor that gave them the output of the mast-mounted sight. Fifteen people shared the icy air with him. Directly before him Casey Schaad had a finger hooked on the transmit lever of the 21MC, ironing out a glitch in the combat direction system with the data processing center. He was keyboarding with the other hand, a phone tucked into the crook of his neck, busy as a fry cook with six short orders going. . . . He caught Dan out of the corner of his eye. "Sir. Track 2378. Another incoming from the west Vigilant Dragon wants us to check out. Picked up by Tiger One Four."

Each incoming contact was assigned a track number by the tactical data system that linked the NATO warships. "Vigilant Dragon" was the screen commander, CTG 60.5. As far as Dan could tell, someone had grabbed a group staff and assorted straphangers and commissioned a scratch task group. They were split off from the battle group aboard USS *Mahan* and placed in tactical command of this barrier operation, which did not yet, as far as Dan knew, have a name, despite having grown hour by hour as more ships joined into what was now one of the largest multinational operations he'd ever been involved in. "Tiger One Four" was the on-station P-3C patrol aircraft, which flew a plodding beat north and south across the western boundary of the checkerboard. It was relieved every eight hours. Over the thirty-some hours the operation had taken shape they'd entered track data on hundreds of crossing contacts to the screen units.

To a disquieting extent, though, he had no clear idea what this immense and unscheduled evolution was intended to accomplish. He could see it was urgent. Every destroyer type in the battle group had been pulled into it, leaving *Roosevelt* operating west of Cyprus with only her escort cruisers, and every NATO navy in the eastern Med except Greece. Another puzzling point was that in contrast to most barrier operations, where warships and large merchant ships were the objects of interest, no one running this operation seemed to care about them. The P-3s were only marking small craft—

fishing trawlers, pleasure craft, small coasting vessels.
Which were of course far more numerous, leading to a den-
sity of data that left the screens looking as if they'd been
blasted with birdshot. Some of the tracks were ruler-straight,
arrow-passages toward fixed destinations. Others wandered,
zagged, even corkscrewed, shadowing schools of fish across
the late summer waters. The radios crackled with transmissions on bridge-to-bridge and calling and distress frequen-
cies. *Horn* herself had intercepted and inspected five fishing
craft of various nationalities and a large Greek power yacht.
They were given a choice: turn back, or submit to boarding
and search. The Greek had been drunk and hospitable, Marchetti had reported, but the others had not been happy at being unexpectedly harassed on the high seas.

Dan shifted to see around Schaad. The center screen
showed *Horn*'s area. All the operating areas began with
"Blockbuster." Blockbuster M was the southernmost, twenty
nautical miles by twenty, butted up almost touching against
the Egyptian territorial sea off El-Arish. Only about ninety
straight-line miles from their previous oparea off Port Said,
so they'd been one of the first ships to report on station.
Along with Bill Brinegar in *Moosbrugger,* now occupying K
to the north, and clearly visible not just on JOTS but on both
surface search radars and once during the night past as a distant masthead light.

To the south the radar showed the smoothly curving coast
of the Sinai, speckled far inland with the furrowed-looking
returns of dunes, till they faded as the earth's curve dropped
them below maximum range. The oporder, which gave every
evidence of hasty drafting, directed all units to stay clear of
national waters. Yet the southern boundary of his area, specified in the same order, overlapped the Egyptian twenty-mile
limit by two miles. So far, this hadn't been a problem. He'd
just stayed to the center of the box.

Another interesting point: none of the tasking messages
thus far had mentioned what the boarding parties were looking for. They were to examine the ship's papers, ascertain
nationality, port of embarkation, destination, and cargo.

Within minutes of radioing the results to Vigilant Dragon the response would come back: cleared to proceed.

The only conclusion he could come to was that Higher didn't know what they were looking for, other than that it was being transported in a small craft. Staring at the screens, a second possibility occurred to him. They knew, but they didn't want to tell.

Schaad was on two phones at once now and, between sentences on the circuits, talking across the compartment to the petty officer on the dead-reckoning tracer. Behind Dan's back another ops specialist was scrubbing down the comms status board. The gabble of speech and blowers and radio noise went on and on until gradually his head rolled forward.

In his chair, the captain slept.

"Sir." A hand, shaking him. Not Schaad. Must be after midnight, then. He blinked, worked his tongue around to scrub out a foul taste. "You awake, Cap'n?"

It was Camill. Dan pushed himself upright, reminders or memories popping up in his mind one after the other like a series of programs loading. His brain was booting up, but it didn't feel like he had a lot of speed on his chip. Barrier patrol. East Med. Off Israel. "Yeah," he said. "What have you got, Herb?"

The black lieutenant said, "We got somethin' that might turn interesting."

Tiger, the patrol aircraft, was data-linking two tracks thirty miles west of *Horn*'s box. They were moving fast, almost thirty knots, in a smoothly altering course that JOTS shortly revealed as a weave twenty degrees to either side of the base course. One contact was echeloned back from the other. Dan contemplated this for several seconds, getting an uneasy sense he'd seen it before. Or read about it . . . a red-backed book, on the right side of the page. . . . Strange how he could remember where on the page but not the title of the volume.

"Have we got voice with the patrol aircraft?"

"Intermittently. He's at the edge of VHF range."

All at once he remembered what he'd read about that weave. It was a Soviet tactic, one they'd passed on to the forces they'd trained.

It was the way a strike group of missile craft approached a surface barrier patrol, screening the approach of a higher-value unit behind them.

"Ask him to look behind them. About fifteen miles behind." Dan picked up the phone beside his chair and ratcheted the barrel switch, by feel, fast, *clickclickclickclick*. "This is the skipper," he told the bridge. "General quarters, no drill, right now."

As that was going out, the incoming track data showed a sudden drop in speed. At the same time the petty officer on the ESM stack, the electronic listening gear, yelled, "Square Tie radar, bearing two-five-two, threat close."

The assistant TAO, Kim McCall, was going through the pubs, but Dan already knew what that meant. Odds were their contacts were Osas or Komars. Small, fast missile boats the Soviets had provided to their third world clients by the dozen. Komars had sunk the *Eilat,* an Israeli destroyer, not many miles from where *Horn* was right now. Cheap to build, fast, and packing two to four heavy, huge warheaded missiles.

The 1MC cut loose, so loud it hurt his ears. "General quarters, general quarters. All hands man your battle stations. This is not a drill." The alarm cut in, the rapid electronic note that haunted the dreams of every man who'd ever heard it for real. "Traffic route is up and forward, starboard side; down and aft, port side. Set material condition Zebra throughout the ship . . . I say again, general quarters, general quarters. All hands man your battle stations."

The intruders seemed to be slowing. Now he had them at ten knots, same base course. He told Camill to set emission control, shutting down the radars except for single sweeps on order. They passed that to the bridge, and a moment later it came over the 1MC as well. Watertight doors slammed. He tucked his pants cuffs into his socks, strapped on his gas mask carrier. The compartment was a bustle of others doing the same, the general quarters team coming on and getting briefed up. Fortunately, Camill was the tactical action officer for general quarters, so he didn't have to turn over or brief anyone, just stayed where he was. Dan saw perspiration reflect blue light between the stubble of his incipient hair.

The radar pictures faded to blank screens. Dan didn't plan to stay in electronic silence, but he wanted to see what these guys had in mind before he laid out his hand. If they were what he thought, they'd be searching out ahead for a target. So far, thanks to the patrol aircraft, he knew about them, while at thirty miles they probably hadn't detected him yet.

"Okay, Kim, where are they from?"

"For the Med region the pub lists Russia, Algeria, Bulgaria, Croatia, Egypt, Iraq, Libya, Syria, Yemen, and Yugoslavia as having Osas and Komars."

"That doesn't cut it down much." But this close to the southern shore, he guessed Egypt or Libya, with Iraq, Algeria, or Yemen more distant possibilities. He slid out of the chair and stood beside Camill studying the display at close range. So far they showed as unidentified. As he watched, *Horn*'s transmitted input took effect, rippling change into the data readouts. "See if Tiger's willing to go over there and get some visual ID. Infrared. A side number or something."

"We could launch Blade Slinger, if they can't. Get a better targeting solution, if we need it."

"If they see us launch a fast mover, they'll know we're a combatant. Don't send it voice, either. Send it on the data link."

They'd drilled all this so many times, it was so much second nature now, that even though most of the crew had been in their bunks, barely six minutes passed before the 21MC said, "Captain, Officer of the Deck. Battle stations manned and ready, Zebra set throughout the ship, time six minutes fifteen seconds. Emcon condition bravo set throughout the ship."

"Very well." Dan studied the display. Even though his

own radars were shut down, he was getting data from Tiger, from *Moosbrugger,* and also from *Kocatepe,* the former USS *Reasoner,* which had the box directly to the north of them. The intruders were speeding up again, but had stopped weaving. He brought *Horn* to a course that would take her across their path.

Assuming they were Osas, the most likely possibility, they carried the SS-N-2, some variant of the infamous Styx. Not welcome news for a Spruance, which wasn't well equipped for hard-core antimissile engagements. The Styx had a maximum range of about forty-five nautical miles. But without over-the-horizon targeting assistance, its practical firing range was no more than twenty-four miles. He doubted *Horn* would show up on their radar at less than twenty miles in this sea state, and with his radars shut down, they couldn't tell he was a warship. If he timed this right, he could simultaneously appear on their radar and issue a voice radio challenge commanding them to heave to.

Unfortunately, one of those prickly questions was starting to loom. His orders were to prevent transit of his barrier area. But so far, he had no rules of engagement, nor did they have a designated enemy, nor instructions on what to do if somebody didn't feel like cooperating.

But if they kept coming, at some point he'd have to either shoot or let them go by. Since he couldn't open fire unless somebody told him to, he'd have to give them a free pass. But he figured first, if they kept coming after the challenge, he'd illuminate them with his SPG-60. It was clearly identifiable even with rudimentary electronic surveillance equipment as a fire control radar. A bluff, a threat he couldn't back up, but the best he could do.

With this in mind he pulled a red handset out of its clip. Keyed the scrambled satellite phone, waited for the beep that meant it was synched. "Vigilant Dragon, Blade Runner, over."

A hiss, a beep. "Vigilant Dragon, over."

"Tracks 2383 and 2384 are approaching Blockbuster

Mike from the west at high speed. ESM tells me they're Osas, but not whose. Unless otherwise directed, I'm going to challenge, then illuminate, but if they don't stop, I'm letting them go by. Advise, over."

"Vigilant Dragon. Stand by, over."

He turned up the volume so he wouldn't miss the call-back and resocketed the handset. The spring popped it out again and he had to reseat it hard to make it stay. The Harpoon engagement planner was twisted round, looking at him. Dan nodded to him. "Take it easy. This isn't a combat situation. But you might as well get set up. Just for grins."

"Double-round engagement?"

He nodded, reflecting that though two rounds per target was doctrine, on two boats it would leave him with only half his loadout of *Horn*'s most effective antiship weapon. His magazines were still heavy with Tomahawks, but he had only eight Harpoons. The Sparrows aft had a secondary anti-ship capability, though, and as a last resort he had the guns. He left the petty officer keying and went over and talked to the EWs about how they'd go about jamming a Styx. Then went back to his chair. 2383 and 2384 were still closing. They hadn't detected him yet.

"All right," he said. "Time for their wake-up call. Cancel emission control, illuminate, and challenge."

As he watched them close in he mentally reviewed tactics and countermeasures against missile boats. Material that was as much a part of the core knowledge of surface line officers as how to tie off an artery was to a surgeon. He'd studied them years before aboard USS *Barrett*. Refreshed when he went to the Gulf in *Van Zandt* as exec, and again during tactical training before taking command of *Horn*. If these were hostiles, and if they were actually running an attack profile, the next thing that'd pop up when they realized he was here would be a Drum Tilt fire control radar. Big ifs, but that was what made the Med interesting. It wouldn't be the first time he'd been shot at out here.

"TAO, EW. I have a Drum Tilt bearing 237. Associated with SS-N-2 Styx missile."

Camill looked at Dan. "Captain?"

Now they were radar illuminating each other. But were they both bluffing? He felt the first tension in his shoulders. "Fight the ship, Herb," Dan told him.

"TAO, EW. Drum Tilt's locked on to us."

The lieutenant cleared his throat. Dan hoped he didn't clutch now, this was where the rubber might just meet the road. He called out, "SWC, Harpoon solution?"

The surface weapons coordinator, five feet from Dan's chair, had been talking into his headset, studying his orange plasma screen. Satisfied he had it under control, Dan twisted where he sat to look past him at the Harpoon plotting team. He asked the chief in charge, "Jay, how's the solution look?"

"Time of flight three and a half minutes, STOT, two Bull-dogs each on targets one and two. Recommend air warning yellow. Recommend weapons posture one on all ASUW and AAW systems. Recommend CIWS in auto air ready and man all gunnery stations. Mount 51, HE-CVT, Mount 52, HE-IR."

Dan watched Camill process this. The chief had just given him a lot to think about. That the Harpoon—its on-air code name "Bulldog"—was ready to engage, with the mis-siles arriving at each target at the same time—STOT meant simultaneous time on target. He'd also recommended telling everyone in Blockbuster an air attack was likely. Next, he was suggesting all antiship and antiaircraft weapons and fire control systems power up, so all it would take to shoot would be "pulling the pickle"—pushing the fire button. He was rec-ommending Phalanx be switched to auto mode, giving the radar-controlled twenty-millimeters permission to shoot down anything that looked like a threat to their computers. His last advice was to load the forward gun with high explo-sive, radar-fuzed ammunition, and the after mount with infrared-triggered rounds.

Camill was still thinking. Dan started to slide forward on his chair. Had it been this hard for his skippers, waiting for him to come through? Three seconds . . . four . . . he opened his mouth to take over.

The lieutenant said, smoothly and distinctly, as if reading from a script: "SWC, CIWS to auto/air. Set air warning yellow. CSRO, set weapons posture one, surface and air weapons. CSOOW, WEPS, CSRO: Set weapons posture one, all surface and air systems." Voices answered with loud "Aye, ayes."

"Whiskey, this is Delta. Air warning yellow, bull's-eye mike delta. Sector one-eight-zero to zero-zero-zero."

"This is Bravo, roger out."

"Charlie, rog out."

A slight pause, then an accented voice. "Golf, roger out." *Kocatepe,* the Turk.

"WEPS, radar two, posture one set."

"Mount 51, posture one set."

"Mount 52, posture one set."

"Mount 51, 52, roger up."

"Very well," Dan and Camill said together.

"WEPS, CIWS. Posture one set mount 21 and 22."

Sparrow rogered up, too. Dan asked for a range to the nearest contact. Thirty-two thousand yards. Well inside Styx range. He forced a deep breath. Another. Just another seagoing game of chicken. Like the ones they'd played with the Soviets in the old days.

"Weps, Harpoon. Tech's en route to Combat. Needs the permission-to-fire key. Soon as he has it, posture one will be set."

"Poon, WEPS, roger."

The weapons system supervisor keyed a different mike. "Posture one set all AAW and ASUW systems with the exception of the PTF key. HER Tech en route Combat to get it."

"Got the key, Herb?" Dan asked him. "Just in case?"

Camill held it up on the chain around his neck without looking back. He was listening to the CSOOW passing the weapons posture information on his interphone. The man turned his head. "TAO, CSRO. Posture one set AAW, ASUW except for HER. Tech should be here in a second or two to get the permission-to-fire key."

Camill nodded as someone reported that CIWS was now in auto air ready. A blue-glittering bead was working its way down the back of his neck.

"Vampire, Vampire, Vampire!" the electronic warfare supervisor and the radar operator called out simultaneously.

Suddenly no one spoke. Time seemed to slow. He could feel it draw out between the very pulses of his heart. If he or Camill or the petty officers on the launch consoles screwed up, the people in this dim compartment had only seconds to live. Styxes were huge, and at this range they'd be full of fuel, too.

"Vampire" meant inbound missile.

"TAO, EW: Vampire emitter is A2Z4, correlates to seeker for SS-N-2-C. I hold two, possibly three emitters. Hard to tell, all on the same bearing and freq."

"I hold Vampire composition two. Vampire one from target one, Vampire two, target two."

Dan didn't hear it fast enough. He yelled, "EW, chaff! Now!"

"Chaff, aye—"

Camill called out, "SWC, take vampires. Engage with Sparrow, shoot, shoot, look. Backup with 51, 52, CIWS."

Dan got a grip on himself. He had to let them do their jobs, and get the word out what was going on. He grabbed the red phone, the Med Satellite High Command net. "All stations this net, this is *Horn* actual. I am under attack. SS-N-2-C. Composition two. Missiles launched from probable Osas, flag unknown, out." He socketed the phone without waiting for replies and pointed to the petty officer controlling the P-3. "Tell Tiger to stand clear during real-world engagement."

"All hands stand clear of weather decks . . . missiles inbound . . . missile firing imminent," the 1MC said over the gabble that was rapidly rising in Combat.

Dan could feel, hear, the main engines revving to full

power. The deck begin leaning. The officer of the deck was
applying the ship's maneuverability to the tactical problem.
Bringing to bear as many weapons as they could, but giving
the incoming Styxes the least possible lock profile. Meanwhile, he had to take out the incoming missiles and destroy
the shooters before they got off the next salvo.

"TAO, SWC. Sparrow locked on to Vampire one. Mark
86 has target two. Stand by."

The flight deck TV showed the Sparrow launcher suddenly slew around. The gun elevated, too, then whipped
around to port.

All at once the noise started. *Slam. Slam. Slam.* Two
guns, each pumping out a seventy-pound projectile every
three seconds. A more rapid drumfire from directly overhead: the chaff mortars, firing rounds of radar reflective foil.
Styx was a big missile, but not a smart one. The chaff would
probably fool it. But it was better to make sure.

A high-pitched wail, the missile fire warning alarm. A
rattling bang, then the avalanche roar of a truckload of
gravel being dumped. On the monitor the missile leaped out,
blanking the image first with a flare of light and then a cloud
of cottony smoke. Another roar, flare, and cloud, and two
mach-three missiles were on their way. The guns had been
firing for some seconds, but they'd pass the shells in the air.
A fire control petty officer began chanting time and distance.
Then called out, "I have target bloom, Vampire one . . .
Evaluate as kill!"

"Vampire two turning left . . . no . . . seems to be seeking," Camill told him.

Dan nodded. One hard kill. But the second Styx was trying to decide on its target. The small, hard blip its mother
fire-control computer had told it to attack? Or the big new
ones that had suddenly appeared? It turned away again, then
back toward *Horn* once more. The guns were still banging
away. Camill was gearing up for a second Sparrow salvo.

"TAO, Guns: radar video consistent with target breakup.
Evaluate Vampire two as kill."

"TAO, EW: Emitters ceased."

Camill called, "Cease fire. Cease fire!"

"Ninety seconds from launch to splash," Dan said, looking at his watch. Both missiles splashed at four miles from the ship, and within five seconds of each other. But it wasn't over yet. Camill was looking at him, waiting.

"Take 'em," Dan said.

"TAO, SWC: I have positive solution both targets."

Camill said, eyes still locked with Dan's, "Kill targets one and two with two Bulldogs each."

"Salvo warning." The SWC activated the salvo warning and vent damper alarms. The compartment ventilation fans spun down in a whirring decrescendo. The siren went off again.

Closer and much louder than the fantail-mounted Sparrows, the departing Harpoons rattled the deck plates and vibrated the tote boards like an elevated train going over their heads. A circuit breaker alarm began warbling. It went on and on. Faintly someone yelled, "Bulldog one away. Bulldog two away. Bulldog three away. Bulldog four away."

Dan concentrated on his Seiko. Despite the closed dampers, a smell like scorched brake linings reached them. Time of flight: about three minutes. "All hands stand clear of Harpoon deck in preparation for launch," the 1MC said. Yerega had gotten a little behind script, but it didn't matter now. What counted was how well the millions of lines of code running in the dozens of linked computers had been written. How carefully some production drone had screwed parts into a missile body on a California assembly line. Maybe they'd get lucky. If they didn't . . .

Sweat was trickling down his back, but he felt icy cold. He was waiting for the next "Vampire, Vampire." Waiting with every muscle in his body drawn taut. But it didn't come . . . It didn't come.

Finally he couldn't stand it any longer. "Targets?"

"Gone," Camill said, staring at the big repeater.

"Turn to short wavelength."

"Okay, now I have small intermittent returns at that range and bearing. Consistent with debris. Five . . . four . . . none."

He waited for the next sweep of the radar. Looked up. "Nothing but sea return."

Dan mopped his face with his sleeve. The Combat team looked at him, to him, he supposed, for some hint as to whether it was okay to cheer. He couldn't give them what they wanted. Frozen, paralyzed by the felt knowledge of how horribly other men had just died. Torn apart by explosive, burned, clawing at the sea as they sank into the final bloody darkness.

He couldn't rejoice.

But neither could he be sorry. Whoever they were, they'd tried to kill him first.

Christ! Agonize about that later, Lenson! The question was, Who the hell had they been? And why had they fired? No state of war existed. No blockade or interdiction zone had been declared. Any regularly commissioned ship of war could have blown off *Horn*'s challenge and passed clear, and there was nothing Dan could have done about it.

The only answer he had was that they'd attacked to protect someone else. Someone who *could* be challenged, and stopped, and searched.

The satellite phone beeped. Dan gave the staff officer on the other end a quick rundown. "You sank them both?" the voice said at last.

"I returned fire. Hard kill on both hostile missiles. I then fired four RGM-84Cs on the shooters and observed impact. Both contacts have disappeared from the screen except for faint returns I evaluate as debris. Now proceeding to the point of impact."

He got a doubtful "Roger, out," and slammed the phone back into its holder. It popped out again, impelled by the spring, and this time he let it dangle.

The men were still waiting. He had to say *something*. "Good reaction, good work," he said to them all. "Especially the Mark 86 and the Harpoon Targeting team. Herb, give the OOD a course and run us over where those missiles hit. We'll see if there's anybody in the water who can tell us what this was all about."

But Camill was looking up from the big scope again, puzzlement clear in his furrowed brow. "What is it?" Dan asked him.

"That third contact," the ops officer said. "It's still on the scope."

"What third contact?"

"The one you told me to check for. Out behind them."

Dan slid out of his chair.

The radar return was faint. It was probably either smaller or lower than the Osas. When he put the ESM operators on its bearing, they picked up a weak emission on a VHF band. When they put it on the speaker, it sounded like Arabic. But by the time they got a translator to Combat, the transmission had ceased. The bands hissed like an empty conch shell.

"Give them a call," he told Camill.

"Unidentified craft, this is U.S. Navy warship. Identify yourself."

No response. They called again, then put Barkhat on. No one answered him, either. One of the trackers reported the contact was coming right. After a smooth wide turn, it steadied up. Running its new course out, Dan saw it was heading for Egyptian territorial waters. Where neither he nor any other U.S. unit could follow. From there it could merge back into the coastal traffic and vanish.

What could it have aboard so valuable men would kill and die to protect it?

"Sir, are we headed over where the Osas went down?"

"No," he told Camill. "Get Brinegar on the line. Vector *Moosbrugger* over there to pick up any survivors. If this is what I think it is, I'm not letting this guy go."

32

He could have intercepted in under an hour at flank speed. But he didn't want to go in blind, at night. So for the remainder of the hours of darkness he paralleled the third contact's slow course, remaining some miles to the north. Updating Vigilant Dragon every half hour, and each time requesting permission to cross the line, if necessary, in hot pursuit. Permission denied, permission denied. At first he took it calmly. After almost getting hammered with Styxes, he was just glad to be alive. Then, as the distance separating the fleeing craft from safe haven shrank, he started to heat up.

At the first sign of dawn he launched Richardson and Conden in Blade Slinger and vectored them southward.

As the light grew over the sea, they made a long-range pass, then checked the fleeing contact out from a mile away. Finally the aircraft made a low pass. They reported a trawler-type with two men on deck waving.

Listening in Combat, Dan had a moment of doubt. Was the attack by the Osas unrelated? Coincidental? No, the tactic, the offensive, had to have been meant to protect this innocent-looking craft.

He couldn't help recalling the dhow attack. It had looked innocent, too. Built around a small craft. They'd never have suspected a thing, if Ar-Rahim hadn't blown the whistle from shoreside. This could be the same tactic. Maybe even the same organization.

His phone, by his chair. "Skipper."

"Sir, XO here."

"Claudia?"

"We need a decision about breakfast."

Horn was still at general quarters, though he'd let the men relax on station. Where there'd been two hostile Osas, there might be more. But it had been hours now. He said reluctantly, "All right, secure. I want to stay at condition three on the bridge and Combat, though."

When the word came over the 1MC, the crew began stretching and stripping off their helmets. Dan sat brooding. Blade Slinger reported another low pass, crew still waving on deck. Estimated speed twelve. Richardson said it was pushing a bow wave. Twelve was probably as fast as it could go.

Which Dan thought strange for a fishing boat. The others had tacked and veered at low speeds, seeking their piscine prey. He went back to the chart table. Camill stood by silently.

"So where's he going now? A straight course, top speed?"

"Home?"

"You think so?"

"You know what I wonder," Camill said.

"What?"

"Not where he's going now. Where he was headed before."

Dan cursed himself. He should have thought of that. He headed for the chart of the eastern Med, rolled out and taped down. Called back, "Read me off the first detected position, backtracking on the JOTS."

He plotted it. Ran a straight line from the posit Camill read off.

Straightened, feeling a chilled knife-edge trace his spine. "You seeing what I'm seeing, Camel?"

"Yessir, sure am. They were running straight for Tel Aviv, till we got in their way."

He picked up the sat phone once more. Now he was going to have to explain he'd sent his embarked helo into the standoff zone dividing his patrol area from Egyptian waters. And that *Horn* herself would be leaving her patrol area in the next few minutes. This time he asked to speak to Vigilant Dragon actual. An older, more deliberate voice came on.

"Sir, Lenson here, CO *Horn*. I'm still seeking guidance as to what to do about this contact we picked up last night. The one I think the Osas who fired on me were running interference for. The one that was headed for Tel Aviv, until we intercepted it."

"Haven't you been told to track and trail?"

"Yes, sir, but that's not going to be viable much longer. We're closing in on Egyptian waters. Sir—"

"What is it?"

"I'm assuming whatever this guy is, he's what this whole operation was set up to catch. Some nasty package intended for Israel. So what is he?"

"We're contacting the Egyptian navy. This is an Egyptian national matter."

"Do they have units en route? We're not seeing any on the scope." Dan gave him a moment to reply, then when he didn't, keyed again. "Sir, two more questions on that. One: what if those were Egyptian Osas? Two: whether they were or not, if it's important enough for somebody to sacrifice two missile units for, do we really want the Egyptians to have it?"

Silence on the other end. Finally the admiral said, "We're seeking direction from NCA now."

NCA was National Command Authority, the White House and the National Security Advisor staff. Dan said, "Sir, we can't sit on our hands much longer. Once they get in among the coastwise traffic, they're gone. If it's dangerous . . . germs, or gas . . . maybe the wisest thing would be to sink it. Designate it to Bulldog, like we did the Osas."

The voice said that was out of the question. "Do not, repeat, *do not* launch on your contact. We're working all the angles you've just touched on, Captain. Believe me. Just carry on with what you're doing."

"Sir, we can't hang fire on this waiting for orders. He's making for the coast. Do you want me to board and search?

Light him up? Follow him across the line? I've got to have a decision soon."

"I told you. Track and trail. Otherwise, no action."

Dan thought about telling him he had his helo over the suspect, then decided not to. Better to beg forgiveness than to ask permission. He signed off and called Richardson, got a better description of the boat. It didn't sound that large.

What could it be carrying? A fugitive? Some fleeing political figure? No, he'd have been safer without the escort. It had to be a weapon of some sort. Explosives, like on the dhow? Or something less conventional? He wondered if this was the waterborne biological attack everybody had talked about so long. A small craft motoring along the coast at night, dispensing aerosolized anthrax to blow inland. Certainly Israel would make the perfect target.

And meanwhile, with each mile, they were getting closer to escape. He started to tell Camill to get the interpreter back up, give the boat another call. But they hadn't answered before. Only churned onward, toward the invisible line that would shelter them.

He was tempted to leave it. Be the good little commander. Do just what he was told. But Nick Niles was right. Dan Lenson had never operated that way. He had to second-guess everything. He'd never accepted an order without wondering why. And that skeptical voice didn't just question others. It doubted him, too; questioned everything he did, and everything he thought was right.

That simply, he made up his mind. At worst, he'd annoy some fishermen, lose his command, and forget about being promoted ever again. At best, he could stop a boatload of terrorists. Maybe even bring them to trial.

He told Camill, "Okay, here's what we'll do. The ship stays just outside the line. But we call away Gold Team for a helo boarding."

"A *helo* boarding, sir?"

"They're used to seeing it over them by now. Chief Marchetti can do a fast-rope or rappel down. Then we'll figure out what we've got and what to do about it."

"You're sure about that, sir? I don't think that's what Vigilant Dragon has in mind."

"He can't order me to cross into territorial waters, Herb."

"He can't?"

"Well, I guess he *could*. But he's not going to, because that'd be illegal. See?"

"Okay . . . so . . ."

"But it has to be done. So, I'll do it. At least, put the helo across."

"They're not going to like it, sir."

"That's why they call it command, Ops," he said, trying to make it light, though he felt anything but. He kept remembering how they'd forbidden him to defend himself in Manama Harbor. He'd acquiesced, pulled his men and his weapons back aboard. And came damn close to losing a lot of people and maybe his ship.

This time, he'd do what *he* felt was right.

Marty was pulling out his chair in the chiefs' mess when the 1MC shrilled 'Attention.' Then, "Now away the visit, boarding, and search team, away. Gold Team, provide. Deck division stand by to hoist out the starboard RHIB."

The chiefs stared at him. "Your song, Machete."

"Son of a *bitch*." He grabbed a fistful of toast off Andrews's plate and stuffed it into his maw, swung his leg over the back of the chair. Then froze as the 1MC crackled again.

"Belay my last . . ."

"Shit, why can't they make up their fucking—"

"Now away the visit, boarding, and search team, away. Gold Team, provide. Flight quarters, flight quarters, all hands man your flight quarters stations. Stand by to receive Blade Slinger One-Niner-One. No hats are to be worn on the weather decks. No eating, drinking, or smoking is permitted aft of frame 292. Stow all loose gear inside the skin of the ship. All unauthorized personnel stand clear aft of frame 292. Now flight quarters."

Still cursing, he was out the door in three strides.

. . .

"One-Niner-One on deck."

"Very well," Dan said. In the minutes since he'd given the order to call away the boarding team, he'd realized he hadn't gone far enough, thought the situation through. He couldn't send the boarding team over without *Horn* backing them up. They didn't have night to cover them, or fog, or much in the way of weapons except the door gun. He wasn't going to leave them out there alone again, like he had with the smuggler. Whoever was conning the trawler needed to see a warship on the horizon when the aircraft made its approach. So he'd just have to cross the line, violate territorial waters, and take whatever consequences followed. He reached up for the 21MC. "Bridge, CO: once we secure from flight quarters, come right and head for track 2385. He bears—"

"One-five-five, twelve miles," Camill said from the JOTS.

"One-five-five, twelve miles. Do your mo-board for a flank-speed intercept and be ready to kick around as soon as One-Niner-One lifts."

He got a roger back and reached for the phone. He wasn't supposed to do this. He was going to, okay, but he wasn't going to hide it under any bushels. If they ordered him back, it'd be time to think it over.

"Vigilant Dragon, this is Blade Runner."

"Dragon, over."

"One-Niner-One clear of the deck," said the 21MC. Faintly through *Horn*'s metal Dan heard the zooming whine of the helo's turbines as she tilted past, going out. The deck began to slant as the OOD put the rudder over to follow her.

"This is Blade Runner. Unless otherwise directed, I'm going in after this guy at this time. I'll report back what I find out."

When he didn't hear anything back but empty air, he smiled sardonically at Camill. Clicked the transmit button twice, and socketed the handset so hard that, this time, it stayed put.

• • •

The Gold Team was mustering when Marchetti ran up the ladder. He didn't have coveralls on, just regular khakis, but there wasn't time to change. Goldstine slammed his Mossberg into one hand, his .45 into the other, looped the ammo pouch stenciled MACHETE over his neck. He slung the shotgun and stuck the pistol in his belt. The gunner's mate dumped an extra handful of shells in his hand, and he moved on. In the hangar he caught the harness Cassidy threw, started strapping it on. No life vests: they caught in the rappelling gear.

"What is it this time, sir?"

"Droppin' on a trawler. Skipper thinks, maybe some of the bastards tried to get us in Manama."

"Droppin' on a hot LZ!" said Lizard Man, eyebrows peaking. "Cool."

"You guys see anybody with a weapon, take him out," Cassidy said. He looked at Marchetti. "That's your line, isn't it?"

"It sounds okay from you, sir." They looked at each other, and for a moment there Marchetti wondered what had happened to the old Cassidy, the scared young ensign. Now he had a Battle Face, too, the mask you dropped over your real self when it was time to load up. He turned back to the team. "You melonheads spring-loaded? Check your buddy. Descenders! 'Beeners! Empty chambers, mags tight! Don't forget your gloves. That rope's gonna hurt if you do!"

They gave him thumbs, good to go. He heard the distant clatter of helo blades, and his pulse started to pound. They'd practiced insertions, but he couldn't say they were hot shit on them. Crack Man, Sasquatch, Lizard, Snack Cake, Deuce, Showboat, Spider Woman. He went down the line, checking boots and weapons and harnesses. When he came to Wilson he stopped.

"You ain't gonna give me any shit this time," she snapped, before he could say anything at all.

"Who—me?"

"Then what do you want?"

"I just was gonna say this might be a little rough today."

"I can rappel as well as you can, asshole."

"Cranials!" one of the squadron guys bawled, handing them out. Marchetti snatched off his cap, tucked it into a pocket. So did Wilson.

"Okay, okay, I just wanted to say if you don't—" Looking at her slitted squint, he decided to save his breath. "Ah, fuck it, never mind."

The howl of engines ate through the hangar door, devoured the hot, close air. He pulled the cranial on, and the din became a muffled Niagara. Cassidy hung up the phone and gave him the go signal. He bent for the static line and slung the coil over his shoulder. "Gold! Follow me."

Open air, blinding sun, buffeting wind, the smell of hot kerosene and a turbine-scream deafening even through the ear protection. A red-vested crewman stood under the shining roaring disk, right hand beckoning, left pointing. Marchetti diagonaled across the flight deck and took a brace by the sliding door, helping the guys in when their gear hung up or their boots slipped. Rolling in last, he crammed himself and the coil of static line into the final cubic inches of space. The crewman slid the door shut, scraping his back. Then they were all heavy, the deck pressing against their backsides, and he saw the ship falling away, a blue slanted sea rotate in to take its place.

There wasn't a lot of room in a sixty. The guys were on each other's laps. But climbing the sunlight, he suddenly knew this was as good as it got. A hammering roar in his ears, a gun in his hand, the smell of hot metal and oil and men. If these were the same assholes who'd tried to get them in Bahrain, he wanted another crack at them. He knew the guys did, too. The only problem was, one of them had his ass right in his face. He shoved at it.

Wilson looked around, grinned, and let one rip. He could smell it even through everything else. "You lousy bitch," he yelled into the overwhelming sound.

He had to read her lips to hear "Fuck you."

• • •

To give himself a few seconds grace if the officer in tactical command called back with another "permission denied," Dan told Camill he was going topside. Swung down with relief—he'd been in Combat almost nonstop all night and all day before—and jogged up the ladder, up to the pilot-house.

Sunlight, warmth, shining space. The whistle of wind. The clack of a Browning bolt seating out on the wing. *Horn* was driving over three-foot seas like a big Peterbilt down a new interstate. He took a deep breath of air that wasn't filtered and cooled and rubbed the bristly prickle on his chin. Alive, damn it. For a few seconds last night, when that second Styx had swung back toward them, he hadn't been sure any of them were going to see the sun again. Yerega shouted, "Captain on the bridge." Claudia Hotchkiss started to slide out of her chair on the port side. Dan pushed his hand down, telling her to stay where she was. He asked the officer of the deck, "Range to—what are you calling it? Roughly ten miles, bearing about one-five-five?"

"Calling that Alfa X-ray, sir. Range—sixteen thousand, five hundred yards. Bearing one-five-zero."

"Distance to the boundary of international sea?"

"Five miles, sir, more or less."

He hoped he hadn't put this off too long. But even if he had to go in the shithouse after this guy, he was going. He'd claim hot pursuit and let the diplomats fight it out. "And what are we on?"

"One-three-five, coming up on thirty knots."

Dan said very well. He got his binoculars out and braced his elbows, pointing the glasses slightly to starboard of where the bullnose lifted and fell as it romped along. On the bow the gray tapered tube of the five-inch aimed smoothly left, then right, testing the train commands. He remembered when gun mounts had held human beings, beefy sailors straining to lift and slam heavy shells into breeches. Now all was automatic, computerized. Sixteen thousand yards was a long way to see, but he might have something out there.

Anyway he wouldn't have long to wait. At thirty knots, every minute brought *Horn* a thousand yards closer. A flash from above the horizon. He squinted and made out One-Nine-One, banking, the sunlight reflecting from the shimmering halo of her rotor.

"Sir, I hold Alfa X-ray altering course to port."

"New course?"

"Not sure yet, sir—seems to be going into a turn—no, wait. He's coming back now."

The talker spoke up, too, confirming that from Combat. Dan rubbed his chin, frowning.

The helo controller said, "Sir, Blade Slinger requests permission to fire a warning burst."

Hotchkiss, looking through her own glasses. "He's trying to shake off the helo."

"Shit, yeah, how are they gonna drop if he starts snaking and weaving?" He was sorry now he'd lagged back. He should have gotten *Horn* over there first, overawed them with six hundred feet of gray steel, *then* put Marchetti over. He told the controller, "Permission granted. Put a burst across his bow."

The man who called himself Mahmoud shaded his eyes, looking up at the huge clattering smoking machine that reeled and swayed in the air a hundred yards behind them.

His men were dressed as simple fishermen. He'd told them to come up on deck at dawn, all except Antar, who had to stay below with the diesel. It had overheated during the night. They'd had to carry water in buckets all night long to keep it running. But it should get them back into Egyptian waters. They could lose themselves until the sardine fishers ventured out again. Then try again, and complete the mission this time.

But now, this helicopter. He had no idea where it had come from. Only that with each pass it edged closer. He could see the pilots' faces now. Looking down through the windscreen.

A door on its side slid back, revealing an open blackness as the aircraft yawed. It banked away, flying out in a wide turn. Then wheeled back crossing ahead of them. A helmeted crewman aimed.

The clatter of an automatic weapon, and bursts of white foam sprang up in their path.

Rasheed leaned from behind the wheel. "They want us to stop," he called uncertainly.

Stroking his beard, he said softly, "Stop weaving. It only wastes time. Steer south by your compass, and put your throttle full ahead."

In the roaring interior of the helicopter, Marty was still thinking about Cassidy. How he'd grown up. How he was probably gonna be all right.

He didn't usually think about zeroes much. They only came in four sizes anyway. There were the ones he called brown-asses. They wanted to be your buddy, but never stood up for the troops when it counted. The second kind were the micromanagers. But some of them were teachable, once they figured out you were as smart and committed as they were. Then there were the ROAD scholars. Retired on active duty. A waste of a uniform and a paycheck, but with a little diplomacy you could run the division around them.

Then there were the real officers. They listened to the chiefs, but they had the conn. Like Captain Lenson. He listened, but he made his own decisions, and they weren't just what'd make him look good at the next promotion board.

Thinking about that, Marty remembered how the CO'd told him to put Spider Woman on the team. Listened to what Marty had to say, then given him his marching orders. And goddamn if she wasn't doing okay . . . not folded like he'd thought she would . . . Wasn't that a kick in the ass?

He was thinking that over when he heard the door gunner shouting something to the pilot. Then Snack Cake was leaning down. Lifting his cranial to yell in his ear, "Pilot says the sumbitch won't stop. Wants to know if we can drop on him while he's under way."

"Tell him Gold can do, if he's not swerving around too much." But he started to sweat nonetheless. They'd never done this for real. Just practice sessions down the cargo elevator. But, fuck!

"All right, melonheads. Mister Machete's going for a walk," he bawled.

The great bird completed its wheel and returned to hover over the wake. He thought it would stay there, as it had before. But this time it kept coming, growing larger, louder, its bulbous body teetering suspended from the whirling disk. Smoke blasted out of its engines. A mist whipped off the sea, brewing over the afterdeck. It was cool and salty. Rasheed cursed from behind the wheel, looking back and up.

A line dropped, uncoiling, and the end hit the water. Then lifted, water running off it. It hung in a curving arc, shivering in the downblast. Then began moving forward. It dipped into the wake, skimming up a fine thin peeling of spray. Dancing along the wavetops toward them.

The little man with the lazy eyelid shaded his eyes, looking up. The man in the doorway was pointing the machine gun directly at him. Behind him another reached out and grabbed the line, snapped something to it.

His eyes went to the gratings beneath Rasheed's bare feet. There were rifles beneath the floorboards. But the steady eye above the machine gun promised they'd never live to point them. Not these ragtag martyrs, these unemployed losers. They'd be shot down. These marines, military, whatever, would descend and capture the ship. Find what lay waiting in her hold.

A sadness swept over him, cool as the blowing mist. He wouldn't retire, or marry, or grow rich. To a devout man, prison was nothing. He could pray, devote himself to Islam. But he'd never been devout, though he'd learned to feign devotion, and face to face with the end, he realized the only thing he'd truly miss and regret. More than the struggle, or the Sheikh, or even service to God. What his heart had truly delighted in was the making of the bombs. The perfection of his deadly expertise. The craftsmanship, and then the bloody harvest.

This, at the end, was the truth, and he trembled at it and bowed his head.

Then, beyond the hovering machine, he glimpsed on the horizon a shape that had not been there before.

He shaded his eyes again, studying it. Still a distance off. But clearly cutting across their path, barring their flight. He studied it for some seconds, watching it gradually close. Until he could make out the numerals only just visible on its side.

He smiled, suddenly filled with a dawning wonder.

He knew this ship.

He recognized its lofty sides and proud towers. Its guns and antennas. The fortresslike power, arrogant and foreign, that had intimidated him when he walked beside it, when he'd stepped aboard.

The one he'd tried to destroy in Bahrain. Delivered back into his hands, as if by some incredible sorcery.

And suddenly all was clear. *Not* by sorcery. By *design*. Truly, all was written from the opening of time. God Himself was speaking to him, clearly and unmistakably, sinful and imperfect as he was. God alone had delivered the Great Satan into his hands, to strike a blow that would resound across time into Eternity.

"Abu! They're coming down!"

He did not answer the panicked cry. In his own heart had come now and forever the absolute calm of unconditional faith. He said quietly, face lifted to the sun, *"Alhamduill'ah."*

Let it be done, in God's name.

Marchetti felt the helo flare out. He snapped the end of the line into the fitting, put his weight on it, then kicked the coil into space. Had to elbow Wilson again, it was so crowded in the compartment he could barely move. He hauled down on the line, testing the shackle. It held. He pulled the descender around on his belt, laid the blue braided line in it, and snapped it shut. Pulled the line forward and back, making sure everything ran free. Cool. Sweet. Good to go. He pushed his legs out the door, pulled the Mossberg around to where he could use it on the way down if he had to. Stand the fuck by, assahollahs.

"Stand by," Snack Cake yelled into his ear. Machete barely heard him. Son of a bitch! God! He loved this. He even had a hard on!

This was the last thought that passed through his brain before, too suddenly even to glimpse the change, the air, the metal around him, and the very atoms of his body evaporated suddenly into incandescent light.

33

Dan was looking away when it happened. But even looking away, everything around him, sea, steel, cloth, turned the brightness of the midday sun. The starboard lookout screamed, dropping his binoculars and clutching at his eyes. The dreadful, burning light went on and on, like someone had opened the scuttle to hell above the eastern Med.

His mind didn't take in what was happening. Instinct drove him across the bridge, slamming into the chart table, to shove Yerega aside and shout into the mike, "Nuclear detonation, brace for shock!" Then diving for the deck.

Which jolted upward as his body met it, whiplashing him several feet into the air. Dust and paint chips leaped out of the overhead and cable runs to fog the pilothouse. An instant later and all together the windows came in on them with a crack like a bolt of lightning tearing an oak apart. Only it went on and on.

As the hellish light waned to a reddish glow *Horn* started going over to port. Clanging reached him through the din, like a boiler factory stood on end and shaken until everything jerked loose. Then the glass crashed down and water came with it, shards and debris raining down on the bridge team as they lay gripping what they'd grabbed for anchor and shelter.

A long groan, and the ship staggered slowly back upright.

She moved in jerks, as if the sea around her hull had turned sticky. She rolled to starboard, then back to port again. As if she'd been punched hard deep in her guts and was trying to feel how hurt she was.

Through the ringing afterblast penetrated dozens of alarms, beeping and buzzing and sirening. And with them, screams.

Dan picked himself up carefully, checking first legs, then arms, then his face. His hands came away unbloodied, except for cuts on his forearm. But there was something wrong with his neck. He stood rubbing it as the others hoisted themselves to their feet, looking around. Hotchkiss was white-faced, slipping and sliding on shattered plastic and pubs and smashed binocular lenses. She got on the phone to Central, asking for damage reports while Dan felt his way from the nav table to the Furuno, then to the helm console, then out onto the wing.

A queer beige fog hung close above the waves. The junior officer of the deck was hugging the starboard lookout, who still had his hands to his face. When he lifted one, Dan saw the swift reddening of a second-degree burn, an eye that stared but did not seem to see. "I was looking at it," the man groaned.

"We'll get you below to the doc. You'll probably start to see again in a few minutes," Dan said. But knowing if he'd focused that flash through the glasses, his retinas were probably burned out.

God! What had that been? *Could* it have been nuclear? He'd seen shells go off at close range, bombs, but never anything like that. He took the binoculars and swept the sea where the trawler had been seconds before. A tan rain was falling. Waves rocked crazily, radiating from an inchoate jumble of boiling whitecaps. A column of dirty-looking vapor towered above the spot, rising from a misty base. No sign of Blade Slinger or the fishing vessel at all.

He turned, and looked the length of his ship.

Horn had been blasted broadside, and the radar-absorbing tiles on the starboard side were peeling like roasted, sloughing skin. All her antennas were gone, snapped off or dangling by swaying lengths of cable. Her life rafts, davits, and lifeline stanchions were swept clear. What few were left were bent at strange angles. He didn't see any windows at all, just holes. The starboard fifties and the twenty-five-millimeter looked unharmed, but their covers were ripped off. Only strings and shreds were left.

With a sudden horror he realized what the gritty mist he was feeling on his face might be, and what might be filtering into the ship with it. He slammed the door behind him, dogged it hard. Roared at the dazed boatswain, "Set Circle William throughout the ship. Base surge incoming. Commence water washdown." Circle William would seal every access to exterior air. And they had to start the cleansing spray before it was too late.

Yet when he peered out again only a few fountains spurted here and there on the forecastle, and none aft of the bridge. Instead of being shriven in cascades of water, *Horn* lurched and wallowed, scorched and naked, as the murky rain pelted down.

He clutched the compass stand as the damage reports came in.

This time when the lights went out, Cobie was ready. She knew they'd been at general quarters all night chasing some boats that wouldn't answer radio calls. She knew they'd fired missiles at the ship but missed and that *Horn* had sunk them, and now they were tracking a suspicious-looking trawler. The captain had reported all that on the 1MC as it happened. So she wasn't expecting it when everything slammed around her and the lights went out, when she found herself lying on the gratings with cold water spraying over her. No. But at least she had a clue what was going on.

So she didn't waste any time looking around to see what everybody else was doing. She just bolted through the spray coming up through the gratings, through the crackling showers of sparks and the deafening blast of suddenly released steam, hauling ass for the ladder. Only she didn't get very far, because somebody was lying across it at the top where it came out at the boiler flat. She heaved a sodden body out of the way and squirmed up past it.

It might be Akhmeed, he'd been heading down to the PLCC flat to get a wrench when the missile, or whatever it was, had gone off. It must have been a hell of an explosion, she realized belatedly. To whip the ship itself back and forth like that. To break pipes and smash valves so they were spraying water and live steam. The hot oily smog was suffocating her. She had to get out.

But then she stopped, looking back.

Steam rose in an enclosed space. Climb and die was the rule after the first fifteen seconds. But she couldn't just leave him. She got the unconscious fireman's leg, then switched off for one of his arms. But no matter how hard she hauled or how mean she swore, she couldn't budge him.

Someone came out of the smoke and spray and blundered into her. Richochet's whine. She grabbed him, yelling, and at last he got Akhmeed's other arm. Together they dragged him to the ladder and with a strength she hadn't ever thought she had, humped him up it, bouncing his knees off the treads.

When they reached the passageway this time the shouting was louder, the thresh and panic of guys tearing by in the dark faster. She felt her way to the remote station, got her flashlight on the controls, and started isolating, like Helm had showed her. But where was he? She and Richochet had got out, they'd gotten Akhmeed, but she hadn't seen Mick Helm or the Porn King.

She hoped they weren't still down there, scalded or knocked out as the steam displaced all the breathable air. She'd glimpsed white water boiling below as they dragged Akhmeed out. She got on the phone, but it was dead. Of course, the power was out. The sound-powered circuit was working, but so many people were shouting on it she couldn't get a word in. Faintly in the background she could hear the Wizard yelling for everyone to shut up, but it didn't do any good. After steering, Aux Two, Main Two were shouting they had steam leaks, flooding; they were evacuating.

To her horror, she realized it wasn't just Main One. It was the whole ship.

Then Helm was there beside her, helping her isolate the space. He must have come up the other way. She felt suddenly better, like everything was in control now. In the beam of a battle lantern she saw he had two guys from the other watch team with him. "Anybody didn't get out?" was the first thing he asked her.

"I think Pascual. The rest of us made it out. Akhmeed's hurt."

"Where is he?" Helm shone his light around, as if they'd left him on the deck somewhere.

"Ricochet took him aft, to Medical."

He reached up and hauled down a big red lever she recognized as the main firemain riser. When you did that, you were supposed to get a rush of water out of the firemain. Only nothing came out. There was no pressure. Which meant none of the ship's six fire pumps was running.

Which meant they were really, really in deep shit.

"Grab an OBA and we'll go in after him. Everything isolated?" He ran his light over the switches she'd thrown. "Good job. Get suited up."

The breathing apparatuses were in racks along the port side, with the green curved oxygen-generating canisters that fit in them, plus hard hats and gloves. She got her mask on and pulled the straps as tight as they'd go. Inside the mask the dark seemed darker. The black rubber interior made her feel smothered. It was big for her face, but she thought she had a seal. She seated the canister, pulled the tab, and set the timer. A smoky smell filled the mask. She sucked it in reluctantly. There must have been oxygen in it, though, because although she felt woozy and scared she didn't pass out.

A click at her waist. She looked down to see he'd snapped

a line on her. Was giving her a thumbs-up. She nodded and returned it, though she was so terrified she could hardly breathe. But she had to see if the Porn King was down there. They'd do the same for her.

Clambering in the heavy gear, the heavy gloves, the hard hat, she followed Helm through the open hatch.

"This is it, sir. Confirmed the format in the pub."

Dan was in Combat, reading the Camel's draft message while the corpsman bandaged his arm. Track Alley was dark under the emergency lighting. The screens were blank. *Horn* was blind and deaf. But that was the least of his worries now. Damage reports were starting to come through. Flooding. Fire. Generators down. Engines down.

His neck was extended stiffly in a plastic brace. The pain had grown since he got up after the blast, and his neck felt warm. Strange tingles, not exactly unpleasant, like when they went to sleep, ran down his legs. The corpsman said he should be immobile. He didn't sound happy about the symptoms. Dan had refused, allowing only the brace and a promise not to exert himself.

He ran his eye down the message. No one had ever sent one of these before, as far as he knew. A NUDET message reported a suspected nuclear detonation. Along with latitude and longitude of the burst, and wind direction and speed, so the course of the fallout plume could be predicted.

"Where'd this true wind come from?"

"Helo control. It's what One-Niner-One launched on."

Obliterated, he had no doubt, along with her crew and everyone on the Gold Team as well. At least it'd been quick. . . . He signed it and handed it back. "Sure you can send it, with the antennas down?"

"We'll get it out somehow."

"Let me know when you get a roger. I'm going to Central. If you can't reach me, Claudia's in command."

He took a last look around, told the chief to keep trying to get the circuits up, and headed for the ladder.

Before he reached it, the corpsman was on him again. "Sir, I told you, you've got cervical damage. You need to be on your back in sick bay till we get you out to the carrier for X-rays."

"If we don't get this flooding stopped, we'll all end up in the water," Dan told him. "Haven't you got anybody else to take care of?"

"I got to tell you this, sir. If you don't minimize your motion, you could end up paralyzed."

"I heard you. Now get out of my way."

Aft and down, head stiffly erect in the brace that was already rubbing his skin raw. Through smoky passageways flickering with the beams of battle lanterns and slippery with water and firefighting foam. He stopped at Aux One to quiz an inspector coming out, face bright red with exertion, skin waxy white where his OBA mask had pressed. Then kept going, easing through scuttles, trying not to twist his spine, till he undogged the door and stepped into Central.

Porter was sitting at the damage control panel. She gave him a quick alarmed glance. "Skipper?"

"Just get me someplace to sit." For a moment he couldn't feel his legs, and it wasn't a good feeling. He groped for the chair someone shoved under him, eyes on the panel. "Okay, what we got."

Porter and the damage control assistant, Danenhower, outlined the damage, using the firemain diagram on the panel as a visual aid. The firemain was the principal means of fighting fire and flooding. A loop of eight-inch pipe circled the ship just below the main deck. Six fire pumps kept the pressure to a hundred and fifty pounds per square inch. Cross-connects running athwartships could divide it into smaller loops to isolate damage. Sitting here he could read the pressure in each loop and monitor the pump and isolating valve status, although you couldn't actually operate them from here.

Danenhower had sound-powered phones on and was relaying information as it came in. He pushed an earpiece back, but Lin was already talking. She went methodically from forward to aft. Dan's unease grew as she outlined the damage.

Main One reported flooding and fire. Aux One reported flooding from either the seawater service piping or from a fracture to the hull. Aux Two also reported flooding. Main Two reported flooding, probably from cracks in the main drainage piping in the bilge. There was also water in shaft alley, most probably, Porter said, from seal failure in one or both shafts as the underwater shock whip-cracked the hull around them. That was why she hadn't restarted the engines. The turbines might spin up, but with flooding in Shaft Alley and Main Two the line shaft bearings were likely submerged. Running a shaft with water in the bearings would overheat it, seize it, destroy it. "I thought it'd make more sense to sit dead in the water a little while and get things straightened out," she told him. "Since there's no more threat topside. Or is there?"

"If there is, we can't do much about it," Dan told her. "How about the generators? Can we get lights and comms back? We need to let somebody know we're in trouble."

"They tripped off with the shock. We're checking Number Three out. If it looks good, we'll try restarting. Number Two, there's something wrong with the fuel lines. Number One's half submerged, so I don't want to screw with it."

Danenhower had more reports from the repair parties and Dan sat back and thought seriously about whether he was going to be able to save the ship. Spruances were supposed to be able to flood out any three of the eight primary watertight transverse compartments without going under. But he had flooding in seven, every one except the pump room, all the way forward. What worried him was, no one knew *where* the flooding was coming from. If it was from piping breaks and valve fractures, they could isolate and repair. But if the hull itself was ruptured, it might not be possible to save her.

"We're going to have to prioritize," he said.

Porter said rapidly, not lifting the phones off her ears, "Not yet. We have to get the teams down into them."

"We can't concentrate on the aftermost spaces now?"

"No. If we let any of them flood solid, it's going to leak into the adjoining spaces. Or what I'm really afraid of, one of the bulkheads is going to give. We've got to find out where the flooding's coming from before we do anything."

This sounded right. Or maybe he just didn't feel like arguing. The tingling prickle was working its way up his legs. Maybe he should do like the corpsman said, and lie down.

No. The ship came first.

Porter said, "Stand by on generator number three. Are we lined up? Battle circuits only. High pressure air start, start number-three generator."

Chin propped on his hands, he stared at the board as the lights flickered.

Staggering under the spray, Cobie felt the water seep cold into the tops of her boots and flood her feet.

They were on the IR flat, looking down at black, smoggy night. And now and then through the gratings, a wavering tangerine flicker.

She was following Helm in, her right hand on his right shoulder. Somebody else's hand was on her own, she didn't know who. Behind them, like a supple cross, they were dragging the heavy black rubber hose of the AFFF system. The protein compound mixed with water to make a foam that smothered fuel fires. They had pressure back, at least enough to make the foam. She couldn't see much through the little dirty eyepieces. She was navigating by feel. Mainly, following the petty officer. She was scared stiff, but she kept going.

Helm's battle lantern probed downward. The beam lingered on the main space eductor. A heavy piece of steel lay fallen across it. Water was boiling up, foaming like a geyser. The beam held there a few seconds. Then they shuffled forward again, swaying under the weight of the hose, and slowly and clumsily worked their way down the ladder to the level below.

Mick reached back and clamped her hand tight on the handrail. She could read that: Stay here. The guy behind stopped, too. She followed the swing and glow as Helm worked his way through and under the debris to where the water was boiling up. He bent and she saw his shoulder muscles bunch.

He came back, took the nozzle again, and they shuffled forward once more. Everything was slow and clumsy. Water kept pouring in. How much more could it take before all this steel around her just . . . *sank*?

Another ladder. As she wriggled past an obstruction something snagged her coveralls. She jerked free, tearing the cloth, but in the struggle she lost touch with Helm. She hesitated, peering around through the little plastic windows, torn between going ahead and back, and at last shuffled forward. Till she slammed into him.

On the boiler flat the flames were closer, bigger, and a whole lot scarier. She felt the heat through her coveralls. She couldn't tell what was on fire. It might be fuel from the gravity head tank. Even busted, though, it shouldn't be leaking enough for a fire this big. She hoped the seams hadn't split on the main tanks. If those let go, there was no way they were going to get out of here without getting basted and broasted like so many chicken thighs.

Helm was wrestling with the hose. She turned around and started pulling at it, too. It came free all at once and she almost fell backward off the platform through a missing section of handrail. All she could see down there was the orange flames and between them surging black water.

For some time now she'd been smelling smoke and fuel. This meant her mask wasn't super tight, but as long as she was getting enough air to breathe, it didn't matter. But now there was more smoke in what she was breathing and less air. She finally had to let go the hose and of Helm and stagger off and pull at her mask with both hands until it fit her face better. Then she went through the restart procedure, al-

though she couldn't think straight, what with breathing the
smoke and not getting enough air. Bright sparklies began
drifting in from the edges of her vision. She jammed her
face into the rubber and sucked. The candle smell came
back and her head cleared, though she still couldn't see
worth a shit.

But when she groped her way back to where she'd left the
hose, she couldn't find it. She kept running into stanchions
she didn't remember. She sure as hell didn't want to step
into any of these holes. At last she tripped over the hose. She
bent and picked it up and worked her way along it till she
caught up again.

Helm was silhouetted against the flames. She caught the
dark bloom of the foam. He was sweeping it back and forth,
blasting it where the fire glowed and roared. The hose
bucked like the bull at the Daiquiri Palace. He hesitated,
then went forward; paused again. The flames seemed to be
backing off.

Suddenly the rubber went soft in her hands. Helm started
backing out, walking back into her. She felt the hose fill once
more. Then it went soft again and she knew it was no good.
The flames were roaring now, harsh light glaring all around
them. Lord have mercy, she wanted out. They still hadn't
found Pascual. But her mask was so fogged she couldn't see
at all. Couldn't stop coughing. Somebody shoved her. Arms
outstretched, she stumbled toward what she hoped was the
ladder up.

Dan decided to stay in Central. This fight would be decided
here. Besides, his neck didn't want him to go through those
scuttles again. By now Porter had number-three generator
running but there were breaks and intermittents all over the
ship. They'd get light or firemain pressure for a few minutes,
then lose it.

Hotchkiss called down from Combat. She'd pulled
everybody off the bridge and sealed topside accesses. The
radiological sweep team was out checking for contamination. He told her to keep trying to get comms back. She said

Radio was trying to rig an antenna. He told her to keep trying to get through to Vigilant Dragon and Sixth Fleet or at the very least to *Moosbrugger* so Brinegar could relay *Horn* was dead in the water and needed help. Beyond that he couldn't think of anything more to do. Whether they went down or not would hinge on what happened down in the spaces.

At the moment the board showed half the firemain out of commission. It didn't hold pressure even when they had power. That meant it was fractured or holed. Without pressure they couldn't run the eductors, which were the major way to get water out of the spaces fast. They had portable pumps, but faced with the rate of flooding the teams were reporting it was a waste of time to rig them.

Danenhower said, "Main One: Fire out of control. Main space eductor broken and nonfunctioning. Investigating team pulled out. One soul remaining in the space."

Porter told him, "I'm going to Halon-flood Main One as soon as the team's clear."

"What about the missing man?"

"If he's still in there, he's dead by now. There's no breathable air."

A chief called, "Investigators clear in Main One."

"Very well," Porter said. To Dan, "They report rapid flooding through what we thought was a sheared eductor. They got it closed, but that wasn't it. It's still flooding. So it's more than ruptured piping. There's a big, bad fuel leak in there feeding the fire. We have to get the fire out, then address the source of the flooding."

He nodded, feeling both helpless and enraged. Knowing it'd kill anyone left in the space, if they were still alive and trapped down there. But not having any choice.

Danenhower said, "Aux Two reports leak located in seawater service pipes. Closed off . . . no, water's still coming in from somewhere over by the sewage incinerators. Investigating now."

The lights flickered off. Everyone looked up. Then they came on again. At least for the moment. But the ship was protesting. Unsettling cracks and bangs reverberated around them, conducted through her bones. She was settling deeper into the water. Giving up, no, being overwhelmed, smothered, dragged down, inch by inch and gallon by gallon.

Slowly winding the sea around her like a deep blue shroud.

Cobie was back in the passageway, bent over and coughing helplessly. They had to seal off the engine room while the Halon snuffed the flames. At high temperatures bromotrifluoromethane turned into poison gas. If anyone went in after this, they couldn't crack their mask at all. Even if they needed a restart. She felt in her coveralls to make sure she had her little SEED, the pint-sized cylinder of canned air meant for emergency escape. She rubbed her neck, where the mask hadn't protected. Her hand came away black with soot and grime and fuel. Meanwhile Helm and Chief Bendt were arguing over why the firemain wasn't holding pressure. She hadn't been thinking about it, but suddenly she knew.

"You saw it go?" Bendt asked her. "Sure?"

"The flexible coupling, the one that goes from the fire pump to the manifold? It sprayed me when I was trying to get past. It's fucked, all right."

"That might be where all this fucking water's coming from, too," Bendt said.

Helm mused, "If the flex coupling's busted, you'll have flooding from two directions at once. Up from the sea chest, down from the firemain system."

"Sure, we're pumping it in at the top, it's running out at the bottom. That's why it's not holding pressure," Bendt said. He took the sound-powered phones from one of the talkers, spoke to Central. Then gave it back, looking grim. "The remote valve doesn't work on the sea chest. None of the remote valves are working. The hydraulics are fucked."

Helm looked around, past her, pointed to Sanders. "Ricochet. Remember where the fire pump discharge valve is?

Yellow wheel? Lower level? Under the main engine enclosure?"

"Uh—sort of."

"Sort of. And the suction valve?"

He shook his head. Helm looked frustrated. Finally he
looked to her. "Okay. Cober. *You* remember where the fire
pump discharge valve is?"

She nodded. "And the sea suction valve's the red one,
with the wheel. Under the deck plates, by the fire pump."

He studied her. "We got to close both those valves. First
the yellow one. Then the red one. You up for going back in?"

"But it's flooded down there."

"I know. But we're all gonna be playing tag with the
sharks if we don't get those valves closed."

She was scared. She didn't want to go back in there. But
Mick was right. They had to do it. She put her head down
and shrugged.

Hotchkiss called down that Radio had rigged a whip antenna and raised a merchant out of Cyprus. She was asking
him to relay the information about their sinking condition to
any warship that answered up. Dan said that was fine, would
he alter course to stand by them? Hotchkiss told him the
master said he had to request permission from his owners to
alter course more than ten miles. Dan thought this was bullshit, but couldn't think of anything he could do about it. He
told her to keep trying to pass traffic to *Moosbrugger* and
Kocatepe.

"How's the flooding?"

"It's not going too great down here, Claudia. We'd better
start a life raft inventory."

"I sent Yerega out to check, but I don't want anybody exposed outside the skin of the ship long. He says most of the
rafts got blown over the side. Some of the containers are
cracked but they might still inflate."

"*Faith? Fear?*"

"Gone. Wait one." She went off the line, then came back.
"Bad news from the radiological team. There's heavy alpha

contamination all the way up the starboard side. Very heavy—some patches count at three hundred rads an hour."

"*Three hundred?*"

"Uh-huh. So it was a nuclear burst, all right—and a really, really filthy one. We'll stay at Circle William and try to get the washdown system going. Are we going to have firemain pressure anytime soon?"

"That's kind of up in the air right now."

"Okay, but we got to get this stuff washed off. The longer it stays, the higher dose we're accumulating. I'm stripping everybody who was topside and sending them through decon. I've got to rotate my radiological team, they're over safe stay time already. Everybody else needs to go to deep shelter stations, right now."

Dan held the phone, overcome by a sense of disorientation. The U.S. Navy had drilled and trained for nuclear war for nearly fifty years. Now, just as the enemy they'd feared most had gone away, he was facing it for real.

Suddenly all the material about isotopes and half-lives and biological damage that had seemed so esoteric had become a deadly reality. Three hundred rads an hour was serious contamination. On *Horn,* the maximum permissible exposure was a hundred and fifty rads, and the dose to be rated as a casualty was two hundred and fifty. The book said half the men who got six hundred rads would die.

Radiation from a nuclear burst came in two forms. Initial radiation, emitted during the first seconds of the fireball's existence, came from the actual fission of the warhead. It was powerful but transient, gamma rays and neutrons. No way to estimate how much the personnel topside had gotten from that source. The second wave was residual, from the base surge and the fallout cloud . . . mainly alpha and beta particles, slower acting but longer-lived.

Whatever had just gone off had obviously been intensely dirty, grossly radioactive, and *Horn* had been caught square under the area of maximum fallout. But if they couldn't stop the flooding, they'd all be in the water with it. He looked at his watch. Only twenty minutes had passed since the detonation.

"You there? Concur with deep shelter?"

"Yeah." He told her to get that word to the battle dressing stations, make sure they knew any wounded from topside were probably contaminated, too.

As he was talking, a decon team had come in. They stood waiting behind him. He told Danenhower to start double-checking Circle William settings, make absolutely sure some neglected fan or topside access wasn't sucking contamination into the ship. Then he pushed back the chair and stepped into a trash bag one of the masked and suited team spread on deck.

Working from both sides with heavy shears, they cut his uniform off down to the skin, dropping the scraps into the bag. He stepped out of his shoes and stood naked except for the neck brace. Porter was talking into the phone, not looking at him. Letting the decon guys help him, he went clumsily through the portside hatch and up to the main deck level and aft, still inside the skin of the ship, until he got to after decon. He caught his breath as the spray of cold water hit him, and they started scrubbing.

This time the air in the engine room was much hotter. Cobie figured heat rose, it might not be so bad at the lower levels. At least she hoped not. They weren't pulling a hose now, so it was easier to shuffle along. Fear gave her energy, but she felt fatigue growing under it. She kept pulling the mask straps tighter, till it felt like it was crushing the back of her head. Her skin itched where she'd buttoned the collar and wristcuffs of her coveralls. She wondered if that was the toxic gas, or what.

Main One was no longer the place she'd worked and stood watch in. Except for the dying glow of the remaining emergency lights it was completely dark. They had power back in the passageway but couldn't put power back into the space. Not with wires dangling loose in saltwater. At least the fire was out now. She and Helm had to feel their way,

point their lanterns where they were going to step. They got
to the boiler flat and inched along to the ladder down to the
PLCC flat. Then looked down to see the water surging there,
black, oily-looking, absorbing light. She couldn't tell how
deep it was or what was underneath.

Mick put his face close and yelled through the speaking
diaphragm, "Me first."

She nodded. He slid down the ladder, letting boots, then
legs, then lower body in little by little, like inching into a
chilly pool. Only this one was covered with oil and smoking in the heat. If it reflashed they'd die screaming, clawing
at their faces as the pure oxygen they were breathing ignited.

When he let go of the ladder, he was waist-deep. He
glanced back, and she saw the fear in his eyes. Somehow it
gave her the courage to go down after him. Only her boots
slipped on the slick treads, her hands let go and she
splashed down and floundered around, almost falling. It was
up to her chest. Hell, almost to her neck, when the ship
rolled and a black wave came out of the dark and surged up
toward her face.

She pointed her lantern the length of the flat. Gauge faces
flashed at the far end. The water sloped slowly back and
forth above the counter level. She remembered how the Porn
King used to sleep under it with his jacket over his head.
Where was he? They should have seen his body by now, at
least. Unless he was *under* this stuff.

Helm started wading toward the panel. She forced her fingers to unclamp from the handrail and waded after him.
Hoping she had a good seal on the OBA mask. They'd told
her never to let the canister touch oil or fuel. But it was all
over the water, a thick brown viscous coat of it. With hydraulic oil and that synthetic shit she wasn't supposed to
touch and everything else mixed in, too.

Finally she got to the console. To her left was the main
engine enclosure. To her right a short ladder leading down to
the generator flat. But now it was invisible under the black
undulating blanket. One more level below this. Where the

firemain valves were. But they were back under the main engine, and deep under water by now. How the fuck were they going to get to them?

In the darkness she felt Helm pull her head in close to his. Like for a kiss. Only he was yelling, through the creak of the ship and the hammer of her heart, through the buzzing diaphragm: "I'm going for the firemain suction. That's the first one we got to close."

She nodded, already figuring that. Once it was closed, Main Control could pressurize the loop without pumping more water into the engine room. But each time she'd looked, the water level was higher. It was already almost to where Helm had once shown her the outside waterline was.

She shouted back, "What you want me to do?"

"Wait here."

That didn't sound too demanding. She watched as he peered down, trying to figure which way he'd go. She'd guess down the ladder to the generator flat, duck under the deck beneath the PLCC—it looked like there was a couple inches of air space yet under it—and down three more steps to the lower level. Then across to the lube oil coalescers, around them to the right, then hang a left.

It'd take about six seconds to walk it. If it wasn't underwater, with who knew what crap fallen down from above blocking the way. You'd be right under the big main engine bracing. The mass of the reduction gear aft of that. Nothing but solid steel bulkhead forward. And no way out except back the route you'd just come.

Helm was pulling off his OBA. Her light flashed off the stainless steel of one of the emergency escape canisters. He was looking down into the smoothly rolling surface. Then he was gone, and she was alone in the echoing and clanging and the rush of water and the slamming of her heartbeat in her ears. She couldn't even see his lantern. She was shaking, and not just with the cold of the sea.

"Shit, shit, shit," she mumbled around the mouthpiece. She tried to slow her breathing. Like Lamaze when she had

Kaitlyn. In, two, three. Out, two, three, four. Her heart slowed a little and she sloshed over to the engine enclosure and knelt in the smoking fuel that covered the deck plates, trying to see past it to where he ought to be by now. But she couldn't see anything.

She realized she should be timing him. The little SEEDs, the emergency breathing devices didn't hold much air. Three, at the most four breaths. Just enough to get you out of a space. She brought her wrist above the water. Hard making out the sweep hand through the eyepieces. The plastic was going foggy, as if something was eating at it. But at last she acquired it and followed it around. Once. Then again.

She was beginning to feel frightened. More scared than she'd ever been before in her life. Except maybe when she'd gone into labor, surprised at the pain. The doctor had told her it wouldn't hurt. Like *he* would know . . . She started to back away from the black water that nibbled at her boots as the ship rolled and things clanked above her. Heavy things, sounding like they were getting ready to come down on her head.

A hammering rose from the darkness. It grew louder. Then faded. Till at last there was only silence again, or as close to silence as the creak and bang of a dying ship could approach.

She passed her beam over the black, and saw no sign of Helm. No bubbles. Nothing. There wasn't any other way out. The noise must have been his last despairing effort to escape.

She looked back up the way they'd come, seeing that already, in the time they'd been down here, the water had risen at least another foot. The emergency lamps were fading, cherry filaments slowly being eaten by the dark. Her own beam searched panels, hydraulic lines, the blank vertical tombstone of the console. The ship was dying. And she was deep in it, buried beneath the machinery and decks that towered above.

Her hands went to the mask. Her breath seemed to have a

mind of its own, sucking in the rubber cheekpieces again and again. She couldn't get enough air. She had to get out.

She turned and began wading back toward the ladder. The viscid mixture tided toward her, reaching nearly to her knees.

Then she stopped. Stared upward into the dark. At a gleam of light far, far above.

Somebody still had to close that valve.

Mouth dry, mind a dreadful milling of fear, she looked back again toward the sullenly waiting water. She saw the way she had to go, like a jerky handheld camera shot from a horror movie in front of her rapidly blinking eyes. Down, and to the left, and straight, and left again. Down to the valve, under the deck plate by the bulk of the fire pump. Turn it. And then back.

She knew the way. But she didn't know what else was down there. What Helm had run into. That had trapped him. And killed him.

She took another step. Then stopped again. Grabbed the mask and wrenched at it with both hands, forcing her face down into it. Sucking desperately at the smoky dregs.

Then she turned around, and waded back to the ladder. The water came to her knees again. Then to her waist.

She heard a gurgle as she sucked, and knew the water had reached her breathing tubes. OBAs weren't made to be submerged. She panted rapidly. Getting all the air she could. Before there wouldn't be any more.

She groped in her coveralls, and her gloved fingers felt the rounded hardness of the SEED.

Under the deck it was blacker than a starless night in Louisiana. She still had the heavy waterproof battle lantern in her hand. She waved it back and forth as she pushed her way under the steel deck, caught a gray smooth gleam ahead.

Unweighted now by the heavy breathing apparatus, she kept floating upward, to bump the back of her skull into the steel above. There was only about four inches of air space

between the surface and the cables and valves that hung
down. She pushed away quickly, afraid of snagging her coveralls. She was floating above the lower-level walkway. She
pulled herself toward the engine. She'd left the OBA hanging back on the handrail. She'd better not get turned around.
No matter how dark it was, or how confusing. This was for
real, and nobody could help her if she fucked up.

Her kicking steel-toes slammed into rounded metal
domes. The coalescers, with only a narrow air space above
them. A tide of fuel-covered water slid out of the darkness
and covered her face. She clawed oil out of her eyes as they
started to burn. She strained to lift her head but hit steel
again. No room to go over the coalescers. If she got snagged
she'd panic, she was barely hanging on as it was. The fuel
was really starting to hurt even with her eyes squeezed shut.
So she dog-paddled to the right, and twisted around the coalescers and her outstretched fingers brushed the rough steel
webbing that held up the main engine.

She was under it now. Her face was crammed right up
against its foundations. Her searching fingertips felt the fire-
pump manifold where it rose out of the water. She felt the
sea currenting up around her kicking legs. This was where it
was coming in, right below her. She opened her eyes a second, moaning with the pain, and saw yellow at the level of
her face. She scissored her lantern between her legs, grabbed
the handwheel with both hands, and cranked around on it.

It didn't move. She tried again, but couldn't brace herself.
All she was doing was twisting her own floating body instead of turning the wheel.

No, she thought. It's not working. And she only had a
couple of breaths left. Fuel was leaking around her clamped
teeth, a sickening nauseating taste. She yanked angrily at the
wheel but anger didn't work either. It just wasn't gonna turn,
that was all.

Okay, but this wasn't the only valve . . . and the yellow
one wasn't the most important one, either. The red one, on
the sea chest, was the one that really absolutely had to be

closed. That was where the sea was coming in from. The water she felt cold under her legs, reaching up under her coveralls. That valve was below her. Under the water. Under the deckplate. Open to the sea.

She was thinking about that when the air stopped. All at once. She'd figured on getting some kind of warning, but there wasn't any. Just suddenly . . . no more. She sucked so hard pain knifed her chest, and got maybe a quarter lungful.

So that was that. She opened her teeth and let it slip out. Time to go back and try to find her OBA, before the Halon got to her. She just might make it.

But then the ship'd go down.

Her ship. That she was supposed to be down here saving. Her. Cobie Kasson.

So that instead of going back, knowing that doing this she might not make it back, she duck-dived under the water and started pulling herself down.

Into black black darkness. No, there was a glow . . . her lantern, where it'd fallen from between her knees when she was wrestling with the firemain valve. It lay on the deck plates. Yellow light parabolaed the finned cylinder of the fire pump. She pulled herself down to it and got her hand on the fire pump and pulled herself the rest of the way down.

She couldn't see. Her eyes were going. But she knew where that deck plate was. Right at the base of the fire pump. Which she had her right hand tight on. She groped out with her left and felt over the diamond patterns in the metal till her fingers hooked in the lift hole. The plate came up slow-motion under water, and she pushed it away to clang somewhere off in the dark, and reached down till she felt the smooth cold rim of the handwheel.

She was out of air. Time to go up. But there was no air up there to breathe. And she had her hands on the wheel now. So she drew her knees up under her and bent over the valve and said in her mind *Left to loose, right to tight,* and put her shoulders into it hard and broke it free. Shifted her grip and got it over another quarter turn and then another. Closing it.

Closing off the ruthless inflooding sea. Thinking: Kaitlyn. Remember me. Your mom did what she had to do.

Stars shooting away from the edge of her vision. She couldn't see anything, only those stars. But she kept turning the wheel, until all her strength would turn it no more.

34

Dan was still at the damage control board hours later, when word came up at last that flooding was under control in Main One. The water level was dropping around the submersible pumps that had been lowered down the escape scuttle.

"What about the people?" he asked harshly.

"Nothing yet, sir. We searched down to the internal waterline." Another voice on the far end of the line; then the first one, the repair party talker, came back on. "Sir, just got the word we have firemain pressure back. Rigging the portable eductors."

"Dewater fast as you can. Check for any air pockets." But he knew as he took the phones off there probably wouldn't be any.

He slumped, rubbing his eyes with utter weariness and near despair even though that last news was good. They'd fought flooding and fire all this time and for many hours it had looked like they'd lose. If any of the bulkheads had ruptured, it would have been over. With Main One starting to dewater maybe they'd turned the corner at last. But he couldn't stop thinking of the helo crew, the Gold Team, the guys who'd been topside when the blast hit. The investigators and repair party people he'd sent down into the spaces, who'd never made it back up.

Porter came off the phones. "Starting from forward going aft: Flooding in Main One under control, commencing dewater. Dewatering complete in Aux One and Two, starting cleanup. Main Two, water cleared, smoke cleared. Shaft alley, three feet of water left, but lube oil restored to main shaft bearings. Port shaft seal checked and cleared for one-third power. Permission to light off main propulsion engines one-alfa and one-bravo. Permission to restart gas turbine generator number two."

"Granted."

"And test the engines?"

"Check with Commander Hotchkiss first, in Combat. Then come ahead slow with the port shaft and check the stern tube seal for leaks."

She passed that word and he watched her profile for a few seconds. Then called Combat himself.

"XO here. Are we gonna float, sir?"

"I think so. So far anyway. Anything yet from Bill Brinegar?"

"We just got him. Get this: on a secure compartmented-intelligence net. The Evinrude guys tinkered it up and got a message out. I passed our position. He was already on his way; his sonar guys reported the explosion and he wondered why we dropped off the net and didn't answer his calls. He passed our status to Sixth Fleet. Orders are to head for Crete if we can, Port Said if we can't."

"Copy that."

"The chief corpsman says you have to get off your feet and on your back. Are you gonna do that? Or do I have to relieve you of command?"

"Lin says we might have steerageway in a couple of minutes. I'm going to tell after steering to put us into the wind and start the washdown system, start decontaminating from the bullnose aft. Pass that to Bill. When he gets here, we're gonna want to borrow his decon guys, damage control teams, and some of his hose and patching kits. We'll have to use his boats, ours are gone."

He signed off and went over to the propulsion control panel and stood watching as the engineers started the main propulsion engines. One-bravo lit off. One-alfa wouldn't start. But even one engine would give them steerageway and they already had enough generators to run the vital load. When the second engine lit off, he told them good job. Then undogged the door and went forward.

But after a few steps he had to stop. His neck felt warm. The tingling in his legs was worse. He had to lie down. Sick bay. No. His at-sea cabin. Just a couple of ladders.

He leaned against a fire station, alone in the passageway, and closed his eyes.

It had been very close. A lot of his people had died, been hurt, taken doses of radiation. But they'd come through. The guys, the girls, every one of them. He was so fucking proud of them. It looked like they'd saved her.

And having that bomb go off out here at sea, not where it had been intended, had probably saved a lot of other lives.

The trawler had been headed for Tel Aviv. With a tremendously fallout-enhanced nuclear device of some sort. Probably enough, if the wind was right, to contaminate most of Israel. Where had it come from? Who'd been behind it?

He didn't know. But he looked forward to finding out.

A sailor came from aft, bedraggled and wet. Their eyes met. "Gonna make it, Captain?"

"I'll make it."

"How about the ship, sir? She gonna make it, too?"

"We're hurt. But I think we're going to come through. Thanks to our shipmates."

"That's good, sir," the seaman said. He hesitated, then reached out and slapped his arm. "You doin' good, my man."

He went on forward, leaving wet tracks on the deck. But Dan stood there still as the lights came back on, the ventilation kicked on, as far beneath him he felt the first rumbling vibration of the turning screw. As he felt the sting of loss,

and the exaltation of survival, and the cold certainty of re-
venge. As around him, like him, hurt but still afloat,
wounded but because of that even more dangerous, USS
Horn came slowly back to life.

The Afterimage

The ship came home under an autumn overcast. Her starboard side was dished in between her stringers. Here and there sheet-steel patches were welded on. Her antennas were bent and some were still missing. She moved, not under her own power, but at the end of a long wire from a stubby tug.

Her crew had flown back ahead of her weeks before. She was still too hot for round-the-clock manning. The weapon in the intercepted trawler had been modified in some as-yet-unclear way to generate an enormous fallout plume of radioactive cobalt 60, enough to contaminate hundreds of square miles. The plan had been ruthless but artfully conceived, one of the techs flown out to meet them in Soudha Bay had told him. Detonated off the coast, dispersed by the prevailing winds, the isotope would contaminate air and drinking water, making Israel—the presumed target—uninhabitable for years. The current population would have had to evacuate to Europe, North America, Latin America. And once resettled, how likely was it, speaking realistically, that they would ever be allowed to return?

As to the ship, her sea life was over. Once home, she'd be left to cool in some shipyard backwater for years, then scrapped. But still she moved with the deliberate grace of a cared-for thing. She was like a living being, though she was not alive. She was something more and something less; enduring only so long as those who had loved her lived, but for that period of time granted an individuality of her own.

Almost, a soul.

She'd left the country that had built her, to defend that country. Now she returned. But she'd never be the same.

Like every creature who voyages, she'd undergone the sea change.

The man who stood on the tug's fantail, fingering a neck brace as he watched her plodding submissively astern, had tried to define exactly what that change was. Most of it he couldn't put in words. Some he'd probably never understand, because it was not given to men to understand all about their lives, or even, perhaps, the deepest things about their lives.

But he had some idea. For one, that his hopes about young American men and women had been justified. The counsels of fear and intolerance had been proven wrong. That maybe it was purely and only that—the willingness to accept change—that set his country apart from so many that preferred the certainties of the past to the possibilities of the future.

He also suspected, to his astonishment, that he was beginning to answer a question he'd always asked of himself.

He'd always questioned authority. Distrusted those above him. Searched for a standard he didn't have to believe in because it was handed down, or inherited, or imposed; but only and simply because it was the truth. Now, to his surprise, he was beginning to suspect he didn't need someone else to tell him what was right. That his own anchors, when the strain came, would hold against the storm wind.

He didn't feel wise. He certainly didn't feel infallible. But something had stood up in him that hadn't been there before. He couldn't say what it was, or where it had come from. Maybe just from being tested, and coming through. But in some mysterious way, he'd left the fear behind.

Ahead rose the upperworks of other ships, the shattered, shifting glitter of the sun on the river as the overcast thinned away. The jut of the piers, and visible on the nearest, as he raised his binoculars, the colors and flags of a waiting crowd. Blair would be there, fresh from what she saw as a victory: Following congressional lifting of the ban on women's assignments, the secretary of defense had directed the services to open virtually every career path to them except direct ground combat and submarines. And with a house in Arlington she wanted to show him. To take up a life together at last.

But *was* this home? Or was home the battered metal astern? His family, the men and women he served with?

He smiled at the realization he was questioning again. Doubting. And probably, always would.

But maybe that wasn't a bad thing. Maybe it was only those who were most certain they were right who were guaranteed to be wrong. And that maybe, just maybe, those who questioned the most were in the end those who came closest to being wise.

Lowering the binoculars, he looked toward home.